'Don't look at me like that when it's a lie,' Rio urged with staggering abruptness, fiery sparks illuminating his stunning eyes to smouldering gold.

The sudden apparent change of subject disconcerted Ellie. 'What's a lie?'

'You looking at me with dislike when you would really much prefer to rip my clothes off me!' Rio contended, without an ounce of doubt in his dark, deep drawl. 'I don't do pretences, Principessa.'

Ellie stared back at him in genuine fascination. 'Oh, my word, Rio—how did you get through the door with an ego that big?'

'I hate the way you beat around the bush,' Rio told her, lounging back against the bedroom door, his sudden slumbrous relaxation screaming sex and the kind of bad-boy attitude that set Ellie on fire with fury. 'I was talking about us having angry sex.'

Ellie reddened again, her green eyes luminous with disbelief. 'You did *not* just say that to me!'

Rio laughed with unholy amusement. 'I did. Why  may not like each other... the chemistry... bed on fire...

Brides for the Taking

With this ring...

At their mother's deathbed
Polly and Ellie Dixon are given a name, a ring
and the news of a half-sister they've never met!

The search for their heritage leads these three sisters
into the paths of three incredible alpha males...and
it's not long before they're walking down the aisle!

Don't miss this fabulous trilogy,
starting with Polly's story...
The Desert King's Blackmailed Bride
February 2017

Continuing with Ellie's story
The Italian's One-Night Baby
April 2017

Finishing with Lucy's story
Sold for the Greek's Heir
June 2017

THE ITALIAN'S
ONE-NIGHT BABY

BY
LYNNE GRAHAM

First Published in Great Britain 2017
By Mills & Boon, an imprint of HarperCollins*Publishers*
1 London Bridge Street, London, SE1 9GF

© 2017 Lynne Graham

ISBN: 978-0-263-92515-9

Lynne Graham was born in Northern Ireland and has been a keen romance reader since her teens. She is very happily married to an understanding husband, who has learned to cook since she started to write! Her five children keep her on her toes. She has a very large dog who knocks everything over, a very small terrier who barks a lot, and two cats. When time allows, Lynne is a keen gardener.

Books by Lynne Graham

Mills & Boon Modern Romance

Bought for the Greek's Revenge
The Sicilian's Stolen Son
Leonetti's Housekeeper Bride
The Secret His Mistress Carried
The Dimitrakos Proposition

Brides for the Taking

The Desert King's Blackmailed Bride

Christmas with a Tycoon

The Italian's Christmas Child
The Greek's Christmas Bride

The Notorious Greeks

The Greek Demands His Heir
The Greek Commands His Mistress

Bound by Gold

The Billionaire's Bridal Bargain
The Sheikh's Secret Babies

The Legacies of Powerful Men

Ravelli's Defiant Bride
Christakis's Rebellious Wife
Zarif's Convenient Queen

Visit the Author Profile page at millsandboon.co.uk for more titles.

My husband, Michael,
for his constant support and kindness over the years.

CHAPTER ONE

RIO BENEDETTI SET his even, white teeth together hard and suppressed a very rude word as his godfather cheerfully chatted on about his plans to entertain his unexpected guest. Beppe Sorrentino was a naïve man, trusting and generous to a fault, not at all the sort of man to suspect his self-invited guest of a hidden agenda. Luckily he had a godson like Rio, determined to shield the older man from anyone trying to take him for a ride.

Rio, the billionaire veteran of many triumphant wins in the business world and a man cynically unimpressed by women, knew he had to proceed with discretion because Ellie Dixon had powerful, wealthy friends, and most important, she was the sister of Polly, the current queen of Dharia—a country which rejoiced in oil wealth. Even worse, on paper at least, Ellie was impressive. Nobody knew that better than Rio, who had met her at his friend Rashad's wedding to her sister Polly. She was a beautiful, intelligent and hard-working doctor. But saintly Dr Ellie's profile took a fast nosedive if you had her past history exhaustively checked. At best Rio knew her to be a thief and a gold-digger, at worst she could be the kind of doctor who befriended the elderly to persuade them to change their wills in her favour.

Ellie had had a disciplinary action brought against her at work after an elderly patient had died endowing Ellie with all her worldly goods. Not surprisingly, the old lady's nephew had filed a complaint. But then there had been indications that Ellie might have an unseemly lust for money earlier than that, Rio acknowledged, thinking of the section in the investigative report relating to her grandmother's diamond brooch. The valuable brooch should've gone to Ellie's uncle but Ellie had somehow acquired it instead, causing much family bitterness.

No, nothing about Ellie Dixon was straightforward, not least her surprising approach to his godfather in a letter in which she had asked to visit because Beppe had apparently once known her late mother.

Of course, it was equally possible that Rio himself was the actual target in Dr Ellie's sights, he conceded with a certain amount of cynical satisfaction at that idea. Perhaps Ellie hadn't realised just how very rich he was at the wedding and, knowing where he lived, had come up with this vague connection as an excuse to visit his godfather, Beppe. Women, after all, had often gone to quite extraordinary lengths to try to reel him in, and he was as slick as an eel when it came to avoiding commitment.

He refused to think about what had happened with Ellie at Rashad's wedding because Rio did not believe in reconstructing unpleasant past events. With women he was very much a 'hit it and quit it' kind of guy. He didn't do serious and he didn't do long-term. Why would he? He was thirty years old, rich as sin and very

good-looking and his female options were so many and
varied that, had he wanted to and without effort, he
could have slept with a different woman every night of
the year. So, if he was Dr Ellie's target she was in for
a severe disillusionment. In any case, the woman was
an absolute shrew with a streak of violence, he recalled
sardonically.

'You're very quiet, Rio…' Beppe remarked. 'You
don't approve of Annabel's daughter visiting, do you?'

'Why would you think that?' Rio parried, surprised
that the older man had seen through his tolerant front.

Beppe simply grinned. He was a small man with
greying hair and rather round in shape. Perched in his
favourite armchair, he had the cheerful air of a playful
gnome and Rio's shrewd dark eyes softened the instant
they settled on him because Beppe Sorrentino was as
dear to Rio as any father could have been.

'I saw you wince when I mentioned how disappointed I was that Ellie wouldn't agree to stay here
in my home as my guest. She's a very frank young
lady. She said she wouldn't be comfortable because she
doesn't know me and would prefer to stay at the hotel.'

'It wouldn't be comfortable for you either to have
her here. You're not used to having guests,' Rio pointed
out, for Beppe had been a childless widower for almost
twenty years and lived a very quiet and peaceful life in
his family *palazzo* a few miles outside Florence.

'I know but I get bored,' Beppe admitted abruptly.
'Bored and lonely. No, don't look at me like that, Rio.
You visit plenty. But, Ellie's visit will be stimulating.
A fresh face, different company.'

'*Dio mio…*' Rio rhymed thoughtfully. 'Why are you

so reluctant to tell me anything about Ellie's mother and yet so excited about her daughter coming here?'

Beppe's rounded face locked down so fast it was like a vault sliding shut and his dark eyes evaded his godson's. 'It's not something I can discuss with you, Rio. Please don't take that the wrong way.'

Rio's even, white teeth gritted again. He had even considered the idea that in some way Ellie could be engaged in an attempt to blackmail his godfather about some dark secret, but even optimistic Beppe would hardly look forward so happily to the visit of a blackmailer. Furthermore Rio couldn't imagine that Beppe *had* any dark secrets because he was the most open, transparent personality Rio had ever known. Yet Beppe had known great unhappiness and loss in his private life. His delightful wife, Amalia, had given birth to a stillborn son and had then suffered a severe stroke. From then on right up until her death, Beppe's wife had endured precarious health and the confinement of a wheelchair. Beppe, however, had remained utterly devoted to his beloved Amalia and, although now pushing sixty, had evinced not the smallest desire to meet another woman.

Rio, in strong comparison, had never been open or trusting with other human beings. He was naturally suspicious and naturally complex. He had been abandoned in a dumpster at birth, born to a heroin-addicted mother and an unknown father and he had spent his formative years in an orphanage until Amalia Sorrentino took an interest in him. Through Amalia he had met her kindly husband, his benefactor. He knew very well that he owed almost everything he had become and everything he had achieved to the man seated by the fireside who had first recognised his intelligence and there was little he would not have done to protect Beppe from any potential harm. And Rio was absolutely convinced that in some way Ellie Dixon was a harmful threat.

Evil temptress? Gold-digging harpy? Hard-nosed feminist? Thief? Scam artist with the elderly? At Rashad's wedding, he had been treated to giggly, amusing Ellie and enraged Ellie. He had also been led down the garden path right to the door of his hotel room and then assaulted. He hadn't forgotten the experience. He hadn't forgiven it either. Insults lingered with Rio. For too many years of his life he had been a nameless orphan, bullied and abused and dismissed as unimportant. And Ellie Dixon had cut him down to size as effectively as the most terrifying nun at the orphanage, Sister Teresa, who had struggled to overcome Rio's stormy and essentially vengeful temperament.

No, Rio wasn't the forgiving and forgetting sort. He still occasionally dreamt about Ellie twirling on the dance floor in her diaphanous green dress, her glorious mane of red curls tumbling round her animated face, and he would remember how he had felt and it stung him like salt in an open wound. He had felt that night that he would die if he didn't have her. Lust multiplied by wine and wedding fervour, he dismissed now with still-gritted teeth. Now all he had to do was sit back and wait for Ellie and her character of many divergent colours to emerge into the unforgiving glare of daylight…

So, would she be the temptress, the prim doctor, the clever academic or the friendly, casual tourist? And just how long would it take for Rio to find out what her game was?

Whatever, it was still game on…

* * *

Ellie surveyed the vast cache of clothing in sheer wonderment.

'Yes, your pressie has arrived,' she confirmed to her sister Polly, with the phone tucked in her nape. 'What on earth were you thinking of?'

'I know you don't do shopping, so I did it for you,' Polly responded cheerfully. 'You need a holiday wardrobe for Italy and I bet you haven't had the time to buy anything... Am I right?'

On that score, Polly was right but Ellie, picking up a floaty white sundress with a designer label, was gobsmacked by her sister's generosity. Correction, her sister's embarrassingly *endless* generosity. 'Well, I'm really more of a "jeans and tee" sort of girl,' she reminded her sibling. 'In fact, I think the last time I put on a sundress was when I was visiting you. You know I'm very, very grateful, Polly, but I wish you wouldn't spend so much money on me. I'm a junior doctor, I'm not living on the breadline—'

'I'm your big sister and it gives me a lot of pleasure to buy you things,' Polly told her unanswerably. 'Come on, Ellie... Don't be stiff and stuffy about this. We never got much in the way of pressies and treats growing up and I want to share my good fortune with you. It's only money. Don't make it change things between us—'

But it *was* changing things, Ellie thought, suppressing a sigh. She might always have been the kid sister in their duo but she had also always been the leader and she couldn't help missing that familiarity and her sister, who now lived half the world away in Dharia. Polly didn't turn to her for advice any more. Polly no longer needed her in the same way. Polly had Rashad now, and a gorgeous little son, and unless Ellie was very much mistaken there would soon be another little royal prince or princess on the horizon. Her sister also had a pair of adoring grandparents in Dharia, who had welcomed her into her late father's side of the family with loving enthusiasm.

And that was why Ellie was travelling out to Italy clutching the emerald ring gifted to their by her late mother, Annabel, whom she had never known. Annabel had died in a hospice after a long illness while her daughters were raised by their grandmother. Ellie's mother had left behind three rings in separate envelopes for her daughters.

That there were *three* envelopes had been the first shock because until that moment Ellie and Polly had not realised that they had another sister, younger than they were, raised apart from them and most probably in council care. A sister, Lucy, completely unknown to them. In each envelope their mother had written the name of each girl's father.

Polly had flown out to Dharia to research her background in the hope of finding her father, only to discover that he had died before she was even born, but she had been compensated for that loss by the existence of welcoming, loving grandparents. In the midst of that family reunion, Polly had married Rashad, the king of Dharia, and become a queen. As soon as she had married she and Rashad had hired a private detective to try to locate Lucy but the search had been hampered by officialdom's rules of confidentiality.

Ellie had received an emerald ring along with two male names on a scrap of writing paper... Beppe and Vincenzo Sorrentino. She assumed that one of those

men was her father and she already knew that one of
them was dead. She knew absolutely nothing else and
wasn't even sure she really *wanted* to know what kind
of entanglement her mother had contrived to have with
two men, who were brothers. If that made her a prude,
too bad, she thought ruefully. She couldn't help her
own nature, could she? And she didn't have unrealis-
tic expectations about what she might discover about
her paternity in Italy. Neither man might have been her
father, in which case she would simply have to accept
living with her ignorance. But the discovery of *any* kind
of relative would be welcome, she conceded sadly, because since Polly's marriage she had missed having a
family within reach.

At the same time she asked herself why she still
cherished that idealistic image of 'family,' because the
grandmother who had raised her and Polly had not been
a warm or loving person and her mother's brother, her
uncle Jim, had been downright horrible even when they
were children. In fact, recalling how the older man had
treated her in the aftermath of his own mother's death
made Ellie flame up with angry resentment, which
made her wonder if she would *ever* share that sad story
with Polly. Probably not, because Polly preferred only
to see the good in people.

In the same way Polly had blithely declared that her
marriage would change nothing between the sisters but,
in fact, it had changed *everything*. Ellie didn't even like
to phone her sister too often because she was very aware
that Polly had far more pressing and important commitments as a wife, a mother and a queen. Ellie loved
to visit Dharia, as well, but the long flights would eat
up a weekend off and she often spent her leave simply

catching up on sleep because junior doctors routinely had to work very long hours. At her most recent training rotation she had been working at a hospice and her duties and her patients had drained her both mentally and emotionally.

Indeed as she packed the new wardrobe Polly had had delivered to her into a pair of suitcases Ellie was too weary even to examine the garments and belatedly very grateful that her sister had saved her from an exhaustive shopping trip. No doubt she would look a lot fancier and more feminine in clothing Polly had picked than she would in anything she would have chosen for herself, she thought ruefully, because she had never been interested in fashion.

Far more importantly, Ellie was much more excited about even the slight prospect that she might find her father in Italy. Even Polly, with whom Ellie had played it very cool and cynical on that topic, had no real idea how much Ellie longed to find a father at the end of the Italian trail.

Two days later, Ellie walked down the stairs of the small rural hotel she had chosen and was shown out to a delightful three-sided patio, which was festooned with flowers and overlooked a rolling section of the green, vine-covered Tuscan landscape. She breathed in the fresh air with a smile of pure pleasure and relaxed for the first time in many weeks.

Tomorrow she had an appointment to meet Beppe Sorrentino at his home, but today she was free to explore her surroundings and that lack of an actual to-do list was an unadulterated luxury. She settled down at her solo table, smoothing down the light cotton skirt and top she wore in mint green, only momentarily thinking that the uneven handkerchief hems Polly loved were very impractical. Fashion isn't about practicality, she could hear her sister telling her squarely, and she smiled fondly as a brimming cup of cappuccino coffee arrived along with a basket of pastries.

Ellie powered through her usual work schedule on snatched coffee pick-me-ups and the fresh cappuccino was glorious, as was the croissant, which melted in her appreciative mouth. Indeed it was as she was brushing tiny flakes of pastry from her lips that a tall, dark silhouette blotted out her wonderful view. She blinked behind her sunglasses, supposing it was too much to have hoped that she would be allowed to have the patio and the view all to herself. After all, it was a very small hotel but still a hotel and naturally there would be other guests.

A liquid burst of Italian greeted the new arrival, whom Ellie could not yet see because of the sunlight. The waiter seemed to be falling over himself in his eagerness to greet the man, which probably meant he was a regular or a local, she thought idly. He responded in equally fast and fluent Italian and there was something about that voice, that dark chocolate honeyed drawl, that struck a dauntingly familiar note with Ellie and she paled, dismissing that jolt of familiarity with brisk common sense. After all, it couldn't be the same man, simply couldn't be! *He* lived in the city of Florence and she was miles outside the city, staying in a village hotel convenient to Beppe Sorrentino's home. No, it absolutely couldn't be the male who had totally destroyed her enjoyment of her sister's wedding festivities and left her filled with self-loathing and regret.

Even fate couldn't be cruel enough to sentence her to a second meeting with Rio Benedetti, her worst nightmare cloaked in male flesh.

'*Buongiorno*, Ellie…' Rio murmured silkily as he yanked out the vacant chair at her table and sat down.

Shock, mortification and anger seized Ellie all at once. 'What the heck are you doing here?' she demanded baldly before she could think better of such revealing aggression.

Rio Benedetti angled his handsome dark head back, his dazzling dark golden eyes veiled by his ridiculously long black lashes. He had blue-black hair that he wore cropped short but the strands still revealed a striking tendency to curl, which gave him a tousled, sexy aspect. He had beautiful eyes, a lean straight nose and bone structure that belonged in an oil painting of a dark angel. He smiled back at her in complete silence.

That fast, Ellie wanted to slap Rio all over again and tell him what she thought of him even though she had already done that two years earlier. He was gorgeous and he *knew* it, a hanging offence in her list of the attributes of a decent man. In reality she had never met such a stunningly good-looking male as Rio and when she had, she had caved as fast as a brick shed built on sand foundations, she recalled with an inner shudder of revulsion.

Why? she still asked herself occasionally, because that kind of impulsive recklessness was not Ellie, not her way with men, not her style, nor even how she was prepared to behave. Unfortunately she hadn't counted on meeting a Rio Benedetti blessed with such extreme magnetism, intelligence and charm. At least that was how she had excused herself for having very nearly succumbed to a one-night stand that had no prospect of any future but she was still ashamed of her misjudgement, still unable to forget that awful moment when that hotel bedroom door opened and she saw what was already waiting on his bed for him…

Rio didn't want to smile. He didn't want to fake it, he wanted to glower at her, and he hadn't planned to sit down either. No, standing over her, intimidating her with his much greater height had been his intention. But then he had seen her and all bets were suddenly off. Watching the tip of that little pink tongue chase stray flakes of pastry from her full pink lips had been more than his libido could bear. And his libido rode him like a runaway express train around Ellie Dixon, his arousal enforcing the necessity of sitting down to conceal his condition. What was he? An uncontrollably horny fifteen-year-old again? Dark colour lined his hard cheekbones. Regardless of the fact that he disliked and distrusted Ellie, she was a real beauty with skin as translucent as creamy porcelain, luminous eyes as green as any emerald and a wealth of tumbling Titian curls. Although smaller than average height, she had stupendous sexy curves matched with a tiny waist. Her proportions were truly breathtaking.

Rio had been sexually entranced with Ellie Dixon from the instant he'd laid eyes on her and when he had been rejected for the first time in his adult life the bite of that experience had stayed with him. Ellie had returned to his hotel with him the night of her sister's wedding but, on the very brink of intimacy, it had all gone wrong. In departing, Ellie had slapped him and insulted him. Rio gritted his teeth at the recollection of that experience. Far too many people had treated Rio with contempt when he was younger for him to easily overlook that kind of slur.

'What do you think I'm doing here?' Rio enquired smoothly, turning her own question back on her.

Ellie shrugged a shoulder and concentrated on her cappuccino. She didn't even want to speak to him but could she be *that* rude? After all, he was her brother-in-law's best friend and she liked Polly's husband. 'Did Rashad tell you I was going to be here and ask you to check up on me?' she asked abruptly, thinking that that was just the sort of protective thing Rashad would do, believing that he was doing her a favour when she was staying in an unfamiliar place.

'No. I don't think Rashad knows you're in Italy,' Rio admitted.

'So, I don't need to be polite, then,' Ellie assumed with satisfaction, reaching out for another pastry.

A sizzling smile slashed Rio's wide, sensual mouth. 'No, neither of us need be polite.'

That smile of his engulfed Ellie like a blast of sun on a wintry day and she wanted to turn into it and smile back in reward. Suppressing that reaction took the exercising of several seconds of strained self-control. But Rio had still won in one sense because although she didn't return the smile her whole body was reacting to him in the most unnerving manner. Her teeth gritted as she recognised the stinging tightness of her nipples and the warm liquid feeling between her thighs. He could tempt her wretched hormones with just a glance and she hated him for having that much power over her treacherous body. Had she no pride? And after what he had done to her, had he not a single honourable streak in his character?

'So, if we don't need to be polite…' Ellie hesitated only for a second before giving him a very honest response. 'Go away, Rio.'

A very faint stab of bewilderment penetrated Rio's sharp-as-a-tack brain. He had decided in the absence of any other evidence that Ellie had most probably dreamt up some vague link between her late mother and his godfather purely to gain fresh access to *him*. And either she was now playing ridiculously hard to get in the hope of stoking his interest…*or*, he was actually nothing whatsoever to do with her reasons for visiting Tuscany.

'I don't believe in coincidences,' Rio asserted, his sculpted lips compressing as his coffee arrived along with the hotel owner, who lingered to exchange greetings both with Rio and Ellie.

'I don't believe in coincidences either,' Ellie told Rio with a freezing smile once they were alone again. 'I mean, it was bad enough meeting you at Polly's wedding…but *this*—this is overkill of the worst kind—'

'Is it really?' Rio was fearful of getting frostbite from that smile, marvelling that Ellie could dare to treat him with such disdain, and his strong and aggressive jawline clenched hard.

'Yes, I do appreciate that this is your home country but I can't believe we're running into each other again… accidentally,' she admitted.

'And you would be correct. My presence here is no accident,' Rio confirmed softly as he sipped his espresso, contriving to look relaxed.

But Ellie knew he wasn't relaxed. Rio had certain tells. She had picked up on them at Polly's wedding. His eyes were veiled, his jawline tight, his fingers too braced round the tiny cup he held. Rio was tense, *very* tense, and she wondered why and then she wondered why she would even care. He was the man whore she had almost slept with, and she was very grateful that she had found him out for what he was *before* she shared a bed with him. Having carefully ensured that she'd never visited Dharia when he was also visiting, there was no reason for her to waste further words or time on him.

'So, why are you calling on me? And how did you know where I was staying?'

'I want to know what you're doing here in Tuscany,' Rio informed her flatly without answering her questions.

'I'm on holiday,' Ellie told him with a roll of her fine eyes.

'I don't think that is the complete truth, Ellie,' Rio scoffed with a sardonic smile.

'Well, it's the only truth you're likely to get out of me,' Ellie responded as she stood up, her fine-boned features stiff with restraint and annoyance. 'It's not as though we're friends.'

Rio sprang upright with fluid grace. At her sister's wedding, his grace of movement had been one of the first things she'd noticed about him: he stalked like an animal on the hunt, all power and strength and purpose. 'Would you like to be friends?' he asked lethally.

Ellie stiffened where she stood, quick to pick up on the husky erotic note edging his enquiry. 'No. I'm very choosy about the men I call friends,' she declared with deliberate cool, not caring whether Rio assumed that she meant friends with benefits or not.

Heat flared like a storm warning in Rio's dark golden eyes. 'You chose me in Dharia,' he reminded her with satisfaction.

Ellie's hand tingled as she remembered slapping him hard that night. It occurred to her that a fist would have been better and less forgettable on his terms. She was outraged that he could remind her of that night when in her opinion, had he had any morals at all, he should've been thoroughly ashamed of how their short-lived flirtation had ended. But then Rio Benedetti was a shameless sort of guy, arrogant and selfish and promiscuous. That he should also be as hot as hellfire enraged her sense of justice.

'But I wouldn't touch you even with gloves on now,' Ellie traded without skipping a beat and, turning on her heel, she walked back into the hotel.

'Ellie… We will have this conversation whether you like it or not,' Rio ground out with a low-pitched derision that nonetheless cut through the sunlit silence like a knife. 'Walking away won't save you from it.'

'And you coming over all caveman and beating your chest won't get you anywhere,' Ellie murmured cuttingly over a slim shoulder. 'I've never been one of those women whose heart beats a little faster when a man turns domineering.'

'But then you hadn't met me,' Rio imparted in a raw undertone.

'And once met, never forgotten,' Ellie traded, saccharine sweet laced with acid. 'I live and learn, Rio… *Don't you?*'

With that final scornful comment, Ellie vanished into the cool gloom of the hotel. Rio wanted to smash something, break something, *shout*. It reminded him that that was yet another trait he loathed in his quarry. She got under his skin, set his teeth on edge, made him feel *violent*. And that wasn't him, had never been him around women, where he was usually the essence of complete cool and sophistication in his approach. At the same time Ellie sent disturbing cascades of sexual imagery tumbling through his brain. He would picture Ellie in his bed, all spread out and satisfied, Ellie on her knees, Ellie across the bonnet of his favourite sports car. *Troppa fantasia*...too much imagination, again a trait that only she awakened, and annoying. After all, he wasn't sex-starved, anything but. Possibly he had become a little bored with easily available women, who clung and flattered and pawed him like a trophy to be shown off, he reasoned impatiently.

But he didn't want Ellie Dixon except in the most basic male way and he had no intention of doing anything about the effect she had on him. And she might live and learn but she had still to learn that he didn't let *anyone* walk away from him before he had finished speaking. Without further hesitation, Rio strode indoors.

Ellie closed the door of her room behind her and leant back against it in a panic that nobody who knew her would ever have credited. Her heart was racing and she was sweating. She straightened her slim shoulders and stomped into the en-suite to wash her hands and put herself back into her usual calm, collected state of mind. She did not allow men to rattle her. She had never allowed men to rattle her.

But two years back, Rio Benedetti had pierced her shell and hurt her, she acknowledged grudgingly. He had contrived what no man before him had contrived and she had almost made a fool of herself over him. Wouldn't he just love to know that? Ellie grimaced. A man she had known for only a few hours had deprived her of her wits and defences and come close to ridding her of her virginity with her full collusion. And then he had unlocked his bedroom door and she had seen that his hotel bed was already occupied by not one, no, not one but *two* giggling naked women, twin sisters she had noticed at the wedding. Appalled, she had stepped back.

And Rio had smirked and laughed as if it was of no consequence that two other women were already waiting to entertain him. Even in retrospect she marvelled that she had slapped him instead of kicking him somewhere unforgivable because she had been devastated by that revealing glimpse of his lifestyle, his habits, his lack of scruple when it came to sex. The rose-tinted glasses had been cruelly wrenched off when she was least able to cope and vulnerable, forced to see with her own eyes how sleazy her chosen partner was. Awash with disgust, she had called him a man whore and stalked away with her head held high, concealing her agonised hurt. And it had been *agonised*, she conceded painfully. Rio Benedetti had knocked her for six and unravelled her emotionally for months after that night.

It had been too sordid a story to share with Polly, who would have been even more shocked to the extent that her sister might have discussed Ellie's experience with Rashad, and Ellie had not been able to bear the prospect of her humiliation being more widely known. At least what had happened had happened more or less in private.

Someone rapped on her bedroom door and she opened it, expecting it to be the maid because she had said she was going out after breakfast and the room would be free. She didn't use the peephole and was sharply disconcerted when she realised that Rio had followed her upstairs to her room.

Fixing her attention doggedly on his red silk tie, she said curtly, 'I don't want to speak to you... Leave me alone—'

'No can do, *principessa*. If only this living and learning life were so simple,' Rio intoned mockingly.

'Don't call me that!' she snapped. 'And you're not coming in—'

A brown lean-fingered hand curved round the door in silent threat and he moved forward but Ellie stood her ground. She had faced drunks in A & E, dealt with drug addicts and violent people, and she wasn't about to be intimidated by Rio Benedetti.

'I don't think you want me to say what I have to say out here where I could be overheard,' Rio murmured sibilantly. 'It won't embarrass me—'

'*Nothing* embarrasses you!' Ellie snapped with very real loathing.

'It's about Beppe... Beppe Sorrentino,' Rio extended, watching her face like a hawk.

And Ellie surprised herself by stepping back to let him into the room because she absolutely *had* to know what he had to say on that subject. She knew he didn't know the mission she was on in Italy and that she wanted to try to establish her father's identity. She was convinced that Rashad was far too reserved and protective of his own wife's privacy to have shared anything but the sketchiest details about Ellie and Polly's background. But that Rio should even know Beppe's name disturbed her.

'You can come in for five minutes...five minutes

only,' Ellie negotiated thinly. 'And then I want you to go away and forget you ever knew me.'

Rio's beautiful mouth curled, his whole carriage screaming that he wasn't convinced by that claim.

'And I warn you… If you smirk, I will slap you again.'

CHAPTER TWO

'I DO NOT SMIRK,' Rio retorted very drily.

'Oh, yes, you do… You always look awfully pleased with yourself!' Ellie snapped back, her nerves all of a quiver and her brain no longer in control of her tongue because Rio in a confined space was too much for her.

It wasn't a large room. She had gone for cheap and cheerful in the accommodation stakes because she was planning to stay for an entire month in Italy and a classier room would have swallowed her budget within two weeks. But in a room already crowded with a double bed and a big wardrobe, Rio stole all the available space because he was very tall, at least six foot three and large from his broad shoulders to his lean hips and long, powerful legs. Her momentarily distracted gaze ran over the entirety of his sculpted physique, outlined as it was by a wickedly tailored suit that was sufficiently sophisticated to strike a formal note, but which also sensually delineated his muscular strength with fidelity. Colour flared in her pale face as she suddenly realised what she was doing and glanced away, her mouth running dry, her breathing disrupted and her thoughts overpowered by the stricken fear that he could somehow guess what she felt by the way she looked at him. Guess that she hated him but *still* thought he was gorgeous and incredibly tempting and incredibly bad for her like too much ice cream…

'Let's cut to the chase. What are you *doing* in Tuscany?' Rio demanded and it was a demand as only Rio could make it, every accented vowel laced with command and hostility.

'That's none of your business,' Ellie told him flatly.

'Beppe's my business… He's my godfather.' Lustrous dark eyes landed on her like laser beams, watching her face, keen to construe her expression.

Ellie froze in receipt of the very bad news he had just dropped on her from a height and in a defensive move she lowered her eyes. Rio actually *knew* Beppe Sorrentino and, even worse, had a familial relationship with the older man.

'You wrote to him looking for information about some woman he met well over twenty years ago,' he prompted doggedly, his dismissal of the likelihood of such a request clear in every word.

'Not some woman, my mother,' Ellie corrected, seeing no harm in confirming a truth he was already acquainted with. It was quite probable that Rio had already read her very carefully constructed letter to his godfather. Naturally she had mentioned nothing about boyfriends, pregnancies or putative fathers in it. She had been discreet, fearful of ruffling feathers and causing offence, but she did plan to question the older man to establish whether or not he knew anything about her paternity. It might be a long shot but it was the *only* shot she had. Beppe's friendly response to her letter had encouraged her and lightened her heart but the discovery that Rio Benedetti could be involved in any way in her very private quest for information infuriated her. Was she never to escape the shadow of that misguided night in Dharia?

'A mother whom you somehow know nothing about?' Rio pressed in a disbelieving tone.

'I was a newborn when my mother placed me in my grandmother's care. I never knew her,' Ellie admitted grudgingly, throwing him a look of hatred because she deeply resented being forced to tell him anything personal.

'Don't look at me like that when it's a lie,' Rio urged with staggering abruptness, fiery sparks illuminating his stunning eyes to smouldering gold.

The sudden apparent change of subject disconcerted Ellie. 'What's a lie?'

'You looking at me with dislike when you would really much prefer to rip my clothes off me!' Rio contended without an ounce of doubt in his dark deep drawl.

'Is that how you get women?' Ellie asked drily even while the betraying colour of mortification was creeping up her throat in a hot, seething tide. 'You tell *them* that they want you?'

'No, I only need to see you blush like a tomato to know I've hit pay dirt,' Rio countered with satisfaction. 'I don't do pretences, *principessa*.'

Even while betraying red climbed her face, the absolute curse of her fair colouring, Ellie stared back at him in genuine fascination. 'You honestly think I'm here for you and that my letter to your godfather is just some silly excuse to see you again? Oh, my word, Rio, how did you get through the door with an ego that big?'

'I hate the way you beat all around the bush instead

of just coming to the point. It is a very *simple* point, after all,' Rio told her impatiently, wondering how the hell his dialogue with her had suddenly turned personal but somehow unable to stop it in its tracks.

'We're not having this conversation,' Ellie responded icily.

'You're not my teacher or my doctor, so you can drop the haughty chilling tone,' Rio advised, lounging back against the bedroom door, his sudden slumberous relaxation screaming sex and the kind of bad-boy attitude that set Ellie on fire with fury and curled her fingers into claws.

'We were talking about Beppe,' she reminded him in desperation.

'No. I was talking about us having angry sex—'

Ellie reddened again, her green eyes luminous with disbelief. 'You did *not* just say that to me—'

Rio laughed with unholy amusement. 'I did. Why wrap it up like a dirty secret? We may not like each other but, *per meraviglia*, with the chemistry we've got we would set the bed on fire—'

Ellie focussed on him because she refused to let her gaze drop, lest he take it as a coy invitation. But it *was* a mistake to meet those stunning dark golden eyes of his, a mistake to be close enough to note the luxuriant curling length of his black lashes and the hint of stubble accentuating the shape of his full-modelled mouth. Rio Benedetti made her think of sex. It was instinctual, utterly brazen and when she collided with his eyes it was as if he were operating a gravitational pull on her. Ellie's body turned so rigid that her muscles hurt but even that reality couldn't block the tide of physical awareness flooding her every skin cell. With deep bitter chagrin, she felt the pulse at the aching heart of her thighs and the swollen sensitivity of her breasts.

'Angry sex could be a lot of fun, *principessa*. It would loosen you up. You are very, *very* tense and I know exactly how to take care of that,' Rio purred, cool as ice water, his pride soothed by her dilated pupils and revealing flush. After all, if he had to tolerate being constantly aroused around her, why shouldn't she have to suffer the same? But in contrast to him why couldn't she be practical and honest about it? Did she still expect and demand the fake flowers-and-diamonds approach from the men in her life?

'That's enough.' Ellie lifted her chin and closed a hand into his sleeve to yank him off the door so that she could reach for the handle, but it was like trying to move a very large and heavy boulder and he didn't budge an inch.

'You really do enjoy getting physical with me in other ways, don't you?' Rio derided huskily, looking down at her from his intimidating height, wicked amusement dancing in his beautiful dark eyes. 'Is that a hint about your preferences? I'm not into bondage but I can definitely picture you in one of those dominatrix outfits, twirling a whip—'

And that was it for Ellie. He wouldn't move from the door and he wouldn't shut up and frustration made her temper spontaneously combust inside her and shoot up through her like a rocket. 'If you don't get out of here, I'm going to call the police!' she screamed at him.

Rio flicked an imaginary speck of fluff from the sleeve her tight grip had creased infinitesimally. 'Fortunately the *polizia locale* are unlikely to arrest a native for making a pass at a beautiful woman—'

'I don't care!' Ellie lashed back at him, all patience and restraint stripped from her. 'I hate you...I want you out of my room...*now*!'

'When you tell me what you *really* want from Beppe I'll leave,' Rio bargained softly. 'I want the truth.'

'It's private and it's none of your business and I won't allow you to bully me!' Ellie retorted angrily. 'Does your godfather even know that you're here tormenting me?'

Rio fell very still, reluctantly recognising that he was dealing with a quarry worthy of his mettle. Beppe was an old-fashioned gentleman and particularly protective of the female sex and he would be shocked by Rio's interference.

'I didn't think he did,' Ellie declared in the telling silence. 'The letter he sent me was kind and friendly. So back off, Rio, or I'll—'

'Or you'll what?' Rio growled in raw interruption. 'You think that you can threaten *me*?'

'Unlike you I'm not in the habit of threatening people,' Ellie countered, lifting her chin, her green eyes deeply troubled.

'Well, then let us reach an agreement here and now,' Rio suggested silkily. 'I could approach Beppe with the results of the investigative report I've had done on you and, if I did so, you would be turned away from the door tomorrow because there are enough dynamite allegations against you in that report to make him very wary.'

Ellie took an uncertain step backwards, hugely disconcerted by that accusation coming out of nowhere at her. 'I haven't done anything wrong, so I can't imagine what you're talking about—'

'Of course you're going to say that,' Rio parried, unimpressed. 'But the point is that serious allegations have been made against you and by more than one person.'

Ellie fell silent because, although she was innocent of any wrongdoing and had been cleared during an internal enquiry, a serious allegation *had* been lodged against her, which could have had a most negative impact on her career as a doctor. Fortunately for her, she was protected by National Health Service rules there to safeguard staff in such situations and the allegation had been withdrawn and the complaint dismissed. Tears stung the backs of her eyes because that same allegation had caused Ellie a great deal of stress and many sleepless nights before it had been settled and she had viewed her Italian holiday as a much-needed period of rest and recuperation. To have that unpleasant business, in which she had been truly blameless, flung in her teeth by Rio Benedetti was seriously offensive.

'Those allegations were dismissed a week before I flew out here,' she spelt out curtly, struggling to control the wobble in her voice. 'And what were you doing getting an investigative report done on me, for goodness' sake?'

'I will always protect Beppe from anyone who could take advantage of him and I don't trust you or the coincidence that brings you here,' Rio stated grimly, noting the sheen in her eyes, wondering if it was fake, deciding not to be impressed because tears in a woman's eyes were nothing new to his experience. Virtually every woman he had ever been with had done the crying thing at some stage and all it had ever done was chase him off faster.

'That's not my problem,' Ellie traded with an unapologetic little sniff that strangely enough impressed

Rio much more than the hint of tears. 'And why would it even occur to you that I would *try* to take advantage of Beppe? Obviously you don't believe it but I'm not a dishonest person—'

At that claim, Rio quirked a sardonic ebony brow and thought about the diamond brooch she had somehow prevented her uncle from inheriting. 'Aren't you? Even though you can't even bring yourself to admit that you want me—'

'You know why—because nothing is going to happen between us,' Ellie told him piously, superiority ringing in every syllable. 'Why acknowledge it?'

And there it was again, that intonation that made Rio want to do or say something totally outrageous. It shot him straight back to his misspent youth when he had been regularly carpeted for his sins in Sister Teresa's school office. There was something so incredibly frustrating about Ellie's blanket ban on normal sexual behaviour, he reasoned angrily. He could not understand why a woman with so much pent-up passion should repeatedly strive to ignore the sizzle in the air between them. As if attraction was a weakness? Or a risk she wasn't prepared to take?

His own convoluted and uncharacteristic thoughts on that score exasperated him as much as they had in Dharia. The evening of her sister's wedding had been a washout but that hadn't been his fault, had it been? Ellie had been totally unreasonable and unjust when she'd blamed him for that episode. He had been honest with her, as well, *too* honest, and where had that got him? A slap on the face and a shedload of insults. They would never have worked anyway, he told himself impatiently, not with a woman seemingly hardwired to be touchy, angry and super judgemental.

'*Non c'è problema...* Don't worry about it,' Rio advised drily as he swung round and pulled open the door. 'But when you fall, I'll still be the one to catch you.'

'I won't be falling. Can I hope this is the last I'll be seeing of you?' Ellie dared as he strode out into the corridor and involuntarily she too stepped over the threshold.

'You have nothing to fear from me unless you distress or damage Beppe in some way,' Rio warned, his voice roughening at the mere thought of any harm coming to the older man. 'I don't know why you're being so secretive anyway. Beppe will eventually tell me what this was all about.'

Pretending sublime indifference to that prospect, Ellie shrugged a slight shoulder. 'Why would I care?' she said breezily, keen to discourage his suspicions that she was hiding anything of a serious nature.

But she *did* care. Rio could see it in her unusually expressive and anxious gaze. He realised that there was definitely a secret of some sort that connected Ellie to his godfather and that disturbed him because for the life of him he could not imagine any likely connection. Beppe, for one thing, had never travelled outside Italy and was very much a home bird. It occurred to him for the first time that perhaps he should have investigated the mother rather than the daughter, but unwisely he had overlooked that option because Ellie inspired greater curiosity.

'You *do* care,' Rio traded softly, moving slightly closer.

In a skittish move, Ellie backed up against the door

of her room. 'I'm a very private person,' she stated in a stubborn refusal to admit even the smallest weakness, because Rio was 100 per cent shark and she knew the blood in the water would be hers if she gave so much as an inch.

'Not always,' Rio disagreed, suddenly right there in front of her, eating her alive with his black-lashed smouldering eyes. A lean brown forefinger trailed gently down the side of her hot face.

She felt every tiny second of that fleeting caress like a brand burning right through to the centre of her body. She wasn't used to being touched, she told herself bracingly, should've been dating more, should've been less of a perfectionist, should've been less sensible. His eyes above hers flamed gold and she recalled a moment exactly like that on the dance floor in Dharia, and in a clumsy movement she tried to peel herself off the door into her room and safety but it was too late, way too late when Rio's beautifully shaped mouth came crashing down on hers.

And that kiss was something between a car crash and a shot of adrenalin in her veins. Her body came alive with a great whoosh of physical response and her hands flew up into his hair, touching, shaping, *clutching* the springy strands. And she wanted him as a dehydrated woman wanted water, as if he were the only thing that stood between her and death. That ferocious, screaming shout of need that instantly controlled her absolutely terrified her. The spear of his tongue in her mouth electrified her beyond all thought and the flick against the roof of her mouth was pure licking temptation by a maestro of sensation. He knew how to kiss, he knew how to do all the stuff she didn't and that drew her helplessly, that and the merciless craving making her heart beat too fast, making her body tremble and her legs weak.

'*Inferno*, Ellie…' Rio growled against her swollen mouth, rocking his hips ever so slightly against her.

And she could feel him through their clothing, long and hard and urgent with the same need that had already overwhelmed her and she shuddered, fighting for control against all the odds and without words, knowing that no, whatever happened, she just couldn't do this with him.

But Rio, womaniser that he was, kissed her again and again; being Rio, he had upped his game. Slow and tormenting had become rawly passionate and demanding and every skin cell in her body lit up in neon as if she had met her perfect match. The pulsing damp heat between her thighs was coalescing into a generalised burning ache that tortured and tempted and screamed. The sound of a metal bucket scraping across tiles was almost deafening and Rio sprang back from her at the same instant that Ellie literally forced her hands down to his shoulders to push him away.

And for once, Rio didn't have anything super smart to say, she noted with only the smallest amount of satisfaction because she had nothing to boast about either. Rio dealt her a scorchingly angry glance and swung away.

'I'll be in touch,' he said grittily.

'Not if I see you coming first,' Ellie quipped weakly, ducking back into her room under the curious appraisal of the cleaner and closing the door on legs that felt as limp as cotton wool. But *no*, she was not going to do that thing she usually did when she did something wrong.

She wasn't going to dwell on it and go over it endlessly. She had made a mistake and it was already behind her and that was all the brooding Rio Benedetti deserved. No more self-loathing, no more regret, she told herself squarely. He was like a cup of poison that tasted sweet, created only to tempt and destroy. Paranoiac…much, she asked herself then.

CHAPTER THREE

THAT MORNING, ELLIE explored the village, bought a small gift for a colleague and walked in the glorious sunshine through the *piazza* to the café to take a seat. She was beginning to enjoy herself, starting to recognise that beating herself up about Rio was counterproductive because it kept him in the forefront of her mind. One kiss… What was a kiss? *Nothing!* Well, unless it made your knees go weak and threw your brain into la-la land—then it was a threat.

While she sipped her coffee, crossly policing her thoughts, she watched an opulent cream sports car park. The driver, who had a little dog with him, hailed several locals seated outside the café and his attention lingered on Ellie before he strode across the *piazza* to enter the shop there. The dog, however, a bouncy little Yorkshire terrier, hurtled straight across to Ellie and bounced up against her legs, craving attention.

The dog's owner shouted what sounded like, 'Bambi!' in an exasperated voice but the dog wouldn't budge from Ellie's feet and, with an audible groan and a wave that promised his return, the young man went on ahead into the shop.

'You're not the most obedient dog,' Ellie scolded

softly a few minutes later as pleading little round eyes appealed to her from knee height. 'No, you can't get up on my lap. I'm not a doggy person—'

'You could've fooled me,' the owner remarked from beside her and she glanced up and laughed.

'Well, I suspect your dog's not very fussy,' she teased.

'Bambi belongs to my mother and I'm looking after the dog all week.' He rolled his eyes in speaking suffering. 'She hasn't been trained and prefers women.'

'But that's not her fault,' Ellie pointed out, scratching a blissed-out Bambi behind one flyaway ear.

'I'm Bruno Nigrelli.' He extended a friendly hand. 'Join me for a glass of wine—'

'A little early,' Ellie began before she recalled that she was on holiday and not on duty. 'No, that's a good idea,' she told him with a sudden smile. Loosen up, she told herself irritably.

Bruno stayed with her for about half an hour, making easy comfortable conversation, and it was so relaxing after the emotional angst of dealing with Rio, Ellie acknowledged ruefully. Bruno was a contracts lawyer based in Florence and he was currently staying at his mother's home to look after it while she was away. When he asked her to dine with him the following evening, Ellie agreed. Polly's voice was ringing loudly in her ears. 'Attractive man—tick. Employed—tick. Good manners—tick. Stop looking for what's wrong with every man you meet!' Polly had told her that the reason she rarely dated was that she was far too fussy. But Ellie didn't think that was fair because when it came to men, Polly had proved equally hard to impress.

The following morning, Ellie drove her little hire car

to Beppe's impressive *palazzo*. The huge gates stood wide in readiness for her arrival. She drove slowly through the elaborate gravelled gardens that fronted the big house and parked, climbing out, smoothing damp palms down over the casual white skirt she had teamed with a navy-and-white tee and canvas espadrilles. She walked up the shallow steps to the front door and a youthful manservant in a very correct black jacket opened it before she could even reach for the bell.

'Ellie Dixon for Mr Sorrentino,' she said helpfully.

'Yes,' he said gruffly in English. 'He waits for you.'

Ellie was a mass of nerves and trying not to show it. Could Beppe *be* her...? No, she refused to think about that because it wasn't very likely when Beppe had been married at the time. The more likely scenario would be Beppe telling her that he hadn't known her mother well enough to give her any useful information as to who her father might be.

'Miss Dixon...' A small man near her own height greeted her at the door of a book-lined room with a warm smile. 'Come in and sit down. Adriano will bring us morning coffee.'

With a soft sound of pleasure she sat down in the chair overlooking the beautiful garden. 'This is such a comfortable room,' she told him cheerfully. 'All these books and bits and pieces are fascinating and when you throw the view in, as well—'

'I'm a lifelong collector and passionate gardener,' Beppe admitted as he sat down opposite her.

'Thank you for being willing to see me like this,' Ellie said a little awkwardly. 'I can only hope that I'm not about to say anything that may make you regret it—'

'I don't take offence easily,' Beppe reassured her.

'But I confess that I'm very curious about your mother. What happened to her after she left Italy?'

'I didn't even know for sure that she *had* been in Italy, although it was a fairly obvious assumption,' Ellie admitted, opting for complete honesty as she dug into her bag and extracted the emerald ring. 'My mother left me this ring...'

Beppe paled, his easy smile slipping for an instant. He scooped up the ring at the same time as the door opened and Adriano brought in a tray. He spoke to the young man with a couple of hand signals. 'Adriano's deaf,' he muttered absently, his attention still fixedly focussed on the emerald.

'He's a great lip-reader,' Ellie remarked.

'He's had a lot of training over the years. Once he's acquired the necessary experience working here, he hopes to find a more exciting position abroad,' Beppe told her and he leant forward to deposit the ring back on the table beside her cup. '*I* gave your mother this ring. It once belonged to my mother,' he added heavily.

'Okay.' Taken aback by that admission, Ellie nodded acceptance. 'So you knew her well?'

'Better than I should have done in the circumstances,' Beppe confided in a weighted undertone of discomfiture. 'Annabel spent that summer working for an English family who had a holiday home not far from here. My brother, Vincenzo, met her first and they got engaged before I even met her. I think you would call it a whirlwind romance because they had only known each other for a few weeks.'

Ellie sighed, thinking of what she had learned about her mother from her sister Polly. 'What year was that?'

Beppe told her and the timing dovetailed in Ellie's

mind. Her older sister would only have been a toddler when Annabel came to work in Italy.

'How do I describe Annabel to you…her daughter?' Beppe sighed. 'She was full of life and tremendous fun to be with but she was a little impulsive when it came to love.'

'Yes,' Ellie agreed, wondering what was coming next.

'I was married to a wife who was disabled. That is *not* an excuse. There can be no excuse for what happened,' Beppe continued with unconcealed regret. 'I learned that I was not the man I believed I was. I fell head over heels in love with your mother and it was the same for her. I was thirty-five then, hardly an impressionable boy, and I fully believed that I loved my wife. Amalia was a wonderful wife. It was not an unhappy marriage yet I broke her heart and my brother's. But mercifully, *generously* my brother did not choose to publicly accuse me of what I had done and my wife was not humiliated. Together, Amalia and I concentrated on restoring our marriage, locked away that secret affair and moved on.'

'I honestly don't know what I can say to what you've just told me because I know none of the people involved,' Ellie said carefully. 'But I am sorry to hear that other people were injured by my mother's actions.'

'Annabel injured herself most of all. She could've had a good life with my brother but she gave him up because she met me,' Beppe admitted with remorse. 'Vincenzo was still estranged from me when he died. It was a horrible mess for all of us—'

'I'm very sorry,' Ellie breathed, feeling inadequate in the face of such honesty and a very personal story, which she had never expected to hear told.

'The last time I saw your mother she was very angry with me,' Beppe confessed unhappily. 'I had told her from the outset of our affair that I would not leave my wife but she refused to accept that. My love for my wife was a different kind of love but no less real to me. Although I was an unfaithful husband, Amalia forgave me and we stayed together and we were blessed by many more happy years before she passed away...'

'My goodness...I genuinely didn't come here to cause you distress, but I can see that I've done nothing but rake up disastrous memories!' Ellie exclaimed guiltily, seeing the tears that shone in Beppe's dark eyes. 'Unfortunately, I came here with a very different angle, Beppe. I'm trying to find out who my father is—'

'In Italy?' he cut in, his surprise unconcealed. 'Surely you are far too young to believe you were conceived *here*? When were you born?'

And she told him and his face became very sombre. 'I believed you were several years younger, but it is certainly a possibility that I could be the man you seek. *Dio mio*, that could explain why your mother told me that I would live to regret not leaving my wife for her.'

Ellie fell silent, disturbed by the harsh nature of what she was learning about the mother she had never known.

'*We* will have to look into this more. With tests? That is how it is done, is it not?'

'Are you willing to do that?'

'*Certamente*... Of course,' Beppe responded. 'Now perhaps we should discuss something less challenging while we consider what we have both learned.'

Ellie's hand shook a little as she lifted her cup because she was marvelling at his calm manner.

Beppe chuckled. 'I must be on my very best behaviour now in case you turn out to be a relative.'

And Ellie's hopes soared, that he was the man, that he would turn out to be her father and that a lifetime of frustrating speculation would be ended. They parted an hour later with Beppe promising to contact a doctor he was friendly with, who would advise them discreetly on their quest. Tears rolled down Ellie's cheeks as she drove back to her hotel. She was in a daze and she was praying that Beppe would be the man she sought because she had really, *really* liked him and it would be beyond wonderful to discover a father she could actually connect with as a person.

Rio, however, had a very different experience when he joined his godfather for lunch. After what transpired there, bitter anger consumed him and when he left he headed straight to Ellie's hotel, determined to confront her. Learning that she had gone for a walk to a local landmark, he set off to follow her in his car.

Ellie paused halfway up the very steep hill and wiped the perspiration from her brow, registering that in such sultry heat, she had tackled a challenge too great for her fitness level. Hearing the sound of an approaching vehicle, she stepped back onto the verge. She was disconcerted to see Rio at the wheel of a very racy scarlet sports car. He braked and leant across to open the passenger door. 'Get in!' he told her uninvitingly.

'No, thanks,' Ellie responded. Her day had been demanding enough without adding him into it.

Without a word, Rio shot her an intimidating glance from molten gold eyes and sprang out of the car, stalked round the bonnet, and before she could even guess his intention he had scooped her off her startled feet and dropped her into the passenger seat, slamming the door after her.

'What the heck do you think you're playing at?' Ellie yelled at him in disbelief as she struggled to open the door to get out again and failed because he had already engaged the child lock to prevent her from doing exactly that.

Rio shot back behind the wheel, his lean, darkly handsome face granite hard. 'We have to talk—'

'No, we don't. I have *nothing* to say to you!' Ellie proclaimed vehemently. 'Let me out of this car—'

'Put your seat belt on!' Rio growled at her as if she hadn't spoken.

'No, I won't. I refuse to go anywhere with you!' Ellie yelled back at him.

Rio leant across her to wrench the seat belt round her and she was so taken aback by the second act enforced against her wishes that she studied him in shock. 'This is kidnapping and assault,' she informed him furiously. 'I will go to the police and make an official complaint about you!'

'Go ahead!' Rio bit out rawly.

'You are out of control,' Ellie informed him. 'You're not thinking about what you're doing!'

'*Sì*... If I'd thought about it, I would have come armed with a gag!' Rio slung at her wrathfully.

'Much good that would do you. I'm a judo black belt,' Ellie countered. 'Had I known you were planning to kidnap me, I would have defended myself to stop you grabbing me.'

'Don't kid yourself,' Rio practically spat at her as he raked the car on up the hill she had been struggling to climb. 'If you were assaulted, you would be far too busy assessing the pros and cons of acting aggressively to take action quickly enough to defend yourself!'

And Ellie was stunned by that eerily accurate reading of her character. Rio was the single exception to her abhorrence of violence in all its forms and even when it came to him she didn't want to actually *hurt* him, just hold him at bay or make him go away. 'Where are you taking me?'

'Somewhere we can talk in peace,' he grated.

Ellie skimmed an infuriated glance at his set profile, noting the classic slope of his nose, the definition lent by his perfect cheekbones, the outrageous sweep of his black lashes. 'You're driving too fast—'

'I am within the speed limit.'

Ellie flung her head back with a sigh of frustration, her wild mane of hair blowing in the wind. She would look like a rag doll with corkscrew curls by the time she got out of the car but what did that matter? The breeze against her overheated skin was wonderfully cooling. Kidnapping and assault? Rio had a temper worse than her own and that was a revelation that had a surprisingly cooling effect on Ellie's own temper. She had learned young that she had to learn to control and contain the ferocity of her feelings. Rio, evidently, had not. The oddest sense of compassion flooded her because she had not a doubt that he would be very embarrassed when he looked back and fully thought through what he had done to her.

Rio, however, was in a rage to surpass all rages and he was well aware of it. Beppe's distress had provoked a visceral reaction in him that he could not deny or fight. He *loved* that man, would have done anything for him! That he had failed to shield Beppe from whatever nasty business Ellie had somehow involved him in slashed Rio's proud protective spirit to the bone. He was going to get the truth out of Ellie if it killed him. *Inferno*... This mysterious nonsense everybody was refusing to discuss had to end right now because his patience was at an end!

Rio turned the car off the road down a long track. Dense clusters of ancient oak trees prevented Ellie from seeing more than a few yards ahead and when the car rounded the final bend she had no inkling that they were heading for a house until she saw it right there in front of her. It was a breathtaking *palazzo*, with a remarkable resemblance to an elaborate dolls' house, and it fitted into the landscape where it had clearly held its commanding position for centuries. It was built on a hill and undoubtedly had views that stretched for miles. She unclasped her seat belt and climbed out with a look of exasperated tolerance in Rio's direction once the child lock was finally disengaged.

'You can apologise now,' Ellie said.

'Apologise?' Rio practically roared at her in disbelief. 'Beppe was in *tears* over lunch! I haven't seen him in such a state since his wife died. What did you do to him?'

Ellie froze beside the car, her fine-boned features locking tight, her pallor noticeable. Clearly she had upset Beppe Sorrentino and yet she had never wanted to do that. Had she ever truly considered what her quest to discover her father would do to the man involved? No, she hadn't, she conceded guiltily. In fact, she had believed that it would be *safe* to approach Beppe because he was a childless widower who seemed to have no close relatives. Of course, she hadn't known about

Rio's connection to the older man then and, seeing the intensity of Rio's fury, she instantly recognised that he was attached to Beppe and it hit her hard. Rio might not be a blood relative but the way he was reacting he might as well have been.

'I didn't do anything to Beppe. I simply gave him some information he wasn't expecting to hear,' Ellie countered uncomfortably, because what on earth was she supposed to say to Rio?

If Beppe hadn't told his godson the truth, it was certainly not her place to do so. And she quite understood the older man's reasoning. He had had an affair while he was married, an affair that more than twenty years on he still obviously regretted. He was ashamed of his affair with her mother and Ellie had to respect that reality. It hurt to appreciate that, even if tests were done and Beppe did prove to be her father, he might well want the existence of an illegitimate daughter to remain a secret. She couldn't fairly complain about that, couldn't possibly resent it because Beppe had the right to guard his privacy and make his own choices. That he had agreed to DNA testing was more than enough, she told herself doggedly, scolding herself for the fantasy of having a *real* father, which she had rather naively begun to entertain. Really, how likely was it that Beppe would seek an ongoing relationship with her now that she was an adult and fully independent?

'Ellie!' Rio raked back impatiently at her as he stalked back from the front door he had unlocked. She had once watched a tiger pace a cage in the same way and it was distinctly unnerving. For the first time it dawned on her that so volatile a personality should have frightened her and she was even more surprised to ac-

knowledge that, not only was she unafraid, but also ridiculously attracted by Rio's sheer sizzling intensity. Even so, she wished that like a difficult piece of technology Rio came with a useful book of instructions because she didn't know how she was supposed to calm him down when she wasn't in a position to give him the explanation he so plainly wanted.

'The raised voice is getting really *old*,' Ellie told him drily instead.

Dark colour scored his razor-sharp cheekbones. 'Come inside—'

'Said the kidnapper to his victim,' Ellie added.

Rio swore in a flood of Italian.

'Yes, I give as good as I get,' Ellie pointed out, moving out of the sunshine into the shadow of the building because calling Rio's bluff was one thing, but baking alive while doing it would be foolish.

'I brought you to my home because I desired privacy in which to speak to you,' Rio framed with obvious difficulty in being that polite.

Ellie pondered her options, which were few. She had neither her phone nor any money on her person. Rio had stranded her in the Tuscan countryside. 'I'll come inside but there will be no more shouting and you will not put your hands on me again,' she warned him.

'I can't promise that I won't shout because I am very angry with you,' Rio admitted in a low-pitched growl as he watched her move towards him, her skirt fluttering above her slender knees, making him very aware of the long shapely legs beneath. His gaze filtered involuntarily upward, lingering on the soft fullness of her pink lips, and shifted with a jerk as she moved, the luscious sway of her full breasts below her top making his mouth run dry. 'And I wouldn't promise to keep my hands off you because I'm not sure I could ever deliver on that one, *principessa*.'

That honest response and possibly the reuse of that mocking label worked for Ellie and released a little of her nervous tension. In fact, she went pink while inwardly admitting that she wasn't that much better at keeping her hands off him, regardless of whether she was slapping him or kissing him. Rio awakened very strong reactions inside her. The usual barriers that she employed to keep a careful distance from people were shockingly absent with Rio Benedetti and that awareness rattled her nerves.

Ellie followed Rio into a cool, tiled hallway that was strikingly contemporary and into a vast reception room furnished with pale leather sofas and several dramatic modern paintings. The gorgeous house might be ancient but the cool interior decor and modern furnishings were in stark contrast.

Rio spun round to face her again, a dark shadow of stubble accentuating his beautifully shaped mouth and the raw tension etched in the hard line of his lips. And she found herself wondering for the first time if he was ever gentle or tender, traits that seemed far removed from his aggressive, competitive nature. And did it even matter, another voice mocked, when he looked the way he did? That mocking inner voice shocked her because it steamrollered over everything she believed she knew about herself, for since when had she been impressed by appearances? Yet when she looked at Rio, everything sane and sensible vanished from her brain as if it had been wiped. And then there was only room for glorying in his tempestuous male magnificence, room to marvel at the precise arrangement of his lean, darkly charismatic features and the stunning clarity of his smouldering golden eyes. She sucked in a startled breath to fill her deprived lungs.

'All I'm asking you to do is come clean with me,' Rio murmured lightly, as though what he was asking should be easy for her to do. 'Tell me what's going on...'

Ellie's slim figure tensed. 'It's not that simple, Rio.'

An ebony brow quirked in disagreement. 'It is a very simple matter that you are making difficult out of sheer stubbornness.'

'No, it is a private matter between Beppe and me,' she countered. 'Ask *him* to explain things.'

His intent gaze narrowed. 'You must know that I will not do anything more to upset him.'

'And I will not break his confidence without his permission, so we're at an impasse—'

'Have some wine,' Rio suggested wryly, strolling over to the drinks cabinet and giving her a choice.

'Rosé, but it won't loosen my tongue,' she warned him doggedly, but the extreme tension in her knees holding her stiff gave way a tad, reminding her that her meeting with Beppe and the walk had exhausted her.

'Help me out here... I am *trying* to be civilised,' Rio informed her.

'There was nothing civilised about the way you stuffed me in your car,' Ellie reminded him drily as she settled down on a sofa.

'*Per l'amor di Dio*, I never said I was perfect, *principessa*.'

'Why do you call me that?' she demanded abruptly as he settled a moisture-beaded wine glass into her hand, momentarily standing so close to her that the scent of him assailed her: hot, musky male laced with a hint of spicy cologne. A very faint shiver ricocheted through her.

Rio grinned and it was an unexpectedly boyish grin of keen amusement. 'Because the way you walk with your little superior nose in the air gives you that look. You remind me of the rich girls I used to watch when I was a penniless teenager. Oh, they looked at me, but they wouldn't have dirtied their lily-white hands by *touching* me.'

'I was never a rich girl,' Ellie parried uncomfortably, studying him with grass-green eyes that were luminous in the filtered sunshine and alive with curiosity. 'I grew up in my grandmother's working-class home and there were no airs or graces there.'

'*Cio nonostante...* Nonetheless you ooze that rich-girl quality of disdain,' Rio told her with assurance. 'And it sets my teeth on edge—'

'Everything about me sets your teeth on edge,' Ellie pointed out wryly while she wondered about his background, because she was surprised that he had ever been penniless and on the outside looking in at the more prosperous. '*We* annoy each other.'

'Beppe,' he reminded her darkly. 'Talk.'

In a sudden movement, Ellie stood up again because he was making her feel trapped. She understood exactly where he was coming from but she couldn't answer his questions. His godfather *could* have enlightened him and had chosen not to. Beppe's silence spoke for him. Clearly he had no desire to admit to Rio that he had had an extramarital affair or that that liaison could have led to the conception of a child.

'I don't back down, Ellie,' Rio murmured from close

by and every skin cell in her body jumped at the knock-on effect of that deep accented drawl of his, goose-bumps rising on her bare arms. 'I won't let you go until you fill in the blanks—'

'Well, then, you're going to be stuck with me!' Ellie exclaimed in growing frustration. 'Because I'm not going to talk—'

Rio removed the glass from her fingers and set it aside. 'Maybe talking's a total waste of time for us, *principessa.*'

'And what's that supposed to mean?' Ellie demanded thinly even though she had a very good idea.

Rio scored a light forefinger across her compressed lower lip. 'You're pushing it defying me. I don't have your patience—'

Ellie threw her head back, corkscrew curls tumbling across her pale brow, green eyes sharp with frustration and defensiveness. 'Don't touch me!' she warned him curtly.

'No, not a shred of patience,' Rio asserted with hypnotic quietness, reaching for her with scorching dark golden eyes of sensual threat.

CHAPTER FOUR

'I CAME INTO this house with you because I trusted you,' Ellie declared starkly, twisting away.

'No, you don't. You don't trust me,' Rio assured her with grim amusement. 'You most probably came into the house because you don't like arguments in public and you are nervous of how far I would go to win.'

'Well, doesn't that just say it all about you?' Ellie quipped.

'You know nothing about me yet you still judge,' Rio condemned.

Ellie stilled, disconcerted by that criticism, and Rio took advantage of her momentary abstraction. His arm curved to her spine and he yanked her close, bringing her up against the hard, unyielding strength of his lean, powerful body, and her hormones leapt as though he had electrified her. His mouth nibbled along the plump fullness of her lower lip and all of a sudden she couldn't breathe for anticipation. Her lips parted for him, letting his tongue plunge deep, and an aching sweetness that drowned every thought rose from the very heart of her. Something in the furthest reaches of her brain was saying no, no, *no*, but all the rest of her was in open rebellion.

It was the kiss to end all kisses, fit to eradicate any previous kiss because no man had ever made Ellie's head swim with a kiss before. She felt dizzy and delirious, utterly unlike herself, adrenalin charging through her veins and lighting her up as though she had crossed the finishing line of a race. Her fingers delved freely into his springy black hair, sheer delight at the freedom to touch him consuming her.

Overwhelmed by her response, Rio tensed, wondering when it would end and abandoning any plan to stage a slow seduction scene. He had never wanted any woman as he wanted Ellie Dixon. Need was already flaming through him like a burning torch. One hand at the shallow indentation of her spine, he ground against her, so hard, so ready, so overpoweringly hungry for the damp release of her body that he trembled. It didn't make sense to him. Yes, she was a challenge, but no woman had ever come between Rio and his wits. He was in control, he was always in control, but this one time, he *wasn't*. Shouldn't that worry him? He shelved the question, too much lost in the moment to waste time considering the drawbacks and inconsistencies. He brought Ellie down on the sofa and kissed her with unashamed passion.

'What are we...doing?' Ellie mumbled through swollen lips as Rio whipped off her top, exposing the heavy-duty white lace confection she wore to confine the breasts that she considered to be too large. It was a stupid question and she knew it and the sight of her own almost bare flesh unnerved her and filled her with discomfiture.

'*Sta' zitto*... Shut up!' Rio urged, burying his face between those utterly magnificent breasts while wrestling with a bra that had more restrictive hooks than a corset. If she talked, she would talk herself out of it, he thought in consternation, and he looked down into her beautiful eyes, emerald as the most precious of jewels, and told her to close them.

'You are incredible' was wrenched from him, breaking his self-imposed silence as he studied the lush creamy swell of her glorious breasts. An awed fingertip brushed a large pink nipple already pouting for his attention. He wanted to carry her up to his bedroom, spread her out and enjoy her as she should be enjoyed but he didn't want to break the spell.

Instead he bent his dark head and succumbed to the considerable allure of her breasts. He whisked his tongue over a rigid bud the colour of a tea rose and teased the tortured peak, loving the way she shifted under him, instantly responsive to his every caress.

Ellie had fallen so deep that she was drowning in the world of sensation she had always denied herself. The hunger in her for *more* was unbearable. Her breasts throbbed, sending messages to the lush damp place between her shifting thighs. Her hips lifted in frustration. She wanted Rio everywhere at once. She wanted the impossible. She also wanted his clothes off with a strength of craving that shook her because it was not as though she was a stranger to the male anatomy. In frustration, she hauled at the shoulders of his jacket and he reared back from her with a sudden surprised laugh and peeled it off to pitch it on the floor.

'And the shirt,' Ellie instructed him shakily, scarcely believing what she was doing, what she was participating in, and unable to dwell on it lest her caution yank her back from the edge. And she wanted Rio, she wanted him so much that she was weak from the wanting and the never-ending wondering and longing that had dogged her since the day they had first met.

A couple of shirt buttons came loose of their stitching as Rio ripped off the shirt with an almost joyful air of abandonment. He was all lean muscle sheathed in sleek bronzed skin from his wide shoulders to his narrow waist and she stared helplessly entranced and surprised at her visceral reaction to his masculinity. As the shirt dropped, he smiled at her in a way he had never smiled before and that slanting, teasing grin was purebred enticement on his darkly beautiful face. Indeed that smile had so much appeal that she sat up and hauled him down towards her to claim his devastating mouth for herself again.

He lay on his side, kissing her breathless and she revelled in every kiss and the brush of his skilled fingers over her wildly sensitised breasts. He pushed up her skirt and traced the edges of her panties, teasing, tormenting, making her agonisingly aware of just how desperate she was to be touched. A finger slid beneath the lace and stroked her swollen folds. She was wet, so wet she was embarrassed by her body and its screaming eagerness. A fingertip circled her and suddenly there was no room for embarrassment, no room for anything but her own gasping, jerking response. He took away that final barrier and explored her.

He shimmied down the sofa and used his mouth on that tender place between her thighs and if lying still had been a challenge before it soon became an impossible challenge for Ellie. Her fingers clawed into his luxuriant black hair, her body dancing and twisting to the powerful drumbeat of desire. The sensations he evoked were excruciatingly intense and only heightened the tormenting ache of need building deep in her pelvis. Heat gathered and mounted uncontrollably at the heart of her and then, taking her entirely by surprise, exploded outwards in a violent climax of sweet, shattering pleasure.

'*Madre di Dio*... I can't wait to be inside you, *bella mia*,' Rio said huskily, rearranging her and sliding fluidly between her parted thighs. 'I am so hungry for you.'

Do I want this? Ellie asked herself and she knew she didn't need to ask that question because when she looked up into Rio's gorgeous dark eyes she was ready to agree to do anything he wanted to do. It was as though she were in a dream without a past or a future or even a present. She felt as though there was nothing but that moment and she liked it that way.

Rio tilted her back and drove into her with a single powerful thrust. And Ellie twisted her head to one side and bit her lip because it hurt, it hurt much more than she had expected, and that burning sting of pain wrenched a muffled little moan of discomfort from between her gritted teeth.

'Something wrong?' Rio rasped, lifting his tousled dark head. '*Dio mio*, you are so tight you feel like a virgin!'

'I *am*!' Ellie gasped before she could think better of making that admission.

Rio had already sunk as deep as he could get into her tiny body and he froze in shock to gaze down at her. 'A virgin?' he echoed in ringing disbelief. 'How can you be a virgin?'

Ellie wrinkled her nose. 'Oh, just get it over with, for goodness' sake,' she told him in desperation.

Stunned by that irreverent urging, Rio took several seconds to absorb what had happened. She was a virgin? How was that possible? And why hadn't he noticed anything different about her? He shifted position, withdrawing and then slowly gliding back. *Get it over with?* What was he? An ordeal to be endured?

The friction of his movement created a little hum of pulsing sensation low in Ellie's body. She shut her eyes tight, refusing to think, indeed terrified to allow herself to think about what she had just done, what she had just allowed him to do. And while she was battening down her mental hatches, Rio was putting every atom of skill he possessed into rescuing the situation. But he was hugely aroused and working alone because Ellie lay there under him like a little felled tree.

He pushed her knees up and ground down into her, delving deeper, setting an insistent rhythm that she couldn't ignore. Her hips lifted but much against her will because she was set on simply tolerating him. A frenzied heat began to build and she fought it off as though it were a forest fire. Her hips rose involuntarily and he slammed down into her, sending a startling pulse of pleasure through her. Her heart thumped like crazy, the ability to breathe stolen from her as he picked up speed and force and dominated her. Wild excitement surged and gripped her but much against her will. Her hands bit into his shoulders and then slid caressingly down his muscular back as this time she sensed the peak she was reaching towards.

A chain reaction of convulsions claimed her and she cried out as the ripples of ecstasy spread in a blinding moment of release that consumed her. Rio shuddered and held her tight and bit out something raw and rough in Italian, his powerful body surging into hers. Within seconds, however, she was free again, watching in a daze as Rio sprang off the sofa to fix his trousers and reach for his shirt.

'You were a virgin?' Rio repeated incredulously, because innocence and Ellie were a combination that refused to compute in his brain.

Wincing, Ellie sat up and pushed down her skirt. Her panties were lying on the tiles but she had no intention of trying to reclaim them in front of him. She was shell-shocked and shattered by what had taken place. She couldn't believe she had had sex with Rio. Just then in the aftermath it looked like the worst decision ever after a lifetime of vigilant caution.

'A virgin?' Rio prompted again as if a virgin were as improbable as a glimpse of a unicorn. 'So, why give it up to me?'

'Maybe I wanted to lose it with someone who would put me off further experimentation,' Ellie suggested with honeyed derision. 'Stop acting as if you've been grievously assaulted by a virgin, Rio. I can't be the first you've been with—'

'You *are*!' Rio contradicted accusingly, taken aback by her gutsy attitude.

Ellie stood up, very discreetly retrieved her underwear and, quite deliberately ignoring him, went off in search of a cloakroom. It actually hurt to walk, she acknowledged in shock. She ached as though they had had sex for hours. The experience felt less like an introduction and more like a lesson. Be careful of what you wish for, she told herself unhappily. He had leapt off that sofa as though he had been electrocuted. Innocence was clearly a hanging offence in Rio's book.

Another much more worrying fact was screaming along the edge of Rio's ragged nerves while he paced the hall, waiting impatiently for Ellie to reappear. He had never met a woman like Ellie and he was very certain that he never wanted to meet another. She drove him crazy. She made him do and say things he never did or said with anyone else. She screwed with his brain, unleashed his temper and sent him racing off the edge of sanity. She had the seductive powers of a temptress and yet how could that be when she had self-evidently had no sexual experience whatsoever? He was terrific in bed and he knew that but she had behaved as though he were useless. So, why did he want her to stay the night? Simply to rescue his ego? And what about Beppe? *And what about the lack of a condom?* He groaned out loud in frustration and raked his fingers through his cropped black curls. Rio felt *raw*.

Only innate courage persuaded Ellie out of the sanctuary of the cloakroom because in reality she wanted to curl up and die somewhere well out of Rio's sight and reach. She didn't want to see him again; she didn't want to have to speak to him again either. She simply wanted to forget what had happened and continue her holiday.

'Please drive me back to my hotel,' she said woodenly, refusing to look directly at him.

'Are you on the pill? Or any other form of contraception?' Rio asked her with startling abruptness.

Ellie almost flinched. She had spent a year taking contraceptive pills after her sobering experience with Rio at her sister's wedding. She had feared meeting that level of temptation again and as a result had taken sensible precautions to protect herself in the future. Sadly, however, she had suffered side effects from the medication and had stopped taking the pills.

'No. I'm not.' Ellie shook her head slowly and walked back into the reception room to sit down again, because she felt literally weak with shock and anxiety. 'How could we both be so stupid?'

'There are still…options,' Rio selected in a grim undertone.

Ellie's head reared up, fiery corkscrew curls tumbling back from her white forehead, accentuating her bright green eyes. 'Don't you dare suggest options to me! I'm a doctor, sworn to protect life,' she shot back at him.

'I didn't say that *that* was what I wanted. *Accidenti!* We are not reckless teenagers but we behaved as though we were,' Rio intoned in open exasperation. 'When we get together it is as though we are cursed. Let us hope there are no consequences…'

CHAPTER FIVE

ELLIE BREATHED IN deeply and slowly released her breath in the hope of chasing away the brain fog afflicting her ability to think. She was struggling to perform little mental calculations around her menstrual cycle, very quickly realising that their timing had been little short of catastrophic. She had chosen the worst possible moment to abandon her usual caution, she recognised in steadily deepening dismay.

What if Rio made her pregnant? The consequences of unprotected sex were not something she wanted to contemplate, particularly when she had a very poor relationship with the potential father. She suppressed a fearful shudder and told herself to be strong. Whatever happened, it would happen and she couldn't change that. In the meantime it would be best to go on as though nothing had changed.

'Please take me back to my hotel or call me a taxi or something,' Ellie muttered in desperation.

'You still haven't told me what you've done to Beppe—'

'I haven't done anything to him!' Ellie proclaimed in a sudden fury roused by the stabbing of her conscience. After all, if Beppe Sorrentino was troubled, it *was* her

fault because she had told him something that had upset
him. She had been selfish and thoughtless, dwelling
only on her right to know who her father was without
ever considering the cost that that information might
inflict on anyone else. Even worse, Rio was Beppe's
godson and Beppe had no idea that Ellie had already
met Rio and was currently involved with the younger
man. But *was* she involved with him?

Ellie grimaced at the concept because that word, *involved*, lent a gravitas to their entanglement that it didn't
deserve. They had engaged in a foolish and irresponsible sexual encounter, nothing more. They weren't in
a relationship, nor were they likely to be. And how did
she feel about that reality? And the answer was that that
reality saddened and wounded her heart and her pride.
With Rio, she was slowly and painfully learning that
she was more vulnerable than she had ever appreciated.
She had made a mistake with him two years earlier and
almost unbelievably had made an even bigger mistake
this time around. Sex might be a field that Rio played
in but Ellie didn't play at anything she did. She didn't
do casual either.

'Ellie…' Rio breathed impatiently.

Ellie rose from her seat to move back out to the hall.
'I can't discuss Beppe with you. I'm sorry but that's
how it is—'

'What are you hiding from me?' Glittering dark eyes
full of suspicion locked to the pale triangle of Ellie's
face.

Ellie lifted her chin. 'People have secrets, Rio. Secrets they don't want to share. Dragging them out into
the light of day isn't always the right thing to do,' she
reasoned uneasily.

'Beppe has no secrets… He's not that kind of man,' Rio argued with sublime assurance. 'So, if you're not judging, you're preaching. Are you so perfect?'

'No, I know I'm far from perfect and I wasn't preaching. I was just speaking my thoughts out loud. I'm a little confused right now,' Ellie admitted tightly, her eyes suddenly stinging while she wondered if her entire trip to Italy had been an outsize blunder. Maybe she should have left the past buried, maybe she should've tried harder to suppress her curiosity. All she knew was that she felt very guilty at the knowledge that Beppe had been distressed by her visit. He had dealt with her kindly but perhaps she hadn't deserved that kindness.

'I'll take you back to the hotel,' Rio murmured without any expression at all. He had reached the conclusion that it would take a hacksaw to extract anything from Ellie that she did not want to share. What secrets was she concealing? What he had read in that investigative report? Or was there more?

'Yes, thank you. I have a da—' Ellie bit off the word before it could reach the tip of her tongue but she saw Rio's dark gaze switch fast to her face and she felt her cheeks burn.

'You have a date?' Rio pressed in growling disbelief, staring at her as she stood there in the comparative dimness of the hall, a glowing beauty with a sexily tousled mane of vibrant coppery curls, translucent skin and a mouth that would've tempted a saint. And he had never been a saint. Even less was he known as a possessive lover, because he didn't allow himself to become attached: once bitten, twice shy. So why did the very thought of Ellie becoming intimate with another man infuriate him? Disconcerted by that rush of anger, he tamped it down hard and gritted his teeth.

'A guy I met in the village invited me out to dinner tonight,' Ellie confided in a rush.

'His name?' Rio demanded.

'Bruno Nigrelli.'

Rio's nostrils flared. 'I think he did some work for Beppe once. Lawyer?'

Ellie nodded uncomfortably.

Rio gritted his teeth even harder in the smouldering silence. Was she expecting him to object? Even waiting for him to do so? Wasn't that how women sucked a man in, by assigning strings and conditions and making him want and demand more?

'I'm not much in the mood for dinner now, but I don't like letting people down—'

Rio's dark eyes flared golden as the sunset. 'Then cancel him and spend the night here with me instead.'

Ellie froze in bewilderment, green eyes flying over his lean, darkly handsome features. 'Spend the night?' she repeated shakily.

'It would make more sense—'

Ellie dropped her gaze defensively. 'Nothing about us makes sense—'

'We make perfect sense. You decided I was a *bastardo* two years ago and even if I saved the world you wouldn't budge an inch from that conviction,' Rio derided.

'I think a lot of women would think the same after that night at the wedding, but let's not get into that,' Ellie counselled heavily as she yanked open the hefty front door. 'We have enough differences without raking up the past. I can't stay, Rio—'

'Ellie… When will you know?'

Ellie dropped her head as she settled into the passenger seat of his sports car. 'In ten days to two weeks,' she framed jaggedly. 'I'll do a test as soon as I can.'

In the sunlight, Rio stood very still. What would he do if Ellie conceived his child? He recalled his own sordid origins with an inner shudder of recoil, knowing in that instant that there would be no sacrifice too great were it to mean that his child could look back with pride and contentment on his or her early years. Only when Beppe and Amalia took an interest in him had Rio learned what it was to have self-respect. Being cleverer than everyone around him had only attracted the bullies. Being prettier as a boy had also drawn the abusers. His lean, strong face was stamped by the grim lines and hollows of bitter recollection and experience. As an adult, Rio Benedetti might be as rich as the fabled Croesus but he had never forgotten his humble beginnings in that dumpster.

Ellie glanced up to see what was preventing Rio from joining her in the car and ended up staring, because it was a revelation to see that Rio, all lean, mean and magnificent six-foot-plus of him, could look haunted and almost vulnerable. She scolded herself for that imaginative flight as soon as he started up the car but his rebuke about her tendency to judge was still nagging at the back of her mind. Sometimes she was kind of black-and-white about situations, she acknowledged uneasily, but just as she had learned all her life to follow rules she *had* learned to compromise and understand what motivated people to do the things they did, as well. She supposed she *was* still holding the events of two years earlier against Rio because his colourful sex life had shocked her. As someone who had never pushed against conventional boundaries, possibly she *was* a little too conservative for a passionate free spirit like Rio.

Rio pulled the car to a halt in the hotel car park. He shot Ellie a glance, noting the fineness of her delicate bone structure and how clearly it showed beneath her pale skin. She was exhausted and he could see it and he compressed his mouth on the urge to make another comment about Beppe. He refused to think about the dinner date she had. He refused to admit that the idea annoyed him. After all, he wasn't possessive and he wasn't jealous. He didn't *ever* get attached to a woman—well, at least he hadn't in almost ten years.

And when Rio *had* got attached—to Franca—it had been a disaster, he recalled grimly. Treachery laced with infidelity and a woman's greed. Rio had learned the hard way that loving could be a one-way ticket to hell.

No, he definitely wasn't jealous. He already knew that Ellie was a gold-digger, he reminded himself resolutely. He would only care about Ellie Dixon's future if she became pregnant with his child. In the short term his *sole* interest in her lay in uncovering her mysterious connection to Beppe.

Rio sprang out of the car and strode round to open the passenger door. Disconcerted by that unexpected attention, Ellie climbed out and as she looked up warily into his glitteringly beautiful dark golden eyes, the sunlight hot on her skin, her conscience screamed like a fire alarm. She had been downright nasty about the sex even though he had been considerate and concerned and, bearing in mind that he had given her two climaxes, she had been unjust. Her skin flushed beet red.

'*Che cosa*... What?' Rio pressed in the strained silence.

'I shouldn't have said what I said back at your house,' Ellie gabbled before she could lose her nerve. 'It was a train wreck... Us, I mean, and me being...well, you know what. But you were good, I mean—'

Rio wanted to laugh but he fought the urge because she was so embarrassed, so utterly different from him in her attitude to sex. 'Okay...'

'I'm sorry,' Ellie said curtly. 'I was... I was upset.'

And with that apology she spun on her heel and walked into the hotel. Her head had a natural tilt, her hips a shapely sway, the skirt dancing above her long slender legs and, that fast, Rio was hard as a rock again, his hands clenching into fists by his sides. She drove him crazy, he reminded himself unnecessarily. But he had had her now and that should be that, game over. Hit it and quit it, he repeated to himself. He didn't *still* want her. Of course he didn't, so walk away, a little voice in his brain instructed.

Rio swung back into his car. The sound of Ellie moaning as he kissed her engulfed him, the surprised look of ecstasy on her face when she came, the exquisite feel of her soft, satiny skin. He swore vehemently, emptied his mind and dug out his phone. He needed a woman, *any* woman just as long as she wasn't Ellie.

In a daze, Ellie went for a shower. She still ached. There would be no forgetting what she had done. And the incredulous way Rio had looked at her in the car park would stay with her until the day she died. Her face burned afresh. She should have kept quiet, she shouldn't have said anything, should have left that short-lived intimacy and all memory of it back in his house in the hills where it belonged. A mistaken moment and not an important one in her scheme of things. Only sex. Although it would not be *only* sex if she fell pregnant, she conceded wretchedly, and refused to think about that angle on the grounds that it was stupid to worry before she knew she actually had something to worry about.

Although for the first time ever, Ellie desperately wanted to confide in someone and she thought about phoning Polly. She didn't think Polly would tell her husband, Rashad, about *that*. But how did she know for sure? She covered her face with wet hands, all the stress of the past forty-eight hours piling up on her along with every doubt and insecurity she possessed. She still didn't know how she had ended up having sex with Rio, but she knew she had wanted it to happen as much as he had. Being unable to put the blame on him stung, as well. He hadn't sweet-talked her, filled her up with booze or seduced her—*my goodness, anything but*, she conceded ruefully.

Beppe called her on her mobile and asked her to meet him at a doctor's surgery on the outskirts of Florence the next day. She refused the lift he offered her and assured him that she had satellite navigation and was happy to drive herself there. He invited her to dine at his home in the evening and she agreed, keen to take the opportunity to get to know him a little better, regardless of how Rio might feel about it. Should she tell Beppe that she knew Rio? Or would it be wiser to remain tactfully silent? She brooded about that while she got dressed to dine with Bruno.

It was a long evening. Bruno might have ticked all

the basic boxes in the tally of what made a man attractive but he bored on about his work ambitions while asking little about Ellie. He kissed her on the cheek outside her hotel. He invited her out again and she made a polite excuse and she didn't linger, speeding indoors, keen to get to bed.

Opening the door of her hotel room, she drew back with a sound of consternation when she saw the light burning beside her bed and the male reclining there. 'How on earth did you get in here?' she demanded.

Rio uncoiled fluidly off the bed and stretched with lazy assurance, not one whit perturbed by her attitude. 'It wasn't difficult. The staff know we're…close,' he selected with precision and the angry flush on her cheeks bloomed hotter still with chagrin. 'I also own a large stake in the hotel.'

'We are *not* close!' Ellie contradicted, tossing her bag down on the chair in the corner.

Rio shrugged a broad shoulder, gracefully and silently evasive. He was as effortlessly beautiful as a dark angel sent to tempt even with his black hair tousled, his jawline shadowed and his tie missing. Her heartbeat had picked up speed. Her tiredness had taken a mysterious step back and she was already breathing as if she had run up a hill. And there was the craziest melting sensation in that place where she still ached from his sheer sexual energy. Yet she didn't want *that* again, did she? It was a badly timed thought to have in Rio's presence because her entire body quickened as if she had punched a button to switch it on to supersensitivity. Her nipples stung and her thighs pressed together as if to silence the squirming readiness low in her pelvis.

'Are you planning to tell me what you're doing here?' Ellie enquired stiffly, tamping down all those disobedient thoughts and responses.

'I wanted to be sure you came back alone,' Rio told her.

'And how is that your business?'

'You were with me today,' Rio murmured.

Ellie tilted her chin, emerald eyes gleaming like chips of ice. 'Doesn't mean you own me.'

Rio shrugged again. 'I'd still have beaten the hell out of him had you brought him upstairs.'

Ellie's lips parted and then closed again because there really wasn't much she could say to that. 'You do a lot of that sort of thing?' she prompted a split second later, honest curiosity gripping her.

'Get physical? Once it was a regular activity.' Dark eyes spilling a glittering gleam of gold from below lush curling black lashes, Rio strode past her to the door. 'I had to, to protect myself. I grew up in a tough environment.'

'You're leaving?' Ellie framed in disconcertion and then could have bitten her tongue out because she was making it sound as though she wanted him to stay. And she didn't.

'Sì...' Rio treated her to a slow burning appraisal. 'Somehow I doubt that you'd be up for anything else tonight, *principessa*.'

Fury splintered through Ellie. Leave it to Rio to tell it as it is. He would stay for sex but not to chat or share a drink or supper or anything more civilised. The claustrophobic silence of the room enclosed her, increasing her nervous tension. The tip of her tongue stole out to moisten her dry lower lip.

'I *love* your mouth,' Rio husked soft and low, his attention locking to the sultry fullness of her pink lips.

Gooseflesh pebbled Ellie's arms and a wicked little quiver snaked down her taut spinal cord. She was so aware of him that her very skin prickled and tingled with it. For an insane moment she imagined pushing him backwards down on the bed and teaching him that he didn't know everything about her. And then she blinked, sane Ellie swimming back to the fore, and she spun and opened the door for him so that he would leave more quickly.

'Sometimes you crack me up, *bella mia*,' Rio confided with unholy amusement, recognising her defensiveness in that almost desperate pulling open of the door to hasten his departure. 'When you're thinking about me in bed tonight, will you be kissing me or thumping me?'

Ellie breathed in so deep she almost spontaneously combusted while she watched Rio clatter down the stairs without an ounce of discomfiture in his bearing. She had never met anyone quite like Rio Benedetti before and that was probably why he knocked her for six every time she saw him, she told herself soothingly. He was bad, he was brash, he was incredibly sexy and insolent and he had the kind of charismatic confidence that burned like a solar flare. She was too polite and inhibited to deal with him as he *should* be dealt with. Her hands clenched into fists.

He embarrassed her too. The staff had seen her going out with Bruno Nigrelli and now knew she had returned to find Rio waiting in her bedroom. Ought she to complain about that invasion? Or, having already been seen in Rio's company and kissing him, perhaps it was wiser to ignore the situation lest she end up even more embarrassed. Had Rio made her look slutty? Or like a femme fatale? She went to bed on that thought, deciding that Rio's pursuit, if she could label it with that word, made her look like a much more exciting woman than she actually was. But she still wanted to kill him for being so careless of appearances, so arrogant and incomprehensible.

Why would he have beaten up Bruno had she brought the other man back to her room? Presumably that had been a joke, although she had not seen the humour in it. She could not credit that Rio could be jealous or staking some sort of male claim to her. He wasn't the type. And instead of finding the sleep she badly needed the riddle of his complex personality ensured that she couldn't stop her brain running on and actually relax enough to drift off.

The following morning she met up with Beppe outside a smart suburban surgery near Florence. The older man looked perfectly calm and collected and there was no sign of strain or distress in either his expression or his friendly, easy manner. Had Rio exaggerated? Overreacted? They went inside the surgery and swabs were taken. Beppe passed over a tiny gold locket, which he quietly admitted contained a lock of his brother's hair. Ellie flushed and made no comment. After all, her mother, Annabel, had named both brothers as her daughter's possible father, and to do so, she had presumably been uncertain as to which had fathered her child.

'We will know within twenty-four hours,' Beppe assured her with quiet satisfaction. 'And now that I have you here in my beloved Firenze, I will play tourist with you and show you the sights as they should be seen.'

Relieved by his mood and the welcome offer of his company, Ellie relaxed and over a cup of coffee and a pastry in a sun-drenched square found herself admitting that she knew Rio and had first met him at her sister's wedding.

The older man did not hide his astonishment. 'He should've told me that—'

'To be honest,' Ellie added hurriedly, 'Rio and I didn't get on very well, so it wasn't an acquaintance either of us was likely to pursue.'

Beppe sighed. 'You surprise me. Women are drawn to my godson. Obviously you've seen him since your arrival—'

'He called in at the hotel on my first day. I didn't tell him anything,' Ellie assured him, her cheeks colouring when she was forced to think of what else she had done with Rio since that day, but it was a major relief for her to admit simply that she knew Rio.

'Rio put me on a pedestal a very long time ago,' Beppe confided wryly. 'If you and I discover that we are related by blood, it will be a huge shock for him and that is why I have told him nothing as yet.'

'Were you friends with his parents? I know he's your godson.'

'No, my wife and I never knew his parents,' Beppe admitted dismissively and changed the subject to ask her to choose where she would like to go first with him.

Beppe took her to see Michelangelo's sculptures in the Galleria dell'Academia before showing her his favourite paintings in the Uffizi. Her frank admission that she knew nothing whatsoever about art did her no disservice in his eyes and when she liked something he asked her *why* she liked it, evidently set on forming her taste. He also told her a little about his own family background. The *palazzo* had been in his family for several generations and the Sorrentino prosperity had originally been built on the production of internationally acclaimed wines. His younger brother, Vincenzo, had once managed the vineyards. Beppe had always been academic and had worked as a university professor before his wife's ill health had forced him to take a step back from his career. From that point on, he had become more involved in his wife's charitable endeavours, which had been very much focussed on the needs of disabled and disadvantaged children.

'What time is dinner this evening?' Ellie asked when Beppe had finally returned her to her car. She noted that he was out of breath and perspiring and she scolded herself for letting him do so much on a hot day when he was clearly by his girth and indoor habits not usually a physically active man.

'Nine o'clock. And it will be formal,' Beppe warned her. 'But don't worry about that if you have no formal wear with you. Everyone will understand that you are on holiday.'

Ellie smiled at that recollection as she returned to her hotel. Thanks to Polly's holiday shop, Ellie had a dream of a dress hanging in the wardrobe. In fact, uninterested though she had always been in fashion, it was the sort of dress that brought stars to her eyes because it was wonderfully feminine and flowing. Fashioned of peach lace, it was a daring colour for a redhead, but remarkably flattering against her pale skin and bright hair. She showered and paid more heed than usual to the minimal make-up she wore while wondering if Rio would be at the dinner. Would he be annoyed that she had gone ahead and told his godfather that they already knew each other? Staying silent on that score had become impossible for her because Beppe was so very straight-forward and plain-spoken and she did not want to risk losing his good opinion by keeping secrets from him.

The gravel in front of Beppe's home was a sea of luxury-model cars, which disconcerted Ellie because evidently the dinner party was a much bigger, fancier event than she had assumed it would be. Her fear that she would prove to be overdressed receded as soon as she was shown into a crowded salon filled with clusters of very elegant laughing and chattering guests. Beppe hurried straight over to welcome her and tucked her hand over his arm protectively as he took her to join the group he was with. Within a few minutes, Ellie had relaxed.

And then the door opened again and she glanced across the room to see the new arrivals and saw Rio entering with a tall willowy blonde clinging to his arm. Her heart sank and she couldn't stop it from doing that. Her pleasant smile lurched and her tummy flipped and all of a sudden she felt ridiculously sick and shaky. What the heck was the matter with her? She was not in a re-lationship with Rio, was she? Why should it bother her that he was already showing off another woman? After all, she had known from the outset that he was a noto-rious womaniser with few moral scruples.

Rio was taken aback by Ellie's presence because Beppe hadn't mentioned that his visitor would be at-tending. Nor did it help that Ellie looked stupendous in an apricot dress that smoothly shaped her lush curves at breast and hip while highlighting her porcelain-pale skin and the sheer vibrancy of her coppery tumbling mane of hair. His physical response was swift and urgent, the swelling at his groin an unwelcome reminder that 'hit it and quit it' hadn't worked for him where she was concerned. Above her breast, she had fastened a diamond brooch in the shape of a star and it was the only jewellery she wore. So, she *did* have the diamond brooch her uncle had accused her of stealing, Rio recognised in sudden disgust, the brooch she had denied all knowledge of after her grandmother's death. For Rio, it was a timely reminder of the kind of woman he was dealing with in Ellie Dixon. At heart she had to be a greedy, gold-digging liar who had learned how to put on a good show as a caring, compassionate doctor.

Rio strode straight up to Beppe and introduced his gorgeous companion, who seemed unable to take her eyes off Ellie's dress. The blonde's name was Carmela and she was unquestionably beautiful and very different in style from Ellie. She was taller, thinner, blue-eyed and possessed enviably straight, long silky blond hair. Her dress was much more revealing than Ellie's but then she had a perfect body to reveal. A long slender leg showed through the side slit in the dress while the plunging neckline showed a great deal of her improbably large, high breasts. Gorgeous but kind of slutty, Ellie decided, discomfited by the speed with which that shrewish opinion came to her mind.

'Of course, Ellie needs no introduction to you, Rio,' his godfather, Beppe, pointed out smoothly as an opening salvo. 'Since you first met at her sister's wedding.'

Rio was transfixed by that bombshell reminder coming at him out of nowhere and unadulterated rage roared through his big powerful frame as his attention shot to Ellie, who evaded his gaze while slowly turning as red as a tomato, her guilt writ large in her face. Ellie had chosen to come clean with Beppe and had dropped him in it without conscience, Rio registered grimly. A power play? Or was it a warning? What else might she choose to tell his godfather about him? Shot through with anger and frustration at his inability to respond with the truth, Rio was incapable of even forcing a smile.

'We didn't hit it off,' Ellie said abruptly. 'That's why he didn't mention it.'

Shot from rage to wonderment at that apparent intervention on his behalf, Rio dealt Ellie a suspicious look from glittering dark-as-jet eyes semiveiled by his lush lashes and shrugged. 'First impressions are rarely reliable,' he quipped as he turned away to address someone else who had spoken to him.

Ellie was appalled that something she had revealed had caused tension between Rio and Beppe. Her trip to Italy and her search for her father were definitely beginning to feel like a minefield she was trying to pick her way across.

As Rio moved to grasp a glass from a tray and pass it to her, Carmela hissed, 'That redhead's wearing a Lavroff!'

Rio shot the fashion model on his arm a blank appraisal.

'That dress was the star of the Lavroff show I walked for in the spring.'

A designer gown, surely a little rich for a junior doctor's salary? Although perhaps not too expensive for a doctor whose dying patient had left her everything she possessed, Rio reflected sombrely. It was starting to occur to him that he had underestimated Ellie and how much trouble she was capable of causing. He could see at a glance that she already had Beppe wrapped round her little finger. In fact, her hand was resting comfortably on the older man's arm. Rio dragged in a sudden breath, his lean, darkly handsome features tensing into tough lines of restraint. Was *that* what he had to fear?

Ironically that risk hadn't even crossed his mind because Beppe lived a celibate life and had never been known to seek out female companionship. But Beppe had been acquainted with Ellie's mother, and if Ellie's mother had been even half as beautiful as her daughter, she would hardly have been forgettable. Back then, however, Beppe had been safely married and now he was not and he was making no attempt to hide his delight in Ellie's company. Rio stationed himself where he could watch his godfather and he was sharply disconcerted by the level of familiarity he could already see developing between the pair. Ellie whispered something in Beppe's ear and he chuckled and patted her hand fondly. He moved her on with him to another group of guests, giving her no opportunity to stray.

At his elbow, Carmela was still whinging on enviously about the Lavroff gown. Rio wasn't interested. He often paid for the designer clothes his lovers wore but he took no interest in the names or the cost, writing the expenses off as the cost of maintaining a reasonable sex life. His entire focus remained on Ellie. He listened to her making intelligent conversation, heard her laugh several times and learned that she had toured the Uffizi gallery with Beppe. *Inferno*, she certainly didn't need to be taught how to best please a much older, lonely man with a lifelong love of art. But she would soon learn her mistake if she persisted on her current ambitious trajectory. Rio would destroy her before he would allow her to hurt Beppe Sorrentino.

And what if she's pregnant? Rio backed away a step as Carmela tried to get closer to him. He studied Ellie as they were seated at the dining table and strove to imagine that shapely body swollen with his child. The idea unnerved him but it also excited him in a peculiar way, which only had the effect of unnerving him even more.

Ellie barely touched the food on her plate. She eavesdropped on Carmela's airheaded views on suntans as affected by climate change. She noticed that Rio didn't listen to a word his companion said and appeared to be tuning her out like an irritating noise. She watched him, as well, catching the downward slant of his beautifully shaped mouth, the tension in his exquisite bone structure that hardened his exotic cheekbones and placed hollows beneath them. He was furious with her, she *knew* he was. Rio had a temper like a flamethrower and he was boiling like a cauldron of oil.

But Ellie was angry too. Only the day before he had been with her and last night he had been waiting for her in her hotel room. And now he was with a beautiful blonde model, who operated off one very talkative brain cell. Why was she hurt? Why the hell was she hurting over his rejection of her as a woman? Time after time over the years Ellie had learned that men didn't really want career-driven, independent women. She wasn't feminine enough, she wasn't *soft* enough, she could deal with a spider just fine but a mouse sent her screaming. She was stubborn and contrary and choosy and he didn't fit the bill for her either, so why was she agonising? Why would she want a gorgeous, arrogant, shameless man whore in her life anyway? She was far too sensible and strait-laced for a male of his ilk. Sheer lust had put her in his arms and she had got what she deserved, she told herself repressively.

Beppe took her and several other guests to admire his latest painting acquisition in the hall. Rio and Carmela joined them. Carmela wondered out loud if the seventeenth-century subject of the portrait was wearing hair extensions. Ellie whispered a polite, 'Excuse me...' in Beppe's ear as he guided the group into his library to show them something else and she walked down the corridor to the cloakroom instead. Freshening up, she grimaced at her anxious reflection in the mirror. Why was it that when Rio was around he dominated everything? Including her thoughts?

When she emerged, Rio was standing waiting for her, his lean, dark face stormy and tense. 'I want a word,' he told her grimly.

'But I *don't*,' Ellie told him as he snapped a hand round her wrist and pulled her outdoors onto the cool, formal *loggia* with pillars that ran along that side of the house.

'You're such a bully, Rio!' Ellie objected, rubbing her wrist the instant he released it as though he had bruised her.

Rio backed her up against the stone wall behind her by the simple expedient of moving forward, shutting out any view of the gardens and forcing her to tip her head back to look up at him. 'What did you tell Beppe about us?' he demanded in a raw undertone.

'Very little. That we met at the wedding and that you called on me at the hotel the day I arrived,' Ellie proffered. 'I didn't tell him what you said or threatened or anything of that nature. I simply wanted to clear the air. Pretending we were strangers…I mean, why would I mislead Beppe like that? I've got nothing to hide—'

'Not according to the report I had done on you,' Rio reminded her darkly.

Ellie bridled at that reference, fully convinced that any close and proper check on her background would reveal that she was innocent of any wrongdoing. 'I didn't intend to cause friction between you and Beppe. I didn't think of that angle,' she admitted guiltily. 'But I'm sorry that I embarrassed you like that—'

'Are you really?' Rio lifted a sardonic ebony brow, staring down at her, noting the mere hint at her neckline of the pale valley between her full breasts and entranced by the new discovery that showing so little could actually be sexier than showing a lot. As he tensed, inescapably recalling his own response to those luscious curves the day before, he whipped his gaze up to her face in the hope of lowering his temperature. 'I think you dropped me in it deliberately to cause trouble,' he contended.

'But then you would think that because you always think the worst of me,' Ellie shot back at him in exasperation. 'Exactly what is your problem, Rio?'

Rio ran his fingertip along the succulent curve of her lower lip and watched a tiny pulse flicker fast at the base of her elegant white throat. 'You're my only problem, *principessa*,' he told her huskily. 'We had our moment and that was supposed to be it—'

'It *is* it!' Ellie seethed, furious that he was cornering her when he had brought another woman to dinner.

'Not for me,' Rio confided, letting a coppery corkscrew curl coil round his finger like a vine, his stunning dark golden eyes hot and hungrily gripping hers by sheer force of will. 'I'm not done yet—'

'But I *am*,' Ellie spelled out thinly. 'You're ruining my holiday—'

'When we're done, I'll *tell* you,' Rio asserted, bending down to nip at her full lower lip with the edge of his teeth.

A violent shiver ran down through her taut body, that tiny sting of pain somehow setting off a chain reaction of electrified awareness and sensitivity. He lowered his head and he took her mouth with a raw sexual demand that momentarily stole Ellie's wits. She fell back against the wall, knees weak, melting heat surging in her pelvis.

'Rio!' a voice interposed curtly, and both of them froze.

Rio lifted his dark head and stepped back to study his godfather, keen to interpret his expression. Beppe looked angry and protective. Ellie straightened, her face flushing as mortification consumed her.

'Carmela's looking for you,' Beppe murmured flatly. 'I suggest that you take her home. I would also suggest that you stay away from Ellie.'

Rio released his breath in an audible hiss. 'Although I'm always ready to listen to suggestions, Beppe,' he conceded, 'I've always forged my own path.'

With a nod of acknowledgement to Ellie and the older man, Rio strode back indoors, not one whit perturbed by the scene Beppe had interrupted. Or, at least, if he was bothered, he wasn't showing it, Ellie acknowledged.

'I have no right to interfere,' Beppe said uncomfortably to Ellie. 'I love Rio like a son but I also know him.

He had some unfortunate experiences with women in his youth and I would advise you to keep your distance. He plays with women. He doesn't take them seriously. He would hurt you and I would hate to see that happen. Furthermore, if you prove to be either my niece or even my daughter, you will often meet Rio and that—'

'Could get very awkward,' Ellie filled in ruefully for herself. 'It's all right, Beppe. I kind of worked out that stuff about Rio anyway, so don't worry about me. I'm a big girl and I can look after myself.'

Rio and Carmela were nowhere to be seen when they rejoined the rest of the guests. Ellie stayed quite late but insisted on returning to her hotel when Beppe offered her the use of a guest room. She drove back in a contemplative state of mind and wondered if she would find Rio in her room again. Not this time however.

Soberly she lay in bed, wondering about the results of the DNA test. Would she prove to be half-Sorrentino? Or was she in for a shock on that score? It was perfectly possible, after all, that some time after Beppe's rejection her mother had spent a night with some other man. Well, at least she would soon know one way or another, even if she didn't actually manage to identify her father, she told herself soothingly.

But how would Rio react if she was a Sorrentino? Ironically she didn't want to upset him but nor was she willing to apologise for an act of fate. She was already wondering what Beppe's mention of Rio's 'unfortunate youthful experiences' with women had entailed. But then surely no intelligent male could be so innately distrustful and cynical about her sex without cause?

And what did it matter? She relived the teasing sting of his teeth on her lip and a forbidden little quiver snaked through her. With a groan she rolled over and pressed her offending mouth into the pillow. Rio was as potent as poison and equally toxic and Beppe was right, she *needed* to keep her distance. To do anything else would be to court disaster because Rio had no off switch, no respect for boundaries…and probably even less respect for her, she conceded unhappily.

CHAPTER SIX

BEPPE CALLED ELLIE bright and early and asked her to come to his home. Ellie surmised that he had bad news and she took her time over her breakfast in the hotel courtyard, trying not to stress over what could not be changed. Beppe had been wonderfully approachable and kind and helpful and she wanted to thank him for that. He could've denied any knowledge of her late mother but instead he had told her the unvarnished truth, even though doing so had raked up guilty memories and regrets.

Ellie drove over to the *palazzo* and Adriano showed her out to the shaded *loggia*, quickly reappearing with a tray of coffee and biscuits. Beppe appeared then, rather flushed in appearance and with eyes that were a little shiny.

He studied her and he then smiled widely, a smile brimming with happiness and appreciation. 'Ellie,' he began emotively as he handed her a sheet of paper to study. 'You *are* my daughter and I cannot begin to describe how much that discovery means to me.'

Lively with excitement, Beppe could hardly be persuaded to drink his coffee as he ignored her medical training to explain rather unnecessarily the 99.99 recur-

ring percentage of accuracy established by the success-
ful DNA test. 'I would've been delighted to discover
that you were my niece but to discover a daughter, a
first child after all these years, is an unimaginable joy!'

Ellie reached across the small circular table and
grasped his hand to squeeze it. 'Thank you for saying that.'

'It comes from the centre of my heart,' Beppe told
her warmly. 'Amalia give birth to a stillborn son just
weeks before she suffered her stroke. We were devastated. I don't believe, though, that I could have told her
about you were she still alive. It would have hurt her
too much and my affair had already caused her enormous grief.'

'How do you think Rio will take this news?' Ellie
asked, dry-mouthed.

Beppe emitted a heavy sigh. 'He will be here for
lunch and I will tell him then. He will be happy that I
am happy but very disappointed to hear that I once betrayed Amalia. If only we had adopted him as I wished,
he would have been more certain of his place in the
family.'

Ellie sat forward, brow furrowed, her curiosity engaged. 'You wanted to *adopt* Rio?'

'*Sì*. I will respect his privacy by not giving you details but he had neither parents nor a home and I wanted
to take him in, but Amalia refused to set another child
in what she always viewed as our stillborn son's place,'
he confided heavily. 'There were also elements of Rio's
background which disturbed her and she could not be
persuaded to change her mind. He never knew that I
wanted to adopt him though. Our contribution to his life
became less direct as he grew up. We advised him, en-

sured he got a good education and supported him when he needed us but we could have protected him a great deal more had we adopted him and brought him up here.'

'That's unfortunate but Rio has still done very well for himself, hasn't he?'

'If you measure success by prosperity, his wealth reached stratospheric proportions after he won the oil contracts in Dharia. He is very much a self-made man,' Beppe declared with pride. 'But he is also a man damaged by a traumatic childhood and a tough adolescence. I should've done more for him.'

'By the sound of it, you did the best you could in the circumstances,' Ellie remarked soothingly, troubled more than she liked by the reference to Rio's traumatic childhood and troubled adolescence. Yes, she could imagine how such experiences would have hardened him and what a difference a loving, supportive home background could have made. After all, she knew that she too was marked by the lack of love in her childhood. Her grandmother hadn't wanted to raise her daughter's two illegitimate children and had only done so because Annabel had paid her handsomely to take on that responsibility. When that flow of money had stopped, presumably because Annabel had suffered bankruptcy and ill health, her grandmother had complained bitterly about how much of a burden her granddaughters were. Polly's affection had provided the only love Ellie had experienced during those years.

'I think I'll go back to the hotel now,' Ellie announced, hardening herself to Beppe's look of disappointment. 'Rio will be arriving soon and we both need some time to think. This is a lot to take on board and so much more than I ever expected to learn.'

'I hope you will pack and come here to stay with me for what remains of your holiday,' Beppe admitted. 'And perhaps someday you will feel comfortable enough to call me *Papà*.'

Ellie's eyes prickled with tears as she left. She felt ridiculously emotional and when Beppe gave her a small, almost daring hug on the doorstep it almost made the pent-up tears spill down her cheeks. He was willing to be her father and she was in a daze of shock and happiness. It bothered her to appreciate that Rio was unlikely to celebrate the same news. Rio didn't like her and didn't trust her and the revelation that she was his precious godfather's daughter would hit him hard. Would it hurt him that she had the blood tie with Beppe that he had been denied? She flinched from the thought, marvelling at how oversensitive she was to any thought of Rio being hurt.

It was so ridiculous, she thought ruefully. Big, tough, angry, hostile Rio would not be so easily hurt. Why was she even considering how he would feel about her parentage? What business was it of his? After all, the scene had been set before she was even born by Beppe's affair with her unhappy mother. By the sound of it that extra-marital affair had caused tremendous unhappiness for all the parties involved, but surely after so many years Beppe could begin to forgive himself and both of them could now concentrate on forming a relationship? That conviction at the forefront of her mind, Ellie packed her case and then walked down to the village to kill some time and allow Beppe to speak to Rio in peace.

Rio departed from Beppe's home reeling from what his godfather had dropped on him. An adulterous affair and a daughter? No, he had certainly not seen that possibility on the horizon and it changed everything, his own position most of all. Ellie had played a blinder of a game by concealing her true motivation for being in Italy right to the very end, Rio acknowledged bitterly. In fact, she had trussed him up like a chicken ready for the roasting pot. Beppe had openly voiced his concern that Rio nourished dishonourable intentions towards his newfound daughter. Beppe had no idea that Rio had already gone much further than that and if he found out it would destroy his relationship with Rio. Worse still, if she was pregnant, Beppe would be digging out a shotgun.

It was time to take the initiative, not a time to sit back and vacillate over what-ifs and maybes, Rio reflected sardonically. Left in ignorance, he had dug himself into a deep hole and he had to dig himself out of it again and to do that he needed Ellie's help whether he liked it or not. Raging resentment surged up through the cracks inside him and there was no healing balm of acceptance to soothe it. Beppe was, after all, the only true family Rio had ever had, the only adult who had ever shown him love, consideration and understanding while he was still a child. And now Beppe had a daughter, whom Rio had wronged. That she could well be a money-grabbing young woman keen to feather her own nest scarcely counted now that she was about to become Beppe's heir. Furthermore, Beppe would never believe the allegations made against Ellie for there was virtually no proof of misconduct on her part.

Rio had hired a second agency to check and update the evidence he had originally been given. The hospice enquiry *had* cleared Ellie of any wrongdoing and she *had* refused the inheritance left to her by one of her patients. The only dirt left in the first investigative report relied heavily on her embittered uncle's tale about the diamond brooch and, as the police had refused to prosecute, the whole story could easily be written off as being more rumour and backstabbing than actual fact. And furthermore, if Ellie *was* a gold-digger, Rio was about to make her feel as if she'd won the lottery.

When he learned that she had checked out of the hotel he was taken aback until he noticed that her hire car was still parked outside. The receptionist told him that Ellie had walked down into the village. He found her in the cool of the ancient stone church, studying a much-admired triptych of the Madonna and Child.

When he spoke her name, she whirled round, a figure of light and movement in the dim, dark interior. Her dress was the ice blue of diamonds and the sunlight cascading through a stained-glass window high up the wall showered her in a dancing rainbow of colour that only emphasised the vibrant copper of her tumbling hair. She wasn't quick enough to hide the dismay and anxiety that crossed her face when she saw him and the tense expression and attitude that took over to stiffen her into stillness was no more welcoming.

Welcome to your biggest challenge yet, Rio thought grimly, trying not to notice how beautiful she was in that naturally beautiful way that so many women tried and failed to achieve. He froze there, suppressing his body's equally natural instincts, none of which felt appropriate in the House of God.

'Rio...' Ellie whispered uncertainly, mortified by the nerves that had stolen the volume from her voice.

He could have been carved from stone as he stood

there, still and quiet as a predator, sheathed in a light grey designer suit. He resembled a stone angel with cutting cheekbones, a hard-hewn jawline and a mouth as wilful, stubborn and passionate as sin. His eyes were a pure dazzling gold in the light and she blinked rapidly, striving to shut the sheer intensity of him out and to be polite but distant, treating him the same way she usually treated men. But how could she achieve that when she knew in her heart that he had sought her out because he was shocked and agitated by what Beppe had shared with him?

'Are you a believer?' he prompted lightly.

'Yes. Are you?'

'I was raised by nuns in an orphanage and spent more time on my knees than in school. Of course I am,' Rio told her wryly.

And it was as though he had squeezed her heart at the same time as he filled in some of the blanks in her repeated attempts to understand what made him what he was. An orphanage, she thought sadly.

'I bet you were always in trouble,' Ellie remarked without thinking.

'Pretty much. Beppe and his wife raised funds for the home and did a lot to help the children, particularly the disabled ones amongst us,' Rio admitted. 'Although that home is closed now and conditions are greatly improved in its replacement. Beppe is still very much involved in finding employment and educational opportunities for the less fortunate. He is a good man.'

'Yes,' Ellie agreed tightly.

'And you are his daughter,' Rio declared without any perceptible emotion at all. 'I must assume you take after your mother since you don't look much like your father.'

'She was tall, red-haired and pale-skinned like me. I think I get my lack of height from Beppe,' Ellie breathed uncomfortably. 'You're angry that I didn't tell you why I so particularly wanted to meet Beppe.'

'It wasn't your secret to share,' Rio conceded, surprising her. 'But I must confess that I was completely unprepared for what he admitted to me. I shouldn't have been. There must have been times when he felt trapped in his marriage. He is only human.'

'Let's not talk about that,' Ellie advised. 'I don't think we can ever understand that sort of situation unless we've actually lived the same experience—'

'*Porca miseria!* That's a very compassionate comment from judgemental Ellie!' Rio commented, an ebony brow slanting up in apparent wonderment.

'Let's also try not to argue.' Ellie sent him a rueful look of appeal. 'You're shocked right now, of course you're shocked. You thought you knew everything there was to know about Beppe—'

'I don't want judgemental Ellie *or* Dr Ellie right at this moment,' Rio interposed.

The pale triangle of her face flushed as though he had slapped her. 'I'm not sure I know how to be anything else—'

'We'll have coffee…and talk,' Rio framed, extending a lean, long-fingered hand to her in invitation.

Ellie hesitated as if a shark had bared its teeth at her. And then she forced her arm to lift and she grasped his hand, a frisson of quivering awareness shimmying down her spine. He was trying to accept her and because he was making the effort, she had to make it too. His attitude thoroughly disconcerted her because she had expected only anger, condemnation and suspicion from Rio and he had just as swiftly proven her expectations wrong.

She had expected Rio to walk her across the square to the local café but instead he tucked her into the car illegally parked outside. Belatedly it occurred to her that the busy little café would scarcely be a good choice for a private chat.

'Where are we going?' she asked.

'My home. Have you had lunch?'

'No, but I'm not really hungry… Too much excitement today,' she extended wryly.

His long brown fingers flexed smoothly round the steering wheel and she remembered those fingers skimming across her body, expert and deliberate. She dragged in a short sustaining breath but she could still feel the tingling in her swelling breasts and the pulse of damp heat between her thighs. He had stripped her bare of every conviction she had once had about herself, she acknowledged reluctantly. She was a much more sexual being than she had ever dreamt but it had taken Rio to awaken and set free that side of her nature. It was terrifying to feel so vulnerable and yet Rio was currently on his very best behaviour, she recognised suddenly. Why was that? What was he planning? Why had he not yet said a single angry or insulting word to her?

'Who did this house belong to before you bought it?' she asked to break the silence as he steered the Ferrari down the long drive.

'An ancestor of Beppe's, who kept his mistress here—'

'How novel,' Ellie said drily.

'Yes, he was considered the rotten apple in the very respectable family barrel and after he died the house was left to go to rack and ruin because no one in the family thought it acceptable to live in what had once been the mistress's home. I bought it at auction and restored it. It's convenient to have somewhere close when I visit...*your father.*'

He voiced the designation with cool clarity. *Your father.* It shook her to accept that she finally had a father and that the ancestor who had kept a mistress had actually been one of her ancestors, as well. It was as though a family tree had suddenly unfolded in front of her and she smiled at the wonderful sense of security that gave her. 'I thought you would've stayed with Beppe when you visited—'

'Not if I wanted female companionship. You may not have noticed it but Beppe is rather old-fashioned in spite of his liaison with your mother,' Rio commented. 'It's simply easier to keep that side of my life away from him.'

Ellie climbed out of the car in the sunlight, grateful to have movement to distract her from thoughts of Rio's chequered past. None of her business, she reminded herself doggedly as he led the way into the big house. A housekeeper greeted them at the door and Rio addressed her in Italian.

'I ordered a light lunch for you,' Rio told her. 'You shouldn't be skipping meals.'

Ellie compressed her lips on a hasty reply.

'And you know I'm right,' Rio added with unblemished assurance.

He guided her out to a shaded terrace and pulled out a comfortable padded chair for her. 'Sit down...'

'You're so bossy,' Ellie complained, settling down and kicking off her canvas shoes to flex her overheated bare feet on the cold stone.

His housekeeper arrived with freshly squeezed orange juice for her and a glass of wine for Rio. She wondered if she was being deprived of the alcohol option because she could be pregnant but said nothing because she had been avoiding alcohol since their moment of madness. She liked that label. A moment of madness suggested a crazy once-only impulse that was out of character, but then everything that had happened with Rio had been out of character.

'What did you want us to talk about?' she pressed boldly, not wanting him to think she was tongue-tied in his presence.

'I brought you here to propose to you but I'm not quite sure how to go about it,' Rio murmured lazily. 'If I got down on one knee, you would laugh. If I told you how much I'm worth, you would accuse me of being boorish—'

Her lashes lifted high on her bright green eyes as she stared at him fixedly. His lean, darkly handsome features were sardonic and she frowned in bewilderment. 'Propose…propose what exactly?'

Rio gazed steadily back at her, dark eyes glittering like black diamonds. 'Marriage…obviously.'

'Are you out of your mind?' Ellie gasped sharply.

'No, possibly I'm foreseeing Beppe's reaction if he discovers that I've got his wonderful new daughter pregnant,' Rio extended quietly. 'And, yes, I'm aware that we don't know as yet whether you have conceived but it would be much worse to wait and see in the current climate.'

'You *are* insane,' Ellie exclaimed, gulping down a reviving swallow of orange juice.

'Not at all. I know that Beppe will never forgive

me if I've got you pregnant. He will blame me entirely
for it because I have a rather raunchy reputation with
women—'

'*Raunchy?*' Ellie rested her head to one side as if she
was considering that word. 'Do you think rumours of
your three-in-a-bed sexcapades have spread?'

Rio groaned out loud and sprang upright while
shooting her a reproachful look. 'Can't you please put
judgemental Ellie away for a while and have a serious
conversation with me?'

Ellie winced. 'Not really. I can't take a marriage pro
posal from you seriously.'

Rio backed up against a stone pillar like a cornered
lion and studied her with scorching golden eyes. 'That
night in Dharia, I did not invite those women to my
hotel room. They bribed their way in—'

Ellie pushed her stiff shoulders back into her comfortable seat and inclined her head. 'Oh, I guessed that,'
she admitted. 'I assumed you wouldn't have double-
booked yourself.'

The faintest colour scored Rio's hard cheekbones.
'You can't blame me for what *they* chose to do—'

'No, but what they did and what they assumed was
acceptable said a great deal about the nature of your
prior relationship with them,' Ellie pointed out with
hot cheeks.

Rio swore long and low in Italian and finished his
wine to set the glass down with a jarring snap on the
table. 'I didn't have a *relationship* with either of them!'
he fired back. 'I had sex with them on one drunken
night years before the wedding. I admit that I did stuff
when I was younger that I wouldn't do now—'

Her face stiff as she struggled not to betray any reaction, Ellie nodded.

'Just because you never felt the urge to experiment doesn't mean we're all the same...or that you're better than me!' Rio raked back at her.

'I don't think I'm better than you in any way. But that kind of experimentation doesn't appeal to me,' she confided.

'I can't lie and say I'm surprised,' Rio breathed, watching her like a hawk. 'Now we've got that out of the way and I can disclose that I have no plans to involve you in any form of sexual deviancy, can we concentrate on the marriage proposal?'

Ellie stiffened. 'Why would you want me to marry you?'

'If you do turn out to be pregnant I would have been asking you anyway,' Rio advanced. 'There is no way I would allow any woman to raise my child without me—'

'Rio... These days, single and separated parents are common—'

'I want my child to have everything I *didn't* have. A home, a solid background, two caring parents, security,' Rio extended almost argumentatively. 'It's only when you don't have those advantages that you realise how very important they are.'

'I understand that and I understand how you feel,' Ellie assured him, relieved that she knew more about his background than she had. 'But there's a reasonable chance that I *won't* be pregnant—'

'I don't want to wait and take the risk that you are because Beppe will judge me for that, as well, and regard me as an unwilling husband and a very bad bet.

It would be much easier just to tell him that we have fallen in love and wish to get married as soon as possible,' Rio argued. 'He will understand that and he will see nothing wrong with it.'

'I'm here on holiday,' Ellie reminded him helplessly. 'In a little over three weeks, I have to go home and return to work—'

'I will not come between you and your medical career. I own property in England and if you have to be there to complete your training, I will make that possible, whether you are pregnant or not,' he asserted.

That argument taken from her, Ellie slowly shook her buzzing head because he had taken her so much by surprise that she could barely think straight. 'So, you want to marry me to help take care of any child we might have and to keep Beppe content... Am I correct?'

'Sometimes you have the tongue of a viper,' Rio condemned in a harsh undertone. 'I want you for myself and for my own reasons and you know that! You know it every time you see me look at you, every time I touch you and struggle to *stop* touching you...'

Her pale skin flamed red at the dark liquid intensity of his deep voice. She lowered her head, finally acknowledging that she was equally out of control around him. In that they were equals. One kiss, one touch, one moment of madness wasn't enough to sate the craving. But marriage, marriage was something else entirely, wasn't it? It was forging a future together as partners, trusting each other.

'You don't trust me,' she reminded him. 'How can you marry a woman you don't trust?'

'With care,' Rio fielded. 'You don't trust me either. Time and better understanding would take care of that.

I'm sure we would both try to make the marriage a success—'

'People try that all the time with marriage and fail.'

'But there is honour in the trying,' Rio declared without hesitation. 'At least we would be doing the best we could to give our child a brighter future.'

'What if there is no child?'

'Then we eventually divorce and blame your long hours as a doctor and my business trips for keeping us apart too much,' Rio told her smoothly. 'Getting married now is a precaution for our potential child's benefit. The right start, the right environment—'

Ellie held up a hand to silence him. 'Yes, I get it but living with you would be a little like living on the side of a volcano waiting on the next eruption. You're very volatile—'

'And you're *not*?' Rio tossed back, watching her closely as her fine-boned hand closed round her orange juice to raise it to her peach-coloured mouth. 'If I had you in my bed every night I would be a lot less volatile—'

Ellie almost choked on her drink and, spluttering, set it down, her face flushing.

Rio shrugged and dealt her an amused look. 'Well, it's true. Having Beppe warn me off you doesn't improve my mood and makes it almost impossible for me to be with you.'

'We don't even have a relationship—'

'Then what *do* we have? You're splitting hairs, being too cautious. Take a risk on me,' Rio invited.

And she so *wanted* to do that, Ellie realised in astonishment. She had never done a reckless thing in her life but Rio tempted her to the edge of foolishness. What if she *was* pregnant? It would upset Beppe and mess up his relationship with Rio. It would be virtually impossible for her to manage to work and care properly for a child without a partner and a settled home. But to make that decision now when she had no idea whether or not she had conceived? She glanced up at him, at the strong face that sent her heart racing and turned her resolve to mush. Was it wise to give into that side of herself? Or would she live to regret it?

'Ellie…' Rio prodded impatiently.

'I don't rush major decisions!' Ellie responded.

Rio shot her a wicked smile. 'We could go to bed and think about it—'

'Another version of angry sex?'

'But you're not angry with me right now. You're attempting to work me out,' Rio surmised, uncoiling with fluid grace from the pillar he had been lounging back up against. 'But I'm really quite basic. If I didn't want you I wouldn't be suggesting this.'

The silence smouldered with unspoken undertones. In the interim, Rio's housekeeper reappeared with a tray. A plate of delicate and ridiculously enticing little sandwiches and a pot of tea were set down in front of Ellie.

'Think of how simple all this could be…if we do it my way,' Rio urged silkily. 'We say we're in love. We marry in haste. Beppe tries to dissuade us but is secretly delighted… And a baby, if there is one…would be the icing on the cake for him.'

Ellie snatched up another sandwich, registering that listening to Rio weave his arguments with such panache and conviction improved her appetite. He had drawn an attractive picture. If she didn't marry him and then discovered she was pregnant, how much damage would she do to her new relationship with Beppe? And could she really stand by while Rio took the blame when she knew she was just as much to blame? In addition, if she was pregnant, she would definitely be seriously considering Rio's marriage proposal because no one knew better than Ellie that raising a child alone was hard. In the course of her work she had met a lot of exhausted single parents struggling to keep work and family afloat. Her grandmother had struggled with that burden, as well, and both Polly and Ellie had been made thoroughly aware of that fact.

'I'm thinking about it,' she told Rio, who was emanating a wave of silent impatience. 'I won't give up work, you know. I'll never be a trophy wife. I don't like shopping or fussing with my appearance either,' she warned him.

'I'll shop for you,' Rio countered smoothly.

'Stop being so reasonable!' Ellie exclaimed in frustration. 'I'm not used to it—'

Rio stole the last sandwich and grinned at her. 'Stop being so sensible and so negative in your outlook.'

Ellie breathed in slow and deep. 'All right… I'll do it. I'll marry you. Are you happy now?'

Rio treated her to an approving appraisal. *'Finally.* We'll go and tell Beppe straight away and I'll get my staff on to organising the wedding—'

'I have to phone my sister first…and I want to do it in private,' Ellie told him squarely, sounding a great deal more sure of herself than she actually felt.

'And then we go and buy a ring,' Rio informed her. 'We'll go the traditional route—'

'Will we?' Ellie looked at him uncertainly, for she

certainly hadn't expected to be offered what she assumed to be the equivalent of an engagement ring.

Was the ring to impress Beppe with the reality of
them as a couple? Or was it supposed to please her? And
what was she going to say to Beppe? And how was she
going to explain to Polly that she was suddenly rush-
ing into marriage with a guy she had said she loathed?

CHAPTER SEVEN

'I JUST NEVER thought I'd see the day,' Polly carolled with a misty smile as she stepped back to scrutinise Ellie's appearance. 'You're getting married. I thought you were all set to be a spinster with a string of important letters after your name and a cat.'

Ellie had thought that too but she didn't admit it. She had never compromised on what she wanted from a man until Rio had literally crashed into her life at Polly's wedding. And that encounter had altered her image of herself and softened her rigid views. She had gradually begun to appreciate that she was lonely and that there was something hollow about achievements and more painful about trials when she had nobody to share those experiences with. Only now she was putting herself out there in a way she never had before, taking a risk on getting attached to a male who against all the odds appealed to her more than any other for no sane reason that she could find.

For Rio, she had lied for the first time in her life. She had told her father that she loved Rio but in actuality she had no idea what she felt for him. At first she had thought it was a mad infatuation but her thirst for information about him and her craving when he was absent had not faded. Surely an infatuation would have long since died from lack of fuel? All she really knew for certain was that Rio absolutely fascinated her, drew her and compelled her. And he made her feel more with him than she had felt in a lifetime of sensibly repressing strong emotions that unsettled her. And Rio had always specialised in seriously unsettling her.

She had been impressed even more when Rio had accurately forecast her father's every reaction to their marital plans and the stages of it. Beppe had initially been taken aback and had urged her not to rush into anything, but then Beppe had also confided that had he been free when he had met Ellie's mother he would have rushed to marry her. He had also admitted that he thoroughly understood the powerful life-enhancing effect of falling madly in love. And ultimately he had decided that as far as family growth went he could wish for no more than to see his daughter married to a young man he had always valued.

'Rio will grow with you by his side,' Beppe had forecast loftily. 'You make him think, you make him question what he truly wants from life. And what he has always wanted most of all is a family.'

Ellie gazed into the mirror and wondered if she was pregnant, if she could give Rio what he supposedly most wanted. But *was* that what Rio most wanted? Cavorting with all those women seemed a funny way of going about attaining a stable family life. Tomorrow morning, however, she would carry out the pregnancy test she had already purchased. She was both excited and scared by the idea. But most of all she was wondering how Rio would feel, regardless of what the result was.

She had naively assumed that she would see a great

deal more of Rio once their relationship was out in the open, but Rio had flown out to Dharia to settle some complicated dispute about oil well rights and although he had urged her to accompany him and she would've loved to see her sister sooner, she had refused. Why? Girly though it was, she had wanted to work with the wedding planner Beppe had hired and make her individual choices while also being available to ensure her gown fitted perfectly. After all, she was only planning to marry once.

And her dress fitted like a dream. The corset top had been chosen with Rio in mind. She just knew Rio would revel in hooks and laces and cleavage. The long skirt skimmed down in a flattering cut over her curvy hips and fanned out below the knee. Her feet were shod in Polly's gift, a pair of enchanting high-heeled sandals studded with pearls.

'Rashad really likes Rio and the men will be able to go off together when you visit and give us peace to gossip,' Polly remarked happily.

Ellie hid a smile because Polly was sometimes so innocent. The very last thing Ellie could imagine wanting just then was to be deprived of Rio's company. After all, he had been more absent than present since the wedding fervour kicked off. Beppe had held a series of social evenings to introduce his long-lost daughter to friends and relatives. Rio had dutifully attended those evenings before he flew out to Dharia, but Ellie's need to respect Beppe's boundaries had ensured that the bridal couple had little time alone together. Predictably, Rio had been much less accepting about the simple reality that she did not feel free to leave the *palazzo* to spend the night with him and possibly Ellie's insistence on restraint had kept him from hurrying back to Tuscany.

'When you have me wondering if we could contrive to have sex in my car without being picked up on a charge of public indecency, we have a problem, *principessa*,' Rio had complained the night before when he had joined them with Polly and Rashad for a quiet prewedding dinner. 'You need to learn to be more selfish and put us first.'

'No,' she had said. 'You need to learn that anticipation can act as an aphrodisiac.'

'But I don't need one of those,' Rio had responded with sardonic bite.

An abstracted smile tilted Ellie's lips now.

'You're nuts about him. I don't know how I didn't spot it at my wedding—'

'Your attention was elsewhere…on your bridegroom? And I'm not what you call "nuts" about him—'

'Oh, you so *are*,' Polly contradicted. 'Everything you've done just screams it, Ellie. You are not the sort of woman who meets a man and marries him within a couple of weeks unless he rocks your world…'

'People change,' Ellie argued and, eager to change the subject, added, 'isn't it really sad that we still haven't managed to find our missing sister? She could have been with us here today…'

Tracking down Lucy had so far proved difficult because she lived a travelling life, moving around a lot and surviving on casual jobs.

'We'll find her eventually,' Polly said soothingly. 'And it'll be very exciting when we do. Haven't you been tempted to look in her envelope and see what ring she was left and what name is attached to it? It could possibly help us to locate her.'

'No, I was trusted with that envelope and I wouldn't open it,' Ellie swore. 'How would you ever explain that to her when we finally met?'

'We could use steam to open it,' Polly suggested, colouring lightly at Ellie's raised brows.

'No, we should respect her privacy,' Ellie decreed.

Ellie descended the stairs smiling at her father, who stood at the foot beaming with pride. Beppe could not compliment her on her appearance enough. They travelled to the church in a limousine. She paused on the steps in the morning sunshine and she breathed in deep and slow, recognising that the elation she was feeling was happiness and marvelling at it while also fearing the undeniable storms ahead. She knew that she and Rio would argue and tussle and that there would be many times when she wanted to strangle him. That was normal life, she told herself prosaically, but true happiness was so rare a sensation for her that she wanted to make the most of it while she was feeling it.

Rio turned from the altar to get the full effect of his bride. And Ellie was stunning with her coppery hair swept up and her green eyes gleaming with intelligence above her sultry mouth. As for the dress, well, he was extremely impressed by that surprisingly sexy corset, which defined his bride's splendid curves to perfection. No, getting married didn't feel half as bad as he had dimly expected. He had thought he might feel trapped but the prospect of peeling Ellie out of that corset was more than equal to the challenge of surrendering his freedom.

Her hand trembled in his when he grasped it to

thread on the wedding ring. She had worn her engagement ring on her other hand. And like Beppe's family
emerald, which she had brought out to Italy with her,
it was another emerald to reflect the colour of her eyes,
an emerald teamed with white diamonds but not over
large because Ellie didn't like flashy jewellery and had
wanted something she could occasionally wear to work.
So sensible, his Ellie, Rio thought wryly, wondering
just when he had started thinking of her as *his*. When
he'd imagined her pregnant with his child and liked the
idea? When he saw her walking down the aisle towards
him? Or when he realised that he was her first lover and
strangely determined to be her *last*?

Of course, he knew why he was marrying her. With
Ellie, the sex was on another level even though it had
gone wrong the one and only time it had happened. She
stood up to him, she talked back, she was his equal in
every way. But more importantly she had signed a pre-
nup contract ringed with so many iron hoops of protection that an escape artist couldn't have undermined
it. If Ellie liked money, he had plenty of it and there
were worse weaknesses for a woman to have, he reasoned. She could have been the unfaithful type, forever
in search of the next big thrill. She could've been the
uncaring, uncommitted type but he'd already seen her
bonding happily with Beppe and witnessed just how
close she was to her sister. And if there was to be a baby
Rio was convinced that she would always and without
hesitation do right by their child. The ability and the
desire to be a good mother was the most imperative
trait of all that a woman could have, he reflected with
sombre conviction.

Ellie emerged from the church on Rio's arm. A crowd

of people were crushed into the street outside. Fleeting introductions were made while the photographer fluttered around. They were congratulated and showered with rice.

In the midst of the noise and excitement, Ellie suddenly noticed two blondes wielding their camera phones and giggling like drains as they urged Rio to look at them and smile. And it was *them*, unmistakably the identical twins who had gambolled naked on Rio's bed in that Dharian hotel two years earlier. Ellie's throat convulsed. She couldn't have been mistaken, she thought angrily. They were highly noticeable women, blonde, beautiful twins, whippet thin and impossibly sparkly and effervescent in a way that was seen as ultrafeminine. Rio had actually *invited* the twins to their wedding. Ellie paled and compressed bloodless lips while the perplexed photographer urged her to smile.

She settled almost dizzily into the limousine beside Rio and looked at him. How could he do this to her? How could he be so insensitive to her feelings? Those blondes reminded her of the most humiliating moment of her life. Before Rio had opened the door to that hotel room she had been on a high, feeling like a sexy, attractive woman for the first time ever and ready to move forward, no longer feeling like the drab, clever redhead whom few men approached. And her first glimpse of the giggly twins on his bed had cut her like a knife, making her feel ridiculous and pathetic and useless.

'*Cosa c'e di sbagliato?* What's wrong?' Rio asked as the car moved off to whisk them back to the *palazzo* where the reception was being held.

And Ellie didn't know what to say. After all, he was

entitled to a sexual past and in marrying him she had accepted that past. Exes at a wedding, well, not exactly what you wanted but not always avoidable either. But did the twins recognise her as the shocked woman in that doorway two years back? And would they mention that to anyone? Have a good giggle about it? She cringed inside herself and said nothing.

'Nothing's wrong,' she assured him quietly. 'It's just all the wedding hullabaloo. When it comes all together, it leaves you feeling shell-shocked.'

'I didn't invite Becky and Roz,' Rio breathed impatiently, cutting through her pretence.

So, he had noticed the twins. Well, really, how could he have missed them bouncing up and down with excitement only a few feet from him, determined to be noticed by him? Yet he had somehow contrived not to look once in their direction, nor had he shown the smallest hint of self-consciousness. But then why would he?

'Is that their names?' Ellie queried with a wooden lack of expression.

'I told the wedding planner to contact Rashad for the list of our university friends because I haven't kept up with their addresses,' Rio explained. 'They were invited to your sister's wedding and that's probably how they ended up at ours. If I'd taken a greater personal interest, I would've left them off the list.'

If anything, Ellie had grown even stiffer. 'Of course, if they're uni friends, why would you leave them out?'

'Ellie, you're putting out more sub-zero chills than a freezer,' Rio said with sardonic bite. 'But I can't change the past and neither can you.'

'I didn't realise the twins had ever been actual friends of yours,' Ellie admitted stonily, not best pleased to hear that information. 'Probably because I've never slept with any of my male friends.'

'Sadly, I wasn't quite so particular,' Rio countered in the same measured tone. 'And neither were they. In those days I could only cope with casual—'

Her smooth brow indented. 'And why was that?'

Rio squared his broad shoulders and settled back with a sigh. 'I set up a property venture when I was nineteen. Beppe was pressuring me to go to university to study business but I thought I could take a shortcut to success,' he admitted wryly. 'My business partner, Jax, had the security of a wealthy background. The property market was booming and we were doing very well, which is when I met a gorgeous brunette. I fell in love with Franca, asked her to marry me and we moved in together.'

Ellie dragged in a startled breath, for what he had just admitted was the very last thing she had expected to hear from him. After all, she had simply assumed that Rio had *always* played the field without ever pausing to settle on one particular woman. Learning different shook her up, learning that he had found that one particular woman years earlier and presumably lost her again filled her with insecurity.

Rio skimmed narrowed dark eyes over the pale, still triangle of her face and his shapely mouth twisted. 'The property market stalled and I was overstretched. I still believe I could have made it through but Jax pulled out and hung me out to dry…and Franca, who had been screwing him behind my back and who very much liked the luxuries of life, ran off with him.'

Ellie winced and dropped her gaze, imagining the sting of that double blow of financial loss and treach-

ery. 'I'm really sorry that that happened to you,' she
murmured ruefully. 'It must've been very hard to pick
yourself up after that experience.'

'It taught me a valuable lesson. At university I
learned enough to ensure that I would never leave myself that vulnerable in business again,' he confided. 'I
succeeded but after Franca, I avoided any kind of serious involvement with women. What the twins offered
suited me at the time. No strings.'

'I can understand that,' she conceded reluctantly.
'You know…er…that night at Polly's wedding, after
we parted…I've always wondered what happened—'

'You don't want to know,' Rio cut in succinctly, his
tone cold as ice water.

And in telling her that he had told her everything
there *was* to know, she acknowledged in consternation, just as suddenly furious with him. She had rejected him that night and had raced back to her room
at the palace to take refuge in time-honoured tears and
self-recriminations. But Rio had taken solace where he
could find it and what right had she to object? Finding
that out annoyed and disturbed her though. Rio could
divide sex from emotion and treat sex like an athletic
pursuit and he had done so for years before he met her.
Could Rio really change? Could he switch back to the
young, optimistic male he must once have been when
he fell in love with Franca? And what exactly did it take
to make Rio fall in love?

Rio was watching Ellie as the limo drove through
the *palazzo* gates. Her delicate little profile was set,
her brain running at a mile a minute on thoughts he
didn't want to share. Maybe he should have lied. But
lies would catch up with him sooner or later. Did she

realise that she really wanted him to be perfect? Prince Charming straight out of a fairy story? And that he could never be perfect? Frustration and growing anger raged through his lean, powerful frame. He could not pretend to be something he was not in an attempt to impress her. And why would he want to anyway? Ellie would smell a rat sooner than most women because she was always looking below the surface, weighing pros and cons, picking up on inconsistencies, seeking out flaws. And he had still to confess his biggest flaw of all to a woman who had chattered animatedly about how her discovery of Beppe would now enable her to chart the previously unknown paternal half of her medical history.

In the greeting line, Becky and Roz made much of Rio and their previous acquaintance while acting as if they had never laid eyes on Ellie before. They didn't recognise her, she registered with relief, didn't remember her at all from that fleeting glimpse of her in the hotel doorway that night. But instead of being relieved at that realisation, Ellie was angry with Rio and angry with herself. She had agonised so much over that night and she had been so hurt but their backfired encounter had not had a similar effect on Rio's tough hide. She needed to guard herself from being too emotional and vulnerable around him. She had to toughen up, she told herself urgently.

Polly whisked her off after the meal. 'What on earth's wrong between you and Rio?' she demanded.

'There's nothing wrong—'

'Even Rashad's noticed the atmosphere and to be honest he's not usually that quick to notice that sort of stuff,' her sister admitted.

And Ellie spilled the whole story from its start two years earlier to the presence of the twins at the wedding. She was too upset to hold it all in any longer and Polly's shocked face spoke for her. It was several minutes before she could even move her sister on from repeatedly saying '*Both* of them?' as if she had never heard or dreamt of such behaviour before. Her attitude did nothing to improve Ellie's mood.

'And that night you met...?' Polly pressed. 'He told you that?'

'Yes, Polly,' Ellie confirmed wearily. 'I've married an unashamed man whore.'

'If Rashad had ever done anything like that, nothing would persuade him to admit it to me,' Polly declared wryly. 'But at least Rio is honest, well, brutally so.'

'I think he was just thoroughly fed up with me asking awkward questions.'

'I suspect he's already heard more than enough about that night and you shot him down in flames, which is not the sort of treatment he's used to receiving from women,' Polly pointed out grudgingly in Rio's defence. 'Let it go, Ellie. It's in the past and you weren't dating him or anything, so you can't fairly hold it against him. He didn't cheat on you. As for those blondes, ignore them, forget they're here!'

Ellie knew that was sensible advice but something stubborn in her refused to back down. Hard reality was steadily taking the bloom off her wedding day.

Rio tugged her stiff, resisting body close as he swept her out onto the floor to open the dancing. He bent his arrogant dark head and whispered, 'Do you know just how annoyed I'm getting with you?'

'Do you know how annoyed I am with you?' Ellie whispered back, unimpressed.

'Are you always going to be this jealous and possessive of me?' Rio enquired silkily.

A current of rage travelled through Ellie as hotly as a flame. 'Are you? I seem to remember you threatening to beat up Bruno for buying me dinner—'

'That was different,' Rio asserted without hesitation. 'We were already involved.'

Angry tears prickled behind Ellie's lowered eyelids and she finally knew what was really wrong with her. She had got involved with Rio on an emotional level the very first night she met him. But he hadn't got involved with her until she entered Beppe's life and became what he initially saw as a threat to someone he cared about. Was he even involved with her now that he had married her? Or had he only married her to please Beppe and because she might be pregnant? And why was she only asking herself that now and worrying about the answer?

Rio caught her hand firmly in his as they left the floor, deftly weaving them through the clusters of guests addressing them, never pausing longer than a few polite seconds. Only when they reached the foot of the main staircase did Ellie question where he was taking her and she tried to wrench her hand free.

'We're going to sort this out in private,' Rio delivered in a driven undertone.

'There's nothing to be sorted out,' Ellie protested, trying once again and failing to free her fingers from his.

Determined not to be sidetracked, Rio headed for the opulent guest suite where Ellie had dressed for the wedding. He thrust the door shut behind him in a movement that sent dismay skimming through Ellie. She had not expected Rio to turn confrontational because she had assumed that the presence of their guests would control and inhibit him. The message she was getting now was that Rio's temper was rarely repressed.

He dropped her hand and Ellie immediately made for the door. 'We can't do this in the middle of our wedding,' she argued.

Rio cut off her escape by stepping in front of the door, which in turn sent Ellie stalking and rustling angrily in all her finery across the room towards the window. She flipped round, colour accentuating her cheekbones, green eyes very bright and defiant.

'It's our wedding and it's almost over and we can do whatever we like,' he told her grittily.

'Do you have an off button?' Ellie asked helplessly. 'Because I think it's time to hit it. Yes, this is our wedding and we have had a slight difference of opinion but I have done and said nothing anyone could criticise—'

'I'm criticising you!' Rio bit out harshly.

Ellie stared at him in shock, her lips falling open, because once again, Rio was blindsiding her and catching her unprepared. He had the most amazing eyes, stunning dark gold fringed with black curling lashes, and for a split second she was held fast by them while noting the aggressive angle of his strong jaw line, the faint black stubble already shadowing his bronzed skin and, finally, the ferocious determination stamped into his amazing bone structure.

'I'm not perfect, Ellie, and I'm never going to be but I was prepared to give this my best shot—'

'I never expected you to be perfect, for goodness' sake!' Ellie spluttered uncertainly as she moved warily back towards him. 'Look, maybe I was a bit oversensitive but there's absolutely no need for us to start having this out now! Let me go back downstairs before anyone notices we're missing—'

'No,' Rio breathed with finality.

'You don't just tell me no like that and expect me to take it!' Ellie argued furiously, trying to push him away from the door.

'I keep on hoping that you'll learn from experience,' Rio growled, scooping her up, nudging a giant vase of flowers out of his path and planting her down squarely on the marble-topped side table behind her. 'But you never do.'

'This is getting ridiculous. Let me down,' Ellie told him forcefully.

Rio pinned her in place even more effectively by pushing her knees apart and stepping between them to wedge himself even closer.

'You may be physically stronger but you can't bully me,' Ellie informed him tartly.

'I don't want to bully you, *principessa*. I want you to start using your brain,' Rio bit out impatiently, settling his big hands down on her bare shoulders. 'It's time to put sulky, moody Ellie away, ditch the negativity and look forward.'

'I am neither sulky nor moody,' Ellie pronounced with as much dignity as she could summon while seated as she was on a table, being held still. His hands were hot on her bare skin, sending odd little prickles of awareness travelling through her.

'Bear in mind the fact that I'm not sulking about having had to marry a woman who *could* be a scheming little gold-digger,' Rio urged, stunning her with that statement as his long fingers flexed expressively over her shoulders.

Her lips opened. 'A...a *gold*—'

'But I gave *you* the benefit of the doubt. When do you extend the same privilege to me?' he demanded grimly.

Ellie tried to slide off the table but he forestalled her. Flushed by the undignified struggle and enraged by the label of gold-digger, she snapped, 'Let me go!'

'No. I'm keeping you right where I can see you and we're having this out right now,' Rio decreed.

'How *dare* you call me a gold-digger?' Ellie slung at him an octave higher.

'What else am I going to call you when you still haven't explained yourself? You see, I may not be perfect, Ellie but the news is that *you're* not perfect either. You've had serious allegations made against you and although I'm now aware that an enquiry dismissed one set, there are still others in your background made by a family member,' Rio reminded her caustically. 'But I was prepared to overlook that history to marry you and give you a fair chance.'

Ellie had frozen where she sat and she didn't know what to say or even where to begin. 'You said you'd *had* to marry me,' she said, instead of tackling his accusations head-on. 'But you didn't have to. I didn't demand it. I wouldn't have allowed my father to demand it either. It wasn't necessary—'

'It was necessary to me,' Rio cut in ruthlessly. 'I could not live with the chance that you could be pregnant. I had to ensure that we were a couple and that if there is a child, he or she will not grow up without me.'

'So, this really is a shotgun marriage,' Ellie breathed painfully.

'No, it's what we make of it and so far you're doing your best to undermine us,' Rio condemned.

'You know the enquiry cleared my name,' Ellie reminded him sharply. 'How can you still think I could be a gold-digger?'

'It's all those shades of grey that lie between black and white,' Rio commented reflectively. 'What was your true intent when you befriended that old lady at the hospice where you were working?'

'I didn't befriend her. I was doing my job, acting as a sympathetic listener when there was nobody else available!' Ellie told him angrily.

'Maybe you would've got away with that inheritance had a complaint not been lodged against you and maybe you thought you could get away with it. Maybe you only looked up your father after you found out that he was a reasonably affluent man,' Rio murmured lethally. 'Who can tell? That's what I mean about shades of grey. How can I know either way? But I still took a chance on you—'

Ellie relived the stress and worry she had endured when quite out of the blue, one of the patients she had been tending had altered her will and left her estate to Ellie instead. It had been wholly unexpected and she had not felt in any way that she deserved that bequest. She had reported it immediately but naturally the old lady's nephew had lodged a complaint. It had been a nasty business and there had been nothing she could have done to avoid the ordeal. Rage and distress over Rio's suggestions roared through her taut body. 'I hate you!' she gasped chokily.

'No, you don't. You just don't like being questioned

and judged without a fair trial but it's exactly what you do to me,' Rio condemned levelly.

'I don't want to be married to you!' Ellie slung at him wildly.

'You don't mean that,' Rio assured her, the hands on her shoulders smoothing her delicate skin as he bent his head. 'You want me as much as I want you.'

'Stop telling me what I want, what I think!' Ellie exclaimed in seething frustration.

'Maybe I'm talking too much... Maybe I should be *showing* you,' Rio husked, tipping her back a little and burying his mouth hotly in the smooth slope of her neck while his hands delved beneath her skirt and swept up over her thighs.

'Stop it!' Ellie hissed, struggling against the great wave of quivering weakness that assailed her as the heat of his lips and the teasing nip of his teeth grazed her sensitised flesh. 'You're not allowed to do this when we're fighting!'

In answer, Rio crushed her angrily parted lips beneath his own, his tongue flicking the roof of her mouth and tangling with her own. The forbidden pulse at the heart of her pounded faster and hotter while honeyed liquidity pooled in her pelvis. His hands firm on her thighs, she squirmed on the table.

'Rio!' she cried in frustration.

He ripped the delicate panties out of his path and traced the damp wet folds between her parted thighs, and so much excitement surged up inside Ellie that she feared she might go up in flames. He had distracted her, she knew he had distracted her with sex and she knew she had to defend herself but in that instant nothing was more important to Ellie than the fierce, urgent demands of her own body.

'We *can't…*' she moaned for her own benefit as much as his.

Rio sank his hands below her hips and lifted her to him as though she were a doll. He sank into her hard and fast and the sudden fullness of him boldly stretching her made her shudder and gasp. And then he moved with brutal efficiency, hitting some magical spot inside her that knew no shame and the treacherous excitement came in a drowning, remorseless flood that overwhelmed her. Her teeth dug into the shoulder of his jacket, her hands clawed any part of him she could reach. The pleasure was unbearable, pushing her relentlessly to the edge. Her body careened into a teeth-clenching climax that left her bereft of breath and he freed her as the final convulsions trammelled through her weakened body.

He disappeared off to the bathroom leaving her sagging on the table. He had taken precautions this time around, she registered in surprise. So, he was no longer willing to take that risk of conception with her, even though they were now married. Did Rio *still* want an escape route? Was he hoping she wasn't pregnant? That he could still walk away?

And why wouldn't he when he was convinced that she was a shameless gold-digger? Anger sizzled through Ellie. She had lost another battle with Rio. She slid, almost limp with satiation, off the table and retrieved one of her shoes, which had fallen off. Her torn underwear was nowhere to be seen and she had no spare clothing in the room since her suitcase had already been removed. With a grimace she smoothed down her dress and staggered slightly on cotton-wool legs in front of a mirror to check her hair.

'You look fantastic, *principessa*,' Rio said huskily, lazily, catching her hand in his. 'And you're my wife now—'

'Not sure I want reminding of that right now—'

'I *like* reminding you,' Rio murmured, studying her with hungry dark golden eyes. 'Smile, Ellie—'

'No, Rio—'

'Smile,' Rio insisted. 'It's our wedding day and we should be making the most of it—'

'Oh, I think you've already done that,' Ellie told him before she could think better of that comment.

And Rio laughed with unholy amusement. 'You're mine. I needed the proof of it.'

All shaken up and fizzing with conflicting feelings and emotions, Ellie returned to the wedding festivities. Rio kept a hold of her, not letting her stray far from his side. Her body still felt hot and alien, the aftershock of forbidden pleasure and excitement still trapped inside her like a shameful secret. There was wanting and then there was wanting Rio, and he had just taught her that she was the one without the off switch when she needed it. That knowledge made her feel achingly vulnerable.

CHAPTER EIGHT

Rio scooped her out of the helicopter with precision. The flight had taken less than an hour.

'Why won't you tell me where we're going?' Ellie demanded.

'In a few minutes you'll know exactly where we are—'

'I wouldn't bet on that. I haven't travelled much,' Ellie admitted as he walked her a few steps down a quay and assisted her into a motorboat.

But as he had forecast, Ellie recognised where she was even though it was a place she had only previously seen in pictures. The view of Venice as the boat sped across the lagoon was breathtakingly beautiful. 'It's just like the paintings Beppe showed me,' she whispered, entranced.

On the Grand Canal, the boat slowed amidst the busy water traffic and nosed in at a smartly decorated landing stage. Climbing out, she accompanied Rio into a magnificent foyer ornamented with huge Venetian glass chandeliers. 'Welcome to the Hotel Palazzo Sorrentino,' Rio murmured. 'The jewel in the crown of my hotel chain.'

'Sorrentino?' she queried in surprise.

'Yes, it once belonged to your family but it was last used as a home by your great-grandfather and even he only lived in a tiny corner of it. Beppe was quoted millions for the repairs that were needed and he sold it to me,' Rio explained. 'It was being used as a warehouse by then because it wasn't fit for habitation. Converting it into an exclusive hotel took years but it was a worthwhile investment. Now it's fully booked years in advance.'

Recognising that almost every eye in the reception area was on them, Ellie went pink, suddenly conscious of her wedding finery. A little man in a smart suit approached to welcome them and handed her a beautiful bouquet with the compliments of the staff. Rio accepted a key from him and guided her across the foyer and down a corridor.

'We're staying here?' she asked.

'Not in the hotel. The *palazzo* came with a couple of attached buildings and I retained one of them for personal use. Beppe uses it regularly. He loves Venice, particularly in the winter when it's quiet,' Rio told her, leading her outside and along a wisteria-clad walled alley to a narrow door flanked by Venetian gothic windows. 'It's very private here and the staff service it so we don't have to worry about housekeeping or cooking.'

Ellie walked into a charming wood-panelled reception room that overlooked a tiny lush green garden at the rear. Beyond the garden, a gondola sailed past on a narrow waterway. It was a magical scene.

Rio removed the bouquet from her hold. 'I'll stick the flowers in the sink.'

Ellie knew she should go with him and deal with

the flowers but the diverse traffic flowing past on the canal commanded her attention and she stayed where she was.

'I'll show you round now,' Rio said lightly, and in a great gilded antique mirror she caught a glimpse of her answering smile that softened her face, and looked away again, dismayed that she could look happy in the company of a man who had implied that she could be a gold-digger.

'I need to tell you about Violet... The lady in the hospice, who changed her will in my favour,' she said tightly.

'Not now, we've had enough stress. Leave it until later,' Rio urged as he opened the door on a dining room where food already awaited them on the table, fearful that any sudden revelations from Ellie would set them at odds again on a night that he very much wanted to be special and all about 'them.' 'We should eat first. You didn't have much earlier.'

'I wasn't hungry,' she admitted as he pulled out a chair for her. 'I didn't think you'd notice—'

'I notice everything about you,' Rio incised drily.

'If that was true, you'd know I'd never have sought out Beppe simply because he was well off,' Ellie contended uncomfortably. 'It didn't matter who or what he was. I just wanted to fill in the blank I've lived with all my life and know what happened between my parents. You couldn't possibly understand how much it means to me to know who my father is and to actually feel a sense of connection with him. It's so much more than I ever hoped to have.'

'I understand a lot more than you appreciate,' Rio countered, his lean dark face setting into grim lines. 'I will never know who my father is and, frankly, I don't *want* to know. I met my mother as an adult and that killed off any sentimental delusions I might have had. My mother and I didn't have a single thought or feeling in common.'

Ellie studied him in shock at that revelation.

'You were very lucky to find a man like Beppe waiting at the end of your identity trail,' Rio remarked wryly.

He had met his mother and it hadn't worked out? But he had grown up in an orphanage. Where had his mother been when he was a child? And why didn't he know who had fathered him? Consternation gripped Ellie and she veiled her eyes. Rio managed to be incredibly sanguine about realities that would have seriously disturbed her and it made her all the more aware of how very little she knew about him and how unwittingly tactless she must have been while she was happily rambling on about what finding Beppe had meant to her. Of course, what had she ever personally shared with Rio? Discomfiture filled her. As a rule, Ellie was reserved and she kept her secrets close. She didn't share personal stuff except with Polly but that had to change now that she was married. Didn't it? It wouldn't be fair to expect more from Rio than she was prepared to give herself.

'Yes, I was incredibly fortunate,' Ellie agreed ruefully as she took another appreciative bite of her delicious pasta salad. 'Can I ask you about something?'

'Anything...'

'Earlier when we were together, you...you used a condom,' Ellie reminded him.

'Isn't that what you wanted?' Rio responded, his

ebony brows drawing together in a frown. 'If you are pregnant, we'll make the best of it but if you're not, well…it gives us more options.'

'You mean, we wouldn't have to stay together,' Ellie framed, her heart suddenly beating with a dulled thunderous thud against her breastbone.

Rio lounged back in his chair with his wine glass and settled frowning dark golden eyes on her. 'Don't put words in my mouth. I said options and I *meant* options. I believe that babies should be planned and greeted with joy on their arrival.'

Ellie nodded woodenly, thinking about the pregnancy test waiting in her case. 'I agree. The circumstances weren't ideal.'

'Ideal isn't everything, *principessa*.' A slow-burning, wicked smile slanted Rio's beautiful mouth. 'But I did notice that day at my house that the idea of getting pregnant turned you as white as a sheet. It's not a risk I'll run with you unless you ask me to…'

And how likely was that? Yet that unexpected offer soothed her in some strange way. He wasn't slamming the door in her face. He had not said that if she wasn't pregnant they would eventually separate and divorce. His outlook wasn't that simple or that final. So why was she relieved? What had she feared? She searched his lean, darkly handsome features, her mouth running dry as she struggled to look beyond the sleek dark beauty of him into her appalled reaction to the threat of being parted from him. Polly had seen what she had hidden even from herself: she had got attached, dangerously attached to Rio Benedetti. Recognising that reality hollowed her out with fear. She was afraid of getting hurt and very reluctant to want more from Rio than he was likely to give.

She went upstairs to explore and discovered a dreamy spacious bedroom swathed in opulent fabrics and a divine four-poster bed. Their luggage had arrived in advance and had been unpacked for them. Off the bedroom there was a splendid marble bathroom with sumptuous heated towels and very fancy fittings. Champagne and flowers awaited them. She filched a chocolate off the silver dish beside the champagne flutes and bit into it with so much pleasure that she closed her eyes.

'You like chocolate,' Rio said huskily from the doorway.

'Correction—I would *kill* for chocolate,' Ellie admitted with a sudden laugh.

His amusement ebbed as he looked at her, the sheer stunning elegance of her in her gown, stray copper curls showing round her hairline now, the heavier make-up she had worn for the wedding faded, a faint streak of eyeliner at the side of one eye where she had rubbed. And yet she was still so beautiful with her clear green eyes and lush pink mouth. 'I think I would kill for you,' he breathed, stunned and unsettled both by the thought and the feeling.

Unfortunately Rio was being forced to work without a script. He was out of his comfort zone. Hit it and quit it was no blueprint for a marriage or a woman like Ellie. If she was pregnant, she would be with him for a long time, he reminded himself darkly. She would make demands, the sort of demands he had never had to deal with before. She would restrict him. She would also probably and regularly drive him nuts. But on the other hand, every pleasure came with a price tag and she was clever, amusing, passionate and ridiculously sexy.

Ellie plucked the pins from hair and let the thick mass fall to her shoulders. Then she spun round. 'I need your help to get out of this,' she admitted, turning and indicating the lace ties. 'It's beginning to feel very tight.'

Rio removed his jacket and cravat and unbuttoned his shirt. He was thinking about the curves inside that corset, the wondrous curves that bad timing had forced him to neglect that afternoon. Raw hunger roared through him afresh. 'I love corsets,' he confided.

'Thought you would,' Ellie murmured a tad smugly.

He released the ties and the hooks and let the garment drop to the floor while she exhaled in relief that the constriction had gone. He kept his arms round her, dipped his mouth to the smooth slope between her neck and shoulder and dallied there, lifting his head to nip teasingly at her earlobe at the same time as he raised his hands to cup her full breasts.

Ellie rested her head back against him, tiny flames of arousal dancing over her skin as long fingers tugged and teased at her swollen nipples. She was so sensitive there that she pressed her thighs together as if she could contain the rush of damp heat at her core. He backed her down on the bed but she demurred, pausing to unzip her skirt and let it fall, momentarily forgetting that she was bare beneath.

'Memories,' Rio teased with a wicked grin, disposing of his shirt to reveal a corrugated abdomen, hard with lean muscle.

'You work out,' Ellie guessed, studying him closely, faint colour feathering into her cheeks.

'Every day. I'm at a desk too much. Ah…is that a look of approval from Dr Ellie?'

Ellie scrambled onto the bed and beneath the smooth white linen sheet and immediately felt better about hiding her overlarge behind and sturdy thighs. She didn't think there was anything wrong with her body, she simply wished that when she had been blessed with curves she had also been blessed with more height to carry them. Rio undressed, dropping everything in a heap while Ellie watched him like a hawk, thinking that it had never occurred to her to wonder what it would be like to have her own male stripper. He had a really great body. Broad shoulders, lean hips, the inverted V of muscle running down to…*that*! Ellie stared, reddened, no longer marvelling that she had been sore in the aftermath of her introduction to sex. He wasn't small anywhere and, being Rio, he was already primed for action.

'We can do without this,' he told her, yanking the sheet back. 'I plan to make you very hot, *principessa*.'

Ellie rested back on the pillows. 'And I plan to make you equally hot,' she warned him.

Grinning, Rio came down on the bed beside her. 'You've already achieved that…or didn't you notice?'

Ellie stroked the velvet-smooth thrust of him with wondering fingers. 'I noticed—'

'A little less of that,' he censured as she explored him.

'No, you don't get to hand out orders in bed,' Ellie told him.

And Rio laughed with startled appreciation and looked at her, the humour slowly draining from his lean dark face to accentuate the black diamond glitter of his slumberous eyes and the feverish colour lacing his exotic cheekbones. 'Am I being treated to bossy Ellie now?'

'I have more than one setting. I can't have you getting bored,' Ellie murmured intently as her hand spread over his chest. 'My goodness, I'm so pale I must look like a milk bottle beside you—'

Rio rolled over and pinned her half beneath him. 'A very, very sexy, curvy milk bottle—'

'In the mood you're in you'd find anything female sexy,' Ellie protested.

'No, you really don't get it, do you? Growing up, you were probably too busy polishing your brain cells to look in the mirror,' Rio quipped, running a fingertip along the peach-soft curve of her lower lip. 'You have the body of a goddess and a very beautiful face. Did I mention the gorgeous hair…?'

'I hate the hair. I went through school being called "ginger,"' Ellie muttered. 'And "clever clogs."'

'But you still triumphed, *bella mia*. Passed all your exams, married me—'

'Marrying you counts as a triumph?' Ellie gasped.

'See how you feel about me in the morning,' Rio murmured with lashings of sexual assurance.

'That you're tiring me out?' Ellie teased, her fingers dancing over a smooth bronzed shoulder, enjoyment lighting her eyes for such intimacy was very new to her and unexpectedly wonderful to find.

And then he leant down and he kissed her and it was exactly what he had promised, hot and hungry and wildly intoxicating. The heat of his long, lean, powerful frame against hers sent a current of prickling awareness flying across her entire skin surface. The plunge of his tongue electrified her, sending tiny shivers darting through every pleasure receptor. Her breasts tingled and swelled, the tips straining.

His mouth roamed over her, tugging at the sensitive buds, seeking out delicate spots and lingering. He worked his way down her body to explore the most responsive place of all and her hips writhed and her lips parted on tiny cries. She had never felt so much pleasure or such a relentless drive for release. It was as if something deep within her were screaming impatiently for satisfaction. She twisted and turned, drowning in sensation, her body programmed to leap and rise to fever point at his every caress. Slowly she could feel her control being torn away from her but this time it didn't frighten her. She didn't fight, she let go, rejoicing in the strong waves of pleasure convulsing her and thrumming like a euphoric song through every skin cell.

'You're really, really good at that,' Ellie whispered, limp and breathless in the aftermath.

'I'm good at a lot of things,' Rio husked, all sexual promise and dominance as he rose over her, rearranging her singing body to his satisfaction.

And if he was set on proving the fact, he proved it as he plunged into her tender depths with passionate force, reawakening her to arousal. Her heart hammered, her adrenalin kicking in as she arched beneath him, deepening his penetration, and suddenly she was greedy to experience every thrilling sensation. He moved faster, lithe and potent. Her excitement climbed with every compelling thrust. Perspiration dampened her skin, a furnace-like heat rising from the heart of her as the desire for fulfilment clawed at her. And then she was there at the summit and the blinding surge of heart-stopping pleasure seized her body and soul. She jerked and shuddered and cried out, thrown over the boundary between reality and fantasy.

Afterwards, Ellie wrapped her arms tight round Rio, feeling madly affectionate and happy.

'What are you doing?' Rio asked, tensing.

CHAPTER NINE

'I'M HUGGING YOU,' Ellie said witheringly.

'I don't do hugs.'

'I do a lot of hugging. You'll have to get used to it.' She sighed, blissfully unconcerned by his objection. She loved the hot, damp heaviness of him against her and smoothed her fingers gently down the long line of his spine. 'If I'm pregnant, you'll have a child to hug.'

She felt the charge of tension that stiffened him in her arms.

'That day…you went pale at the prospect too,' she pointed out sleepily, exhaustion weighing heavily on her.

'Of course I did. I haven't a clue how to be a parent,' Rio pointed out feelingly. 'How could I? I never had one—'

'Just like me. You'll learn as you go along,' Ellie told him drowsily, the words slurring slightly.

Rio lifted his tousled dark head. 'You can't go to sleep yet… It's our wedding night.'

But Ellie was already sound asleep. He went for a shower and eventually climbed back into bed.

Ellie wakened while it was still dark and suppressed a sigh. Her sleeping pattern had been disrupted by ever-changing shifts and a regular shortage of sufficient rest while she worked. Knowing that she was unlikely to drift off again, she got up and put on a comfy dress while scrutinising Rio as he lay sprawled in bed. He was taking up more than his share of the space, she noted without surprise. It was as well for him that he could look so good doing it, she acknowledged with tender amusement, noting the black hair curling against the pillow, the angular bone structure shaded in by stubble, the relaxed line of his mouth. Asleep he looked younger than his thirty years.

Dragging her attention from him, she went downstairs and the first thing she noticed in the sink of the elegant little kitchen was the bouquet of flowers, and guilt shot through her. A trawl through the cupboards produced a vase and she settled the blooms into water and put them on display in the sitting room. A search of the fridge revealed bottled water and savoury pastries and she ate standing up, watching the dawn light rise over the building on the other side of the canal and slowly illuminate the little garden.

'What are you thinking about?' Rio asked from behind her.

Ellie turned her head to take in Rio clad only in a pair of ripped blue jeans, his feet bare. 'Violet,' she mused wryly. 'The old lady who died in the hospice. She loved to see the dawn. If I was on duty I'd open the curtains early for her. I was thinking of how much she would have loved Venice but she never got to travel because her husband liked home best and in her day husbands ruled the roost—'

Rio grinned. 'Dare I hope it'll be the same for us?'

'Wouldn't hold my breath on that one,' Ellie advised.

'Why are you out of bed so early?'

'I've always been an early riser,' she confided. 'But then I'm not used to having the freedom to sleep in. If I wasn't working the past few years, I was studying for exams. The pressure is constant.'

Rio groaned out loud. 'Tell me about Violet while I order breakfast.'

'She was lonely. She'd outlived everyone who mattered to her,' Ellie told him. 'She had no visitors. Her nephew came once when she first entered the facility but he didn't come back. Some relatives can't handle the last stages of a terminal illness. You can't judge them for it. We're supposed to stay detached…and I never thought I'd have a problem with that.'

'Sometimes you get involved whether you want to or not.'

Ellie squared her slight shoulders. 'When I had a few minutes free I kept Violet company. That was all. She reminisced about her past and I would listen and it made her happy. Once she was asleep I would tiptoe out again. I knew nothing about her changing her will until her solicitor contacted me after her death,' she admitted. 'I couldn't have accepted anything from her anyway because it's against the rules of the trust that employed me for medical staff to make a financial gain from patients. Even though I'd turned it down, the nephew made an official complaint against me and the whole business dragged on for months before it got to the enquiry stage and I was officially cleared. Why would I have wanted her money anyway?'

'What do you mean?'

'Rashad and Polly insisted on paying off my student loans but they also tried to persuade me to accept a large lump sum off them to buy a property. It was very generous of them but I turned it down because, while I can deal with the extravagant gifts they insist on giving me, I don't want to be the family charity case,' Ellie admitted ruefully. 'Polly buys all my clothes as it is, but she's married to Rashad and I'm not. That's *her* life, not mine.'

'And now you've got a life with me,' Rio murmured, tugging her backwards into the circle of his arms.

'I'm not sure how much of a life I can have with a man who thinks I'm after his money.' Ellie sighed just as a loud knock sounded on the front door.

Without responding to that leading comment, Rio went to answer it.

It was a waiter with a covered trolley and at Ellie's instigation it was wheeled out to the small patio, which was now bathed in early morning sunshine. The screening shrubs in the garden gave it all the charm of a forest glade.

Ellie poured the coffee. 'So now you know about Violet. It was a storm in a teacup but it had long-lasting repercussions. Mud sticks. People I trusted made nasty comments. I was worried it would damage my career and I got very stressed.'

'Naturally,' Rio conceded, wondering why it hadn't occurred to him that, had she been mercenary, Ellie could have chosen to rely on her seriously rich brother-in-law for financial support. Rashad was very generous and very family-orientated. Had she so desired, Ellie could have given up work and lived the life of a rich socialite. Why had that very obvious fact never crossed his mind at any stage? Had he preferred to think of Ellie as a gold-digger? And if so, why was that?

'That's why this break in Italy was so important to me. I needed a holiday—'

'And instead you got me—'

A natural smile tilted Ellie's lips as she looked at him, lounging back shirtless in his seat, a beautiful, self-assured and ruthless work of art, who continually surprised her. 'Yes, I got you.'

'When do we find out whether or not you're pregnant?' he prompted without warning.

'I was planning to do a test now,' she confided.

'For *yourself*?' Rio queried in visible consternation. 'No, that won't do at all. We'll go and see a doctor, get it done properly—'

'I am a doctor—'

'*Sì...*' Rio gave a fluid, very Italian shrug '...but this is an occasion and it requires special treatment.'

Midmorning, following their visit to a very charming private doctor, they sat down to coffee and pastries in the atmospheric Piazza San Marco. Both of them were shell-shocked, Ellie most of all, because she had believed she would recognise some tiny sign and somehow *know*. But she hadn't known, hadn't recognised anything that different with the exception of being more tired than usual, and with all the fuss of the wedding that hadn't seemed worthy of note.

'So, now we know,' Rio pronounced without any expression at all.

And Ellie recognised the dazed light in his eyes and knew that he was just as stunned as she was to learn that he was going to become a parent in a few months.

'I just didn't really think it could happen that... *easily*,' he admitted in an almost embarrassed undertone.

'I've met a few distressed teenagers who made the same assumption,' Ellie admitted, smiling to herself, quietly pleased with the knowledge that she was carrying her first child. And no, their baby hadn't been planned and was likely to drive a horse and cart through her career choices, but neither of those facts mattered when set beside the wonder of conception, which she had watched give such great joy to Polly and Rashad. She would gladly make space in her life for her child, she acknowledged, recognising that in the blink of an eye after hearing that news that her goals had changed.

'Saying we would make the best of this development if it happened wasn't the most supportive or sensitive approach,' Rio conceded belatedly. 'I want to celebrate now but not only can you not drink, you've even been warned off coffee.'

There it was again, that ability to surprise her that made her love Rio all the more, Ellie reflected. In fact, loving Rio seemed to have been stamped into her genes like a no-escape clause because, of course, she loved him, didn't know quite when it had happened and certainly not *how*. She smiled, happiness bubbling through her that he was so flexible, so willing to happily embrace their unplanned baby. 'I'll drink decaf—'

Rio grimaced at the idea for he had a true Italian love of unadulterated coffee.

'There are other ways of celebrating,' Ellie pointed out, lashes screening her eyes as she covertly studied him, recognising that she would never tire of this particular view. Rio, hair blue-black and gleaming in the sunshine, stunning dark golden eyes welded to her with an intensity she could feel, sprawled back with indolent grace in his seat, his shirt pulled taut across his broad chest, his trousers straining over his powerful thighs. Her mouth ran dry.

'Eat your ice cream, Signora Benedetti. I love your curves—'

'Just as well. My curves will be expanding—'

A slashing grin curved his sculpted mouth. 'I can only look forward to it, *principessa*. But when it comes to celebrating—'

'You could take me out on a gondola,' Ellie suggested with enthusiasm.

Rio looked pained. 'Seriously uncool. That's a touristy thing—'

'*Please...*' Ellie urged.

And she got her gondola ride the whole length of the Grand Canal. Rio had caved and she was touched. He was much more comfortable sweeping her into a fancy jeweller's store afterwards, where he insisted on buying her an emerald pendant to mark the occasion. They lunched back at the house and he watched her smother a yawn.

'You should lie down for a while—'

'Only if you lie down with me,' Ellie murmured softly.

Disconcerted, Rio flashed her a glance as if he couldn't quite credit the invitation. But without hesitation he lifted her up out of her seat and crushed her ripe mouth under his own, all the seething passion of his intense sexuality rising to the fore.

He tumbled her down on the bed but he unwrapped her from her clothes like a precious parcel, pausing to admire and tease what he exposed, and she writhed like a wanton on top of the silk bedspread in the full glare of the Venetian sunlight, utterly lost in passion and equally lost to all shame. He took her from behind then, hands firm on her overheated body as he drove into her with a roughened growl of satisfaction. His urgent rhythm was wildly exciting. Heart pounding, breathing forgotten, Ellie reached a peak and her body detonated in an explosive charge of pleasure. She slumped down winded on the bed with Rio on top of her.

He released her from his weight and settled down beside her, reaching for her to pull her into his arms.

'Thought you didn't do hugs,' Ellie commented.

Rio splayed a large hand across her flat stomach and said piously, 'I'm hugging my child.'

Ellie laughed, feeling amazingly relaxed and at peace. Her fingers lifted and fiddled absently with the emerald she still wore round her neck.

'You can tell me about your uncle now,' Rio informed her in the tone of someone doing her a favour.

Ellie wrinkled her nose. 'Jim Dixon? My mother's brother? I guessed he would be the family member you mentioned. I take it he's still peddling his sob story about how I ripped him off?'

'You're not surprised?'

'Jim's vilified me everywhere and no matter what I said to him, he refused to listen. He doesn't *want* the truth. He didn't get on with my mother and he never liked Polly and me, but my grandmother was living on the poverty line when she agreed to raise us. Our mother gave her a lot of money to take care of us and the arrangement suited them both from that point of view. Unfortunately my uncle always resented us being there.'

'Tell me about the brooch,' Rio urged with typical impatience.

'Oh, the *famous* diamond brooch, the family heirloom for several generations and the only item of worth the Dixons ever owned,' Ellie recounted ruefully. 'My grandmother sent me a letter during my first term at medical school. In it she told me she wanted me to have the brooch because she was so proud that I was going to be a doctor. She gave it to me the first weekend I was home after that. I didn't tell Polly, well, I couldn't *bear* to—'

Rio had sat up, glorious dark eyes locked to her expressive face and narrowing. 'Why not? I thought you and your sister were really close.'

'Oh, come on, Rio, think about it! Polly was the eldest and the brooch should have gone to her if it had gone to anyone!' Ellie argued. 'Polly sacrificed her chance to go to art college to get a job and help out financially and when Gran developed dementia, it was Polly who looked after her. She deserved the brooch, *not* me, and I was astonished enough to get it because our grandmother wasn't a warm woman. She didn't neglect or abuse us but she didn't love us either. Polly would've been hurt by me getting the brooch, so I decided to sell it and split the proceeds with her and make up some story about where I got the money from.'

'Women... Why do you always complicate things?' Rio groaned. 'A man would just have told the truth. It wasn't your fault that your grandmother chose to give it to you.'

Ellie rolled her eyes, unimpressed. 'But when I tried to sell the brooch, I discovered it was only paste, not real diamonds, which made better sense to me. I mean, why *would* a poor family have held on to a valuable diamond brooch all those years? It was worth so little that I didn't bother selling it but I still haven't told Polly about it,' she completed guiltily.

'Where does your uncle come into this?'

'Our grandmother left her son the contents of her house when she died and, of course, he assumed that the brooch would be there and when I told him she'd given it to me a couple of years earlier, Jim accused me of being a thief. While Polly was out applying for the death certificate and making burial arrangements, I was wrangling with Jim. I told him the brooch was only a costume piece but he wouldn't believe me and he stomped off and wouldn't speak to us at the funeral. A few weeks later he got the police involved,' she revealed wryly. 'They came to see me at university. I showed them the letter. They were satisfied—'

'But your uncle wasn't?'

'No, he'll probably go to his grave convinced that I deprived him of his prized inheritance. I tried to sort it out with him and he wouldn't listen and by that stage I was past caring. I was sick and tired of the whole stupid business,' she confessed.

Rio traced a fingertip over the shadows below her eyes. 'You look tired, *principessa*. Have a nap.'

He owed her an apology for having entertained the ridiculous idea that she could be a gold-digger, Ellie thought in annoyance, but she was *still* waiting for that apology. He was far from perfect, she mused, and he was too strong to find it easy to own up to being in the wrong. On the other hand, he had wonderful taste in emeralds, had endured a gondola ride at her behest, was learning to hug and he was happy about the baby, she reasoned with sneaking contentment while swallowing another yawn.

Rio watched Ellie sleep and heaved a sigh. Had she noticed his moment of sheer panic when her pregnancy was confirmed? His blood had run cold. He had asked himself how he could possibly be a decent parent when his own parents had had more in common with the dregs of humanity. He didn't know what was in his genes, never would know, but that sort of stuff was important to Ellie. Was that why he *still* hadn't told her about the dumpster? Pride? He had always told himself that where he started out didn't matter; indeed that all that really mattered was where he ended up.

And where had he ended up? Married to a woman he had treated badly! His sins had come back to find him out and haunt him. So, he had to reinvent himself again, just as he had as a boy, as a young failed businessman, a student and, finally, a success story. He would change and adapt to his new lifestyle. He would be *the perfect husband*. That was what Ellie deserved. He owed her that. All her life, Ellie had only had her sister Polly to rely on but now she had him. He smoothed a corkscrew curl back from her pale brow, careful not to wake her, and abstractedly wondered if it would be too soon to visit a toy shop. Probably as uncool as that awful gondola ride, he conceded ruefully. But then wasn't he supposed to be reinventing himself?

'So how do you think my Italian is coming on?' Ellie enquired in the language.

'You are learning quickly and the accent, it is good,' Beppe told her cheerfully. 'Rio must be a better and more patient teacher than I expected.'

'He's been very patient but we only talk in Italian for a couple of hours a day. I find it exhausting,' she admitted. 'But I have a good memory. Outside of maths and science, languages were my best subject.'

'When will you be home?' Beppe asked plaintively. 'I miss you both.'

'Tomorrow. We'll join you for dinner,' Ellie promised and she finished the call because Polly had already texted her twice asking her to ring.

'What's happened?' she asked her sister worriedly minutes later.

'You *have* to open Lucy's envelope,' Polly told her and then she explained why and Ellie came off the phone again looking worried.

'What's wrong?' Rio pressed, lifting his handsome dark head from his laptop.

'Well, that kid sister we've been trying to find?' She sighed. 'It turns out that we didn't really think things through properly at the start. Because we didn't know who our fathers were, we assumed Lucy would be in the same boat. But Lucy's had access to her original birth certificate since she was eighteen and her father's name is probably on it. After all, he was living in London with our mother when she was conceived. All the investigator has been able to discover from enquiries is that Lucy's father is Greek and he thinks it's possible that the reason we can't trace her is that she could be in Greece.'

'That's reasonable, so stop fussing and open the envelope. It's only a name and a ring, nothing more important.'

'It just feels wrong,' Ellie muttered, going upstairs to extract the envelope from her case and clattering back down into the sitting room. She opened the envelope and extracted a ruby ring and read the name. 'Kreon Thiarkis,' she sounded out uncertainly.

'I think I've heard that surname before. I'll look into it. Text the name to Polly so that she can pass it straight on to the investigator,' he urged unnecessarily because she was already doing exactly that.

'Stop with the bossy stuff,' she warned him.

'Have you ever listened to yourself talking to Beppe? Telling him to eat more vegetables and drink less wine? Urging a man, who is physically very lazy, to go for walks? It's not going to kill him to be a little overweight at this stage of his life,' Rio opined. 'You climb on your healthy-living soapbox every time you're on the phone.'

Ellie winced. 'Have I been overdoing it?'

'No. Beppe enjoys being fussed over. He's never had that before. And if it's any consolation, you're giving him very good advice but he's very set in his ways.'

Afternoon tea was served to them out in the little garden and Ellie sat watching the canal traffic wend past in all its tremendous variety while she ate a divine slice of blackberry-limoncello tart. She was thinking about how very happy she was and that it seemed downright incredible to her that she had only been married for four short weeks.

After all, she had made some very major decisions during those four weeks. Finding Beppe, marrying Rio and discovering she was pregnant had forced her to have a serious rethink about her future. She had withdrawn at the last minute from her scheduled placement in London and was officially unemployed. But she was learning Italian as fast as she could and with Rio's assistance had already collected up the documents required for her to register as a doctor in Italy. Her career wasn't taking a back seat, she reasoned, she was simply on a go-slow diversion for a few months. Obviously, her priorities had changed.

She didn't want to leave Italy now that she had found her father. With Polly married to Rashad and living in Dharia, she had no family waiting for her back in London. She wanted the time and the space to get to know Beppe, as well. And she loved Italy and saw no reason to demand that Rio live in the UK when it was perfectly possible for her to work in Italy. That decision had removed much of the stress and the fear of the future weighing her down.

And she was so happy with Rio, even though he was the sort of near-workaholic who brought his tablet out even for afternoon tea in the sunshine. They had still contrived to enjoy the most incredible honeymoon exploring Venice. Well, she had explored and he had guided, occasionally complaining bitterly when she dragged him into old buildings or shot what she thought were interesting historical facts at him. They had wandered hand in hand off the beaten track and eaten wonderful food at little restaurants known only to the locals.

Many a morning had drifted long past noon before they got dressed. He was insatiable or maybe she was, she reflected ruefully, but they at least seemed well matched in that field. For the first time ever Ellie was learning what it was to have time to waste, to be indolent, to read a something that wasn't a textbook or a research paper.

And throughout every step of that most entertaining renaissance of hers, Rio had encouraged her and supported her. He made her happy: it was that simple and that was probably why she loved him. They still argued though. After she had told him the story of her grandmother's brooch, Rio had made the very extravagant gesture of buying her a star-shaped brooch studded with enough diamonds to sink the Titanic. 'You *deserve* it,' he had told her while she was trying to remonstrate with him over the expensive jewellery he kept on buying for her even though she rarely wore jewellery because she had never had much to wear. Stone Age man went hunting and dragged a carcass home to his cave to feed his woman. Rio's equivalent was inviting exclusive jewellers to visit the house to show her an array of fabulous gems worth a small fortune. And if she said no, he looked frustrated and hurt, and it was the hurt she couldn't bear to see.

If she made any sort of comment relating to gold-diggers, he froze and changed the subject. No, he still hadn't apologised but she was bright enough to know that the flood of expensive jewels was Rio's way of telling her that he no longer nourished such insulting suspicions about her. And the one thing he wouldn't talk about was his time in the orphanage and his dealings with his mother as an adult. For some reason the story of his early years was a complete conversation killer.

Ellie stirred that night soon after she heard the phone ring, for working in the medical field had wired her to take greater note of alarms and phone calls. Coming sleepily awake, she sat up and watched Rio pace the floor naked. He was speaking in Italian and far too fast for her to follow, shooting urgent questions to whoever was on the other end of the call. And he was upset, lines grooved into his lean dark features, mouth a thinned tense line. Disturbed by what she was seeing, Ellie breathed in deep, bracing herself for trouble of some kind.

Rio made another call and then looked across at her with unconcealed anxiety. 'We need to go home. Beppe's in hospital. He had a heart attack while one of his friends was dining with him. He received immediate attention…which is good. *Isn't it?*' he demanded jerkily, seeking reassurance.

Ellie braced herself, fighting the strong emotions tearing at her at the very thought of losing the father she had only recently found. 'Yes, it will greatly improve his chances of making a full recovery,' she muttered hollowly, striving and failing to be more upbeat.

CHAPTER TEN

'SILLY FUSS,' BEPPE said again as Ellie gripped his hand. 'No reason to come back early.'

Even though Ellie was no stranger to the environment of an Intensive Care Unit, she was having a first-hand experience of how very intimidating it could be to see someone she loved lying in a railed bed, and Beppe looked so small and shrunken. She breathed in deep and slow, composing herself, because she was determined not to inflict more pressure on her father by overreacting.

Beppe had had an emergency angioplasty to clear a blocked artery soon after his arrival at the hospital and his prognosis was good if he followed the rules on how best to maximise his recuperation. But her father's heart attack had given him a terrible fright because he had not spent even a day in hospital before and had enjoyed excellent health.

Rio, however, had suffered an even worse fright, Ellie acknowledged. For during the flight that had whisked them back to Florence in time to see the dawn, Rio, sky-high on anxiety, had sat lost in his thoughts and barely speaking. Right at that moment he was poised at the foot of Beppe's hospital bed trying to act strong and optimistic for Beppe's benefit but Ellie could spot a pretence when she could see one. One of Rio's hands was clenching and repeatedly unclenching in a betrayal of stress that could not be hidden. And for the first time—and she scolded herself thoroughly for it being the first time—she finally recognised that Rio loved Beppe as much as she did, indeed probably more because Beppe Sorrentino had been a part of Rio's life since he was a child.

'Want to live to see grandchildren,' Beppe told them apologetically, his speech abbreviated and slurred by the medication. 'Never had family, want that now.'

'And you'll have that family,' Ellie assured him soothingly.

'Maybe sooner than you think,' Rio slotted in, ready, Ellie could see, to expose her there and then as a pregnant bride if it helped his godfather to look forward and raised his spirits.

'Hopefully we'll have news of that nature sometime soon,' Ellie delivered to silence Rio.

A nurse adjusted the machinery surrounding Beppe and a more senior nurse with a clipboard questioned her quietly from the doorway.

'Franca…' Beppe murmured with a weak smile in the direction of the woman in the doorway. 'Wondered when you'd visit.'

Ellie watched Rio freeze in patent disbelief and then slowly turn round. Her own brain, drained by the sleepless night and the stress, seemed to be refusing to function. The nurse in the doorway was Rio's ex? Or another Franca entirely? Could she possibly be the woman Rio had once planned to marry? The same one who had run off with his one-time business partner, Jax, when

Rio's property venture failed? It was a moment when Ellie would happily have given ten years of her life to be seated in the right place to actually see Rio's face and interpret his reaction.

'Franca...' he acknowledged after a noticeable pause and he addressed her in quiet Italian, moving forward and indeed stepping outside into the corridor to speak to her at length. She was a small, fragile brunette with big dark eyes and ridiculously pretty and right at that moment she was gazing soulfully up at Rio as though he had hung the moon for her.

Beppe squeezed Ellie's limp fingers to attract her attention and her shaken eyes darted back to him. 'She's been working here for years,' he whispered. 'I knew and never said. He didn't know.'

'They're old friends though,' Ellie pointed out with forced casualness, deliberately avoiding any hint of discomfiture for the older man's benefit.

Beppe patted her hand. 'Good girl,' he mumbled. 'Sensible girl.'

Ellie watched his eyes drift shut and slowly breathed in again, feeling almost giddy as the oxygen hit her lungs. Switching her attention back to Rio and Franca, she saw a doctor joining them and she rose from her chair quickly, keen to join the medical discussion clearly taking place in the corridor. But as she straightened she lurched and stumbled, a sudden wall of blackness closing in around her. And her last thought was, *How could you be so stupid?*

Rio scooped up Ellie at such speed that he almost tripped over Beppe's bed in his haste to reach his wife. 'She's pregnant,' he announced in a panic to anyone who cared to listen.

Guilt slashed at Rio as he carted Ellie out to the waiting limousine. He had dragged her out of bed in the middle of the night and she hadn't eaten in hours. That combined with the stress of Beppe's condition had been too much for a newly pregnant woman. Why hadn't he paid more attention to Ellie's needs? As Franca had explained, Ellie was probably experiencing low blood pressure and low blood sugar at this stage.

Ellie began to try to sit up in the car, saying limply, 'What are you doing? I don't want to leave the hospital—'

'Beppe is asleep. For the moment, the crisis is over and there's no reason for you to stay by his bedside,' Rio argued forcefully. 'Right now, you need to eat and rest. And *no*,' he instructed, actually daring to rest two long fingers against her parted lips in reproof. 'Don't bother reminding me that you're a doctor when you can't remember to look after yourself.'

A furious flush mantled Ellie's cheeks. She felt the sting of his censure all the more because it was warranted. But there had been no food on the private jet because there had not been time to restock it for the emergency flight from Venice, so eating had not been an option during the flight, and since their arrival she had only seen the inside of the ICU.

'Beppe didn't see me faint, did he?' she pressed worriedly.

'No, he was fast asleep—'

'What did his doctor tell you?'

'That he's on the mend but that he needs to make the changes you mentioned.' Rio swore under his breath in driven Italian. 'I feel guilty now. I should've tried to talk to him too—'

'At the end of the day, it's his life and his decision,' she said tiredly. 'I think he'll be practical, especially once he realises the next generation is on the way, although how he didn't guess from the way you were talking I'll never know!'

'Dio mio...' Rio growled out of patience. 'We *are* talking about a man who had an adulterous affair with your mother! Beppe wasn't perfect. Why would he expect us to be?'

Ellie sniffed, still reluctant to be exposed as the loose woman who had ended up on a sofa with Rio within days of her arrival in Italy. Not even in a bed, her censorious alter ego reminded her darkly. Rio made her reckless but he also made her happy...well, when he wasn't annoying her or worrying her.

'So was that the same Franca you once planned to marry?' she simply shot at him, going straight for the jugular, in no mood to contrive a subtle approach.

Rio flexed his broad shoulders and sprawled back in his corner. 'That was a surprise but I gather Beppe knew and never mentioned it.'

'I didn't know she worked in the medical field—'

'How would you?' Rio parried. 'It's not relevant in any way.'

Ellie pursed her lips. No, it might not be relevant on his terms, she was thinking grimly, but that one little fact of Franca's nursing profession and her treatment of him could certainly shed some light on Rio's reluctance to view medical staff as being 'caring' and the suspicious reception he had given Ellie.

'How did you feel seeing her again?' Ellie asked baldly, knowing it was intrusive but unable to kill the question before it leapt off her tongue. Because, in truth, the answer to that one little question was literally *all* she wanted to know.

Rio treated her to an incredulous appraisal. 'I'm not going to answer that. It's a stupid question.'

Ellie nodded, mouth compressing harder than ever.

And Rio thought quite spontaneously that Beppe would never have got the chance to stray from his marital vows with a wife like Ellie around. Ellie picked up on every nuance, dissected it, stressed about it and absolutely had to *talk* about it immediately. And sometimes it drove Rio crazy because his brain didn't work like hers. Why would he even *want* to talk about Franca? Aside from the reality that that liaison had happened what felt like half a lifetime ago? Women discussed feelings but he had never felt that need, had he? He very shrewdly kept that kind of nonsense to himself. Why did Ellie always want something from him that he couldn't deliver? Time and time again she showed him that he was failing to meet her expectations.

His jawline setting like granite, Rio brooded about yet another major flaw in his character. He didn't know how to talk about feelings, where even to begin, never mind end. He had had lots and lots of feelings when he was a boy, but he had learned through hard experience that it was wiser and safer to suppress them. He was resolutely practical and always had been. There was no point wanting what you couldn't have and even less point in wasting energy agonising over life's misfortunes. That creed had served him faithfully for thirty years. So, how *had* he felt seeing Franca without warning? Surprise and curiosity. Nothing wrong with those reactions, was there?

'You go to bed while I make you something to eat. What would you like?'

'You can cook?' Ellie gasped.

'Proficiently,' Rio assured her with satisfaction.

'Could you manage an omelette? Omelettes are kind of complicated, aren't they?' Ellie said in the tone of a woman who lived off salads and ready meals.

'Not that complicated,' Rio told her.

He led Ellie up to the master bedroom in his house and her luggage was brought up. She studied her surroundings with tired interest. Luxury fabrics and pale oak furniture lent the bedroom a traditional, almost feminine opulence that disconcerted her because it was very far from what she had expected to find in a rampant womaniser's intimate lair. Had she been less tired she might have noticed that Rio was scanning the bedroom, as well, in a manner that suggested he was equally unfamiliar with it.

And so he was, having hired a decorator to chuck out his man cave accoutrements and decor while they were in Venice. Everything was new, fresh and Ellie approved even though she didn't know it because he had made note of her favourite colours and the style of furniture she liked. She didn't like cutting-edge contemporary and she didn't like flashy and his former bedroom decor would have qualified in both categories. There had also been the serious risk of inadvertently encouraging Ellie to think about how many other women could have visited his home and slept in that bed. No, Rio was convinced that keeping Ellie happy meant acting as if that past of his didn't exist. He understood her passionate possessiveness, in fact, it warmed him as much as the hottest day, but he didn't want any element of his libidinous past coming between them.

And that included Franca. If he talked about Franca, he would be clumsy and he might well say the wrong thing. For that reason it was much better not to discuss Franca at all. Thinking that that was the troublesome topic of Franca now as done and dusted as a gravestone in a cemetery, Rio went downstairs to make an omelette worthy of a cordon bleu chef because he never missed out on an opportunity to impress Ellie and he had just realised that she couldn't cook.

As removed from the real world as a zombie, Ellie opened her case, extracted the necessities and went into the bathroom. She had a quick shower, discovered she had left her toothbrush behind in Venice and searched the drawers in the storage units. She found several new toothbrushes, a giant box of condoms, a choice of several different lipsticks and make-up containers and two unmatched earrings. All had clearly been left behind by previous visitors. Tomorrow she would dump them. Right at that moment, she was reminding herself that Rio was her husband, that, yes, he had had a past with other women, but that that was nothing to do with her, certainly not something she should be worrying about.

Rio presented her with a perfect golden omelette and she was undeniably as impressed as though he had owned up to being a rocket scientist. Washed and fed, she was taken over by exhaustion again and she slid down in the blissfully comfortable bed, quite unaware that Rio went for a shower and then slid in beside her.

When she wakened it was afternoon the next day and she was alone. She was shocked that she had slept so long and anxious to get to the hospital and see how her father was doing. When she came downstairs, Rio's housekeeper appeared, introduced herself as Sofia and brought her lunch on the terrace. Marooned without transport, she went into the large garage off the rear courtyard and discovered a stable of vehicles. Rio liked sports cars, she thought with amusement. *Boy*, did Rio like sports cars. Sofia showed her where the keys were and she picked a car in fire-engine red that appealed to her mood.

Navigating the many turns in the sweeping road that led down to the main route was more of a challenge than she had expected because she had never driven such a powerful car before but she made it to the hospital in good time and went straight to the ICU. Beppe, however, had been moved out of intensive care to his own room, a sign that he was making good progress, and she greeted him with a smile when she found him sitting up in bed and much more able to talk than he had been in the early hours of the morning.

'Rio's gone for coffee in the canteen,' he explained. 'You've just missed him.'

After she had been with him about thirty minutes, Beppe began to flag and she suggested he have a nap, reminding him when he argued that he was recovering from surgery and that it would take a few days for him to regain his strength. Ellie went straight down to the canteen in the basement to find Rio but it was very busy and she bought herself a cup of hot chocolate as a treat, while she queued and scanned the crowded tables.

When she finally located him, she stopped midway on her path to joining him because he was not alone, he was sitting with Franca. Reluctant to interrupt out of the fear that Rio would deem it jealous and posses-

sive behaviour on her part, Ellie slid into a corner table
nicely shielded by a tall fake potted plant and waited
for his companion to leave. She barely sipped her hot
chocolate while she watched the pair of them, former
lovers, looking much more friendly than anyone would
have expected in the circumstances as they sat opposite each other, both leaning forward to get closer and
talking intently.

In not treating Franca like an enemy, Rio was acting
like an adult, she told herself soothingly. It was downright nasty of her to think that Franca was looking at
him with much more appreciation than the occasion
could surely require. Slowly it sank in that they appeared to be having a quite emotional conversation and
that unnerved her, but all the signs were there. Franca
reached across the table and gripped one of Rio's hands
at one point and then brushed away tears. Rio did not
go into retreat. In fact, none of the barriers that most
would expect to be present between lovers who had
parted on very bad terms were to be seen.

Stop being so blasted jealous and suspicious, Ellie
urged herself in exasperation. Obviously Rio and Franca
were catching up on the past and had discovered that at
heart they were still friends. But it really, *really* bothered Ellie that Rio was clearly having the sort of emotional chat with his ex-girlfriend that he refused to have
with his wife. And for how long had he been chatting
to Franca? All that time she had been upstairs sitting
with Beppe? And he was *still* with her?

Ellie drank her hot chocolate, refusing to allow herself to watch Rio and Franca any more since she was
obviously too susceptible to paranoia. She had fallen
insanely in love with Rio, married him and turned into

a maniac she didn't recognise. Every hour of the day she wanted Rio *so* much. It was frightening, mortifying, but she had to get control of her craving, her suspicions, her insecurity. One last look at them and then she would go and check on Beppe again, she bargained with herself.

And Ellie glanced, only allowed herself that one glance, and she saw Rio reach over the table to grip Franca's hand in a heartfelt gesture that felt like a knife plunging into her own heart. Franca put one of her hands on top of his and gave him a wobbly, tearful smile full of warmth and admiration. Ellie's glance became a stare and then she literally tore her gaze away at the same time as she stood up, abandoning her drink, and walked out of the canteen to wait for the lift.

Right, so, Rio had some weird new connection with his ex, not necessarily a sexual or romantic connection. Who was she trying to kid? She had sat watching a woman crying and smiling and holding hands with her husband. What was she supposed to think? A woman he had once loved enough to want to marry. But he had never loved or wanted to marry Ellie, had he? And now he was stuck in a marriage with a woman he didn't love, who was pregnant.

Ellie's eyes prickled like mad. She hardly ever cried and right at that moment she had a crazy urge to howl and sob, and holding all that pent-up emotion in was a challenge. Rio was so intense in everything he did and yet, unless he lost his temper, he didn't let that emotion escape, at least not around Ellie. But what had really seriously hurt was seeing Rio demonstrate unashamed emotion with Franca, Rio taking part in the kind of emotional exchange he had denied Ellie. So what had they been talking about?

Had they discovered that they both still had feelings for each other? Franca must have been Rio's first love and first loves, with all the memories involved, were notoriously hard attachments to shake. Ellie breathed in slow and deep to calm herself and checked on Beppe, but he was sound asleep and, according to the nurse she spoke to, likely to be for some time. There was no reason for Ellie to remain at the hospital, particularly not when she wanted to avoid Rio, who she knew very well wouldn't tell her anything about his encounter with Franca. If she taxed him he would think she was a jealous, suspicious cow and he would be right. She *was*...

As she drove off from the hospital she struggled to calm down. Only a couple of hours earlier, aside of her ongoing concern for her father, she had been blissfully happy and Beppe did seem to be improving. She was making a mountain out of a molehill, she told herself soothingly. She would say nothing, do nothing, wait and see how matters went.

But inside herself, Ellie felt as though her heart were breaking. She kept on getting a flashback of Rio holding hands with Franca, Franca staring back at him with so much brimming emotion. Was that love she had seen between them? Why not? Why shouldn't he love Franca? Seeing his former love in such a crisis as Beppe's illness had created when Rio had been in a very emotional state of mind, even though he wouldn't ever admit the fact? Had Franca and Rio recognised that they both still had feelings for each other?

And, yes, she had believed that Rio was happy with her in Venice, but what if all along from the very outset of their marriage Rio had only been making the best of things? The best of a bad job? He found her sexually

attractive but was there any more to their connection
on his side than that? Meeting Franca again could well
have made Rio appreciate the difference between love
and sex. Her stomach turned over sickly.

So *why* should she keep quiet about what she had
seen? an angry voice inside her demanded.

After all, how would Rio have reacted to seeing her
holding hands with another man? Rio would have gone
up in flames, created a scene and demanded an immediate explanation. That was the truth of it. Rio was as
hot-headed and impulsive as she was invariably sensible
and cautious. So, if Rio wouldn't swallow that kind of
behaviour, why should she?

Ellie drove back to the house, steadily getting more
and more upset and tearful. Whatever she did, she had
to make a statement. She had to make it clear that she
would not tolerate any kind of flirtation because if she
didn't Rio might go on doing it. He needed boundaries,
no, he needed a giant wall built round him to keep him
within acceptable behaviour limits, she decided furiously. So, it was better to overreact now in the hope that
the fallout from her anger ensured that there would not
be a *next* time, she reasoned in growing desperation.

A preventative gesture in mind, Ellie began to pack
her cases again. She would move into Beppe's house for
a few days and Rio would appreciate that she was seriously annoyed with him. But was that the right thing to
do? What if Rio had realised he was still in love with
Franca? A terrible frightening sensation of emptiness
spread inside Ellie, because if she lost Rio, she felt as
if she would lose everything.

And that was sad, really, *really* sad, she told herself
bracingly. She loved him but that didn't mean that she

intended to be a doormat or throw wild, volatile scenes whenever he did something she disliked. Walking out on him for a couple of days was a better, quieter option and he would realise that she was serious. Screaming at Rio would be unproductive because he was as stubborn as a mule.

Rio drove back to his house, still surprised that he had somehow missed Ellie at the hospital. He was in an extraordinarily good mood. Beppe was on the mend, Ellie was pregnant and certain misconceptions he had once held had been cleared up and had left him feeling more in tune with the world than he had felt in a long time. He was in the wrong place mentally to reach home and have a troubled Sofia indicate the envelope left on a coffee table while learning that his wife had departed with cases.

He tore open the envelope. It was an Ellie letter, very succinct and to the point. There was only one sentence, telling him that he had failed to demonstrate the commitment she required from a husband. What the hell was that supposed to mean? Rio swore and then he swore again. It was as if electric shocks were going off in his brain. Ellie had walked out on him and moved into Beppe's *palazzo*. Outrage roared through him. He had made a huge effort to meet Ellie's high standards and yet now she was trying to ditch him like an old shoe.

Rio reacted by doing something that Ellie had not foreseen. He phoned Rashad and asked to speak to Polly. But within a minute of speaking to Ellie's sister, he realised that she was as shocked as he was and had no idea what could have fired Ellie up to that extent.

'Ellie's really not the dramatic type,' Polly told him

unreassuringly, because that only suggested that he must have been guilty of some giant sin that had provoked sudden and uncharacteristic behaviour.

'But I haven't *done* anything!' Rio raged, pacing round the hall in sizzling frustration. 'Do you think it could be pregnancy hormones or something weird?'

Polly's astonishment at that news only convinced Rio that phoning your wife's sister for insight into an unfathomable development could be a seriously bad and undiplomatic move. But then it had never occurred to him that Ellie could have kept quiet about the baby even with her sibling. After all, she and Polly talked most days! It finally dawned on him that Ellie was a much more private person in nature than he had appreciated—someone who didn't share personal stuff unless forced, as he had had to almost force her to tell him about the diamond brooch and the old lady at the hospice. She held all her distress in, *hid* it, trying to stay strong. Until that moment he hadn't recognised just how similar they were in that category and he suppressed a groan because it only complicated his situation more. Maybe she was deeply unhappy living with him. How was he to know? She wasn't a talker or an emoter... *Per l'amor di Dio*, he was *so* grateful for her restraint in that line. After all, Franca had almost talked him into a trance.

Initially, powered on anger, fear and a desperate need to take a stance, Ellie had expected Rio to rush straight to Beppe's home to confront her, but as time wore on into the afternoon she started to worry that he wouldn't even *try* to get her back. In fact, maybe she had played right into his hands by leaving, maybe he had reached the conclusion that he didn't want to be married any longer. For a male as rich and gorgeous as Rio the grass always had to look greener on the *single* side of the fence.

What had she done in walking out like that? What way was that to save a marriage?

She *loved* him, for goodness' sake, even if it turned out that he was the biggest flirt imaginable!

Suddenly feeling distinctly nauseous for the first time in her pregnancy, and shaky and damp with nerves, Ellie went upstairs to lie down. She knew the stress was bad for her and her baby and she beat herself up more for the decision she had made. Since when had she been a drama queen? And walking out on the assumption that the man you were leaving would follow to beg you to return was almost suicidal if he didn't love you. Tears prickled and stung behind Ellie's lowered eyelids. What had persuaded her that she had to make such a theatrical challenge to Rio of all people? A fit of temporary insanity?

Rio walked through the bedroom door and surveyed his wife. She was fast asleep and his keen gaze could detect the faint redness round her eyes that suggested tears had been shed. His confidence rose. If his unemotional Ellie had been crying, that was a healthy sign. He sat down on the side of the bed and gently shook her shoulder.

Luminous green eyes flew open and settled on him in strained silence. Her lush lips parted and closed again as she regrouped and sat up to hug her knees. 'What are you doing here?' she asked coolly.

'You're here,' Rio said simply.

'You can't stay here,' Ellie argued, thoroughly disconcerted by that declaration. 'It's Beppe's house.'

'It's not. I bought it from him years ago when the upkeep was becoming too much for him. I begged him to stay on and look after it,' he explained with a casual shrug. 'It was a property investment for me—'

'You're such a liar!' Ellie told him helplessly. 'You did it because you love him!'

'That too.' Rio looked uncomfortable. 'Can we get to the point of what that stupid note you left behind meant? One sentence? I get *one* sentence of explanation?'

Ellie stiffened, more challenged than she had expected because Rio wasn't shouting or raging, giving her the fight she had subconsciously craved and yet feared with every atom of her being, lest it lead to the end of their relationship. She lowered her legs and slid off the other side of the bed. 'After the way you spent your morning, I should think the note was self-explanatory...'

'After the way I spent... Franca? You *saw* me with Franca?' Rio thundered without warning as he finally made the connection. 'Why the hell didn't you rescue me?'

Taken aback, Ellie froze. '*Rescue* you?'

'*Sì*... I'm sitting in a public place while a woman weeps and sobs and talks about the kind of stuff I really don't want to know and I can't *decently* escape!' Rio recounted wrathfully. 'You think I was enjoying that? Are you out of your mind?'

It began to sink in on Ellie that she could have made a huge error of judgement.

'I can't believe this is all about Franca!' Rio exclaimed with rampant incredulity.

'You were holding hands. I thought you were flirting with her—'

'You need to learn what flirting entails, *principessa*. I assure you that there was no flirting whatsoever. Franca lost her eldest daughter to leukaemia only weeks ago and has only recently returned to work after compassionate leave.'

'Oh, my goodness...' Ellie whispered in shock. 'That poor, poor woman.'

'Yes, even Rio with the heart of a stone was not going to get up and walk away from that!' Rio grated. 'And that was only a part of the doom and gloom rehash of the previous nine years that took place. She said it did her good to get it off her conscience but it only made me realise that my sense of moral superiority over events back then was entirely unmerited.'

Ellie nodded. 'Okay. You contributed to the breakup and her going off with your business partner. I assumed that some of it must've been your fault.'

Rio dealt her an exasperated look. 'I *didn't*. I blamed Franca and Jax, but then I didn't know what was going on behind the scenes. Her fling with Jax only lasted about five minutes, and at her lowest ebb she ended up homeless.'

Feeling guiltier than ever for her wrong assumptions, Ellie backed down into a corner armchair and sighed. 'That can't have been easy for you to hear—'

Rio's gaze was sombre. 'No, even at the time I never wished harm on her, but then she lived with me and I didn't even realise I was living with an alcoholic—'

Ellie's brows lifted in wonderment.

Rio grimaced. 'That tells you how much attention I gave Franca. My sole interest back then was really the business of making money. But to some extent that wasn't *all* my fault. I was driven by the need to show

Franca's family that I could provide well for her. They had done everything they could to try to separate us—'

Ellie was now genuinely interested in what he was telling her and some of her stress had ebbed because she had recognised that her worst fears had been groundless. 'But why?'

'Primarily my background,' Rio divulged stiffly.

'That you grew up as an orphan?' Ellie exclaimed. 'But that's so unfair!'

Rio braced himself to tell the truth and he paled and gritted his teeth. 'It was more sordid than that. I was an abandoned baby, born addicted to heroin. I was left in a cardboard box in a dumpster and found by street cleaners,' he admitted very stiffly. 'The manufacturer's name on the box was Rio. The nuns christened me Jerome after St Jerome but I was always known as Rio.'

Ellie was so appalled that she couldn't speak. She glanced away to get herself back under control but her eyes shone with shocked tears. To think of Rio as a defenceless baby thrown out like so much rubbish absolutely broke her heart. 'Why…a dumpster? Why not somewhere safer?'

'I asked my mother when I met her. She said she didn't want to get in trouble or be asked questions. It was nothing to do with my safety—it was *all* to do with her. I meant nothing to her. She was an addict and a whore,' he confessed grimly. 'Franca's family were convinced that I had to have evil genes. Some people *do* think like that, Ellie, which is why I've always kept the circumstances of my birth a secret. It is not that I am ashamed but that I do not wish to be pitied or thought of as being a lesser person because of those circumstances.'

Fierce protectiveness slivered through Ellie as she looked back at him, all the love she had for him enveloping her. 'I love you no matter what you came from. I love you more than I've ever loved anyone or anything and I *like* Rio as a name. And only now understanding why it was so important for you to give our child a safer, happier start in life…well, it only makes me love you even more!'

Rio was transfixed. He had been prepared for Ellie to flinch and be repulsed by the sleazy facts of his birth and ancestry and then pretend that they didn't matter even when it was obvious that they did. He certainly hadn't expected her to tell him that she loved him without reservation.

'Don't you realise,' she murmured gruffly, her throat thickening, so great was her emotion, 'that you should be *proud* of what you've achieved from such a tough beginning in life? It genuinely makes me feel incredibly proud of you.'

Rio studied her, lustrous dark golden eyes with a suspicious shine, lean, darkly handsome face clenched hard. 'You mean…all that?'

Ellie rose from her seat, empowered by his stillness, his uncharacteristic uncertainty. Never had she loved him more or understood him better. Franca and her family had taught him to be ashamed of his birth and background and she marvelled at their unwitting cruelty over something that he could not have influenced as she crossed the room and wrapped both arms tightly round him.

'Hug time?' Rio interpreted shakily, hoping she didn't catch the break in his voice, because in his whole life he had never known such a relief as the moment when Ellie told him that she *loved* him no matter what. It was the unconditional love he had sought without ever knowing it and suddenly he didn't feel alone and pitched against the world any longer.

'Hug time,' Ellie confirmed unevenly, winding round him like a vine. 'I'm really sorry I misunderstood what I saw with you and Franca. I sort of went haywire. I knew she was your first love and I thought maybe—'

'No.' Rio shuddered at the thought. 'She's happily married to a radiographer at the hospital and has two other children. But she developed a guilt complex about me when she finally got into rehab and started to rebuild her life. She says part of the recovery therapy was the need to mend fences with those she had wronged while she was still drinking but she could never face getting in touch with me after what she had done.'

'So, when she met you again—'

'It all came spilling out.' Rio sighed heavily. 'And I *had* to listen. It would have been cruel to tell her that it was very old history for me and that I no longer cared. I kept on saying that we had both made mistakes and weren't suited in any case but she kept on and on and on talking and crying—'

'I'm glad I didn't interrupt. Listening was the right thing to do. That was kind because I'm sure you were very uncomfortable and if I could've seen your face, I would've known that, but I could only see *her* face. When did you become that sensitive without me noticing?' Ellie asked in honest surprise.

'Oh, that probably happened when I realised I was in love with you. I then decided that I wanted to be the perfect husband—'

'You are…but I'm a very imperfect, distrustful wife,'

Ellie mumbled in shame, burying her hot face in his shoulder, drinking in the familiar scent of him with an enormous sense of relief combined with sheer wonderment. He *loved* her? Her gorgeous, passion-filled, outrageously exciting husband loved her? He didn't find her too boring or sensible? Jealous and possessive? She was ecstatic with wondering happiness. 'So what happened with your mother when you did meet her?'

'There was a piece in the newspaper about me being found when I was abandoned and she always knew where I was. When I began to make money she looked me up,' he confided grimly. 'And that's all she wanted… Money. She told me a lot of lies. I found out that although she had weaned herself off her own addiction, she made a living by dealing drugs to others. I had nothing more to do with her—'

'That must have hurt.' Ellie sighed in sympathy.

'It is what it is. Getting off drugs didn't magically turn her into a nice or caring woman.' Rio shrugged. 'As to my potential father? I was an accident. Probably one of her customers. She had no idea.'

'It really doesn't matter to me,' Ellie emphasised. 'I wasn't only saying that. What matters to me is the man you are now and I love him. I even love you a little more for being kind to Franca, which you must've found trying.'

Rio tilted up her face, dark golden eyes adoring. 'There could never be another woman for me, Ellie. I've never loved like this. I didn't know I even *could* love like this but you're everything I ever wanted in a woman…even if I didn't realise that until I met you the second time.'

'We just fought,' Ellie groaned.

'And I got more of a kick out of fighting with you than I got out of any affair I've ever had,' Rio confessed. 'But the hunger for you was overwhelming...I couldn't fight that—'

Ellie lifted warm eyes to his lean, strong face, glorying in his scorching appraisal. 'I couldn't either. I always keep my feet firmly on the ground and then I met you and everything, including me, went crazy—'

'But we've had so much enjoyment out of each other,' Rio commented with appreciation. 'On levels I didn't even know there could be between a man and a woman. Before you, it was all about sex for me—'

'Oh, I know that.' Ellie flushed. 'In Dharia '

Rio winced. 'I was a jerk...but I had never wanted any woman the way I wanted you that night and I was on a high and then it all went pear-shaped, thanks to the twins—'

'Perhaps we both needed another couple of years to be ready for something more serious,' Ellie suggested forgivingly.

'*Dio mio*, I love you!' Rio swore passionately in receipt of the face-saving, utterly unearned excuse she was giving him and appreciating her generosity. He gathered her into his arms and almost squeezed her with his enthusiasm into suffocation. 'Really, *really* love you and I can't wait for the baby now that I know for sure that I have you by my side...'

'Well, when you ordered that giant train set in Venice and told me there was no reason why a little girl shouldn't enjoy it as much as a little boy I kind of guessed that our baby would be welcomed,' Ellie confided as he smoothly edged her down onto the bed. 'Nap time for pregnant Ellie, is it?'

'No. No rest for the imperfect wife,' Rio teased with a charismatic slashing grin as he looked down at her flushed, smiling face. 'Adriano was so relieved when you and then I showed up. He hates the house being empty because he has nothing to do and he's been fretting about Beppe. He's making dinner for seven, which gives us a few hours to fill—'

Ellie's eyes widened at that implication. 'You mean, you were so sure of yourself when you arrived here that you just went ahead and ordered dinner?' she exclaimed in disbelief.

'I wasn't prepared to leave here without you and if you refused to leave I had a case out in the car to enable me to stay here with you,' Rio explained without hesitation. 'When I want something, *principessa*...I don't quit and I don't surrender and I do believe that I would fight to the death to keep you in my life.'

'At heart you're a romantic,' Ellie told him with satisfaction and approval. 'When I came here, I was fighting for you too—'

Rio interrupted her in Italian to tell her argumentatively that walking out of their marital home had been a dreadful, shocking action to take.

Ellie refused to apologise. 'I was trying to make a statement, draw a line for you. Maybe it was a little extreme but I was hurting so badly—'

'I don't need a damn line, woman...I've got you in the flesh!' Rio told her aggressively. 'And it was not only extreme but also forbidden. You are not allowed to walk out on me ever again in this lifetime!'

'Is that a fact?'

'*Sì*... You're my wife, the centre of my world, my everything. You don't walk out. You stay and *shout*.'

Ellie breathed in deep, helplessly touched by that instruction. 'I'll shout the next time,' she promised.

'There won't *be* a next time!' Rio spelled out feelingly. 'Promise me—'

'*Sì*... I can promise that,' Ellie whispered, running adoring fingers through his cropped black hair and down one proud cheekbone to rest against his wilful lower lip. 'You're mine. I'm never going to walk away from you again.'

'Or drive off in my sports car,' Rio instructed. 'It's far too fast and powerful on these roads when you're not used to it.'

'I liked it—'

'No. I want you safe, *bella mia*.'

And before Ellie could demand that she had the right to influence what *he* drove in the interests of *his* safety, Rio kissed her with all the passion of his relief, love and desire for her and her impressionable toes curled. *Take that, sensible Dr Ellie*, she thought in wonderment that he truly was hers after all her anxiety and distrust, and then a thought occurred and she wrenched her mouth free...

'You never apologised for calling me a gold-digger!' she reminded him hotly.

'Of course I didn't.' Rio slowly shook his handsome dark head in apparent amazement at that reminder. 'That would have been owning up to flawed judgement or stupidity and it would've made you think less of me, so I decided to tough it out because I was trying to win you over to wanting to keep me by that stage.'

'*Nothing* would make me think less of you, you stupid man,' Ellie mumbled before she locked her lips to his again, his instant forgiveness procured, and there was no further conversation or indeed argument for quite some time. The excitement of their reconciliation powered the passion and the promises with buoyant happiness and fresh appreciation of the love they had found where they least expected it.

EPILOGUE

POLLY GROANED. 'I'M OUT of my depth here. What *do* we do about this situation?'

Ellie groaned too. 'Mind our own business for now. If the sister we haven't even met has a thoroughly wicked and dishonest father, it's not our place to tell her so. Lucy doesn't know us or trust us yet. She's found her dad and, at the very least, probably thinks very highly of him and, at worst, really loves him because he's been kind to her—'

'But what if he's just using her for some reason?' Polly proclaimed emotively. 'Doesn't she deserve to know he went to prison for fraud?'

'We need to establish a relationship with her as sisters first,' Ellie opined, crossing the terrace of her Italian home to prevent her fiery little daughter from striking the younger prince of Dharia, tall, sturdy Hassan, aged two, for taking one of her dolls and wheeling his toy tractor over the top of it with little-boy glee.

Across the terrace, his older brother, Karim, the crown prince of Dharia, shouted at his little brother in Arabic.

'He's telling him off,' Polly translated. 'He's so like Rashad, very well behaved.'

'That's never going to be my problem with Teresina,' Ellie whispered. 'She's always ready to fight for what she wants. It's a continual battle.'

'Well, you mix two pretty opinionated people like you and Rio and that's what you get,' Polly pointed out cheerfully. 'She's gorgeous with that hair though.'

Ellie smiled at her daughter, who was two years old now. Born of parents who both had curly hair, Teresina had miraculously straight shoulder-length black hair and eyes that were a lighter green than her mother's. She was small and slight in build and had learned to walk at nine months old. She was lively and quick-tempered and the greatest joy in Ellie's world, for she had never realised just how much she would love her child.

In the three years that Ellie had been married, her whole life had changed and she had not a single regret. She spoke fluent Italian and had secured her dream job in the hospital where Beppe had been treated and where she was now continuing her training as a doctor specialising in children's ailments. Beppe had made an excellent recovery and had, under considerable protest, begun walking to take exercise. She had grown very close to her father and was profoundly grateful to have found him in time to get to know him.

They had finally contrived to trace their long-lost sister to Greece, where she was living with her birth father, who appeared to be a most unsavoury man. But Ellie was convinced that considerable tact had to be utilised where their unknown sister was concerned and Polly and Ellie had yet to work out how to best approach Lucy without frightening her off. Ellie was in favour of sending the ruby ring with a letter introducing themselves and inviting contact. How that would go down was anyone's guess but at least it couldn't be seen as threatening or interfering.

Ellie had grown no keener on shopping in recent years, because if she wasn't at work she was exulting in precious *family* time and certainly didn't want to waste that time shopping and preening. Ellie had always dressed for comfort and she was still doing it. For that reason, Polly was still buying her clothes and now Rio was doing it too and her wardrobe was bursting at the seams with designer garments she only wore at the occasional swanky event Rio attended. On the jewellery front, however, her collection could almost have rivalled the jewellery of Dharia's royal family. Rio never went anywhere and came back without gifts for her and Teresina, and soon he would have a third little person to buy for, Ellie thought with quiet contentment. And she had finally told her sister the story of their grandmother's diamond brooch and Polly had simply laughed and dismissed the matter without concern, more worried that Ellie had had to deal with their uncle's spite without support.

The sound of a car coming down the drive sent Ellie leaping upright.

'I'll watch the kids,' Polly proffered. 'Go on…greet him and make his day! Rio's so romantic.'

Rashad climbed out of the passenger seat. The friendship he and Rio had formed while at university had only deepened when the men married sisters who liked to see each other regularly.

Rio's sizzling smile broke out as Ellie threw herself at him and wrapped her arms round his neck as if she hadn't seen him in a week. He was a little disconcerted because he had only left her early that morning and she wasn't usually given to any public displays of affection.

'You missed me?' he whispered, wondering if something was worrying her.

'A little. I've got news,' Ellie murmured soft and low. 'Let's go upstairs.'

'Is this about your sister Lucy?'

'No, nothing new there. Polly still wants to jump in the royal jet and land on Lucy's doorstep and explode into her life,' Ellie told him ruefully. 'But I think she's beginning to come round to a more diplomatic approach.'

As Rashad, the king of Dharia, strolled past them to join his wife and two sons Ellie gripped Rio's hand and practically dragged him up to their bedroom.

'You're beginning to worry me,' Rio confided, shooting a glance at Ellie's glowing face and registering that whatever had happened, it couldn't be anything bad.

'We're pregnant again!' Ellie announced with delight.

Rio blinked and nodded very slowly. 'I wasn't aware we were even *trying...*'

'I didn't want to put pressure on you so I didn't mention that I wasn't taking anything,' Ellie revealed cheerfully.

Rio almost laughed out loud. *Put pressure on him?* Nothing could keep him away from Ellie. He adored her. But he still compressed his lips and said, 'It might have been nice to be asked…to have discussed this as a couple,' he remarked, rather woodenly because he still wanted to laugh.

Ellie's face fell as if he'd slapped it. 'I didn't think of that. I know how much you love having Teresina and I want to have my family while I'm still young and I

would like them close together in age.' She chewed
uncomfortably at her lower lip. 'I suppose I should've
said something—'

Rio grinned. 'I was only joking. I'm delighted,' he
assured her with heartfelt enthusiasm. 'The more the
merrier—'

'Polly's pregnant again too. She's very keen to have
a daughter,' she confided. 'I'll tell her about me over
dinner, so don't go breaking my news ahead of me like
you did the last time with that phone call.'

Rio linked his arms round her slim waist. 'It's my
news too, *principessa*. I did figure in the conception.'

Ellie beamed up at him approvingly. 'Yes, you're
wonderfully fertile—'

'Good to know I'm useful for something—'

'*And* spectacularly good at the action part,' Ellie
whispered lovingly, hands running below his jacket to
skate possessively over his hard muscled chest and then
lowering in a much more intimate caress.

Rio shed his jacket and his shirt in record time. 'I
won't sulk about not being consulted on the extending-
the-family issue,' he admitted huskily. 'I know Dr Ellie
was in the driving seat worrying that I might suffer
from performance anxiety in bed for the first time in my
life. In short, I'm perfectly happy to be used and useful.'

'I know you are,' Ellie told him cheerfully, shimmying out of her dress even faster, her eyes full of love and
appreciation as she fasted her gaze on his lean, bronzed
body, the passion that always simmered below the surface of their marriage gripping both of them with its
scorching intensity. 'Did I ever tell you how much I
love you?'

'Not since last night.' Rio studied his wife with wondering admiration and marvelled that he had found her, that she had married him, learned to love him and overlooked his every flaw. Loving Ellie had brought him untold riches in the happiness stakes and he would never ever take it for granted because he had lived too long without that security. 'But if you want to be competitive, you couldn't possibly love me as much as I love you...'

* * * * *

If you enjoyed this
BRIDES FOR THE TAKING *story,*
don't forget to read the first part of the trilogy
THE DESERT KING'S BLACKMAILED BRIDE
Available now!

Also, look out for these other great
Lynne Graham reads!
THE GREEK'S CHRISTMAS BRIDE
THE ITALIAN'S CHRISTMAS CHILD
BOUGHT FOR THE GREEK'S REVENGE
THE SICILIAN'S STOLEN SON
Available now!

'I am here to claim my bride.'

Ghizlan loathed his superior, über-confident air, the gloating note in his deep voice. She pitied his bride, whoever she was, but clearly Huseyn wanted her to be impressed. What would it cost her to play along—at least until she got to the bottom of this?

'Who are you marrying? Do I know her?'

His smile widened and she saw the gleam of strong white teeth. Fear scudded down her spine as she read his expression.

'That would be *you*, my dear Ghizlan. I'm taking you as my wife.'

Wedlocked!

Conveniently wedded, passionately bedded!

Whether there's a debt to be paid,
a will to be obeyed or a business to be saved…
She's got no choice but to say, 'I do!'

But these billionaire bridegrooms have got another think
coming if they think marriage will be that easy…

Soon their convenient brides become the object
of an *inconvenient* desire!

Find out what happens after the vows in

The Billionaire's Defiant Acquisition
by Sharon Kendrick

One Night to Wedding Vows
by Kim Lawrence

Wedded, Bedded, Betrayed
by Michelle Smart

Expecting a Royal Scandal
by Caitlin Crews

Trapped by Vialli's Vows
by Chantelle Shaw

Baby of His Revenge
by Jennie Lucas

A Diamond for Del Rio's Housekeeper
by Susan Stephens

Bound by His Desert Diamond
by Andie Brock

Bride by Royal Decree
by Caitlin Crews

Claimed for the De Carrillo Twins
by Abby Green

Look out for more **Wedlocked!** stories
coming soon!

THE
DESERT KING'S
CAPTIVE BRIDE

BY
ANNIE WEST

First Published in Great Britain 2017
By Mills & Boon, an imprint of HarperCollins*Publishers*
1 London Bridge Street, London, SE1 9GF

© 2017 Annie West

ISBN: 978-0-263-92515-9

Printed and bound in Spain
by CPI, Barcelona

Growing up near the beach, **Annie West** spent lots of time observing tall, burnished lifeguards—early research! Now she spends her days fantasising about gorgeous men and their love lives. Annie has been a reader all her life. She also loves travel, long walks, good company and great food. You can contact her at annie@annie-west.com or via PO Box 1041, Warners Bay, NSW 2282, Australia.

Books by Annie West

Mills & Boon Modern Romance

The Flaw in Raffaele's Revenge
Seducing His Enemy's Daughter
Imprisoned by a Vow
Captive in the Spotlight
Defying Her Desert Duty

Secret Heirs of Billionaires

The Desert King's Secret Heir

One Night With Consequences

Damaso Claims His Heir
A Vow to Secure His Legacy

Seven Sexy Sins

The Sinner's Marriage Redemption

Desert Vows

The Sultan's Harem Bride
The Sheikh's Princess Bride

At His Service

An Enticing Debt to Pay

Visit the Author Profile page
at millsandboon.co.uk for more titles.

For my darling Dad

CHAPTER ONE

THE STEWARDESS STOOD ASIDE, inviting her to leave the plane. Ghizlan stood, smoothing her moss-green tailored skirt and jacket with a hand that barely trembled.

She'd had days to prepare herself. Days to learn to mask the shock and, yes, grief. She'd never been close to her father, a distant man, more interested in his country than his daughters, yet his sudden death at fifty-three from a brain aneurism had rocked the foundations of her world.

Ghizlan drew herself up, donning the polite smile her father had deemed appropriate for a princess, and, with a murmur of thanks to the staff, stepped out of the aircraft.

A cool evening wind whipped down off the mountains, eddying around her stockinged legs. Briefly she pondered how nice it must be to travel in comfortable, casual clothes, before letting the idle thought tear free on a gust of air. She was the daughter of a royal sheikh. She didn't have that freedom.

Setting her shoulders, she gripped the rail and descended the stairs to the tarmac, aware that her legs were unsteady.

Falling flat on her face wasn't an option. Clumsiness had never been allowed and now, more than ever, it was imperative she look calm. Until her father's heir was named she was the country's figurehead, a face the people knew. They would rely on her, eldest daughter of their revered Sheikh, to ensure the smooth running of matters while his successor was confirmed.

Who that would be, Ghizlan didn't know. Her father had been negotiating a new marriage when he died, still hoping to get that all-important male heir.

She reached the tarmac and paused. On three sides rose the mountains, purple in the late afternoon, surrounding the capital on its plateau. Behind her on the fourth side the mountain dropped abruptly to the Great Sand Desert.

Ghizlan breathed deeply. Despite the grave circumstances of her arrival in Jeirut, her heart leapt at the familiar scents of clear mountain air and spices that even airline fuel couldn't quite eradicate.

'My lady.' Azim, her father's chamberlain, hurried towards her, face drawn and hands twisting.

Ghizlan quickly crossed to the old man. If anyone could claim intimacy with her father it was Azim, his right-hand man for years.

'Welcome, my lady. It's a relief to have you back.'

'It's good to see you, Azim.' Ignoring custom, Ghizlan reached for his hands, holding them in hers. Neither of them would ever admit it but she had been closer to Azim than to her father.

'Highness!' He darted a worried look to one side where soldiers guarded the perimeter of the airstrip.

Ghizlan ignored them. 'Azim? How are you?' She knew her father's death must have been a terrible blow to him. Together they'd made it their lives' work to bring Jeirut into the new millennium by a combination of savvy negotiation, insightful reform and sheer iron will.

'I'm well, my lady. But it's I who should be asking...' He paused, gathering himself. 'I'm sorry for your loss. Your father wasn't merely a visionary leader, he was the mainstay of our democracy and a protector to you and your sister.'

Ghizlan nodded, releasing Azim's hands and moving towards the terminal. Her father had been all those things, but her country's democratic constitution would continue after his death. As for her and Mina, they'd learned long ago not to expect personal support from their father. Instead they were used to being paraded as role models for education, the rights of women and other causes. He might have been a visionary who'd be remembered as a great man, but the sad truth was neither she nor her younger sister could be heartbroken at his passing.

She shivered, knowing she should feel more.

As they approached the terminal Azim spoke again. 'My lady, I have to tell you...' He paused as some soldiers marched forward.

'Wait. My lady.' His voice was barely above a whisper and Ghizlan stopped, attuned to the urgency radiating from him. 'I need to warn you—'

'My lady.' A uniformed officer bowed before her. 'I'm here to escort you to the Palace of the Winds.'

Ghizlan didn't recognise him, a tough-looking man in his thirties, though he wore the uniform of the Palace Guard. But then she'd been away more than a month and military transfers happened all the time.

'Thank you, but my own bodyguard is sufficient.' She turned but to her surprise couldn't see her close personal protection officers.

As if reading her mind the captain spoke again. 'I believe your men are still busy at the plane. There are new regulations regarding baggage checks. But that needn't delay you.' He bowed again. 'My men can escort you. No doubt you are eager to see the Princess Mina.'

Ghizlan blinked. No palace employee would dream of commenting on the intentions of a member of the royal family. This man *was* new. But he was right. She'd fretted over how long it had taken to get back to Jeirut. She hated the idea of Mina all alone.

Again she turned but couldn't see her staff. It went against every instinct to leave them, but now, finally in Jeirut, her worry over Mina had grown to something like panic. Ghizlan hadn't been able to reach her by phone since yesterday. Her sister was only seventeen, just finished school. How had she coped with their father's death?

Only men attended Jeiruti funerals, even state funerals, but Ghizlan had wanted to be here to take the burden of the other formalities, receiving the respects of provincial sheikhs and the royal court. But tradition had prevailed and her father had been interred within the requisite three days while Ghizlan had been stuck on another continent.

'Thank you. I appreciate it.' She turned to Azim. 'Would you mind explaining that I've gone on to the palace and that I'm in safe hands?'

'But, my lady...' Azim darted a glance towards the guards surrounding them. 'I need to speak with you in private. It's crucial.'

'Of course. There are urgent matters to discuss.' Her father's death was a constitutional nightmare. With no clear heir to the sheikhdom, it could take weeks to decide his successor. Ghizlan felt the weight of responsibility crush down on her shoulders. She, as a woman, couldn't succeed, but she'd have a key role in maintaining stability until the succession was finalised. 'Give me two hours then we'll meet.'

She nodded to the captain of the guards to proceed.

'But, my lady—' Azim fell silent as the captain stepped towards him, deliberately invading the old man's space, expression stern and body language belligerent.

Ghizlan fixed the officer with a stare she'd learned from her father. 'If you're going to work for the palace you need to learn the difference between attentiveness and intimidation.' The guard's eyes met hers, widening in surprise. 'This man is a valued aide. I expect him, and everyone else approaching me, to be treated with respect. Is that understood?'

The officer nodded and stepped away. 'Of course, my lady.'

Ghizlan wanted to take Azim's hands once more. He

looked old and frail. But she desperately needed to see Mina. Instead she smiled gently. 'I'll see you soon and we can discuss everything.'

'Thank you for your escort.' Ghizlan stopped in the vast palace atrium. 'However, in future, there's no need for you or your men to come within the palace itself.' The security arrangements didn't include armed men in the corridors.

The captain bowed, the slightest of inclines. 'I'm afraid I have orders to the contrary, my lady. If you'll come with me?'

'Orders?' Ghizlan stared. The man might be new but he overstepped the mark. 'Until my father's successor is announced *I* give the orders in the palace.'

The man's expression didn't alter.

Ghizlan was used to soldiers. Protecting the royal family was a prestigious rung on the military career ladder, but never had she met one like this. He looked back, fixed on a point near her ear, his expression wooden.

'What's going on here?' Ghizlan kept her tone calm, despite the unease trickling, ice cold, down her spine. She hadn't paid attention before, had been too lost in her thoughts to notice, but a quick glance revealed all the guards were unfamiliar. One new face, maybe two, was possible. But this...

'My orders are to take you to the Sheikh's office.'

'My father's office?' Despite a lifetime's training in poise, Ghizlan couldn't prevent the hammer of her heart against her ribs, or the way her hand fluttered up as if to stop it. An instant later she'd controlled the gesture, forcing her hand down. 'Who gave this order?'

The captain didn't speak, but gestured for her to precede him.

From confusion and shock, anger rose. Whatever was going on, she deserved answers and she intended to get them! She strode forward, only to slam to a halt as the whole squad of guards moved with her.

Slowly she spoke, articulating each word precisely. She didn't bother to turn her head. 'Dismiss your men, Captain. They are neither required nor welcome in this place.' For the beat of her pulse, then another she waited. 'Unless you feel unable to guard a solitary woman?'

Ghizlan didn't deign to wait for his response, but strode away, her high heels smacking the marble floor, fire fizzing in her veins. It should have been a relief to hear the men moving away in the opposite direction, except she knew their officer followed right behind her.

Something was very, very wrong. The knowledge twisted her insides and raised the hair at the nape of her neck.

Ignoring a lifetime's training, Ghizlan didn't bother knocking on the door to the royal office, but thrust it open, barely pausing in her stride.

Her breath escaped in a rush of frustration as she surveyed the room. It was empty. The person who'd allegedly given such outrageous orders to the palace guard, if it *was* the palace guard, was nowhere to be seen.

She swayed to a halt before the vast desk and her heart spasmed as she inhaled the faint, familiar scents of papers and sandalwood, as well as spearmint from the chews her father kept in a box on his desk.

Time wound back and she could almost believe it all a nightmare. That her father would enter from the rear door to his private quarters, intent on some report or new scheme to help his people.

Ghizlan planted her palms on the satiny wood of the desk and drew in a deep breath. She had to get a grip.

Whatever was going on, and instinct belatedly warned her something was, her father was gone.

A shudder racked her so hard she had to grit her teeth so they didn't chatter. She'd known all her life that her father's love was for his country not his children. Yet he'd been vigorous enough to contemplate a third marriage. It still seemed impossible—

Ghizlan straightened. She didn't have time to wallow in sentiment. She needed to discover what was happening. For it had seemed as if the guards kept her prisoner rather than protected her. Unease stirred again.

She smoothed her palms down her skirt, twitched her jacket in place and pushed her shoulders back, ready to face whatever unpalatable situation awaited.

She was halfway to the study's rear door when a voice stopped her. It wasn't loud but the deep, bass rumble cut through her jumbled thoughts like the echo of mountain thunder.

'Princess Ghizlan.'

She swung around, twisting on a stiletto heel. Her pulse tripped unevenly as she took in the great bear of a man standing before the closed door through which she'd entered.

He towered over her even though she wore heels and was often described as statuesque. The disparity in their heights surprised her. He wasn't just tall, he was wide across the shoulders, his chest deep and his legs long and heavily muscled.

He wore a horseman's clothes—a pale shirt and trousers tucked into long leather boots. A cloak was pushed back off his shoulders so she glimpsed the knife at his waist. Not a decorated, ceremonial dagger as her father had worn from time to time, but a plain weapon, its handle gleaming with the patina of use.

'Weapons aren't permitted in the palace,' she snapped out. It was easier to concentrate on that than the strangely heavy thud of her pulse as she met his gaze. It worried her almost as much as the inexplicable behaviour of the palace guards.

The man's eyes were blue-grey. Light-coloured eyes

weren't uncommon in Jeirut's provinces, crossed by ancient trade routes between Europe, Asia and Africa. Yet Ghizlan had never seen eyes like this. Even as she watched the hint of blue was erased and his eyes under straight black eyebrows turned cool as mountain mist.

He had a wide forehead, a strong nose a little askew from an old break and a mouth that flattened disapprovingly.

Ghizlan arched her eyebrows. Whoever he was, he knew nothing about common courtesy, much less court etiquette. It was not for him to approve or disapprove.

Especially when he looked like he'd stalked in from the stables with his shaggy black hair curling around his collar and his jaw dark with several days' growth. It wasn't carefully sculpted designer stubble on that squared-off jaw but the beard of a man who simply hadn't bothered to shave for a week.

He stepped closer and she caught a whiff of horse and tangy male sweat. It was a strangely appealing smell, not sour but altogether intriguing.

'That's hardly a friendly greeting, Your Highness.' His words were soft but so resonant they eddied through her insides in the most unsettling way.

'It wasn't meant as a greeting. And I prefer not to be addressed as Highness.' She might be of royal blood but she'd never be ruler. Despite the modernisation of Jeirut, of which her father had been so proud, there was no question of equality of the sexes extending that far.

The intruder didn't make a move, either to remove his weapon or himself. Instead he angled his head to one side as if taking her measure. His eyes never left hers and heat sparked at the intensity of that look.

Who was this man who entered without a knock and didn't bother to introduce himself?

'Please remove your weapon while you're here.'

One dark eyebrow rose as if he'd never heard such a request. Silently he crossed his arms over his chest.

Make me.

He might as well have said it out loud. The challenge
sizzled in the air between them.

Bizarrely, instead of being scared by this big, bold,
armed brute, Ghizlan's blood fizzed as if trading glares
with him had finally woken her from the curious, dor-
mant feeling that had encompassed her since the news of
her father's death.

She kept her hands relaxed at her sides but allowed her
mouth to quirk up in the tiniest show of superiority. 'Your
manners as much as your appearance make it clear you're
a stranger to the palace and the niceties of polite society.'

His eyes narrowed and Ghizlan felt that stare as if it
penetrated her silk-lined suit to graze her flesh.

Then in one swift movement he hauled his dagger from
his belt and threw it.

Ghizlan's breath stopped in her throat and she knew
her eyes widened but she didn't flinch when the un-
sheathed blade skidded across the desk an arm's length
away.

Slowly she turned her head, seeing the jagged cut in the
polished wood. Her father had prized that desk, not for its
monetary value, but for the fact it had belonged to an ancestor who had introduced Jeirut's first constitution. A visionary, her father had called him. His role model.

Ghizlan stared at the deep, haphazard scratch on the
beautiful wood and anger welled, raw and potent. An anger
born of shock and loss. She knew the stranger's aim was
deliberate. If he'd planned to attack her he wouldn't have
missed.

Why inflict such wanton damage except to make a point
of his rudeness? And, of course, to frighten her. Yet it
wasn't fear bubbling up inside her. It was wrath.

Her father had devoted his life, and hers, to the betterment of their people. He may not have been a loving father but he deserved greater respect in death.

She made no move to grab the weapon. She was fit but no match for the sheer bulk of the man filling her father's study with his presence. He could probably snap her wrist with a single hand and no doubt he'd enjoy demonstrating his greater physical strength like a typical bully. But she refused to be cowed. She swung to face him.

'Barbarian.'

He didn't even blink. 'And you're a pampered waste of space. But let's not allow name-calling to get in the way of a sensible conversation.'

Ghizlan almost wished she *had* lunged for the knife. She wasn't accustomed to such rudeness and for the first time ever her blood surged with the desire to hurt someone. Slapping him would probably only bruise her palm when it came into contact with that high, sharp cheekbone. But with a knife…

She dragged in a fortifying breath and squashed the errant bloodlust. She blamed it on the creeping certainty that something terrible had happened here. Something that brought unfamiliar faces and armed guards to the royal palace that had epitomised the peace her father had worked so hard to win.

Mina! Where was her sister? Was she safe?

Fear skittered through her but Ghizlan wouldn't let it show. She wouldn't reveal it to the man looking so predatory. His eyes never wavered from her face as if he searched for weakness.

Ignoring the tremor in her knees, Ghizlan crossed the fine silk carpet and pulled out her father's chair from the desk. Deliberately she sank onto the padded leather and planted her arms on the chair, for all the world as if she belonged in her father's place.

If she was going to face this lout she'd do it from the position of power.

Too late she realised that while he stood, dominating the space with his size and raw energy, she was forced to tilt her neck to view him.

'Who are you?' She was relieved to hear her voice revealed none of the emotions roiling inside.

An instant longer that clear, cold gaze rested on her, then he bowed, surprisingly gracefully. It made her wonder what he did when he wasn't trespassing and threatening unarmed women. There was a magnetism about him that would make him unforgettable even if he hadn't barged, uninvited into this inner sanctum.

'I am Huseyn al Rasheed. I come from Jumeah.'

Huseyn al Rasheed. Ghizlan's stomach plunged and her brow puckered before she smoothed it into an expression of calm.

Trouble. That was who he was. Trouble with a capital T.

'The Iron Hand of Jumeah.' Fear prickled her nape.

'Some call me that.'

Ghizlan sucked in a surreptitious breath between her teeth. This grew worse and worse.

'Who can blame them? You have a reputation for destruction and brute force.'

She paused, marshalling her thoughts. Huseyn al Rasheed was son to the Sheikh of Jumeah, leader of the furthest province from the capital. Though part of Jeirut it was semi-autonomous and had a reputation for fearsome warriors.

Huseyn al Rasheed was notorious as his father's enforcer in the continuous border skirmishes with their nation's most difficult neighbour, Halarq. It had been her father's dearest hope that the peace treaties he'd been negotiating with both Halarq and their other neighbouring nation, Zahrat, would end generations of unrest. Unrest Huseyn al Rasheed and his father only fed with their confrontational behaviour.

Ghizlan gripped the leather armrests tight, wishing

her father were here to deal with this. 'Did your father send you?'

'No one sent me. My father, like his cousin, *your* father, is dead.'

Second cousin, Ghizlan almost blurted, wanting to deny the connection he claimed, but she was well trained in holding her tongue.

'My condolences on your loss.' Though she saw nothing in that tough, determined face remotely resembling grief.

'And my condolences on yours.'

Ghizlan nodded, the movement jerky. She didn't like the way he stared at her. Like a big cat who'd found some fascinating new prey to torment.

She curled her fingers until her nails dug into leather. This was no time for flights of fantasy.

'And your reason for entering here, armed and uninvited?'

Was it imagination again or did something flicker in those grey eyes? Surely not because she'd called him on his deplorable behaviour? If the rumours surrounding this man were true she needed to tread very, very carefully.

'I'm here to claim the crown of Jeirut.'

Ghizlan's heart stopped then sprinted on frantically.

'By force of arms?' Vaguely Ghizlan wondered at her ability to sound calm when horror was turning her very bones cold. A man like the Iron Hand in control of her beloved country? They'd be at war in a week. All her father's work, and her own, undone.

Pain lanced her chest and her lungs cramped. She blinked and forced herself to breathe.

'I have no intention of starting a civil war.'

'Which doesn't answer my question.'

He shrugged and Ghizlan watched, mesmerised, as those impossibly broad shoulders lifted.

Terror, loathing, anger. That's what she should feel. Yet

that tingling sensation across her breasts and down to her belly didn't seem like any of those.

She ignored it. She was stressed and anxious.

'I have no intention of fighting my own people for the royal sheikhdom.'

The constriction banding her chest eased a little. Yet she didn't trust this man. Everything about him set alarm bells ringing.

'You think the elders will vote for a man like *you* as leader?' She couldn't sit still. She surged to her feet, her hands clenched in fists on the desk as she leaned forward. How dared he walk in here as if he owned the place?

'I'm sure they'll see the wisdom of choosing me.' He paused, long enough for a flicker of heat to pass between them. Banked fury, Ghizlan decided. 'Especially given the other happy circumstance.'

'Happy circumstance?' Ghizlan frowned.

'My wedding.'

Ghizlan opened her mouth but realised she would only parrot what he had said. Instead she stood, tension racking her body as she watched his mouth curve up in a smile that was painfully smug. It transformed his face enough that she wondered how he'd look if something genuinely amused him. Heat drilled through her. She could almost see traces of a handsome man beneath that fierce beard and the threat he represented. Then she reminded herself this man didn't do light-hearted. And even if he did she wasn't interested in seeing it.

'That's my other reason for coming to the capital. To claim my bride.'

Ghizlan loathed his superior, über-confident air, the gloating note in his deep voice.

She pitied his bride, whoever she was, but clearly he wanted her to be impressed. What would it cost her to play along at least until she got to the bottom of this?

'Who are you marrying? Do I know her?'

His smile widened and she saw the gleam of strong white teeth. Fear scudded down her spine as she read his expression.

'That would be you, my dear Ghizlan. I'm taking you as my wife.'

CHAPTER TWO

HER EYES WIDENED and Huseyn's satisfaction splintered. He'd expected shock, but not the absolute horror he read on her face.

He was a rough and ready soldier but he wasn't a monster. Her expression made him feel like he'd threatened to molest her, instead of honourably planning to marry her.

It was his own fault. He hadn't meant to spring it on her like that. But the high and mighty Princess provoked him as no one had succeeded in doing.

He should have expected the unexpected. Selim had warned before he entered the room that she wasn't what they'd thought. She had grit. She'd even scolded Selim, his right-hand man, now captain of the royal guard, about his lack of courtesy and defied him despite the guards surrounding her!

Huseyn would love to have seen that.

But now he had his hands full with a woman who flouted his assumptions.

Steadfastly he refused to let his gaze flick down over her ripe, enticing body. Yet it was too late because the memory of it taunted, threatening to distract him.

He'd entered the room to find her braced over the desk. He'd had a perfect view of shapely legs and a trim, beautifully rounded backside in that tight skirt. When she'd straightened and tugged at her clothes, wriggling her hips as she did, flame had seared him. Then she'd turned and faced him down as if he were something slimy on the sole of her high-heeled shoe.

No man would dare look at him that way. As for

women—he was used to them sighing over his muscles and his stamina.

When the Princess raised those perfect eyebrows at him all he'd felt was heat.

And curiosity.

'That's totally absurd! I'm not your dear. And I didn't give you permission to call me Ghizlan.'

Anger emphasised her beauty, bringing colour to those slanted cheekbones, making her eyes sparkle and her whole being vibrate with energy. He'd known from the photos that she was lovely, but those images of her at royal events, lips curved in a polite smile, didn't do her justice.

He'd underestimated her. The way she'd stood up to him, not flinching when he'd thrown his knife, had made him rethink. She'd defied him even though she must know she'd been outmanoeuvred. Huseyn admired her for that.

'What am I to call you if not Ghizlan?' His voice dropped on her name as he savoured the taste of it. What would *she* taste like? Sugary sweet or spicy hot like those burning, dark eyes?

He'd considered her a tool to be exploited and a necessary encumbrance. He hadn't expected to desire her.

That was one thing in her favour. She was a woman of passion, despite how she strove to hide it. And a woman of experience, that went without saying. At twenty-six, and after living abroad in the US and Sweden, she was no shrinking maiden. His belly tightened in anticipation. He didn't particularly want to marry but since it was necessary, he'd prefer a wife who could satisfy his physical needs.

'*My lady* is the correct form of address.'

Huseyn stared at her chiselled features, her head held high as if wearing a crown. As if looking down on a man who'd toiled all his life in service to his Sheikh and his people. This from a woman who'd never done a day's work in her life. Who'd never held down a job or done anything but live off the nation's largesse.

Deliberately Huseyn let his gaze slide down her hour-glass figure, lingering on the swell of her breasts, the narrowness of her waist, then the lush curve of hips and thighs. When his gaze rose her face was pink but her expression gave nothing away, except for her flattened lips.

She didn't like him looking at her.

She should be grateful he only looked. The way she'd met him challenge for challenge, refusing to be bested, was an enticing invitation. So was the heavy throb of awareness clogging the air. They might be enemies but he sensed there were things they would both enjoy together.

'Does the title make you feel superior to a mere soldier? Even though it was awarded because of an accident of birth?'

Huseyn had met many who'd fancied themselves better than him. He was illegitimate and his mother had been poor and uneducated, despite the looks that had captured his father's eye. But it had been a long time since anyone had dared look down on him. Not since he'd grown old enough to fight and prove himself as a warrior of strength and honour.

'I believe in common courtesy.' Her gaze met his unflinchingly and, to his astonishment, Huseyn felt a niggle of…could it be shame?

'As you point out, my title is honorary.' She stood straighter, lifting her fists from the table and looking down her regal nose at him in a way that, perversely, made him want to applaud. How many women in her position would stand resolute? 'Some would say I've spent a lifetime living up to the title but I'm sure you—' she sent him a smile as cool as cut glass '—aren't interested in that.' She paused for just a beat. 'What should I call you?'

'Huseyn will do.' He was Shcikh of his province but soon he would rule the nation and Ghizlan would be his wife. Even if the marriage was for political reasons, he discovered he wanted to hear his name on her lips.

His brain stalled on an unexpected vision of her naked beneath him, her soft body welcoming, her breathing ragged as she clutched him, crying out his name in ecstasy.

He couldn't remember such instantaneous, all-consuming lust. It must be the result of months too busy even to take a night off to be with a woman.

'Well, Huseyn.' Her voice crackled with ice but strangely he enjoyed even that. 'Whatever your plans, marrying me isn't possible.'

'Why?' He folded his arms and watched her gaze sharpen. In any other woman he'd have put that fleeting expression down to feminine interest. Yet Ghizlan could be masking fear. He needed to remember that. 'You're available since the Sheikh of Zahrat jilted you.'

It had been the scandal of the decade and the sort of snub to Jeirut that Huseyn would not allow once he ruled. It was time the neighbouring nations paid Jeirut respect.

Ghizlan mirrored him, crossing her arms, and for a second he was distracted by the rising swell of her breasts and the shadow of her cleavage.

This woman fought with weapons more dangerous than guns or knives.

'I was not jilted,' she said coolly. 'I met Sheikh Idris as part of my father's push for a trade and peace deal with Zahrat. As for us marrying…' She shook her head. 'I was happy to attend his betrothal ceremony in London.'

'But not his recent wedding.' Huseyn surveyed her keenly, interested, despite himself, in her feelings for the man who'd dumped her when he'd discovered he had a son by an Englishwoman he hadn't seen in years. A woman he'd since married.

'It wasn't possible. I had business commitments elsewhere.'

It wasn't a convincing lie but he gave her marks for trying. What *had* she felt for Idris? The idea of her nursing a broken heart was vaguely…unsettling.

'Business?'

'Strange as it may seem to you—' her eyes flicked from him dismissively '—I do have some business interests.'

That was news but Huseyn didn't show it.

'And you're free to marry.'

Fine eyebrows arched in a haughty show of surprise that made him long to wrap his hand around that slender neck and draw her close enough to kiss. Her touch-me-not air was a surprising turnon. He couldn't understand it. His taste had never run to spoiled rich girls.

'I have no plans to.'

'No need. I've made the plans already.'

'But—'

'Or did I get it wrong? Aren't you up for sale? Willing to go to the highest bidder? Weren't you part of the price your father planned to pay for a treaty with Zahrat?'

Her face remained as unruffled as ever but something flashed across her eyes that made him think he'd hurt her. Yet how could that be? She'd been bred to be a dynastic bargaining chip.

'Contrary to the old-fashioned customs in your province, Huseyn—' his name on her lips was a silky taunt '—I'm not a chattel. Thanks to my father, women have a say in their lives here now. I have a will of my own.'

He saw that, and despite the minor inconvenience of dealing with it, Huseyn was glad. He admired spirit. If he was to be shackled to her, at least it would be interesting, once she stopped defying him and accepted the inevitable.

'You're afraid I can't meet your bride price?'

'I'm not interested in how many camels you offer for my hand.' As if he were a poor herder from a backward province. 'And I'm not afraid. I'm not afraid of any man.' She drew herself even taller, betraying the anxiety she tried to conceal. Reading opponents' body language could save your life in combat. Huseyn had learned that early.

'I won't hurt you, Ghizlan.' He should have said it

sooner, but he'd been too caught up sparring with her, enjoying the cut and thrust of parrying her objections.

Reassuring women didn't come naturally. He led warriors and protected his people. He knew a lot about women, in bed at least, but he wasn't used to negotiating with them. His was a man's world.

She blinked and for a second he thought he glimpsed a vulnerable woman behind the calm façade. Then she was gone, replaced by an arrogant aristocrat.

'And my sister? Have you hurt her?'

'Of course not!' His pride pricked. She really did think him uncivilised. 'Princess Mina is in her rooms.'

If he expected to win thanks from Her Royal Haughtiness he was doomed to disappointment. Her eyes snapped to his as she did her best to cut him down with that cool stare. Yet all he felt was a jolt of sexual awareness. And a sliver of anticipation at the idea of taming this disdainful Princess.

'Thank you for the assurance.' Her tone was lofty. 'I appreciate it given the illegal presence of armed men in the palace.'

Huseyn frowned. He understood she'd had a fright but surely even here his reputation for protecting the weak, including women, was known. His might be a pre-emptive strike to secure the throne but they weren't criminals. He had a legitimate claim to rule. The *best* claim.

'The guards are here for protection.'

Again that supercilious lift of dark eyebrows. 'And the palace guards who were here before?'

'Temporarily relieved of duty.'

'If you've hurt any of them—'

'No one has been hurt.' Except the soldier who'd tried to quieten the younger Princess, Mina, and been bitten on the hand. Huseyn should have realised then that these spoiled women would be trouble. 'There has been no fighting.'

It hadn't been necessary. Huseyn had visited the palace

to pay his respects to his late King. Once inside, and with the Princess Mina a hostage to their good behaviour, it had been easy to convince the palace guard to stand down.

'Good, then you won't object to me seeing the Captain of the Guard. The *real* one.' When he remained silent she tilted her head and assessed him. 'Unless you're frightened to allow me that courtesy.'

This woman knew how to get under his skin. He, the Iron Hand of Jumeah, frightened! No man would dare even think it.

Ghizlan's breath rushed out in a shaky sigh. Talking to this man was like addressing a brick wall. Except for the curious spark of awareness when his gaze moved over her.

She should be petrified. She *was* anxious, particularly for Mina, but at the same time she felt more energised than she had in ages.

Her lips flattened as she tried to suppress gallows humour. Nothing like an armed coup and the threat of imprisonment to shake you up!

'What's wrong?' His broad brow furrowed and, if she didn't know better, she'd almost think he looked concerned.

The idea was beyond laughable.

He was a brute. An opportunist who sought to profit from her father's death.

He saw her as a chattel.

Like your father did.

The memory stabbed. Huseyn was right. Her father had viewed her and Mina as assets to further his plans. Marrying her to a neighbouring sheikh had been part of his negotiations. It had hurt when her father told her, even though she'd been raised to expect an arranged marriage.

For years she'd been obedient, dutiful, putting her country's needs first. Yet not once had that gained her a father's love or appreciation. He'd relied on her as a matter of course, never considering her happiness.

She'd be damned if she'd have this…interloper tell her who she could marry! She might be bound to her country by ties of duty and love, but for the first time she was free to live as she chose. She did *not* choose to tie herself to an uncivilised bully.

Ghizlan stalked around the desk so she stood before Huseyn al Rasheed, tilting her chin to glare into his pale eyes. The evocative scent of warm, male skin filtered into her senses. She ignored it, as she ignored the fact that up close there was absolutely no doubt he was boldly attractive, despite the beard and rumpled hair and arrogance.

'You ask me what's wrong?' She laughed, the sound brittle. 'What could possibly be wrong? Apart from the fact you've taken over the palace in some sort of revolution and demand I marry you. You deny me access to my sister. You won't let me see the staff. How do I know they're all right?'

'Because you have my word. And I haven't denied you access to your sister.'

'I can see her?' She hadn't pressed because she feared most for their staff. Mina's royal position gave her some protection, but the people who worked in the palace had no one but her to fight for them.

Relief was so strong it was a punch to the belly. Ghizlan locked her knees to stop herself swaying. She refused to show weakness.

'You can see her when we finish our discussion.'

'Is that what you call it?'

His mouth twisted and she wondered if it was in anger or frustration. She didn't care. She was dangerously close to losing her cool. She'd fought to keep her composure, knowing it was the only way to make him take her, and her demands for the people relying on her, seriously. But she didn't know how long she could keep this up.

'Of course.' He unfolded his arms and abruptly she was aware of how close they stood, and how very big he was.

Heat emanated from him, warming her despite the chill gripping her bones. It was an insidious warmth, like the strange flutter of awareness rippling through her when his broad shoulders lifted then settled again.

She'd never been close to a man so blatantly *masculine*. Not just in size and brute strength, but with a potent, unfamiliar *something* that made her body want to shiver and melt at the same time.

'I'll see the Captain of the Guard first. I need to check the staff are all right.' She paused as fear for her personal bodyguard struck. She hadn't seen them since the plane. 'And my bodyguard. I need to make sure—'

He raised one big hand, palm out. 'They're unharmed.'

'You'll forgive me for needing to see proof for myself.' She paused, fighting fear that those who'd devoted themselves to protecting her family had been harmed. 'Then I'll see my sister.'

Ghizlan made to walk away but his long arm snapped out and strong fingers shackled her wrist.

Her pulse thudded, staccato and strong. She hated that he could feel it with his bare hand on her wrist. She particularly hated the effervescence that radiated through her from his touch.

'I prefer not to be manhandled.'

'Manhandled?' A jet eyebrow rose and the lips buried in all that undergrowth of beard curved up.

She amused him. The realisation infuriated her.

'I'm not a plaything, Huseyn. You'll find most women prefer not to be touched against their will.'

'Most women enjoy my touch.' His voice was a low murmur of masculine confidence. His eyes gleamed silver. He thought himself irresistible.

The women in his province of Jumeah must be a sorry lot.

Impossible, appalling man. Was she supposed to thank him for planning to marry her?

'If you say so.' She met his look blandly. 'But I can't help thinking most women would *pretend* to enjoy intimacy when a man has so much more…power than they do. Out of self-defence, you understand.'

He dropped her hand as if bitten, his eyes widening in what looked like genuine shock.

'I would never use force against a woman!' His growl scuttled along her spine, drawing her skin tight.

'Is that so?' She stepped back until she felt the desk behind her. It was good to lean on something solid. 'Then what would you call your demand that we marry? If it's a request, I've already declined.'

Ghizlan saw his jaw move. Was he grinding his teeth? She hoped he got jaw ache. A pulse throbbed at his temple and the muscles in those big arms bunched and swelled.

She refused to cower.

Always show a calm face, no matter what the provocation.

'It's an attempt to avoid bloodshed.'

'You'll have to do better than that. Jeirut is a proud and stable democratic monarchy. The new Sheikh will be voted in by the Royal Council, then parliament. There will be no bloodshed. The truth is you want the crown and you're resorting to force to get it.'

'Not force. Just a pre-emptive tactical move.'

Ghizlan remained scornfully silent.

He scowled at her and she knew she should be scared. But to her surprise, she was more intrigued than fearful. Clearly she was jet-lagged and had taken leave of her senses!

'Even you must admit I'm the best choice to rule. I have a solid claim to the crown with my kinship ties. I'm the only one who can say that. More importantly, I'm strong, resolute, a warrior as well as having experience as an administrator. Our marriage will simply make the decision easier and speed the process.'

Ghizlan arched one eyebrow. 'If you're such a perfect choice the Council will vote for you.'

'But that will take *time*. Time Jeirut doesn't have.'

'You may be eager to ascend the throne but—'

'You think this is about *me*?' His shaggy hair brushed his shirt as he shook his head. 'It's about keeping Jeirut safe. With your father's death, Halarq is poised to invade.'

'Nonsense.' Her voice sharpened. 'My father was on the brink of signing peace agreements with both Zahrat and Halarq.'

'Now he's gone the old Emir of Halarq sees an opportunity. His troops are mobilising. Intelligence suggests they'll begin by claiming the disputed territory then pushing as far as they can into Jeirut.'

'That territory has belonged to Jeirut for two hundred years.'

'Yet I've been fighting border skirmishes with his forces since I was old enough to hold a weapon. You may not realise it here in the safety of the capital.' His gaze raked the room as if dismissing its fine furnishings. 'But my province has borne the brunt of our neighbour's ambitions for years. Believe me, he's poised to act and the longer it takes us to choose a new leader the better it suits him.'

Ghizlan opened her mouth to protest then closed it. There was a seed of truth in what Huseyn said. 'Then talk to the Council. Urge a speedy decision.'

He shook his head. 'The majority are in favour of me but the Council likes to deliberate. A quick decision is seen as a bad one. And there are two other candidates, though their claims aren't as strong. If Halarq invades it will throw that process into confusion. I need to act now. Convince the Council to choose the best man to protect the country.'

Ghizlan looked at the determined thrust of that dark jaw, and the gleam in his eyes, and she nearly believed him. Until she thought of her sister and the palace in lockdown.

Her hands came together in slow, deliberate applause.

'That's some performance. I could almost believe you were sacrificing yourself for the country in claiming the throne. But if you expect me to sacrifice *my* liberty and marry you, think again. Your rhetoric doesn't sway me.'

Something flickered across his face. An expression so swift she couldn't read it. Yet it reminded her of a flash of sheet lightning across mountain peaks in the storm season. Her flesh tightened.

'You won't do this for your country?'

'For my country or for you?' She didn't bother hiding her disdain.

He scowled. 'I should have known not to expect too much from you. You didn't even hurry home when your father died. Obviously your priorities lie elsewhere.'

Ghizlan sucked in an outraged breath. It was true she'd avoided returning to Jeirut when her planned betrothal to Sheikh Idris was abruptly cancelled. But that had been at her father's request, to let the scandal die. Since then she'd been cultivating business contacts Jeirut desperately needed if planned new developments were to proceed.

Not that a man like this, a ruthless mountain marauder with no finesse, would understand that.

'Clearly news is slow to reach your province,' she bit out. 'The dust cloud from a volcano in Iceland stopped all flights for days.' She'd almost flown home from New York across the Pacific instead but each day the forecasters had predicted the cloud would clear and aviation would recommence. For two days they'd been wrong. 'I came on the first flight.'

Her voice grew husky. It was ridiculous. She'd never been close to her father. He'd never once indicated he loved her. Yet her chest ached when she thought of not being here for his funeral. Or to support Mina.

'Not that I care about your opinion. I'd simply never marry a man I despised on sight.'

'Despised?' His voice dropped to that bass rumble.

Thunder to the lightning she'd seen a moment ago. She felt its vibration shimmer across her nipples and thighs.

'Absolutely.' Her chin notched even higher. Had he moved closer?

He *had* moved closer. She drew in that tangy scent of stable and man as he stepped in, toe to toe.

'Then how do you explain *this*, my lady?'

Big, warm, implacable hands closed around her upper arms and his face lowered to hers.

CHAPTER THREE

GHIZLAN WHIPPED HER head to one side but only succeeded in baring her cheek to this…this…bandit.

Whiskers brushed her in a totally unfamiliar caress, sending little shivers dancing across her skin. Warm lips, far softer than she'd imagined, nuzzled her cheek, stealing her breath.

She wouldn't scream. She wouldn't give him the pleasure of revealing fear. Instead she stood ramrod straight. Frozen.

Yet it wasn't fear she experienced as his lips moved in a tantalisingly slow trail up to her ear. Ghizlan blinked, surprised at the odd sensation of warmth curling in on itself deep in her belly.

This had gone on long enough.

She yanked her arms back, trying to break his hold, but it was like wrestling a boulder. A huge, warm boulder scented not just with the stables but with an enticing, unfamiliar tang that she suspected was essence of Huseyn al Rasheed.

Teeth nipped her earlobe and she jumped, horrified at the fiery trail zapping from the spot straight to her womb, as if he'd jerked a string and she, like a puppet, responded. Her nipples budded hard and achy against her bra. Did he feel that as his big body pressed against her?

'Stop it, you lout!'

Hands braced on his chest, she leaned back, trying to escape, but he was taller and stronger. In one swift movement he clamped both her hands against that brawny, powerful chest. His other hand grabbed the back of her head, inexorably turning her face towards him.

Ghizlan saw a flash of smoky blue beneath straight dark brows, then his mouth was on hers.

Heat, power, the rich, zesty scent of male skin. The soft prickle of his whiskers against her flesh contrasted with the sheer force of his mouth grinding down on hers. It was a predictably ruthless assault on her senses by a man determined to dominate.

Fear filtered into her stunned brain. Until she realised, astonished, that despite the power in that massive, muscled body, he'd pulled back a fraction. Even as the thought formed, the pressure on her lips eased and his hand in her hair gentled, cradling and massaging.

Ghizlan stared, trying to focus on the blue of his eyes, but he was too close. He shifted his stance, drawing her lower body in against him until there was no mistaking the monumental evidence of his arousal.

She gasped, stunned, and too late realised her mistake. For Huseyn al Rasheed took the opportunity to invade her mouth.

Not to ravage this time but to seduce. His movements were sure but gentle as his tongue swiped hers, learning the feel and taste of her, just as she discovered he tasted like almonds and something else impossibly, horrifyingly delicious.

Her chest cramped as she realised she *enjoyed* the sensation of his tongue tangling with hers.

Foggily she fought the drugging pleasure of those slow, sure, sensual movements of lips and tongue, no longer forcing but *inviting*.

A shiver passed from the back of her skull where his fingers caressed her, down to her curling toes.

She'd been kissed before. Perfectly pleasant kisses from perfectly nice men. Sweet kisses, even eager kisses. But none like this. None that *demanded* so imperiously then gentled to seduce her into feelings that surely were more dangerous than anything else he could unleash on her.

His kiss invited her to relax and follow the unfamiliar lure of pleasure. To be selfish, just once. His hand cupping her head supported but also caressed, sending whorls of languid delight through her.

And his hard body against hers—*that* was a totally new, electrifying experience. Ghizlan had kissed, and dated while a student, but, ever conscious of the high expectations placed on her, and the possibility for scandal if caught out publicly in a love affair, she'd never progressed beyond that.

No man had ever made her feel this potent longing for more.

Ghizlan tried to be strong, tried not to respond. Until she heard, and tasted, Huseyn's low humming growl of satisfaction. It was a sensual assault, as real as his hand in her hair or his tongue stroking hers. The way it vibrated through her, sparking an answering excitement, was unlike anything she'd known.

His kiss slowed, deepened, became positively languorous, and Ghizlan's bones began to soften. Her hands twitched against that powerful chest and before she knew it they'd slid up, over hard shoulders to tangle in tousled locks, tunnelling and tugging then clamping tight on his skull.

She shifted, angling her mouth to kiss him back and losing her breath as his erection aligned provocatively against her.

Another growl from the back of his throat and he roped one muscled arm around her, lifting her against him so the contact became even more blatantly sexual.

And devastatingly delicious.

Ghizlan gasped, her mind, like her body, running on overdrive. One part of her was aware of curving in, inviting more of that heavy, outrageously improper contact. Another revelled in the strength of a man who could lift her with one arm as if she were made of gossamer. But mainly she was focused on the provocative, delicious kiss she didn't want to end.

Except this was wrong. On so many levels she couldn't begin to count them.

The part of her consciousness that had been trained from birth to focus on duty, to be a good example, to do the right thing always, suddenly burst awake and screamed in horror.

Ghizlan dropped her hands to his shoulders and shoved with all her might. She tried to tear her mouth away and only succeeded in inviting him to nuzzle her neck.

Her body trembled and flushed with delight at the sensations bombarding her from his mouth and his hands and that huge body moving deliberately against her pelvis.

'I don't want this. Do you hear me? I don't want it!' Her voice was a raw whiplash, ragged and desperate. 'Let me go.' She gave up pushing and thumped her fists on his shoulders.

Finally, slowly, his head lifted. His eyes pinioned her as effectively as that heavy arm lashing her to him. His gaze was the colour of the sky after sunset, that fleeting blue when the first stars appeared before the sky turned indigo.

He blinked. Once. Twice. His gaze dropped to her lips, throbbing and heavy from that devastating kiss. To Ghizlan's horror she felt that stare like a stroking caress.

'Let me go.' This time her voice was subdued. How she managed to look him in the eye, Ghizlan couldn't fathom. They both knew that despite her anger she'd responded, lost to everything but the magic of his kiss.

Heat roared in her veins. Shame filled her that she should surrender so easily to such a man!

She told herself she'd responded because of her inexperience. If she'd known what to expect she could have prepared herself. She'd known he fancied himself as a lover—that smugness had been unmistakable. Clearly he'd played his greater expertise to advantage.

'Well, that was interesting.' His voice held a husky note that drove a shaft of heat right to her belly.

'You can let me go now.'

His lips curved slowly into a smile Ghizlan wanted to hate because it was prompted by masculine pride. He was pleased with himself because she hadn't been able to resist him. But strangely his smile made her heart thud faster.

'Are you sure you can stand?'

Of all the complacent, self-satisfied...

Ghizlan's knee-jerk reaction, straight for the soft spot where that monumental male ego was centred, should have crippled him. But his reactions were faster than hers. Her knee grazed his cotton trousers but he'd already whipped back out of reach with the lightning reflexes of a man used to fighting. And fighting dirty.

His hands dropped, leaving her free, panting for breath and propped against the desk.

At least that wiped the grin off his insufferable face.

Ghizlan summoned her strength, standing tall, her hands going automatically to her hair and swiftly pinning what he'd turned into a mare's nest. Fortunately she could tidy her hair without thinking about it, like she could descend a grand staircase in a full-length dress without looking down or tripping. Or converse with ambassadors in several languages at the same time. Years of practice made some things easy.

What she found difficult was the realisation her own body had betrayed her.

'You've had your fun at my expense.' She kept her voice even, only because letting him glimpse the depth of her despair at her weakness was untenable. 'Now, I'd like the see the Captain of the Guard, and my bodyguards and then my sister.'

'After we've concluded our business.'

Ghizlan shook her head. 'That can wait.' She hefted a breath, waiting for some tiny sign he relented but none came. He remained immovable, implacable.

She sighed and fought the desire to rub her aching head. 'Surely you understand I must see them. They're my responsibility. With my father…gone, it's my duty to see to their welfare.' She swallowed, hating the salty tangle of tiredness and emotion blocking her throat. She couldn't afford to be weak now. 'You'd feel the same way about the soldiers you command.'

He'd give her points for perceptiveness. Ghizlan understood him better than he'd expected. Appealing to his sense of duty to his men was the approach he'd expect of an honourable adversary, a general he could respect, even if they were on opposite sides.

He hadn't thought a pretty princess, spoiled from birth and raised in luxury, would understand that overriding sense of responsibility. Much less share it!

His gaze raked her. This time he tried to take in more than the mutinous, deliciously kiss-swollen mouth, the delectable figure, flawless skin and glossy ebony hair that had run like silk in his hands.

Huseyn discovered an unwavering dark gaze, shoulders as straight as any guard on patrol, and an expression as cool as the snow on the topmost peaks of Jeirut's highest mountain range. Only the throbbing pulse hammering at her throat belied her calm façade. It ignited a flare of satisfaction that he'd got to her as she had him.

Admiration vied with impatience and lust. He wanted her mouth beneath his, eager and generous, that bountiful body crushed against his still painfully hard arousal.

He shook his head, appalled. This was no time to indulge himself. The future of his province and his country hung in the balance.

'What do you want? For me to beg? Is that what it will take to satisfy you?'

'You'd do that?' Huseyn imagined her on her knees before him, head bent. But the vision swimming before his eyes didn't involve her begging. With a roaring rush of arousal he realised it was something more satisfying, more earthy, that he desired from this proud princess.

She opened those reddened lips, now devoid of lipstick, and abruptly Huseyn had had enough. He'd have her in his bed soon enough, as his wife. Because he must and because he'd do what was necessary to make that happen. In the meantime he refused to toy with her. Her instincts were honourable and he respected that.

'No.' His voice was harsh. 'No, I don't expect you to beg.' He sucked air into constricted lungs and watched as her attention dropped to the rise of his chest, her eyes rounding infinitesimally. As if she liked what she saw.

She'd certainly enjoyed that kiss. She'd been so enthusiastic he'd actually begun to forget why he'd kissed her. To show who had the upper hand, and more, to puncture that haughty air of hers.

Realisation slammed into Huseyn and with it distaste. He'd let her distract him from his purpose. From the vital work that needed to be done.

'Wait here. I'll have them each brought to you so you can satisfy yourself that they're unharmed.'

'It would be easier if I went—'

'No.' A slashing gesture stopped her mid-sentence. There was no way he'd allow her to wander the palace. Not till everything was settled. 'Give me your phone and I'll arrange for them to see you here.'

'My phone?' She looked puzzled.

Huseyn folded his arms over his chest. 'I don't want you contacting people outside the palace till we've concluded our business.' Her gaze sliced to the phone on the desk.

He shook his head. 'The landlines have been temporarily disconnected. All electronic devices have been confiscated.'

'While you stage your coup.'

For a minute, caught up in appreciation of her bravery,

he'd almost forgotten his dislike of the pampered elite who sucked the country dry with their demands.

'While I save the nation.'

Her snort of derision was anything but regal and Huseyn found himself suppressing a smile. Despite everything, he warmed to this blue-blooded daughter of privilege.

She swung round, treating Huseyn to a view of her peach-perfect bottom as she leaned over to grab her purse.

'Here.' She extended her phone. 'But I expect it back intact. I'm in the middle of important negotiations and I want my contacts and messages untouched.'

Negotiations? With her hairstylist? Boyfriends? Huseyn didn't care. She'd be incommunicado till he said so.

His fingers closed around the phone, his big hand scraping her smaller one, and heat shot up his arm. He frowned, lips flattening at that unwanted response.

She pulled her hand back, her face smoothing into the mask of calm he'd learned she wore when something disturbed her. Good. He liked the idea that he disturbed her. For she sure as hell disturbed him!

'The phone will be returned undamaged.' He paused. 'As long as you obey orders.'

Ebony eyebrows arched but she said nothing. She was learning.

'After you've assured yourself no one has been harmed, we'll talk.' With that he turned and left. He had business to attend to. He'd deal with his recalcitrant bride later.

'Truly, I'm fine.' Mina squeezed Ghizlan's hand. 'But I'm glad you're here. It's been pretty grim.'

Ghizlan nodded, the banked embers of fury glowing brighter. Mina was just seventeen. Losing her father was bad enough without being held prisoner in her own home.

'You're sure they didn't hurt you? You'd tell me, wouldn't you?'

'Of course. But they didn't hurt me. Just took my phone

and laptop and told me I couldn't leave the palace.' Her mouth set in a distressed line. 'But I need to access the net, Ghizlan. It's vital.'

'Vital?' It was such a relief seeing her sister okay. First the Captain of the Palace Guard then her own protection staff. Now Mina. It seemed Huseyn al Rasheed was as good as his word. No one had been harmed. The takeover had been accomplished with the ease and precision of a consummate professional.

A professional coup leader, she reminded herself. And a thug. Look at the way he'd groped her.

'Are you listening, Ghizlan?'

'Of course.' She smiled. 'But I'm still getting used to your new look.'

Mina stroked the dark hair feathering her bare neck. 'When Father died I realised that at last I could do what I wanted. Not pretend to be someone I'm not.' Her expression grew earnest. 'I'm not like you, Ghizlan. I can't be the consummate diplomat, following duty and public expectation. I tried to please Father but never succeeded. As for studying economics...' She shuddered.

Ghizlan covered Mina's hand with hers, emotion welling. 'You're fine as you are, Mina. You're bright and enthusiastic and talented.' It seemed like betrayal to think it but with their father's death Mina was free to follow her inclinations and build the life she wanted. Their father couldn't straitjacket *her* into a life designed to fulfil some political objective as he had Ghizlan.

'Actually, I rebelled a while ago. Before Father died, though he didn't know.' Mina's eyes glowed. 'You know I don't want to go to that stuffy school to study economics.'

'I know.' It had been part of their father's plan to show Jeiruti women could achieve in nontraditional fields. Which was why Ghizlan had a degree in chemical engineering, though at least she'd been interested in science in the first place. 'So what have you done?'

'I applied to art school. A fabulous art school in France. You know that's always been my dream. I secretly sent off an application and offers should be out now but I can't check my email.' Her voice rose in distress. 'If they make an offer and I don't reply, they won't wait. They'll—'

'Calm down, Mina. They'll give you time to respond.'

'Not if we're in lockdown for weeks. What if Huseyn doesn't release us for months? What if—?'

'Don't fret. He can't hold us indefinitely. His plan is to get himself declared Sheikh as soon as possible.'

With her as a vital part of his plan. But he'd soon discover she was no gullible pawn. She'd never marry him.

'You really think so? I'd shrivel up and die if I had to do the course Father picked.'

'No one's going to force you to do anything, Mina. Just relax.'

The thought struck Ghizlan with the force of a lightning bolt. It was true. Once a new sheikh was proclaimed they would leave the palace. Huseyn couldn't force her to marry him. All she had to do was remain steadfast. When he'd given up they could do what they wanted with their lives. Mina could go to art school and she could... Her brow puckered. It had been so long since she'd thought about what *she* wanted, rather than what was expected, she didn't immediately know how she wanted to spend her future.

Now freedom beckoned. A whole world of opportunity.

'Ghizlan? You have the strangest look on your face.'

Ghizlan smiled. Not the polite smile she used for official occasions, but a beam of excitement. 'That's because I've realised once Huseyn al Rasheed gets what he wants we'll be free to do what *we* want. No one can stop us.'

'You demanded my presence?' Ghizlan lifted her chin to meet those misty blue eyes. The sheer size of the man would daunt her if she let it. She focused on that rather than the peculiar flutter of her pulse when his gaze met hers.

Antagonism. Distrust. That's what she felt.

The strange excitement she experienced when he turned from her father's desk to face her was due to the realisation she and Mina would soon be free in a way they'd never dreamed possible. It had nothing to do with the memory of Huseyn's lips on hers or that hollow ache in her middle when he'd crushed her to him. Or that, minus the long cloak, his pale trousers and shirt emphasised the breathtaking strength in that beautifully proportioned body.

Ghizlan preferred character to brawn.

'Gracious as ever, I see.' That deep voice was soft, like plush velvet across her skin. He didn't look annoyed either, merely watchful as she closed the study door and approached the desk.

That all-encompassing survey was incredibly disquieting. Ghizlan fought to repress a shiver.

'You expect me to pretend you and your thugs haven't invaded the capital or taken me and my sister hostage?' Ghizlan took a sustaining breath and was momentarily discomfited when his gaze flicked down as if taking stock of her body.

Rubbish. He wasn't interested in her. That scene he'd played out here a couple of hours earlier had been about power, not attraction. Some men got off on that. Men like Huseyn al Rasheed.

'You don't give up, do you?' He leaned back against her father's desk as if he owned it. The raw, jagged scratch he'd made in it was half hidden by papers. Ghizlan was incensed at how he'd made himself at home.

'You expect me to treat you like a welcome guest?'

'Frankly, my manners are the least of your worries, *my lady*. You should be more concerned about the threat to Jeirut from Halarq.'

'Ah, but according to you, I'm merely a waste of space.' She tilted her head as if thinking. As if she didn't recall precisely what he'd called her. 'A pampered princess, wasn't it? It's obvious that as far as you're concerned such weighty issues can only be dealt with by armed men. The sort of men who flout the law and imprison law-abiding citizens.'

Silver flashed in those deep-set eyes and he muttered something under his breath.

She locked her hands together behind her, forcing her shoulders back and her chin up. This was pointless. Much as she enjoyed baiting him, there was nothing to be gained from it except personal satisfaction. She had others in her care to worry about. She couldn't afford to endanger them.

'Might I suggest that, while the citadel is under armed guard, you release most of your hostages? I'll stay, of course, but my sister is just a teenager and the staff could leave while this is sorted out.'

Ghizlan tried and failed to repress the pounding thud of her heart at the thought of Mina at this man's mercy any longer. Mina was young and impulsive, and Huseyn al Rasheed didn't look like he had an understanding bone in his body.

'Sorted out? You speak as if I'm here temporarily. I assure you, *my lady*, that isn't the case. This is now my home.' His wide gesture encompassed not just the room, but the whole palace.

'Once the Council declares you Sheikh.'

'I expect that within a couple of days. I've already informed them of our impending marriage.'

Ghizlan's eyes popped. 'You had no right.'

'I had every right. I'm trying to save our country. Can't you see that?'

'What I see is a man so wrapped up in his bid for personal power he'll do anything to succeed.' It was a miracle she kept her voice even. Behind her back her knotted hands shook with the force of her outrage. 'I wouldn't be surprised to learn you had an army surrounding the city, ready to start a civil war.'

He stopped lounging against the desk. In the blink of

an eye he was standing tall, looming over her, his expression one of hauteur and repressed anger. 'I'll forgive that. *This time*. When you know me better you won't jump to such insulting assumptions.'

'I have no intention of knowing you better. You can't make me marry you.'

He didn't move, didn't lift a finger, but that smoky blue gaze grazed her face as surely as if he'd stroked rough fingers across her flesh. Beneath the whiskers his mouth curved in a slow smile that sent quivers of foreboding through her.

'If you're so set against it, *my lady*, so be it.' He paused. 'I'll simply marry your sister instead. Her royal blood is as good as yours. She's seventeen, is that right?' He paused, his smile widening. 'No doubt I'll find her much more *amenable* to my needs.'

For a second, then another and another, Ghizlan's heart stalled. Her stomach dropped sickeningly. She looked at the implacable man before her, read the determination in the set of his shoulders and the proud tilt of his head. The certainty in that complacent smile. And felt the world tremble on its foundations.

It was one thing for their father to try bartering Ghizlan into an arranged marriage to Sheikh Idris of Zahrat. At least Idris was a civilised, cultured, caring man. But to expect Mina, her innocent little sister, to marry this brute…

Ghizlan's arm swung up and she punched Huseyn al Rasheed full in the face.

CHAPTER FOUR

HUSEYN TURNED JUST in time. The blow glanced across his cheekbone an instant before his hand closed around hers, pulling it away from his face.

Just as well they didn't teach princesses boxing.

And that his reflexes were fast, honed by years of combat and training. She'd taken him by surprise and could have done some damage if she'd had a decent technique.

Huseyn stared into Ghizlan's flushed face. There was no mistaking the bloodlust in her burning eyes. If looks could kill he'd be six feet under.

Who'd have thought she had it in her to take him on?

His respect for her rose. Every minute in her presence she intrigued him more. The combination of ice and fire. The loyalty to and sense of responsibility for those who served her was unexpected too. His image of a self-absorbed socialite was fading fast.

But most of all, her courage amazed him. Huseyn knew grown men, trained soldiers, who'd retreat rather than fight him.

Heat scored his cheek where she'd made contact. Selim would laugh himself sick if he discovered an untrained woman had got past Huseyn's guard.

Serve you right for goading her. For expecting her to agree and make this easy. Since when has life been easy?

He'd had no compunction about threatening to marry Mina, in order to convince Ghizlan. This marriage was the key to success. He'd do whatever it took to keep his people safe.

But he'd been crass, acting like the sort of voluptuary he despised, as if he really wanted a teenager in his bed!

What was it about Ghizlan that made him sink so low? That made him taunt her again and again? He was no schoolboy, teasing a pretty girl to get her attention. This was about the fate of the nation, not some petty struggle for points.

Her eyes were over-bright—not with tears but fury. Her breasts thrust high with each panting breath and a shot of pure lust hit his belly, arrowing to his groin.

He wanted her. Like this. Full of fire and passion. Full of spark and spirit.

His fist closed more firmly around hers as he felt himself harden.

He wanted—

She winced, white teeth baring as she frowned. An instant later her face smoothed of expression.

That's when Huseyn realised how hard he gripped her hand. Instantly he released her, fingers spreading wide.

'My apologies. I didn't mean to hurt you.'

Perfect eyebrows arched on that fine forehead. 'You apologise for that but not for your threat to marry my little sister?'

Huseyn shrugged. Now he'd embarked on this course he had to follow through. 'Marriage to one of you will secure the throne quickly so I can protect Jeirut. It will ease tensions with other factions by providing a link to your father's rule. It's immaterial to me whether I marry you or your sister.'

Which was an outright lie.

Who'd bother with an adolescent when they could have Ghizlan?

She'd be trouble. She was too full of her own importance, too used to having her own way. But against that, she had pluck and more character than he'd expected. Plus a body made for pleasure. He wanted to haul her close and experience again the honey-cinnamon sweetness of her lips, and that unique dark, sultry flavour he'd found so addictive—the taste of her passion.

'Mina's a child!'

'She's seventeen. By law she's old enough to marry.'

'Only a brute would force someone so young into a marriage she doesn't want. Thanks to my father and grandfather we left those traditions behind long ago.'

Huseyn crossed his arms, noting the way her gaze skittered towards his chest. It was the sort of look women had been giving him ever since he'd grown out of puberty and it made him smile inside. She might pretend not to be attracted but the curiosity and the hunger were there, all right.

'Who says I'd be forcing her?'

Her lush lips tightened. 'You think you're irresistible?' She crossed her arms, mimicking his confrontational stance. But he'd bet she didn't realise it drew attention to the ripe curve of her breasts and the shadow of her cleavage. 'I've got news for you, Huseyn. Neither my sister nor I would be stupid enough to fall for a man like you.'

Her gazed raked him from head to toe, like a sergeant inspecting an unpromising recruit. He enjoyed her boldness. It was a new sensation. No woman had ever stood toe to toe against him. Instead they were only too eager to offer what he wanted.

'So you melting in my arms, kissing me as if you'd been starved for a man—that was you demonstrating how immune you are? Is that what you're saying?'

Her breath hissed and her eyes narrowed to slits of hatred that did nothing to diminish her attractiveness. Spitting fire or burning up in his embrace—both incarnations of Her Royal Bossiness were disturbingly enticing. And distracting. He needed to sort this wedding and move on.

'*Know your enemy* is a tried and true tactic.' Her chin shot up, drawing his eyes to the pale golden expanse of her throat. His pulse throbbed hard and low. He wanted to press his lips there again, taste the sweet spiciness of her flesh. And more.

Huseyn opened his arms wide, palms out, inviting her into his space. 'Feel free, *my lady*. I'm happy for you to *know* me in intimate detail if it will persuade you.'

She spluttered and he had to repress a grin. For all her hauteur she was amazingly easy to rile when the discussion turned to sex. Intriguing.

He beckoned her. 'Come. Don't be shy. It's a sacrifice I'm willing to make.'

'You're a cocky bastard, aren't you?'

He didn't hold back his grin then, surprised by her language. Who'd have thought to hear such words from the lips of such a fine lady?

'A bastard, yes, though my father took the trouble to legitimise me before he died.' His voice was bland, giving away none of his feelings on the fact that his father had waited over thirty years to do it. The old man had relied on him for years, had seen his promise early and cultivated it. Yet he'd never had any affection for the boy who'd come to him in rags and proven his loyalty again and again, usually by facing down dangers others baulked at. 'But cocky? No. I know my worth, probably more than the next man. I've spent my life proving it.'

Suddenly his good humour drained away. What did he think he was doing, playing word games with this woman? She had no notion how real people lived. People born in poverty. People living on a disputed border, where any night could bring marauders intent on pillage and death.

Huseyn let his arms drop to his sides.

'Know this, *my lady*. I intend to rule Jeirut and soon. That means marrying either you or your sister. No negotiation, no argument. I don't care if you believe I do it for my own prestige. I care even less if you think I'm a barbarian.'

He stepped forward, into her space, so her head jerked back. Though to her credit she stood her ground.

This time the tantalising honey scent of her skin only fired his impatience. He was more used to the scents of sweat and fear, of hard work and blood and dust. She was a distraction he didn't need.

'I'll give you till tomorrow morning to come to terms with that and agree to be my wife. If your answer is no, then I'll marry your sister instead.'

He paused, reading her fear, swiftly hidden. To his surprise he found himself lifting his hand, stroking a stray strand of hair back behind her ear, his hand big and rough against her silky perfection.

If he'd thought gentleness would win her over he was wrong. She shuddered beneath his touch, her body freezing in rejection. To her he was a savage. It was a timely reminder.

'I'll come for your answer at nine.'

Huseyn spun on his heel and left her.

'You're sure you know the way? We've been going for ages.' Mina's whisper came out of the cellar's darkness behind Ghizlan. Was that fear in her voice, or excitement?

Ghizlan hoped it was excitement. She was scared enough for the two of them after that climb across the sheer stone wall outside their windows. She hated heights. Even now she couldn't quell the sick terror in her belly after forcing herself out over her window ledge. Silently she cursed Huseyn al Rasheed and his thorough ways. The movement sensors on their doors meant the only escape had been out the windows and via the towering walls, which on their side of the palace dropped sheer to the valley below.

'I'm sure it's the way.' She forced the words through clenched teeth. 'It seems a long time because we're going slowly. But we need to save the light for later.' Without their phones they had no light source, save a single penlight torch Ghizlan had found in a drawer. But its light was dim and she didn't trust the battery to last. She'd save it for later.

'We're here.' Her hand, skimming the cold stone of the old cellar, found a corner, the wall turning at right angles. 'This is it!'

Relief coursed through her. After hours desperately considering and dismissing possible escape routes, the abandoned tunnel was their only hope. Cut through the living rock, the ancient passage into the city had been disused and forgotten for ages.

'Brilliant,' Mina whispered. 'This place gives me the creeps.' Light bloomed and Ghizlan blinked. Even the glow of the tiny torch was bright after the inky blackness. 'You need light to work the lock.'

If she could work it. As a child the ancient palace locks had fascinated her with their intricate, decorative metalwork. But it was a lifetime since Azim had shown her the secret to unlocking them. They'd been replaced by modern security devices. All, she hoped, except this one.

Her breath eased out as Mina played the torchlight further along the wall to a hefty door with massive hinges and a familiar, ancient lock.

Ghizlan's heart raced as she traced the metalwork, half-remembered instructions like whispers in her ears.

'Can you get it open?' Mina was at her shoulder.

'I can try.' Ghizlan sank to her knees, breathing deeply. She'd been only this height when Azim had shown her the trick—a lock that, despite the keyhole, didn't need a key if you were one of the very few who knew its secret.

Her fingers moved hesitantly, then with more confidence. There was a click as a hidden lever worked. A quiet curse and a frown as another refused to budge. Ghizlan gnawed at her lip, frowning as she tried and retried the various components. Had she got it wrong or had the lock seized from disuse? Cold sweat broke out between her shoulder blades at the idea they'd lost their one and only chance to escape. How could she protect Mina if—?

With a slow, grating groan, the pieces slid into place and the lock opened.

'You did it!' Mina's whisper was exultant.

Ghizlan stared, amazed she'd managed it. Amazed it had still been there. Luck was on their side. Until now she hadn't let herself actually believe.

'Come on. Let's get out of here.' Mina was already reaching for the huge twisted ring of metal on the door.

'No. Wait. Let me go first. We don't know for sure what's at the end of the tunnel and whether it's still open.' Mina started to protest but Ghizlan continued. 'I've been this way before. Let me test it first. One person will make less noise than two.'

Mina huffed. 'You think I'm still scared of spiders?'

It wasn't spiders Ghizlan had in mind. It was guards. She had no confidence the men Huseyn al Rasheed had brought would respect a pair of unprotected women if they came across them in the dark.

'If I'm not back in fifteen minutes, retrace your steps and go back to your room.'

'You're kidding, right?'

Ghizlan grabbed her sister's wrist, meeting her gaze. 'I'm serious. We don't know what we're walking into.' But she had to take this chance to spirit Mina away. 'Let me do this without arguing. Please?'

Finally Mina nodded, her defiance fading as she handed over the torch. 'Be careful.'

'You can count on it.' Then Ghizlan opened the door, wincing as the old hinges shrieked in the stillness. She switched off the light, her breath stopping as she slid through the door and pushed it almost shut behind her.

The air was different in the tunnel. Fresher? Hope rose but she made herself wait, listening. After a full minute she risked the torch, even then shielding it with her hand. What she saw made her heart leap. A bare tunnel fading into gloom. No blockages that she could see.

Switching off the light she moved to the side, fingertips touching the wall, and began to walk.

She counted three corners in the tunnel. Turning the last one she had to bite back a gasp of excitement. In the distance she saw a sprinkle of city lights, half hidden by what looked like undergrowth. She made herself wait, listening to her pulse pound erratically.

Finally, after waiting several minutes, Ghizlan sneaked to the end of the tunnel. Nothing. No sign of life except for the city's old quarter ahead. She'd go back and get Mina. But she had to be sure first.

Tucking the light into her pocket, she pushed aside a thorn bush, ignoring the darts of pain as it ripped at her hands and caught her clothes. Eyes closed to protect them, she groped her way, relief filling her as the last branches fell away and she stepped free.

Straight into something hard and warm and all too familiar.

Despair swamped her.

She should have known it couldn't be this easy.

Ghizlan's eyes snapped open as two large hands wrapped around her upper arms and tugged her off-balance. She had an impression of glinting eyes, then she landed against him, palms splayed on a muscled chest.

'Well, well, what have we here?' Huseyn al Rasheed's voice rumbled up beneath her hands, making her want to tug them free. *Feeling* that baritone as well as hearing it was far too intimate.

Frustrated tears prickled her eyes. They'd been so close to freedom.

'Stop squashing me!' Her breasts were pressed against him and she was surrounded by an earthy male scent. It was surprisingly appealing after the dank dustiness of the passage. No smell of horse this time, she noted. He must have had a shower.

She reared back. In the starlight she saw his smile. He

looked so complacent, so annoyingly unperturbed. It made her want to wipe that smile away.

'Is this how you get your jollies? Mauling women?'

The smile faded, replaced by a grim frown that made him look more formidable than ever. He thrust her back but still his huge hands shackled her shoulders.

Looming there in the dark he was big, hard and merciless. The hope she'd held like a flame inside flickered and died and Ghizlan tasted ashes on her tongue. Had she really believed she could spirit herself and Mina away from this man? He was like a genie in those old stories, the sort whose powers were unassailable. The sort who mocked the efforts of puny mortals to avoid their fate.

A shudder passed through her. Despite the lump of despair in her throat, Ghizlan met his stare head on. She might be defeated but she would go down fighting.

'You don't give up, do you?' He stared down into her tense face, wearily acknowledging the inevitability of tonight's little scene. He'd known from the first she was trouble with her defiance and that sinfully distracting body.

Of course it was too much to expect hoity-toity Princess Ghizlan to accept the inevitable gracefully. Especially when the inevitable included him, a low-born soldier, in her pristine bed. No doubt she saved that privilege for lovers as blue-blooded as she.

'Would you give up, in my position?' Her voice was low.

Damn her for stirring even a tickle of sympathy. This wasn't about her, or about him for that matter. It was about saving Jeirut from the bloodshed of war.

'I have better things to do with my night than bandy words with you, *my lady*. I don't appreciate being interrupted when I'm busy.' He'd been in the middle of crisis talks with some of the leaders eager to have him claim the throne. With luck they could bring this off quickly and—

'At two in the morning?' she sneered, her chin lifting

regally. 'Don't let me keep you. I hope she's a camp follower you brought from home and not someone from the palace you forced into your bed.'

Huseyn's teeth ground together. She had a knack for riling him—a man renowned for his patience.

'Careful, *my lady*. Even a despicable barbarian has his pride. I'm tired of the implication the only way I can get a woman into my bed is to force her.' He paused, letting her see his displeasure. 'One more crack like that and I'll begin to wonder at your interest in my sexual activities.' Another pause, longer this time. 'I'd also be tempted to demonstrate that no force is needed.'

Despite his anger, he felt the sizzle of erotic heat at the thought of seducing Ghizlan. Though given the shimmering attraction he experienced whenever they got close he wouldn't be surprised if they didn't make it to a bed.

For the first time since they'd met he'd reduced her to speechlessness. He liked it.

'If you'll let me go—'

'What? You'll toddle off about your business?' He bent forward, thrusting his face into her space. 'I think not.' He sucked in the sweet honey scent he remembered from earlier and suddenly anger turned to burning fury.

'What the hell did you think you were doing, climbing the outside wall of the palace? You could have fallen to your death!' He hadn't wanted to believe the report when it came through, except the guard in the corner tower was one of Selim's best and he'd seen the two women with his own eyes.

That had stopped Huseyn in his tracks—the idea the women were so scared of him they'd risk their lives.

No, not scared of him. Scared of being forced to make a sacrifice for their people instead of living in luxurious ease.

'Worried that you would be blamed?' Her eyebrows rose scornfully.

'Worried you might have broken that pretty neck of

yours.' He dragged in another breath, trying to ignore the perfume of enticing female flesh beneath the scents of dust and clean sweat. Inevitably it made him wonder how she'd smell, and taste, burning up in ecstasy. 'You could have killed your sister too, or didn't that occur to you because you were too busy making your point?'

'Don't pretend you give a damn for Mina, or me.' He felt a shudder rack her body but she stood tall, her eyes glittering. 'All you care about is that it would be inconvenient if you had to scrape us up off the cliffs then explain why we'd fled for our lives.'

Huseyn drew in a calming breath. Then a second and a third. He'd grown used to people either obeying him or expressing gratitude for what he'd done for them.

It had been a long time since he'd faced vitriol. Not since he'd been a skinny, bastard kid, dependent on the unstable charity of his father for a roof over his head and food in his belly.

Deliberately he forced down the urge to do something reprehensible like turn her over his knee and spank her. It would relieve his tension but it would incite her to further recklessness. She had no concept how lucky she was to have lived in such privilege and safety, cosseted and protected.

'If you want to know what it's really like to fear for your life, go to my province of Jumeah and stay in one of the border villages. The Emir's men will strike there first when they attack Jeirut. Then you'll know real terror.' His voice was harsh with memories. Memories of arriving too late to prevent a fatal attack. And even older memories from early childhood, ones branded into his psyche. Of escaping such a raid by the skin of his teeth, only to discover his mother hadn't. 'Survive that, then talk to me about fear.'

That shut Ghizlan up. For once her scrutiny was all piercing curiosity with none of the dismissiveness that riled him.

'I'd like you to let me go now. Please.' It was said quietly, as if finally she acknowledged the urgency that drove him. 'I need to go back to my sister. She'll be worried.'

Huseyn forced breath from his lungs, dispelling the scent of blood and despair, as real as if the slaughter had just happened instead of decades ago.

Carefully he pulled his hands from Ghizlan's shoulders, surprised at his reluctance to release her. She was nothing but trouble. And yet...

'Your sister is being escorted to her room as we speak. Politely and with the utmost courtesy, of course.'

Ghizlan nodded curtly. 'Of course. I'd better go and see her.' Her voice was devoid of emotion but even in the starlight Huseyn read the slump of her shoulders.

He wanted to let her go, but he had to be sure there'd be no more lunatic escape attempts. Even now he couldn't quite believe the pair of them had found hand-and-footholds on the most forbidding face of a palace designed to withstand both bombardment and sneak assaults.

'I need your word you won't try to escape.'

Her laugh was brittle, like the scrape of icy fingers across his nape. 'I see no reason why I should give it.'

'It's either that, or I station a guard in each of your bedrooms.'

Her breath hissed in and her eyes bulged before narrowing to assessing slits. 'You really play dirty, don't you?' Disdain dripped from each syllable. At least she didn't waste her breath with protests that he wouldn't dare. He'd dare whatever it took.

'I don't *play*, *my lady*. I'm deadly serious. The sooner you learn life isn't a game the easier it will go for you.'

Surprisingly she didn't flinch away. She looked back steadily, her voice cool and crisp. 'I never had the luxury of believing it was. And the sooner *you* understand I'm not some brainless pawn you can use for your own ends, the better it will go with you. Interfering in people's lives has consequences. You may not like them.'

There was no bravado in her tone yet he heard the threat. Did she think he'd be scared to take her on because she was blue-blooded and born to privilege while he was a plain, honest soldier with only his honour and accomplishments to recommend him?

'That's a chance I'm willing to take.'

'And you'd take my word that we won't try to escape?' Disbelief tinged her tone.

'In the circumstances, yes.' He didn't try to explain his belief that however spoiled and wilful she might be, Princess Ghizlan had enough honour to abide by a promise. Her care for her people was proof of that.

'In that case you have my promise. Until tomorrow morning.' Her eyes never left his. She wasn't giving up.

She was destined to defeat, of course. But he'd be careful not to crush her spirit in the process. Despite her ability to infuriate him, he respected that in her.

With a flourish he gestured for her to proceed him on the path that led round the ramparts to the Palace's main entry. She pivoted on her heel and marched ahead, spine straight and head up, her slim figure intriguingly supple.

Huseyn swiped a hand over the back of his neck, rubbing at the muscles knotted there. He forced his gaze away from the fascinating, frustrating woman with her long-legged, hip-rolling stride and back to tonight's interrupted negotiations.

But it was difficult, more difficult than it should have been.

CHAPTER FIVE

GHIZLAN STRODE THROUGH the passage that led to the stables, her footsteps echoing on the old stones. She'd worn high heels, shiny black patent leather ones that screamed elegance and gave her a few precious inches of extra height. After a sleepless night she'd use whatever advantage she could get when facing Huseyn al Rasheed.

She still hated him. His behaviour appalled and his plans were unconscionable. But last night in the darkness when he'd spoken of fear, the bone-deep certainty in his voice, the realisation he wasn't posturing, had stopped her in her tracks.

He was power-hungry, selfish and brutal, yet she'd responded to the honesty he'd laid bare in the darkness last night. And to the surprising gift of his trust. There'd been no guard within or outside her room or Mina's last night and Mina was still sleeping, as cosy and safe as if there were no strangers patrolling the royal compound. For that at least, Ghizlan was grateful.

Huseyn al Rasheed was an annoying conundrum. A man she shouldn't take at face value. Yet part of her was tempted to think he actually believed what he said, outrageous and appalling as it was.

She twitched the jacket of her suit into place, scarlet this time, for courage. Another prop to help her with what promised to be the most difficult interview of her life.

Unless he'd changed his mind. She couldn't prevent the stray hope. It was past nine and he hadn't appeared in her father's study, apparently too busy in the stables to meet her to demand her answer. Maybe he didn't need a royal marriage after all.

Ghizlan pressed a palm to her sternum, trying to ease the pounding of her heart. She might be an optimist but she wasn't delusional. The chances of him changing his mind were microscopic. More likely he dallied in the stables as a way of putting her in her place, reinforcing how little he thought of her.

A loud whinny caught her ears, a crash and the quick thud of hooves. It was only then that she tuned in to the sound of male voices, sharp with warning and dismay.

She quickened her step, curious. Silence descended, broken only by the jingle of a harness and the percussion of hooves, staccato on the cobbles.

Turning a corner, Ghizlan reached one of the stable courtyards, surrounded by colonnades. Sunlight flooded down and she stood under one of the arches, blinking into the brightness.

Around the perimeter men loitered, intent on the courtyard. Hooves clattered and from one corner a giant horse pranced, chestnut coat gleaming in the sunlight, its muscles shifting with each deliberate, dance-like step. It tossed its head and a mane the colour of raw silk flared. On its back sat a horseman, broad-shouldered and straight-backed. He moved as if he were part of the magnificent beast—hands apparently relaxed, yet his hard thighs bunched beneath pale, dusty trousers and his white shirt was ripped half open across his chest as if he'd been in a brawl.

Without warning, the stallion's hindquarters bunched and it reared high, its eye rolling back towards its rider. There was a gasp from the crowd but the rider clung on, leaning forward as if whispering to it. Mighty hooves thudded down with a clang that struck sparks, then the horse was flying, bucking and wheeling in a desperate attempt to dislodge his rider.

Reflexively Ghizlan stepped back as the pair thundered past. In the flurry of movement one impression lingered— the smile on the rider's face. On Huscyn al Rasheed's face.

A smile of absolute delight, as if battling a horse who wanted to trample him underfoot was the most marvellous treat.

Her breath caught. That smile, the sight of such unadulterated joy, sent unexpected sensations hurtling through her. Energy zapped and adrenalin pulsed. Not just from the danger of what she witnessed, but because of the blinding white grin on the face of the man she abhorred.

Another step took her back till she leant against a pillar, heart pounding. She was still reeling when, with a whinny that might have been defiance or perhaps defeat, the stallion finally dropped to stand docile, its ears flicking, its heavy breaths and twitching muscles the only reminders of its earlier battle.

Huseyn al Rasheed leaned forward, his square hand caressing the animal's neck, and Ghizlan could swear it listened to every word. Finally, with no apparent order from its rider, the stallion stepped neatly and quietly towards a groom waiting in the shadows. With one final pat, Huseyn dismounted and the horse was led away, docile as if there'd been no bloodlust in its eyes as it had tried to unseat its rider.

Ghizlan had never seen anything like it. Whatever else he might be, her tormentor was a horseman of immense skill.

Better to focus on that than Huseyn's smile. Its impact had seared her—a tangible assault.

The groom said something and Huseyn spun round, his smile dying.

She told herself she was glad. She didn't want to like anything about him. Not his infectious smile. Not his sheer, stupid joy at risking his neck on that brute of a horse. Not even his incredible horsemanship.

The onlookers faded back into the stables and he crossed the dusty courtyard with a loose-limbed stride that reminded her not of a soldier this time but an athlete. Maybe

that was because his torn shirt revealed part of a powerful, hair-smattered chest that would have done a weight-
lifter proud. Ghizlan's pulse gave a little dance of feminine
appreciation. Her eyes bulged before she forced them up
to meet his misty blue gaze. It was like the sky over the
mountains after dawn, clear and cool and totally imper-
sonal. As if nothing untoward had happened. As if there'd
been no danger.

'You could have killed yourself! Have you no sense
at all?' Ghizlan wasn't aware of forming the words until
they rang out. She blinked and bit back whatever else was
on her tongue.

He halted, frowning. The sunshine turned his tousled
hair blue-black, a glossy invitation. To her horror Ghizlan felt a corresponding tingle in her fingers and bunched
them tight.

'You were concerned about me?' He looked as stunned
as she.

He stood before her, huge, dusty and dishevelled, a
smear of blood along the tear on his shirt and a look of
disbelief on his face. And all she could think about was
the raw, gut deep horror tightening her insides at the idea
of him lying lifeless on the cobblestones. It was absurd.
Appalling.

'Of course not! What do I care if you break that thick
skull of yours? It would solve a lot of problems. I just...'
She paused, her words petering out. She breathed deeply,
ignoring the scent of horse and clean male sweat that she'd
already told herself she couldn't possibly like, and lifted
her chin. 'It would leave me to deal with your rabble of
followers.'

'Ah. My followers.' He nodded, black curls slipping
against his collar. 'You mean the highly trained, completely
disciplined soldiers who managed to outmanoeuvre your
so-called security staff without a single blow? You were

worried they'd panic and run amok if they saw my dead body?'

Then he smiled, damn him. A slow, drawn-out smile that stretched his mouth wide and spoke of pure amusement. Amusement at *her*. He was laughing at her because she'd been stupid enough to express concern for him, her enemy.

Or was he laughing because he'd somehow sensed her response to his powerful, masculine body?

Anger flooded her. It was bad enough he'd captured the palace with such ease and that he held everyone here at his mercy. The humiliation of his laughter was too much.

'You think it funny?' She stepped forward, into his space, pleased when his smile slid away and surprise tightened those bold features. 'To be at the mercy of a bunch of armed men isn't my idea of fun, nor my sister's. You might think them wonderful but I see a bunch of cowards who overcame men far better than themselves by threatening to harm my sister.' She folded her arms over her chest. 'The sort of men who would hold an innocent girl to ransom aren't ones I could trust.'

His amusement was gone now. His face was like flint, those cheekbones craggy beneath lowering brows.

'Come.' His hand closed round her upper arm. 'This isn't the place for this conversation.'

To Ghizlan's annoyance, even in heels she didn't reach his eye level. When he spun her back towards the corridor she was surrounded by his hot, strong body and spicy scent. She dug her heels in until he stopped, scowling down at her.

'I'm not a sack of potatoes to be dragged from place to place. You only have to ask me to move, not grab me.' She paused, catching her breath. 'Besides, you're the one who didn't have the courtesy to meet me at nine. I had to come looking for you.'

'And in the stables of all places. How that must have

irked your fastidious soul.' His gaze was provocative. 'How far beneath your royal person.'

It was on the tip of her tongue to burst out that she'd once spent hours in the stables. That in her teens riding had been her passion. Until her father had decreed she needed to focus on other, more useful activities, like acting as his hostess, studying and learning to serve their people.

'Does this mean you're ready to talk now? Or does your leisure time take precedence?' She let her gaze sweep him as coolly as if her pulse wasn't doing a crazy double-quick beat. She was determined to conquer this awareness of him as a man. It was simply that, despite meeting men all the time, she'd never met one so unabashedly, so in-your-face *male*. Or one whose lingering stare wasn't at all respectful but held a heat she distrusted.

'If you're ready, *my lady*.' He didn't acknowledge her jibe. With an ostentatious deliberation that mocked her title, he lifted his hand from her arm and put space between them. Pity he couldn't also erase the burning awareness where his hand had clamped her upper arm.

'I'm ready.'

She turned and led the way, conscious of the click of her heels on the stone floor and the curious sensation that skated from her upswept hair, down her spine to her legs then back up again. His stare did that. She didn't know how. She didn't want to know. But she was conscious of it with every step.

It was that awareness, that claustrophobic sense of being tethered to the man behind her, unable to escape, that led her not to her father's study but to a balcony that hung out over the valley below. On this side, away from the city, the wall dropped to the escarpment's sheer cliffs and, if she wanted to make herself sick, she only had to lean forward to see the hazardous route she and Mina had taken last night. She'd never have dared it in daytime. Thinking about it made her feel queasy.

Instead she planted her hands on the balustrade, sucking fresh mountain air into tight lungs. She kept her eyes fixed on the vast desert sprawling from the foothills as far as the eye could see.

'You have an answer for me?' That deep baritone rolled along her bones, shivering into recesses she tried to hide.

'About marrying you?'

'What else?'

Another slow, fortifying breath. She didn't turn to him. This would be easier if she didn't look at him.

If only she could avoid him totally.

Desperate humour stirred at the thought of a bride wanting never to lay eyes on her groom. That would suit her perfectly.

'My lady?' For once she heard no sarcasm when he used her title. Somehow that made this moment even more horribly real.

'*If* I were to agree to marry you I'd have conditions.'

'Go on.'

'First, my sister leaves the country before the wedding.'

'Immediately after.'

'Not good enough.'

'You don't trust me to make good on my promise?' He sounded like a grumbly bear.

'You've done nothing to earn my trust.' Ghizlan focused on a distant blue, razorback ridge rising from the desert. As a child she'd imagined it was the spine of a sleeping dragon. She could do with a dragon right now—some powerful creature to save her and Mina.

But there was no one who could save Mina. Only her.

'I kept my word last night. There were no guards posted at your rooms.'

'True. But even you must see this isn't in the same league. The only way I'd consider this…arrangement is if I know Mina will be free.' Her hands clenched on the balustrade so hard the grit from the ancient stone bit into her palms.

'You have my word as Sheikh of Jumeah.' He paused as if waiting. When she didn't respond he continued. 'On my honour. And my mother's memory.'

Doubt tickled Ghizlan. She knew he was a warrior who took claims to honour seriously. But to promise on his mother's memory, rather than his father's? What did that say about his relationship with the old Sheikh?

'I'll have a plane standing by to take her wherever she wants to go.'

'France. She wants to go to France.' Suddenly it hit Ghizlan that, if she did give in to this man, it might be years before she saw Mina again. She blinked and focused on maintaining a mask of calm while inside she crumbled.

'France then.'

'As soon as the ceremony is over.' She swung around and met that silvery blue stare. She told herself it was as cold and unemotional as ice, yet the shiver racing through her was hot, not icy.

'Agreed.'

'And there'll be no attempt to freeze our bank accounts.'

A frown pleated that wide brow. She could see him wondering how vast a fortune they had salted away. Maybe it would be simpler to explain that was far from the truth, that since the age of sixteen they'd both lived off modest inheritances left by their respective mothers. The royal treasury paid only for official travel and the lavish gowns required for formal court occasions.

'Agreed.'

'And—'

'You've already negotiated enough concessions.'

Ghizlan let her eyebrows arch in a show of astonishment. 'I hardly see the right to travel and to keep our own possessions as any sort of concession. In a civilised environment they would go without saying.'

His eyes narrowed to glacial slivers. She couldn't be sure because of the whiskers, but she suspected he was grinding his teeth. The notion gave her confidence.

'Four more points only.'

'Four?' He scowled down at her. 'Well, spit them out.'

'You release every prisoner you've taken. Unharmed.'

He nodded. 'I'd planned to. *After* the wedding.'

Ghizlan opened her mouth to argue for their immediate release then decided it was better to accept the compromise and continue.

'Mina and I have access to our email accounts from this moment.'

'That I can't allow.'

'Because we'll foment trouble?' She shook her head. 'I have no interest in bloodshed. But I have several commercial matters that need attention. And Mina is expecting news that will determine her future.' Ghizlan knew her sister's talent. Surely it was enough to secure a place at the art school she'd set her heart on. If not, Ghizlan would investigate sponsoring her somewhere else.

His gaze grew assessing and Ghizlan found herself holding her breath. She hated that she had to go cap in hand to this man for the favour of continuing her work.

'Very well,' he said at last. 'But under supervision.'

'Impossible. We need our privacy.'

'I thought you said it was about commercial matters.' His tone dripped disbelief and it hit Ghizlan he had no idea of her work. What had he called her? A pampered waste of space? He probably thought she used the net to gossip with girlfriends instead of initiating projects to improve the lives of her people and open up new opportunities.

She could try explaining about the state-of-the-art waste water systems in provincial towns, the nation's first pharmaceutical factory being built on the far side of the capital and her other pet project, still in the design phase. But a glance at his expression told her he wouldn't believe her.

'How about a compromise? We read our messages privately, but any responses are vetted before sending?'

'Done. That's two points. What are the other two?'

'That I'll be free to go about my business unhindered.' Ghizlan refused to live under perpetual house arrest.

His gaze scrutinised her so sharply she'd swear she felt it scrape her cheeks. 'On condition that your behaviour befits the wife of the royal Sheikh.'

Did he imagine her living a life of debauchery? Ghizlan was torn between the desire to laugh and the desire to smack his face. She'd never in her life been violent before meeting Huseyn al Rasheed. He evoked frighteningly primitive responses, even in a woman who'd spent her life learning to be proper at all times.

'You think I'd drag your name through the gutter?' For a moment the idea tempted.

He shook his head. 'I wouldn't allow it.' There was no doubt in that deep, decisive tone. He believed himself her master. The idea irked more than anything else.

Ghizlan sucked in a deep breath, willing herself not to snap out a response she'd regret. She needed his agreement. She couldn't lose her temper now.

Yet her voice, when she found it, was brittle. 'I have a far better idea than you of what's appropriate behaviour for the royal Sheikh's consort. Believe me, I have no intention of sullying my father's memory or my own good name just to make life difficult for you.'

She'd spent her entire life hemmed in by duty, behaving as a proper princess should, responsibly, courteously, always gracious and calm. If anyone was taking a wrecking ball to the royal reputation it was this arrogant lout.

He had no idea how important her work was, and how much went on behind the scenes to ensure the royal court and the administration ran like clockwork. Huseyn al Rasheed thought leading was about macho posturing and armies and telling people what to do.

He'd learn.

'What are you smiling about?' His eyes narrowed to slits of suspicion.

Her own eyes widened innocently. 'I'm just waiting for your agreement.' When he said nothing she hurried on. 'The people will expect to see me about as usual. It will be a sign that everything's okay and there's been a peaceful handover of power.' The idea choked her and she had to pause and swallow.

'Very well. You'll be free, within the borders of Jeirut. But your security detail will report your movements to me and if I discover anything inappropriate...' His expression was grim and Ghizlan knew a moment of fear, wondering what he'd do if roused to fury. Lock her in a dungeon and throw away the key? 'And your last item, my lady? What is it?'

Ghizlan forced down a sudden thickness in her throat. She'd come this far. She would succeed with this too. She had to. Ruthlessly she squashed those betraying nerves. She let go her hold on the balustrade and tilted her chin to meet his stare head on.

'When the time comes you won't stand in the way of our divorce.'

His dark brows scrunched together. 'When the time comes?'

She huffed out an impatient breath. Surely it was simple enough. 'Once the people have time to accept you and you're established as Sheikh you won't need me any more. You only need me for the transition from my father's reign.' Ghizlan paused, swallowing yet again. She hoped he didn't notice. 'Once that happens you won't want me cluttering up your life. I'll leave and you can choose a wife who suits you better.' Someone biddable and obedient. Beautiful, no doubt, petite and delicate. Someone impressed by his muscles and his masterful air. Someone who wanted nothing more than a man to tell her how to live her life.

Someone not at all like her.

Why the thought disturbed, she didn't know.

Still he didn't respond. That hint of a frown lingered and his nostrils looked pinched. In anger or contemplation? Surely he saw the sense in a clean break?

Finally he nodded and relief was a warm rush, weakening her knees so she put out a hand onto the warm stonework beside her. She'd been strung tight as an archer's bow.

'When I don't need you any more we'll divorce. Is that all?'

Ghizlan nodded. For the life of her she couldn't form the words.

'Good. We'll be married by the end of the week.'

She opened her mouth to protest, saw his expectant look, then shut it again. The end of the week was two days away. She needed more time—to get used to the idea of this objectionable marriage, or to plan a better escape.

A large hand grabbed hers, engulfing then shaking it. Huseyn's gesture was disconcerting. She felt the heat of his flesh, the ridge of calluses across his palm, the surprisingly neat fit of her hand in his big paw. It should have been businesslike, a mere confirmation of their verbal agreement.

Except for the rippling arc of power traversing her body, like circles of waves around a stone dropped in a still pool. Tiny sparks flared under her skin and warmth flushed her throat and face. She hated the insidious awareness he created in her.

She'd hoped to avoid touching him again. The press of his flesh against hers evoked haunting, devastating memories of that kiss. Of how she'd given up fighting and instead capitulated in humiliating eagerness. As if she wanted this man's attention. His touch. His passion.

She backed up a step, tugging her hand free, uncaring whether he read her discomfort.

'Until the wedding.' He nodded once then spun on his heel and strode into the building.

Ghizlan fell back against the sun-warmed stone. What had she expected? To see delight on those sombre features? To hear his thanks for the sacrifice she made?

He'd got what he wanted and that was all he cared about.

The sooner she learned to expect absolutely nothing from her husband-to-be, the better. He didn't like her and she detested him. She intended to see as little of him as possible until the day came for their divorce.

CHAPTER SIX

HUSEYN'S GAZE SWEPT the royal audience chamber. They were all here. Every member of the Royal Council, each provincial sheikh, government minister and senior office holder. Every leader whose opinion counted when it was time to proclaim the new Sheikh.

Some were exuberant, some grim, but all, it seemed, content to wait and see if it was true that Princess Ghizlan had promised to wed him and therefore support him as Royal Sheikh.

Anger stirred his belly. Already there'd been skirmishes on the border. Already men risked their lives, fending off the Emir of Halarq's raiding parties. Huseyn knew how he worked. He was testing Jeirut's defences. But any day now he'd make his move, pushing hard and fast over territory where for generations Huseyn's people had lived.

He was tired of the interminable waiting. Of negotiating and hand-holding nervous old men who should have been pensioned off years ago, and young ones who had no concept of real danger. He wanted to—

A ripple passed through the crowd. About time. He'd been about to send someone to fetch her. Ghizlan had left it until the last possible moment to make her appearance. The guards at the door stepped neatly aside and two women entered. The first was slim and coltish, dressed in muted tones. The second—

Huseyn's breath stalled as Ghizlan strode into the room. She didn't look like any bride he'd ever seen. She looked confident, statuesque as a proud goddess, full of a blazing energy he felt even from across the room.

Head up and stiletto heels clicking an assured rhythm

in the pin-drop silence, she looked regal and powerful and beautiful enough to stop a man's pulse.

She was magnificent. Superb.

Her hair was piled high in some elaborate, elegant arrangement that complemented her tiara of flashing silver-blue fire. Diamonds and sapphires, he guessed. But they were nothing to the bright glint in her eyes as she surveyed the throng grouped in clusters around the room.

Her chin lifted higher as she crossed the marble floor, her sister in tow now, heading directly for him.

Huseyn had never appreciated the sight of a woman as much as he did now.

And soon she'd be his.

No traditional wedding veils for his bride. No long skirts sweeping the floor. No fluttering hennaed hands. Neither did she wear a Western-style wedding dress of white. He hadn't really expected that, but neither had he expected *this*.

His belly clenched hard on itself as she marched across the vast space and he reacted with pure male appreciation.

Flouting tradition, as he'd guessed she would, Ghizlan wore Western dress. A dress that clung to her ripe, perfect body, making her stride a symphony of lush breasts and rounded hips and a waist narrow enough to dry his throat. His palms tingled with the desire to touch and fire wound its way through his bloodstream, tangling with adrenalin in a combustible mix.

The dress ended at her knees, but the subtle sheen of the fabric highlighted long, slender thighs with each step she took. Then there were those calves, shapely in break-neck heels.

Sex on legs. But she was more. Far more.

Power and disdain and absolute challenge.

For his bride hadn't chosen to wear gold or red, the traditional colours for rejoicing. She'd avoided colour completely on this auspicious day. Instead her wedding dress was of rich, velvety black. The colour of mourning.

And she wore what he guessed were royal heirloom jewels at her wrists, throat, ears and hair with a nonchalance that reminded everyone present of her impeccable aristocratic lineage.

Huseyn's lips twitched as she stopped before him. He wanted to applaud her defiance and her courage. Her disdain for him. Her disdain for the crowd of men filling the room who must guess, if they didn't know for sure, that she was here under coercion, yet who did nothing to assist her.

He looked into eyes glittering with pride and defiance and felt something rise inside. Something more than mere lust.

Appreciation. Respect.

Huseyn stepped back on one foot, bowing deeply in a gesture not just of courtesy but of deference.

'My lady. You do me great honour.' He lifted his head and caught a flash of surprise before her face smoothed into an imperturbable, regal mask. 'I've never had the pleasure of seeing such a striking, truly beautiful woman.' For in this moment Ghizlan outclassed every woman he'd ever known. And he'd known a few.

He reached out and took her unresisting hand. Closing his fingers around hers. Her pulse hammered beneath the soft skin at her wrist and his admiration notched higher. Not even by a flicker of expression did she betray her nerves.

If he had to have a wife he'd far rather one like this— one with fire—than all the submissive, eager women he'd known.

He lifted her hand and pressed his lips to her flesh, inhaling the cinnamon-honey scent of her skin, lingering to enjoy the taste of her.

* * *

Ghizlan stared at the man bending over her hand with such courtly gallantry. She had to fight not to goggle.

This couldn't be Huseyn al Rasheed, the arrogant Iron Hand of Jumeah. The man who revelled in boorish aggression and macho posturing.

He exuded suave sophistication in a formal suit that fitted so perfectly it could only have been tailored by a master. Fine fabric clung to broad shoulders and long legs, creating a mouthwatering display of male confidence.

Yet the Western clothes, so surprising in a man of such deliberate barbarism, couldn't hide his essential power.

Ghizlan felt it in the light clasp of his big hand. More, in the spark of response shivering through her from the touch of those warm lips on her skin. She hauled in a breath redolent of shock and testosterone and fought down panic.

He was daunting enough with his beard and traditional horseman's garb. Shaved and dressed like this...

'There's no need to make a spectacle of us both.' She jerked her hand from his grip, rubbing her other palm over the spot where his mouth had pressed her flesh, as if to erase the imprint of his touch.

Slowly he straightened, standing close enough that she had to crane her neck to meet his eyes. More blue than grey today, if she didn't know better she'd say they looked almost approving. The idea made her pulse jerk waywardly.

One jet eyebrow flicked high. 'I was merely according you the formal courtesy you deserve, my lady.' His gaze dipped to the weight of diamonds draping her neck, then lower, to the black velvet that now seemed unaccountably stifling despite the chill of the vast, high-ceilinged space. 'As for a spectacle...' His lips, long and well shaped, curled in a smile she *felt* in her belly, 'I leave that to you.' He lifted his eyes. 'You're magnificent.'

It sounded like a compliment. Except she knew better than to believe it.

Ghizlan had entered the hall full of bravado yet he'd pulled the rug out from beneath her feet.

She swallowed. Hard. No man's smile did that to her. Ever.

Yet, bereft of his beard, he looked less like a merciless marauder and more like a movie star. Not the cute boy-next-door types who'd done so well in recent years, but the red-blooded, swoonworthy ones who could seduce a woman with a smile while fighting off a villain and single-handedly foiling a plot to destroy the planet. Even that broken nose added to his charisma, to the aura of strength and masculinity he exuded.

An aura that turned her poised defiance into a jumble of warring emotions and made her wonder if she'd bitten off more than she could chew, conceding to this wedding. Fear gnawed at her.

In a flash her flesh was prickling at the memory of his mouth on hers, his arms locked around her, body pressed close. Heat licked her insides, sending shivery hot chills through her taut body.

His jaw was as strong as she'd guessed, square and dependable-looking. What she hadn't guessed was the intriguing hint of a cleft in his chin, and the long dimples that creased his cheeks when he smiled.

She blinked. Dimples? Impossible. But still they showed, grooves of pleasure as he smiled down at her, eyes dancing. Frantically she scanned his face. It was still hard, still honed and strong, but that glow of amusement transformed him from beast to human, from bogeyman to hunk.

Ghizlan cleared her throat. It didn't matter how he looked or how elegant his bow. He was a thug. 'I didn't expect to see you in a suit.' Her voice grated. 'Surely you're all about old-fashioned values and traditions.' She paused, tugging in a sustaining breath. 'Like treating women as chattels.'

His smile shut off instantly. Yet for once she was spared his forbidding scowl. Instead he looked merely sombre.

'Perhaps I wanted to match you.'

Ghizlan said nothing, reminding herself he'd had no way of knowing for sure what she'd wear. He'd at least kept his promise and left her and Mina alone to prepare for today. There'd been no guards, no spies in their apartments.

'Or maybe you wanted to make a point of appearing as something more than a leader from a rustic province.' His expression didn't change but something in his eyes told her she was on the right track. 'That's it. You're trying to look the part of a national leader! Someone who can work in an international setting.'

Of course he was. Despite the fact not one of the throng of onlookers made any attempt to stop this farce of a wedding, she knew some among them doubted Huseyn's ability to rule the nation and deal in international relations.

She kept her voice low as she let her lips curve into a cold smile. 'It will take more than a well-tailored suit to turn *you* into a diplomat.'

Annoyingly he didn't seem to register her jibe. Instead he smoothed one large hand down the lapel of his jacket. 'You approve? I'll be sure to inform my tailor. Since he's from a *rustic* province, he'll be delighted to have praise from someone with such expertise in fashion.'

Amusement still lurked in his eyes but there was no mistaking his implication—that her knowledge was shallow, all about fripperies, while his masculine understanding was practical and important.

Obviously he knew nothing about her. If she didn't already detest the man she'd be incensed he hadn't bothered to research her—just assumed her role was decorative and her interests lightweight.

That showed how little he understood the work behind

the scenes to bring about the progress for which her country was admired. But he'd learn. Ruling a nation was hard work and it needed more than a soldier's skills.

His narrowing eyes told her he'd read something in her expression and Ghizlan smoothed out her features. She glanced to one side where Mina stood a little apart, hands gripped tightly together, and instantly shoved aside thoughts of beating him in a verbal battle. What did that matter when her sister's future was on the line?

She took a half step closer, ignoring the tantalising scent of fresh male skin. 'You promise you'll let Mina leave?'

'I gave my word, didn't I?'

The trouble was Ghizlan didn't know if that was enough. This man was renowned for adhering to an old-fashioned warrior code, where personal honour ranked high. Yet in the circumstances, where he held every advantage… Was she mistaken to believe he'd release Mina when she was a hostage to Ghizlan's good behaviour? How ruthless was he? Ruthless enough to stage a coup rather than wait for due process to be named her father's heir. Ruthless enough to break his word to a woman he viewed as a waste of space?

Abruptly heat engulfed her as a callused hand wrapped around hers, completely enfolding it.

Startled, she looked up into eyes the colour of the desert sky after dawn, when the first sheen of pale blue washed it clear.

'Stop fretting.' His deep voice was soft. Oddly, Ghizlan found its timbre reassuring as it resonated through her. 'Your sister will be fine.'

She opened her mouth but before she could speak his grip tightened and he turned towards their audience. 'Come, it's time we got this wedding over.'

Firmly she repressed a shudder of apprehension. If this was what it took to free her sister, she'd do it and be damned if she'd let the cowards surrounding her guess at her anguish. She set her chin and stepped forward.

Ghizlan stood on the tarmac, feeling the cool evening breeze stream by, and worked to keep a smile on her stiff features. She didn't know which was worse, needing to keep up a show of calm encouragement for Mina, or having her new husband watch everything that passed between them.

Even now, as she kissed her little sister and forced herself to step back, she was acutely aware of him looming nearby. As if he didn't trust her not to make a dash for the plane that would fly Mina to France and safety.

Or more probably for the benefit of the onlookers on the edge of the tarmac. There were cameras trained on them and Ghizlan assumed he was making a point of looking like a supportive spouse.

'I'll be fine,' Mina whispered. 'You don't have to worry about me, really.' Her glance darted sideways. 'But will you, Ghizlan? I don't like leaving you.'

Ghizlan shook her head sharply. 'I'll be okay. I'm going to be the royal Sheikha, remember? Besides, there's no point both of us staying. You've got a chance to do what you love and—'

'And what about you? Don't you deserve—?'

Ghizlan raised her hand. 'It was my choice, Mina.' She hadn't told her sister of Huseyn's threat to marry her instead if Ghizlan refused. 'With me here there's a good chance this transition of authority will go smoothly. If I can help keep the peace...' She shrugged. 'It's my duty to do what I can.'

Mina frowned. 'You've done your duty all these years. You—'

Movement beside her made Ghizlan turn. It was Huseyn, his face inscrutable as he approached. 'It's time.'

Beyond him the cabin steward was waiting at the bottom of the steps to the plane.

Ghizlan swallowed a knot of emotion and wrapped her arms around her little sister as Mina leaned in for another hug. 'Don't forget—'

'I know, I know. I'll call you as soon as I'm settled. And I'll ring regularly. And I'll see Jean-Paul for you too and find out how he's going.'

Ghizlan smiled, ignoring the way her cheeks felt pulled too tight by stress. 'Perfect. Tell him I can't wait to hear from him.'

Then Mina was walking away, her baby sister suddenly almost grown up. Yet Ghizlan couldn't help worry about how she'd cope, living away from home for the first time.

'She'll be all right.' To her surprise, the deep burr of Huseyn's voice was surprisingly reassuring.

Ghizlan nodded, her throat tight. She lifted her hand as Mina reached the top of the stairs onto the plane and turned to wave. 'Of course she will.' Yet worry gnawed at her belly.

'I've asked the ambassador to check on her from time to time in Paris. And a friend of mine, a professor at the Sorbonne, is going to invite her to lunch to meet his family. He has teenagers so with luck they may strike up a friendship.'

Ghizlan spun round, her brow crinkling. *She'd* already asked the Jeiruti Ambassador to France to look out for Mina. And Huseyn had done it too? 'You did?' Wasn't all his effort focused on grabbing the sheikhdom?

This wasn't the action of a self-serving thug. It was thoughtful and reassuring. As if he genuinely cared about how her little sister fared.

'Don't look so surprised. She's my sister now.' One eyebrow rose interrogatively. 'Or is it the fact I know anyone as civilised as a professor of languages?'

Both, actually.

Did he really consider himself bound to look after Mina?

The idea of this man in the role of protector was so novel Ghizlan knew she was gawking but she couldn't help it. First his exquisitely tailored suit. Then an act of thoughtfulness.

Had some genie spirited Huseyn al Rasheed away and replaced him with a changeling?

'No, don't answer that. I can guess.' Despite the glimmer of amusement in his eyes, his mouth tightened.

For a single moment the ridiculous idea surfaced that he was disappointed in her reaction. Except that was too patently farcical.

'That's very kind of you,' she said through stiff lips as he took her arm and turned her towards their limousine. Instantly little darts of heat fizzed out from his touch, making her skin tingle and her breath seize.

In the distance there was a flurry of activity as the photographers jockeyed for the best shot of them.

That explained why he touched her, and why he'd made the gesture of concern for Mina—he had a vested interest in them looking like a real couple rather than a brute with his forced bride. The fiction of a solid marriage would help him get what he really wanted—the throne. Everything he did was calculated to achieve that goal.

The knowledge stiffened her backbone and chilled her blood as she marched towards the car. She'd married a man she abhorred and—

'Who's Jean-Paul?'

'Sorry?' She stumbled and he hauled her closer so his heat enveloped her as her hip brushed his thigh. A flutter of unfamiliar sensation turned her pulse to a staccato throb.

'Jean-Paul.' His voice was soft but taut. 'The man you're so desperate to hear from. Is he a lover?'

Ghizlan swung her head round to meet a piercing silvery stare. The trained scientist in her wondered how it could be that his eyes appeared to change colour with his temper. But mainly she was intrigued at his interest. Because he didn't want her doing anything that undermined the fiction of their marriage—like flaunt a lover?

Jean-Paul was old enough to be her grandfather and their relationship, though friendly, was based on business. He was the key to her new venture to revitalise the ancient perfume industry in Jeirut and give it a modern twist that would bring money and work to people eager to better themselves.

She let her lips curve in a slow smile. 'I have no intention of questioning you about your love life, neither do I intend to share any such personal information with you.'

Those long fingers tightened around her upper arm. No mistaking his annoyance.

Ghizlan experienced a flare of unholy delight to have scored even such a small point over the man who'd stormed into her life, taking it over as if she had no right to choose for herself. She might not be able to escape him but there was pleasure in reminding him she was no pushover.

'Afraid it would take you too long in the telling?' His lips widened in what might, at a distance, look like a smile, but which, up close, was no more than a baring of strong, white teeth. Like a mountain wolf eyeing off a juicy lamb.

Ghizlan swallowed hard but refused to look away. She refused to feel fear. No matter how…carnivorous the look he sent her. Besides, the alternative, telling him she didn't have a love life and never had, was unthinkable.

'Isn't it time we headed back?' She shot a glance at the limo waiting for them. 'You don't want to miss your wedding feast, not with all those important people you want to impress.'

Huseyn gritted his teeth as he handed his new bride into the car. He couldn't believe how easily she provoked him. As for the slivers of hot metal pricking at him when he thought of her with her French lover…

His jaw locked as he identified the unfamiliar sensation.

Jealousy.

Impossible, remarkable, unlooked for. He'd never been jealous of a woman in his life. Never cared about one enough to be bothered.

But it was true. The blurred image in his brain of Ghizlan writhing in the arms of some suave Frenchman churned his gut and made him want to lash out. If Jean-Paul were here Huseyn would take pleasure in thrashing him.

Stunned by the well of fury simmering so close to the surface, Huseyn took his time walking to the other side of the car. It was normal, he reassured himself, to feel possessive about his wife, even if they'd only been married an hour. Even if they didn't really want each other.

Ghizlan was his now and what was his he kept. He had no intention of sharing her.

Everything he had was hard won and he valued it. Even his unwilling spouse. *Especially* his unwilling, hauntingly provocative, endlessly fascinating wife.

He should be devising tactics to deal with the power-brokers attending the wedding feast yet instead he was fixated on the possibility his wife had planned a rendezvous with another man.

Huseyn shook his head. Feisty she might be, but she'd met her match. There'd be no other lovers. Not while she was his.

On that satisfying thought he took the seat beside her and reached to take her hand, knowing it unsettled her. It wasn't because he enjoyed the feel of her soft palm fitting snugly against his, or the quiver that passed through her—evidence of the searing attraction she tried so hard and yet failed every time to hide. He knew enough about women to recognise attraction when he met it. No, Huseyn was simply reminding her that she belonged to him now.

'I look forward to having you at my side as we celebrate with our guests, *my lady*.' As ever, she stiffened further, correctly reading the thread of amusement as he used her title.

'I'm glad one of us is looking forward to it,' she huffed, turning her head away to look out the window.

But her fighting spirit didn't annoy him. Not when he held her hand and felt the fast, trembling pulse beating at her wrist. Not when he knew, for all her blustering, it was excitement as much as nerves, winding her so tight.

He'd enjoy helping her unwind.

CHAPTER SEVEN

HER MAID HAD laid out a nightgown for her. It lay demurely stretched across the counterpane—ruby silk with panels of delicate lace. Ghizlan stared at it for a full thirty seconds before swiping it off the bed and stuffing it in a drawer.

First, her maid had never before chosen her nightwear and she wasn't about to start now.

Second, the gesture was clearly designed to help her seduce her new husband. Which she wasn't going to do under any circumstances. He'd be sleeping wherever it was he'd slept since he'd arrived at the palace and, in case he had any ideas to the contrary, her door was securely locked.

Theirs was a paper marriage so he could grab the throne he coveted. She'd played her part for her sister's sake and to secure peace if she could. The last thing her beloved Jeirut needed was civil strife while the Emir of Halarq was threatening them, which official sources had confirmed he really was. Huseyn hadn't lied about that.

Ghizlan yanked out an ancient oversized T-shirt that was anything but seductive. True, she hadn't worn it since studying abroad. True, it was a defiant act no one but she would know about. But the thought of wearing that provocative nightgown sent a chill through her that wasn't about being cold, but an inner heat she didn't want to acknowledge.

Because it led inevitably to images her wired brain supplied too easily. Of Huseyn stripping the ruby lace straps off her shoulders with those big callused palms and kissing his way down to—

'No!' She slammed the drawer and stomped into the bathroom. She refused to think about Huseyn al Rasheed in that way. It was a betrayal of her self-respect. He'd forced her into marriage. He wasn't forcing her into anything else.

No matter how her rebellious body responded to his masculinity. She wasn't *that* masochistic!

A whole afternoon and evening in his company had been more than enough. Yet as she unpinned her hair, unfastened the jewels and put them in their cases, then slipped out of her dress, her thoughts turned to him time and again.

To her annoyance and unwilling admiration, he'd been perfectly at home hosting their formal wedding banquet. Arcane court etiquette and even the ridiculously large choice of cutlery for the multi-course meal hadn't fazed him. Obviously his province wasn't as rustic as she'd supposed. He'd proven a fine host, attentive and urbane. He'd even had the grace to allow Azim, fretful and apologetic, time alone with her. She'd found herself lying to the distressed old man, telling him she was okay, that the marriage was her choice.

Ghizlan finished cleansing her face and splashed cold water over her cheeks. She *wasn't* okay. Not one man amongst those present had made a move to question the marriage or stand up for her rights. Far easier to accede to the fiction she'd chosen to marry a brute intent on seizing personal power.

Except he didn't seem...

No. She wasn't going there. Huseyn presented the persona he knew others wanted to see. As for her unwanted response to that ultra-masculine vibe of his—she'd squash it eventually. All she had to do was concentrate on how loathsome he was.

Her response wasn't really about *him*, but *her*. It was high time she found herself a man. As soon as the divorce came through and she had the freedom to act for herself instead of as a royal princess, always under press scrutiny, that's what she'd do. She'd find a man who attracted and respected her. One she could imagine herself caring for.

She picked up her toothbrush and scrubbed her teeth vigorously.

Despite her exhaustion she was wired. Today's events had awakened such intense emotions, not least indignation, and she was ashamed to say—fear, that she knew she wouldn't sleep any time soon.

Ghizlan turned to the door and raised her hand to the light switch. She didn't feel like reading. She'd turn on her computer and—

'What are you doing here?' Her eyes bulged as she took in the tall form lounging against the bedroom wall, one long finger stirring the diamond glitter of the bracelet she'd discarded on the dressing table. Sparks of light flashed at his touch. Matching sparks ignited her temper and something else, hot and shivery, deep inside.

Her hackles rose. 'How did you get in?' Her gaze snapped to her door, securely shut.

Huseyn shrugged, surveying her from under hooded eyes. 'With a key, of course.' That deep voice was pitched even lower than usual, running like a stream of velvet right through her middle.

Ghizlan bit her lip. Of course he had a key. He'd taken over the Palace of the Winds. It had only been a fiction these last few days that she and Mina had any real privacy in their own home. The realisation smacked her hard in the chest.

She stiffened, torn between the desire to eject him and to cover herself up. Except for the mortifying, infuriating knowledge she could no more force this giant lump of a man to move than she could the Palace itself. And her wrap was in her wardrobe. Besides, her huge T-shirt covered her from neck almost to knee.

Show no fear. Once she showed trepidation he'd have the advantage.

As if he doesn't already have that!

Ghizlan's hands tightened on the velvet jewellery boxes

as she walked towards him, keeping her eyes on his face, not the shadow of dark hair she thought she saw through the fine weave of his open-necked shirt.

Wordlessly she scooped up the bracelet and placed it in its box then shut the lid. She needed to put the jewellery boxes down but that meant she'd have nothing to hide behind and the keen way those silver-blue eyes surveyed her, she wasn't ready to do that.

'You're not Sheikh yet.' The words emerged from between clenched teeth. 'And even if you were, you have no right in my room.'

Balancing the jewellery cases on one arm, she held out her other hand. 'I'll take that key. Whatever you want to discuss can wait till tomorrow. I've played my part in your little farce.' Ghizlan paused, swallowing to banish the wobble in her voice. 'Now I'd like to go to bed.'

'At last,' he murmured. 'Something we agree on.' Before she could stop him he reached out and plucked the boxes from her, placing them on the dresser.

Instantly the air around her sucked tight as if he'd somehow stolen the oxygen she needed.

Her hands fell to her sides as she fought the urge to cover herself as his gaze skated lower, taking in her bare legs and feet, then up to the bulky white shirt she hoped to heaven covered her adequately. Except, even as she assured herself it did, her breasts tightened, tingled, and her nipples puckered.

Abruptly she crossed her arms, high and tight, over heaving breasts. 'Get. Out. Of. My. Room.'

She'd never looked more stunning. In diamonds and velvet she'd been regal and sexily sophisticated. In the trousers and black top she'd worn to scale the castle walls she'd been vulnerable and outrageously provocative.

In a T-shirt that skimmed those amazing curves and gave him his first uninterrupted view of her long, long legs, she was the most voluptuous, alluring woman he'd ever known. His heart hammered his ribs as anticipation welled.

She wasn't even trying to seduce. He guessed she didn't realise how the bathroom light behind her revealed so much she tried to hide. And that spark of hauteur in her eyes, the sulky turn-down of her plush lips…

Huseyn dragged in much-needed air through his nostrils, registering the rich cinnamon-honey scent he'd become addicted to since meeting Ghizlan.

'This is *our* room, my lady.'

As expected, she drew herself up, bristling. He loved her spunk. The way she came out of her corner fighting every time.

'Oh, no.' She backed a step, shaking her head. 'Don't think it even for a minute. That was never part of the agreement.'

Huseyn folded his arms rather than reach for her and tug her to him. 'You agreed to marry me. And now, as my wife, you're—'

'Don't you *dare* preach to me about duty!' Those ripe breasts rose high and flame shot from his belly to his groin. 'I've done what you demanded because I was blackmailed into it. I will *not* be blackmailed into bed.'

Belatedly he raised his eyes to hers, seeing the flash of fury. Had he ever had a woman of such intense feelings? And the combination with her usual iron control made him wonder, as he'd wondered for days, what Princess Ghizlan would be like when she really let herself go. Adrenalin spiked in his blood.

'I have no intention of blackmailing you, *my lady*.' There was no sarcasm in his use of the word. Right now he revelled in the fact Ghizlan was exactly that, or soon would be. It had been that, as much as his concerns for the nation, interrupting his sleep for days.

'Good, then you can get out now.'

Huseyn took a single step, blocking her exit. 'I'm spending the night with my wife.'

She shook her head, luxurious ebony tresses coiling over her shoulders and sliding around her breasts. Huseyn's mouth dried and he swallowed. His need for her was so urgent. He had to rein it in.

'That's not going to happen, Huseyn.' Stupid to enjoy the sound of his name on her tongue. But he was so hungry for her even that was like a flurry of rain on parched, desert soil, accepted greedily. 'Unless you intend to use force.'

Her eyelids flickered and for a horrible moment he thought he read fear. For a moment only, until her body reassured him. Her nipples thrust needily towards him over those fiercely crossed arms. Neither did he miss the subtle perfume she exuded. Her usual sweet fragrance had altered to the light musky note of female arousal.

Fierce elation gripped him. A smile tugged one taut cheek. 'We both know there's no need for force. You want me, Ghizlan, and I want you. It was there when you kissed me—'

'I didn't kiss you!' She shifted away, but found herself backed against the wall. 'You forced yourself on me.'

'And you kissed me back with an enthusiasm that bodes very well for our sexual relationship.'

She was swinging her head from side to side in emphatic denial. 'The only way you'll get sex from me is rape.' She drew herself up to her full height, the fire in her eyes lighting a blaze in his belly.

He stepped forward. 'You know that's not—'

Only nimble reflexes saved him from the massive glass paperweight she shot at his face. Huseyn tossed it over his shoulder to bounce on the floor.

A hairbrush came next. He batted it aside.

Then an antique clock that he caught and placed on the far end of the dressing table, out of her reach.

The marble-framed photo came next, nearly clipping his

ear, making him surge forward to snap his hands around her wrists.

'Enough!'

She was trembling all over, the pulse at her wrist galloping. Huseyn breathed deeply, inhaling the intoxicating scent of her. 'Stop fighting me. You know it's pointless.'

'Because you're strong enough to take me even though I despise you?' She spat the words, her eyes bright, her pale golden skin flushed. Even now she fought what they both felt.

Slowly he shook his head, his eyes never leaving hers. Whatever this connection was between them, he'd never known its like. Never had a woman mesmerised him so. It was clear she felt it too, no matter how she fought it.

He captured both her wrists in one hand and lifted the other to her cheek. She gulped, the movement emphasising the slender, perfect line of her throat. Since when had a woman's throat been so enticing? Her eyelids fluttered as he stroked his knuckle over downy soft flesh. Heat rose to meet him. A tremor jerked through him at the delicacy of her skin. Like a rose petal, far too fragile for the touch of a rough hand like his.

Then she exhaled. A silent, fluttery sigh and her head tilted into his touch. Just for a millisecond. Until she realised what she was doing and jerked away.

'I don't want you. I'd never want a brute like you.'

'Liar,' he murmured, watching her swallow again.

'You come in here, you *force* yourself on me and you accuse me of *lying*!' She looked down. 'What are you doing?'

'Letting you go. You know I won't hurt you.' He opened his fingers, releasing her wrists, repressing a shudder of need as her hands slipped from his. He was strung so tightly it was a wonder he had the patience for these games. But he had to be sure. 'You're free to walk away.' He paused. 'As soon as I get a goodnight kiss from my wife.'

Shining dark eyes, huge and outraged, stared up into his. 'But I—'

The rest of her words were muffled as he bent and kissed her. Not hard, not fiercely, but with a slow, sure sense of rightness that nevertheless blasted the back of his skull like a blow from flying shrapnel.

He'd waited so long—days—since he'd tasted her. And it was as well he had, because falling into the lush softness of those open lips, the world splintered, falling away as he lost himself in her sweetness.

Everything—the sheikhdom, tonight's diplomatic negotiations under cover of their wedding banquet, even the threat from Halarq—receded to nothing when he tasted Ghizlan.

Manfully he kept his hands at his sides, allowing her the freedom to break the kiss, knowing in the marrow of his bones that she wouldn't. How could she resist the powerful attraction that had sparked between them from the very first moment?

Even so, tension ratcheted up as seconds passed and she stood, stoic and unresponsive. As his own need battered at the confines of his self-imposed restraint.

Then, finally, with a sound that might have been a groan or a sob, her lips moved tentatively against his and her eyes closed. Sensation exploded as her tongue tangled with his and she tilted her head, allowing him further in.

With one arm he hauled her to him, up on her toes, so she pressed her whole length against him, cradling him with those gorgeous hips, her belly cushioning his swollen length and her breasts...

He cupped her jaw, angling her face to his, diving into a kiss that sent every sense into overdrive.

She had to stop. She had to force him away.

She had to dredge up her sense, even if it was too late to salvage her pride.

Urgent commands raced through her brain. Rational, logical commands to assert herself and shove him away. Yet Ghizlan couldn't find the strength to obey.

Not when his mouth fused with hers in a kiss that should have been rapacious but instead was lushly inviting, slow yet demanding in a way that shattered all her preconceived notions of what a kiss could be. Even that earlier kiss in her father's study hadn't prepared her for the sheer need that welled within her as Huseyn made love to her mouth with his.

For that's what this was. He didn't plunder, he pleasured. He didn't demand, he invited, tempted, *lured* her into abandoning a lifetime's caution, so sweetly that her blood sang and her defences disintegrated.

It must be the recent trauma, the tension of the last days, a prisoner forced time and again to confront a man who should, on every account, disgust her yet who instead fascinated her. She hated the way he used her to further his ambition, despised his tactics, yet found herself drawn to him, her blood fizzing with an excitement that scandalised, scared and excited.

With Huseyn she felt vibrant, alive and…sexy.

He urged her back to the wall, his solid frame pushing against hers from thigh to breast and her knees liquefied. Never had she been so close to a man. Never felt so delicate and feminine, responding to such flagrant maleness, quickening and softening against powerful hardness.

Ghizlan grabbed his shirt, revelling in the searing heat of his muscled chest, then slid her hands up to his shoulders, hanging on tight.

Maybe this was Stockholm syndrome, the bizarre fixation of a prisoner for her captor. But even as the thought trailed through her brain, it burnt to cinders as one big hand cupped her breast and her brain went into meltdown.

Nothing, ever, had felt so good. Quivers of ecstasy ran through her as his thumb pressed then circled and a betraying moan escaped her lips. That he swallowed the sound of it and responded with his own deep grunt of masculine pleasure only heightened Ghizlan's excitement.

That big, rough hand was so gentle, his touch so perfect, as if she'd waited all of her twenty-six years for this moment, this sensation. This man.

Runnels of fire traced down from her breast, down from her lips fused with his, down from her scalp where his long fingers massaged, to coalesce in a burning heat deep in her pelvis.

Ghizlan shifted, feeling the blatant weight of his erection high against her belly. To her shocked fascination she revelled in the promise of his aroused body.

She shouldn't be doing this. She should be ripping herself from his arms. But there was nowhere she wanted to be more than here, drawing in the almond and spice taste of Huseyn, revelling in all that powerful masculinity, the rock-hard muscle taut against her softer frame. The combination of desire and curiosity was irresistible.

Shuddery ripples of delight rayed from his touch as he caressed her breast and her hair and Ghizlan all but purred.

Never had she ignored responsibility or propriety. Both had been drummed into her since childhood. Letting all that go in a blast of unadulterated sexual hunger was the most intoxicating experience of her life.

Ghizlan lifted onto her toes, slipped her hands inside Huseyn's collar and welded her fingers against the satiny heat of his shoulders, answering his deep, potent kiss with demands of her own.

Seconds later his hands slid around her thighs, lifting her high then pressing her back against the wall, his pelvis hard against hers.

Astounded at how *right* that felt, Ghizlan's eyes popped open to meet his hooded, silvery stare. His mouth lifted from hers, just enough for them to gasp for air, their chests rising together, making her sensitised breasts tingle needily.

Now was the time to demand he let her go. To grab control.

But it wasn't control she needed. It was this man who'd torn away her blinkers and made her feel things she'd never understood existed.

There'd be hell to pay later. Sex wouldn't remove the vast chasm between them. But to turn back now, to retreat into the safety of duty and dignity, was impossible. Ghizlan had fought him with everything she had but now she needed him with every nerve and sinew and muscle and bone in her body. Even her brain craved him.

She should cringe away and beg for a reprieve but she wasn't that much of a coward. Those slumberous pale eyes promised pleasure. So did those deft hands and the sensual mouth that had so thoroughly seduced her.

For once in her life she was going to have what *she* wanted, not what duty dictated, and damn the consequences.

So when he lifted her thigh over his hip, tucking her calf around him, Ghizlan let him. Let him position her other leg too, so she was wound around him, ankles locked at his back. His erection was solid and provocative against her feminine core and it was all she could do not to squirm closer. Her breaths were short, out of control, and her pulse throbbed erratically.

The sight of Huseyn's pulse flickering just as fast at the base of his throat proved this was mutual. She wanted to taste him there, where the sheen of heat burnished his dark gold skin.

'Ghizlan.' He stretched the word out, like the sigh of the wind swirling round the battlements. Or maybe that was her own sigh as he folded one arm around her, drawing her close so her breasts crushed against his broad chest. The glitter in his eyes held a promise she yearned to accept.

When his mouth came down on hers it was hard, almost punishing, yet she revelled in his hunger, meeting it with her own, gripping him tightly with her legs, her hands clamped on his shoulders. She lost herself in it, only vaguely aware of movement till they toppled, her over him, onto the bed.

Limbs tangled, her cheek scraped his hard jaw and her fingers dug hard into his flesh. There was a waft of cooler air as he reefed her T-shirt off, forcing her to let go of him so he could drag it over her head and away. Then flurried movements as he discarded his clothes and came back to her, his super-heated flesh smooth in places, in others tickling with the abrasion of hair, a brand new, wondrous territory to explore.

Ghizlan slid her instep over his calf, fascinated at the texture of coarse hair and solid muscle. Her hand cupped his biceps then slid to his shoulder, silky smooth and broad. Her other hand pressed at the curve of his chest where his heart pounded, then inched down his torso, following the tantalising trail of narrowing hair she'd seen so briefly as he'd hauled off his shirt.

'Later,' he growled, capturing her hand in his.

That searing light gaze held hers and something shot through her. Something she had no name for, but felt right to the centre of her being. Shared purpose. Understanding. Something so elemental and real it was hard to believe they were virtual strangers.

Her husband—the man she barely knew.

But as he tugged her other hand up to his shoulder, at the same time lowering his body to lie within the curve of her hips, as she felt the weight of him where no man had ever lain, it didn't feel as if they were strangers. It was better than she could have imagined.

Her mind overloaded on sensation. His breath, steamy on her lips. His hip bones, hard against her. His erection thick and impossibly long, pressing against her belly. The

intimate fragrance of their hot flesh together. The friction
when he slid lower.

'Easy.' Huseyn's voice sounded clogged. He kissed her
when she jerked and trembled at the powerful sensations
unleashed as his body aligned against hers. As he took
possession of her mouth she melted again, caught up in
delicious abandonment. And when he slid down her body,
cupping her breast, licking it, circling her nipple with his
tongue, then finally drawing the sensitised peak into his
mouth and drawing hard—

Ghizlan dug her fingers into him, her back arching and a
sob tearing from her mouth. So good. Who'd have guessed
it would feel so good? So—

His teeth closed around her nipple with a little tug and
an incendiary dart shot straight to her womb. He did it
again and she heard a sharp, keening cry as pleasure ripped
through her. Once more she arched against him, fingers in
his hair, dragging him closer, and still it wasn't enough.

Pleasure came in waves with each suck and nip of his
mouth at his breast. Then, through the haze, she felt the
slide of long fingers against her body, right down to her
entrance, curling in to where she was slick and hot.

'So eager.' His voice was gravel and velvet, honeyed yet
rough, and it tore at something in her. He kissed her hard,
his tongue delving deep. 'I need you, Ghizlan.'

Of its own volition her body clamped his fingers, shocking her. This was glorious but so fast, so far beyond what
she knew. 'I'm not—'

But Huseyn was kissing her again. Hard, demanding
kisses that stifled her half-formed protest. Words spiralled
away, her doubt lost as her body quickened.

He stroked her deftly, lingeringly, and fire flickered in
her blood.

'Tell me you want this.' His deep voice burred through
her. She felt hollow inside, achy and restless. She'd never
felt— 'Ghizlan?'

'Yes,' she gasped. *Yes, yes, yes.* Her need for him pulsed with every beat of her heart. 'But I...'

He withdrew his hand and she couldn't stop a groan of dismay that he muffled with his lips. She craved him with an urgency unlike anything she'd experienced. Needily she tilted her hips.

She was holding him tight, kissing him back when he shifted. She felt the heat of his erection between her legs, then a surge of movement, impaling her, stretching her impossibly. Her eyes snapped open on a gasp of distress as pain ripped through her.

Diamond-bright eyes bored down into Ghizlan's as she froze, her breath choking in constricted lungs. She read heat and lust in his eyes and a glimmer of something that might have been surprise as he sank into her till they were locked tight.

For a frantic instant she panicked, believing she couldn't breathe.

He was hot, so hot, hard and unyielding. His huge body surrounded her, pushing her down into the bed despite the way he propped himself on his arms. His wide brow crunched in a ferocious frown and his breathing laboured as he held himself still. The weight of him inside her was so foreign she felt dazed.

Ghizlan's hands went to his shoulders as if to push him away and he withdrew, the slide of his body inside hers strange yet tantalising as pain ebbed.

She sucked in a shuddery breath, telling herself it was okay. That pain wasn't unexpected. It would be fine when she had time to adjust.

She stared into glittering eyes, reading regret there and in the twist of his lips. Then her breath stalled as Huseyn thrust again, his hips hard against hers as he surged long and deep, filling her.

'I'm sorry. I can't—' His words tore away.

Then his hand closed around her breast and excitement

jolted through her. She tried to catch it, hold it. A flicker of
response trembled there, where his body joined hers. She
dug her nails into the wide ridge of his shoulders, tentatively lifting her hips, instinctively seeking the friction that
would intensify that fragile flutter of delight.

But with a sudden hoarse shout, Huseyn stiffened
against her. The tendons in his neck stood proud, his eyes
closed in a wince of concentration and his body arched,
pinioning her to the mattress as the heavy pulse of his orgasm filled her.

Despite the dull echo of pain just turning into pleasure, Ghizlan was fascinated by the sight of him, so big
and powerful, lost in the moment of ecstasy. Within her
the rhythm of his rapture continued and she shifted as
arousal surged anew.

But it was too late. Huseyn was drawing away.

To her surprise, Ghizlan regretted the moment when
they separated, feeling something almost like loss. She
wanted to hold him to her, cuddle him and feel the slow-
ing beat of his heart. She wanted to feel again that beat of
arousal and experience her own climax when they were
joined.

But instead of gathering her close, or lying, lost in satiation, Huseyn rolled away. He sat for a moment on the
side of the bed, shoulders bowed and hands braced on the
mattress. Then abruptly he pushed to his feet and strode
to the bathroom.

Ghizlan stared, hating the way her gaze trawled the
dark gold skin of his back, the delicious, tight curves of
his buttocks, and his easy, comfortable-in-his-body gait.

Even when he entered the other room and flicked on a
light she waited, telling herself he'd turn and speak, say
something.

He shut the door between them without turning. It
snicked closed with a finality that lodged a weight in her
chest.

Her body throbbed, but not from completion. Her legs were wobbly and suddenly she was close to tears.

What had she expected? Tenderness? A union of souls?

She flopped back and stared at the high ceiling. There'd been tenderness, at least until he'd got her where he wanted her. But after that? Her brain clung to the moment of apology. *I'm sorry. I can't.* Can't what? Can't stop? Can't give you what you want?

Huseyn was the experienced one. The one who'd bragged about satisfying his lovers. Despite her discomfort she'd felt excitement at his possession and something like awe as he'd climaxed within her. She'd felt the slow bubbling of rapture. But then he'd simply turned away and ignored her.

Ghizlan swallowed, blinking back stupid, hot tears. Had that really been too much to expect? Had she been so wrong, believing they shared a mutual passion?

Of course she was wrong. He'd wed her and bedded her for one reason only—to get power. He wasn't interested in anything else, including a wife who didn't even have the conviction to push him away when he hauled her into his arms.

She'd betrayed herself. She'd given in when she should have fought.

She'd succumbed.

Setting her jaw tight, Ghizlan rolled over and stared at the closed bathroom door. Self-loathing threatened to swamp her but she shoved it aside and focused on determination instead.

Huseyn had played her for the last time.

CHAPTER EIGHT

HUSEYN TURNED THE TAP to full, letting the cold water pound him, hard and needle-sharp. Yet each tiny stab from each streaming shower jet only made him more aware of his body than before, not less. The needling discomfort was nothing to the disgust channelling through his gut, leaving a gaping hollow where his self-respect used to reside.

He sluiced water from his face then propped his palm against the tiled wall, leaning hard as his body sagged.

He shook his head, still horrified at what he'd done. Taken Ghizlan—beautiful, defiant, wary Ghizlan—with the finesse of a rutting ram.

Even when he'd realised she was a virgin, had he stopped? Had he pulled back and made her first time easier?

Huseyn's eyes squeezed shut at the memory of how he'd been unable to restrain himself, so lost in thrall to her glorious body and the drugging hunger that overrode his brain and left his libido in control of his body.

The dazed shock in her beautiful eyes had shot an arrow straight to his conscience. He'd known he had to pull away, but for the first time ever, intending and doing had been two separate things. He hadn't been able to do more than begin to apologise, because he'd been overtaken by the most intense, all-consuming climax of his life.

He dragged a hand over his face, almost surprised to feel familiar features. He felt as if he was no longer the man he'd been. What he'd done—hurting Ghizlan—went against every code of honour. His pride revolted.

He'd brushed off her jibes about him taking unwilling women, about him possibly hurting lovers because of his size, because of course it was nonsense. Aware of his greater bulk, Huseyn always held back, ensuring his lover's pleasure and never letting go completely. Now, unbelievably, he'd done as she'd accused and he didn't know what to do with himself. His skin was too tight and his conscience too big.

Wrenching off the taps, he reached for a towel and began to dry himself.

He couldn't have expected her to be a virgin at her age. Surely not. And she'd spent years in the West, supposedly studying, but, he'd assumed, partying and living a life of idle pleasure.

How could she have been a virgin?

How could a woman who looked like that have reached her mid-twenties and not—?

He was making excuses. As soon as he'd discovered she was a virgin he'd had a duty to withdraw, to soothe and ease her into sex.

Instead he'd succumbed to selfishness. Absorbed in the rapture of Ghizlan's capitulation, he hadn't been able to put the brakes on. He'd lost himself in mere seconds.

There'd been a heady elation in taking his wife's untried body. In the sudden, overwhelming knowledge that he was her first and only lover. It had shattered his control even as he'd ordered himself to stop.

No wonder he hadn't been able to face her afterwards. He could imagine the reproach in those dark velvet eyes. For once her estimation of him had been right. And for the first time in his life he'd run, unable to look her in the face while guilt devoured him.

Huseyn stiffened. Perhaps she was still in pain. What could he do to ease that?

Hell! He knew nothing of virgins, had carefully avoided them. Until now.

He'd go back and take her in his arms, show her the tenderness she deserved. Then he'd give her orgasm after orgasm to make up for the disaster of their first coupling. He'd deny himself all night if he had to, for fear of hurting her again. He'd be gentle. He'd ease her into ecstasy, erasing the memory of what had gone before. Though he knew he couldn't eradicate his shame any time soon.

He reached for the trousers he'd grabbed on the way to the bathroom and dragged them on. One final scrub of his wet hair with a towel, then he was striding to the door. He should have stayed with her, should have—

'What are you doing?' He slammed to a stop in the doorway. From across the room dark eyes met his and he felt the jolt of response right to the bare soles of his feet.

Far from lying, curled in a ball of misery and pain, Ghizlan was on her feet, covered once more by that long white T-shirt that did virtually nothing to hide her luscious body. Huseyn's blood quickened, his groin grew tight as she moved and her beautiful breasts swayed against the fabric, pebbled nipples visible even from here.

Damn it. He should have stayed under the cold water longer. It had done nothing to combat his arousal.

'Ghizlan?' Still she didn't answer, but tugged at the bedding. Already the pillows and bedspread lay tossed on the floor.

He strode towards her, saw her sidelong glance and the way her jaw tightened, and stopped on the other side of the bed.

'What are you doing?' He planted his hands on his hips, welding them there before he was tempted to reach for her. Her hair was a dark, glossy cloud that screamed an invitation for his touch. Her mouth, turned down in a sulky pout, would taste like heaven, he knew. And those legs. The feel of them wrapped around his waist had driven him beyond thought. He locked his jaw and drew on all his willpower to keep his distance. He needed to be calm, gentle, reassuring.

She wrenched the bedsheet free from one corner and

hauled it towards her. That was when he saw the dark stain on its centre. Fresh blood. Ghizlan's blood.

Huseyn stumbled forward half a step before he found his balance. An invisible fist had smacked him in the solar plexus. Another hand chopped the back of his knees, loosening his stance.

He drew a deep breath, telling himself it was a small stain after all, and inevitable. That if it hadn't been him it would have been someone else taking her virginity. But rationalisations didn't work. Not when he felt marrow-deep guilt over hurting her.

But what really fuelled his guilt was that it wasn't just regret he experienced. Reliving those moments when he'd possessed her in that most elemental way excited him.

He wanted her again. Right now.

'What do you think I'm doing?' She didn't bother to look at him. He wondered if the sight of him so disgusted her she couldn't bring herself to meet his eyes.

The sheet tugged free and she hauled it into her arms, turning away not towards the door but the window.

'Talk to me, Ghizlan.'

Now there was a first, asking a woman to talk. But this was different. *She* was different.

One-handed she wrenched aside the curtain and wrestled with the window catch. 'What do you think I'm doing?' She paused and shot a look of pure loathing over her shoulder. 'Hanging the sheet from the window so all of Jeirut can see our marriage has been consummated. The Royal Council will want proof I've been appropriately deflowered and—'

'Stop it!'

It was only as the sound echoed around the room that Huseyn realised he'd roared the order. That stain was proof he'd acted like a savage. He couldn't look at it.

He swallowed hard, banishing emotion, searching for calm. He hadn't even realised he'd moved until his hand closed around Ghizlan's shoulder. She shrank back as if his touch burnt.

Horrified, Huseyn dropped his hand. Her breasts rose and fell with each sharp breath. Her face was hectically flushed, her lips twisted in pain or fury and this close her eyes looked febrile. It struck him that finally he'd broken through Ghizlan's unbreachable control.

But it wasn't triumph Huseyn felt in the coiling, burning pit of his conscience. Watching her reaction, he felt like the barbarian she'd branded him. So much for being a man of honour.

Through everything she'd maintained a proud air of invincibility, even when the odds had been stacked against her. But here in this room, he'd shattered that. He hoped he hadn't destroyed it completely. Her pride and her determination to stand up to him were, he realised, part of what attracted him.

As if she wants to attract you.

Judging by that glare, she'd like to boil you in oil.

'There's no need for that.' He kept his voice low and soothing.

'There's every need!' She fumbled with the latch, never taking her eyes off him. As if she expected him to lunge at her. That made his belly shrink in self-reproach. 'You don't leave anything to chance, do you? You couldn't wait to be made Sheikh the usual way—you had to marry a royal princess to cement your claim. Now it's time to prove you've done your *manly* duty and consummated the match.'

'Ghizlan.' He softened his voice and held out his hand. 'You don't need to do this.'

She shook her head so wildly her hair swung wide, streaming across his outstretched hand.

'Why not?' Her voice was raw and bitter. 'That's all I am now. A means to an end. Not a person with hopes and plans and desires.' Her breath hitched. 'It's time to inform all your yes-men still down in the banqueting hall that you've—'

'Enough!' Huseyn wrenched the bunched sheet from her, lifting it out of her reach. He couldn't bear to hear any more. It shaved too close to the truth. He'd been so focused on the good of the nation he hadn't allowed himself to think about what this meant for Ghizlan. 'That's enough. You're becoming hysterical.'

'Hysterical?' The battle light in her eyes told him she'd cleave him in half if she could. Just as well there were no weapons in the royal apartments. 'It's typical of a brute like you to accuse a woman of being hysterical when—'

Huseyn had no plan other than to stop her tirade, hating the note, not just of anger but of despair, threading her voice. It made him sick to the core. So when she stepped in, reaching over his shoulder for the fine linen, he slammed his mouth down on hers. Anything to shut her up until he worked out how to calm her.

Except kissing Ghizlan had an inevitable effect on his still needy body. One touch of those lips, one taste and his other arm hooked round her, hauling her to him, soft breasts and belly cushioning his rigid frame.

He tried not to fall into the kiss. He tried to keep his head and think things through. But an instant later he was leaning in, delving deep, *willing* her to feel and respond to the same devil of desire that drove him.

His mouth gentled. He could coax her, he knew. Up until the moment he'd lost control Ghizlan had been with him all the way, kissing him with a fervour that had short-circuited his brain, wrapping those long legs around him as if she'd never let go. He deepened the kiss to a languorous caress he knew would seduce. He'd—

The sudden tang of salt on his tongue pierced his thoughts.

'No!' With a violent shove, Ghizlan thrust him off, the

heels of her hands digging into his chest. He rocked back, blinking as she stepped away. 'Get off. I don't want this!'

Over-bright eyes stared up at him.

Stunned, he saw the track of a tear down one pale cheek. It belied her fighting stance, hands on hips and feet planted wide. And it made his heart lurch in his chest.

Her mouth was swollen from his passion and there was a mark on her neck where he must have nipped her with his teeth. He couldn't remember doing it.

Is that going to be another of your excuses?

I didn't know she was an innocent.

I don't remember hurting her.

Hell! He stepped back, bile rising. How close had he come to losing control again?

Huseyn backed away another step. Always, even as a skinny, underfed kid, he'd understood what he had to do. Help his mother scrape a living in their dirt-poor village. Then, when she died, find the father who'd abandoned them. Later it had been to do everything it took to become a warrior. Not simply any warrior but the best in the province, so good his father would finally have to acknowledge him, however grudgingly. Always he'd believed he'd acted honourably. Given his father's appalling example, Huseyn took pride in doing the decent thing always. Until now.

Shame scythed through him, slicing at his self-respect. With this one woman, he'd behaved anything but honourably.

Yet even now, staring into her beautiful drowned eyes, reading the defiant tilt of her chin and the distress turning her breathing into staccato gasps, he hungered for her. The desire, no, the *need* to possess her, hummed through him like wind through a desolate mountain canyon. As desolate as his soul.

He couldn't stay here. He didn't trust himself. He swung on his heel and marched to the door, determined to have himself under control before he faced his wife again.

* * *

Ghizlan stared, blinking, at her husband's unreadable face.

He felt something, she knew he did from the way his mighty chest rose with each deep breath. And the way tiny lines bracketed his mouth and his nostrils flared. But his eyes gave nothing away.

Or maybe the problem was her—she was so lost to the myriad sensations he'd awoken—*again*—with that kiss, she was too befuddled to do more than gawk.

The man only had to kiss her and she lost it!

Even with that dull ache gently throbbing between her legs and disappointment vying with fury for pre-eminence, her one, overwhelming response when he touched her was to lean in and let him do exactly what he wanted.

It was bizarre. But when he'd taken her mouth and pulled her to him, part of her, the largest part, had clamoured a triumphant *Yes!* She'd wanted to fall against him and let him seduce her all over again.

It was only the last, fragile remnants of pride that had saved her from responding.

That's why, to her horror, she'd cried. Because despite everything he'd done to her, despite the fact he was her enemy, using her person, her body, as a political tool, she'd come to crave him in a way that made a mockery of everything she'd ever believed about herself.

How low had she sunk?

She'd known he was dangerous, even if she'd never completely understood the exact nature of that lethal animal quality in his potent personality and rugged frame. But she understood now. The memory of that fleeting pleasure as he'd filled her body flashed through her, a devastating sense memory. She had to squeeze her eyes shut rather than look at his big, beautiful, loose-limbed frame.

She heard the door scrape and her eyes snapped open. She wanted to ask him where he was going. Whether he'd return. She wanted, foolishly, to reach for him.

Rigid, she kept her hands at her sides. 'What are you going to do with the sheet?' Her voice was tight and thin.

He paused but didn't turn. When finally he spoke she could tell it was through gritted teeth. 'Burn the damned thing.'

Then he was gone. Yet the image of him lingered—impossibly wide shoulders, acres of bare golden flesh over muscles that flexed and rippled with every movement, long, powerful legs and tousled dark hair. An erection that even now was as enticing as it was daunting.

Ghizlan was glad he'd gone. She never wanted to see him again. He'd turned her into a woman she despised—weak and needy, on the verge of promising anything to the enemy in the hope of physical pleasure.

She spun away and marched across the room, blinking back tears she'd never shed for her father.

In the bathroom she put the plug in the bath and wrenched the taps on. She locked the door. Surely he wouldn't interrupt her for a while. She had time to…what? Recover? Plan her opposition? Wish he'd made love to her again?

Distraught, she swung around and caught her reflection in the mirror. She didn't know whether to be pleased or worried that she hardly recognised herself.

CHAPTER NINE

'YOU'RE LOOKING VERY regal today, my lady.'

Huseyn didn't utter his actual thought—that she was stunning. So gorgeous she'd made his heart kick as she crossed the vast audience chamber, the crowd parting before her. For an instant his breath had stilled.

'That's appropriate since I'm married to the man about to be proclaimed Sheikh.'

Her voice was cool, in stark contrast to the fiery termagant who'd ripped the sheet off their bed last night, and the lover who'd melted against him as he'd kissed her, her soft mews of pleasure driving him crazy.

Totally unlike the woman whose drowning eyes had driven him from her room, not to return.

The well of self-disgust he'd tapped into last night surged high. Had he done right, leaving her alone? At the time it had seemed the only sensible course.

Not by so much as a quiver did she display that her thoughts strayed to their disastrous wedding night. Instead a casual hand gesture dismissed both him and the treasures she wore: a gold and ruby necklace and a delicate ruby-studded diadem, rich against her ebony hair.

Huseyn surveyed her from the crown of her intricate hairstyle to her satin high heels. He particularly enjoyed the long, square-necked dress she wore—simple yet devastatingly feminine.

He'd never paid attention to women's clothes, except for the mechanics of removing them. With Ghizlan that changed.

His gaze followed the dip and swell of her small waist and rounded hips with a lover's appreciation, the smooth line of her long thighs. The dark red suited her.

Blood red, it was.

A deliberate reminder of last night's disastrous bedding. A warning she remembered exactly why he'd married her and that she refused to give in to him. Marginally more subtle than wearing mourning to yesterday's wedding. This message was for him alone, a private challenge.

Relief filled him. She wasn't broken after all, despite what his conscience had said whenever he recalled her pain last night.

Huseyn's eyes rose swiftly, catching her off guard.

That's when he saw it, the shadow in her gaze, the distress in her too-tight mouth. Proof that despite her brave show, Ghizlan was hurting. Scared? The notion cut like a blade.

'Ghizlan, we need to talk. About last night—'

Her eyes widened and she shook her head. 'There's nothing to say.'

Nothing to say? Then he saw her gaze flick to the crowd of guests. They were far enough away not to overhear but still…

'Very well. We'll discuss it after the ceremony.'

'I'm afraid that won't be possible.' Distress was replaced by hauteur as she angled her chin. Her eyes sparkled and her nostrils thinned in regal disapproval. 'I have some longstanding commitments later. I've already had to cancel appointments to attend this…' her mouth flattened '…ceremony.'

So that's how she was going to play it.

Huseyn knew what she was doing. Masking feelings with a show of unconcern. How often as a kid had he pretended nonchalance when petrified by fear?

Disdain was easier for Ghizlan than bridging the gulf between them. Who could blame her?

Besides, the international situation was so fraught that *had* to be his priority. There'd be time later to fix the damage he'd done last night.

Meanwhile, let her play the disdainful aristocrat. He could weather her scorn. She had no way of knowing her defiance attracted rather than repelled him.

'Let me congratulate you,' he murmured. 'You look every inch the royal consort. The colour suits you.'

Her expression didn't alter but the wash of heat up her throat told him what words couldn't.

'Thank you, my lord. So do you. Very…impressive.' She made a production of scanning him, from his traditional headscarf to the toes of his crimson kid boots, pausing a fraction too long on the ceremonial dagger at his side. 'The broadcast of today's ceremony will be a national sensation since you're the star.'

By all that was sacred, this woman was superb. She stood there proud and serene, a perfect smile on those perfect lips, as if she hadn't a worry in the world. As if calling him her lord wasn't like swallowing bitter aloes.

This was the sort of woman he needed beside him. A woman who wasn't afraid to—

Huseyn stilled. He was a loner and always had been. Their marriage was a necessity forced by circumstance. Yet he found himself enjoying the prospect of getting to know his wife, and not just sexually.

'Is there a problem, *my lord*?'

She was quick. No one else read him so easily.

'None at all.' He reached out and gripped her elbow, feeling the tiny quiver of reaction she couldn't hide.

Her eyes met his, rounding slightly. Once more Huseyn considered broaching last night's debacle. But she wasn't ready. He sensed it was only outrage giving Ghizlan courage to continue. *That* he could accommodate.

He inclined his head, invading her space. 'You can still feel it, can't you, *my lady*? You didn't really think what's between us is so easily destroyed?'

Her nostrils flared as if inhaling an offensive odour.

'On the contrary, I know only too well how binding our marriage is. Until you choose to dissolve it.'

He moved to one side, his mouth against her ear. 'Are you already counting the days? I find the idea of you impatiently waiting for me quite endearing.'

Ghizlan turned her head to stare up at him, eyes dark and fathomless as an abandoned desert well, and he knew exactly how treacherous those could be for the unwary, desperate with thirst. She gave another perfect smile, this one showing even, white teeth and the beast in him, the beast he'd worked to leash since the moment he'd walked away from her bed, sprang to life with a growl of anticipation.

'The day you find me eagerly awaiting you is the day you know I've lost my mind. Which, now I consider, has some attraction as an alternative.'

Huseyn couldn't prevent a bark of laughter. She was priceless. Steely and determined. It was a pity she wasn't a man. She had more gumption than any of those present for today's ceremony.

Except Ghizlan as a man would be a crime against nature.

Last night it had taken more determination than he'd ever needed to walk away from her. He'd distracted himself by spending the rest of his wedding night locked with the nation's powerbrokers. They'd still been downstairs, celebrating his wedding, when he'd stalked in, determined that one thing at least would go as planned that night.

Ghizlan had been right. None of them had looked concerned that he'd left his bride's bed to wrangle over politics and press his case to become Sheikh. None save Azim who'd eyed him the way a sensible man watched a deadly asp.

It was good to know his wife had at least one champion in this throng of self-important men.

Why that mattered, Huseyn didn't know. Except he'd

be busy in the weeks to come trying to pull Jeirut from the brink of war. He didn't like to think of Ghizlan alone.

'Come. It's time.' He looped her hand through his elbow, clamping it with his hand—huge and scarred against her delicate fingers.

Theirs was an unlikely match. A refined princess and a lowborn soldier who knew more about hunger and hardship than banquets or ceremonies, despite his time as second in command and now as Sheikh in his province.

Yet he held her hand firmly as they crossed to the dais where the throne waited. He kept her at his side through the short, all-important ceremony, not because it was custom but because she deserved to be there.

That laugh. Who'd have thought it would make a difference?

But it had. The memory of it even now wound through Ghizlan like sweet syrup, hot and enticing, confusing her.

Who'd have thought Huseyn al Rasheed knew how to laugh? He specialised in glowering and stony-faced determination.

And raw passion. Remember?

Oh, she remembered too well. He was a big, burly brute but no matter how she rebelled at the idea, he had the uncanny ability to make her want as no man ever had. She was drawn to him by forces she'd never fully understood until he'd taken her in his arms, forces she'd blithely believed she could ignore with all the confidence of an untried innocent. Now she knew better.

But one thing hadn't altered. He was still her enemy.

Shame filled her and she set her jaw, trying to concentrate on her schedule for the day. She'd had eighteen days to practise nonchalance. Almost three weeks of Huseyn absent in the provinces, yet in regular contact with diplomatic advisers here in the capital. He'd left immediately after the ceremony that proclaimed him Sheikh and not once in that time had he contacted her.

Ghizlan closed her computer tablet and set it aside on the car's back seat. She turned to look out the window as the vehicle wound slowly through the oldest, poorest part of the city towards the outskirts.

Of course she hadn't expected a message from him. She heard enough from Azim in her daily briefings. She'd been torn between amazement and something almost like pride as she'd learned of Huseyn's success. Not through sabre-rattling or a pre-emptive military strike, but with canny diplomacy and a personal, if foolhardy show of courage.

He'd met the nephew of the ailing Emir of Halarq alone, without even a bodyguard, for hours of talks, in an isolated tent on the disputed border. What had passed there no one knew for sure but it had paved the way for officials to meet over the following weeks and painstakingly nut out an agreement between the two nations. Rumour had it that the Emir of Halarq was terminally ill and his nephew would succeed him soon. While relations weren't exactly friendly, there was solid hope for a longer term rapprochement.

That Huseyn had achieved that, the man who'd monstered and manipulated her, *used* her in ways that must appal any thinking woman, stunned her. Had she misjudged him as he'd misjudged her? Oh, he was still a self-satisfied macho, callous, cold-hearted beast, but he'd saved her beloved Jeirut and the fizz of relief in her veins was palpable.

But she was *not* on tenterhooks at the news he was returning today.

The car pulled to a halt and Ghizlan thrust aside unwanted thoughts of her unwanted husband. He'd done his job, saving the nation. She would do hers as she always had, patiently, painstakingly, even it if wasn't on a grand, international scale. It was still necessary and she was proud of what she and her people had achieved.

Huseyn rolled his shoulders against the padded seat and stretched his legs. He was weary after weeks of little sleep and the need to keep three steps ahead of the soon-to-be Emir of Halarq. The other man was ambitious and clever but not quite clever enough to best Huseyn, who'd won his knowledge of men and their weaknesses in a hard school.

The comfort of the limo, after the luxury of the longest, hottest shower he'd had time for in weeks, almost tempted him into closing his eyes. But it was only late afternoon. There was still much to do.

Like meet his wife.

He'd chosen to do that straight away. He'd spent only a few hours alone with her but the woman had got under his skin, like a thorn too deep to cut out. For weeks he'd thought of her at the oddest times, not only when he'd lain down to sleep and found himself recalling her soft body and the tiny sounds of pleasure she'd made as he'd kissed her into oblivion.

He looked around with interest as the car passed the ragged outskirts of the city. What was she doing out *here*? Azim had spoken of her busy schedule and Huseyn had imagined lunch with ambassadors' wives at upmarket restaurants. Or a goodwill visit to a hospital or charity.

They drew up in an isolated spot, before a new building. Beyond it he glimpsed more buildings and a series of regular round ponds.

Huseyn stared. His wife was visiting a waste water treatment plant?

Not only visiting, he discovered when he made his way, unannounced, into the building, but talking knowledgeably. Huseyn paused in the doorway to what appeared to be a control room, listening to her engaged in a conversation that made little sense to him.

Clearly the woman he'd married was far more complex than he'd imagined. He'd underestimated her.

'Your Highness.' One of the men with Ghizlan bowed, drawing the attention of the cluster of people to Huseyn.

Slowly she turned from the computer and the display panels. She wore an elegant skirt and jacket the colour of dark mountain violets, which skimmed her gorgeous curves. Her eyes held his, totally expressionless. But he hadn't missed the almost imperceptible tightening of her shoulders, or the tiny turn-down of her mouth before she widened it into a polite smile.

A familiar spark ignited in his belly, confirming what he already knew—he'd been impatient to return to her.

Inexplicable. Impossible. But true.

Huseyn never wasted time hiding from the truth. He saved his strength for dealing with it.

'My lady.' He strode across the room and lifted her hand to his lips, breathing in her subtle sweet scent. He felt her hand shake, saw her mouth firm, and repressed a smile. She had no way of discerning the abrupt jolt of energy cleaving his insides as desire soared, and he had no intention of enlightening her. For now it was enough to know she felt it too.

'My lord.' She paused and he wondered if it was to choke back distaste. Yet she continued easily. 'Allow me to introduce everyone. First, the facility manager...'

What was he doing here? Why wasn't he neck deep in treaties and diplomatic wrangles, or bullying some poor hapless servant?

He looked big and bold and stole more than his share of oxygen, leaving her chest tight. He'd shaved and she saw with alarm the flicker of amusement in the long dimple cutting one lean cheek.

'I have a question.' That deep voice purred along her skin, making the fine hairs at her nape rise. She recalled the way it had resonated through her on their wedding night, making her feel things she'd never expected, never wanted to experience with a man like him.

'Yes?' Her voice was too sharp. She sucked in a calming breath.

'What's an anaerobic digester?'

He must have been listening for some time. That unsettled her. What did he want? Why had he come?

'Ah,' said the manager, 'we're very proud of that. It was the Sheikha's suggestion initially—'

'Really? Do tell.'

'Well, given our aim to maximise energy efficiency and Her Highness's special interest in the field—'

'Her special interest?' Huseyn turned to her, one eyebrow raised. Ridiculously she experienced a twinge of guilt, as if she'd been hiding some secret, when the truth was he'd never been interested enough to enquire.

'My degree,' she explained. 'I was one of the first Jeiruti women to study engineering.'

'And still the only female chemical engineer in the country,' the manager added proudly.

Huseyn's blue-grey eyes held hers and sensation kicked high in her chest. 'Quite an achievement,' he murmured. 'I didn't know chemical engineers specialised in waste water.'

'You'd be surprised,' she said. 'We work on all sorts of processes. Anything from power generation, mineral processing or water management to pharmaceuticals, biotechnology or manufacturing explosives.'

'Quite a lethal combination.' Huseyn's eyes didn't leave hers.

'Absolutely.' She let her teeth show when she smiled.

'And the digester?'

'It's working as well as we'd hoped,' said the eager manager. 'It breaks down organic waste to release a gas which we then use to produce electricity. This new plant is generating enough power to meet its own needs and contribute to the city's electricity grid.'

Instead of looking bored, Huseyn began asking questions, pertinent questions that showed a genuine interest. And so they went over it all again, explaining everything they'd already shown her.

Now he was here she was no more than a fly on the wall. Ghizlan swallowed her bitterness. It didn't matter. But the headache at the base of her skull had been building for hours and she'd love to sit. Her period had begun this morning and she felt rotten. Though at least it meant she wasn't pregnant! She couldn't bring a child into this disastrous marriage, which was why she planned to start the Pill tomorrow. Ghizlan was determined never to give herself to Huseyn again. And he'd shown his total lack of interest since their wedding night, but she'd take no chances.

She shifted, wishing she'd worn lower heels, when Huseyn's voice cut her thoughts.

'It's been fascinating, and a credit to you all. Thank you so much.' Then, with a series of swift farewells he was leading her outside where her driver held open the car door.

'Where's *your* vehicle?' She sank onto the seat, suppressing a sigh of relief.

'I sent it away. No point keeping two here when we can return together.'

The driver slid into the front seat. 'To the new factory, my lady?'

Ghizlan bit her lip. She still had just enough time for her planned visit, but with Huseyn beside her—

'That's right.' Huseyn spoke up.

'Surely you don't have time for this,' she murmured, glancing at the driver. 'It's your first day back in the capital. You must have plenty of other—'

'Nothing more important than seeing my dear wife.' At her fulminating stare his lips twitched into something verging on a smile. 'Unless you find my presence too distracting?'

Ghizlan didn't deign to answer. It was too close to the truth. The whole time he'd stood beside her at the water treatment plant she'd been a mass of nerves, unsettled because *he* was there.

Why had he come? What did he want?

Now she shut her eyes and leaned her head back, blocking him out. One more stop then back to her room for a warm shower and a cup of tea and something for the rising pain. All she had to do was put up with him a little longer.

'We're here.' The words tickled her ear. Or perhaps it was Huseyn's lips, soft and warm against her lobe. Ghizlan jerked awake and stared up into slate blue eyes that seemed to bore right down into her soul. She blinked and shuffled to one side, flesh prickling at his nearness as if she'd received a zap of electricity.

The trip could only have taken fifteen minutes. Could she really have fallen asleep with Huseyn beside her?

'And where, exactly, is here?' her husband asked as they stood, surveying the building before them.

A tickle of apprehension traced down Ghizlan's backbone but she ignored it. There was nothing to be nervous about. She just didn't like Huseyn peering into her life and her interests as if he had a right to. But now she was here she refused to turn away. This was important.

'A project of mine.'

'Yours, not the city's?'

She swung round to face him but that severely sculpted face was unreadable. No hint of sarcasm.

'It's a joint venture.' She was putting up the money with the bulk of her inheritance and the Council had supplied the site. 'It will link to some schemes that are already running—one to help aspiring businesswomen and another to provide employment for local women.'

'An all-female enterprise?'

Ghizlan shrugged, too fatigued to rise to the bait. 'If you read the statistics you'd know the bulk of the poor in Jeirut are women, as are the bulk of those without education or employment. This is one, small attempt to turn that around.'

She marched across the newly resurfaced pavement and into the building, not waiting to see if he followed. No doubt he'd view this project as insignificant when measured against his own recent efforts, but it mattered. Not just to her, but to the people whose lives it would change.

He caught up with her as she moved through the vestibule of the old building. His tread was silent, too silent for such a big man, but she knew he was there from the hum of awareness tickling her shoulder and back. It was as if he put out an electrical force that zapped when he got near.

'My lady. Your Highness.' The project manager, Afifa, bowed low and Ghizlan admired the other woman's unruffled demeanour. She was used to Ghizlan and they'd developed a good working relationship but Huseyn could be daunting.

Quickly Ghizlan introduced Afifa then paused, surprised when her husband didn't instantly take over. In fact, he seemed to be waiting for her to take the lead.

Ever-present suspicion rose.

'We're here for a progress check and update on the new extension to the building.'

He nodded, falling in step as she led the way. 'And this building is…?'

'It was used for distilling attar of roses, the essential oil for which Jeirut was famous. It fell into disrepair in the last few decades as demand dropped due to the availability of imported scent.' And because, as part of the country's modernisation, traditional endeavours, particularly those seen as cottage industries, were ditched in favour of new, large-scale enterprises.

She led the way through the old distillation room to the

vast space where once tonnes of rose petals were brought for processing. Even now Ghizlan fancied she inhaled an echo of that lush, intoxicating scent. She breathed deeply, feeling some of her tension ebb.

'You're expecting to restart production with flowers grown locally?' There was scepticism in his tone.

'Of course. We've been successfully cultivating roses since the Middle Ages, if not before. Plus there are native plants ideal for perfume making. Like the iris. You know it grows wild in the mountains? It thrives in arid, cold conditions. This region was once famous for myrrh and frankincense and—'

Ghizlan pulled up short, discomfited at her own enthusiasm. She'd forgotten she needed to keep him at arm's length. Instead she'd rambled about her pet project. He couldn't possibly be interested.

'So you'll make perfumes using only local ingredients. Traditional oils and such.'

When Ghizlan hesitated, Afifa smoothly filled the breach. 'There will be a range of traditional products, both for domestic consumption and, we hope, export. We plan to extend the irrigation at the base of the mountains to grow more raw ingredients ourselves. But as well…' Afifa smiled at Ghizlan '…the Sheikha plans to import ingredients from elsewhere. Cedar from Morocco, bergamot from the Mediterranean, jasmine, orange blossom and so on.'

'Our aim,' said Ghizlan, tilting her chin as she met her husband's unreadable eyes, 'is to establish a couture perfume industry to rival the biggest names in the business.' When he remained silent she continued, provoked. 'There's no reason why Jeirut shouldn't achieve what others have. We have experience in the field and a willingness to learn and innovate.'

'No reason at all,' he said finally. 'I applaud your ambition.' He turned to Afifa. 'So you've extended the building? In what way?'

Ghizlan's shoulders slumped. She hadn't realised she'd been holding her breath until it escaped in a soft sigh of relief.

Because she'd thought Huseyn would belittle the project? His opinion didn't matter. She hadn't let her father's doubts stop her. Yet as she followed Huseyn and Afifa into the new section of the building, still to be completed, she admitted she'd been tense, waiting for some offhand dismissal of this scheme that was so dear to her.

She pressed her palm to her stomach as it cramped. That had to be the explanation. She was tired and vulnerable because of her hormones at this time of month. It couldn't possibly be because *his* approval mattered.

By the time they'd toured the new development, listened to Afifa's enthusiastic update on the business plan and progress on the irrigation programme, Ghizlan was all but swaying on her feet.

Thankful for the silent ride back to the palace, she nodded goodbye to Huseyn and headed to her room, only to find him shadowing her. She said nothing. No doubt he'd taken over the Sheikh's apartment, which lay in this direction.

But when she entered her apartment and found him following, brushing aside her arm when she would have shut the door, temper flared.

'You're not welcome in here!'

'Tell me something I don't know.' He had the audacity to lean back, propping one shoulder against the closed door and folding his arms across that powerful chest.

Something inside Ghizlan contracted, but not, she realised, in horror. It was more akin to excitement. Despite her now throbbing head and the pulling ache in her belly she found this man potently, inexplicably attractive.

Which made her angrier.

'This is my room and I don't want you here. Why don't you go back to wherever it is you've been sleeping?'

'From now on we sleep together, my lady. And I assume you'll be more comfortable here than moving into the royal quarters your father used.'

Seething, she turned her back on him then stopped short as she saw the view through the open door from her sitting room to her bedroom.

'What's happened to my bed?' It had been replaced with a massive, king-sized affair that cut off the oxygen supply to her lungs. If ever a bed screamed sex, this was it.

'I like to sprawl when I sleep.' That deep, rumbly voice rolled through her. 'And you must admit there's a lot of me. We'll be more comfortable this way.'

She swung back to glare at her tormentor. 'I have no intention of sleeping with you.'

The fire in his blue-grey eyes and the slow lift of one dark eyebrow were calculated to annoy. Ghizlan told herself she was angry. Not anxious about him or, worse, about her response to him.

'Or having sex!'

'That's a pity. I've been looking forward to that.' His eyes were pewter now, bordering on silver, and the sight of that sensual light sent a judder of response right to the soles of her feet.

'Because you enjoyed it so much? I don't care. You're not the lover I want.'

That snapped him to attention, all pretence at indolence gone. He stepped forward, crowding her.

'Who do you want, Ghizlan? Idris of Zahrat? The man who jilted you to marry someone else? Or maybe your Frenchman, Jean-Paul?'

Ghizlan stared up into eyes narrowed to gleaming slits. 'Don't be absurd.'

'I'm glad you realise it's absurd, *my lady*. Because the only man you're going to share yourself with is me.'

The way he loomed over her, his wide shoulders hemming her in, the tangy scent of him tantalising her nostrils, should have infuriated her. Yet Ghizlan found herself for a moment transfixed, a shudder of excitement ripping through her at his possessiveness.

Until she realised what she was doing and hauled herself away from him. 'We're not having sex.'

'Of course you don't want a repeat of our wedding night.' He followed her, step for step. 'For that I apologise. If I'd known in advance you were a virgin—'

'Stop!' She raised a hand. She didn't want to go there. Not even to ask what she'd ever done to make him assume she was anything but a virgin.

Living in the spotlight, she'd been cautious about dating. More than cautious, given her natural reticence about putting herself in any man's power. And when she'd lived overseas, studying, the paparazzi had always been waiting for a scoop about her, mingling with 'real' people. They'd approached her friends for tell-all exposés about the exotic, foreign princess. That had put Ghizlan off any inclination to pursue intimacy with a man, knowing the details would probably be splashed across the media.

'I. Don't. Want. Sex. With. You,' she said through clenched teeth. 'Got that?'

'Of course you do.' The nerve of the man left her speechless! 'But you're upset about our wedding night. It wasn't my finest hour but, believe me, I can do better.' His mouth kicked up at one corner and the gleam in his eyes burned so brightly it was like a spotlight, heating her where she stood. 'I promise you, Ghizlan, next time *will* be much better.'

Heat coursed through her, an insidious heat that trickled into places it shouldn't, making her wonder what it would be like if—

'There won't be a next time. Unless you intend to use force again.'

If he felt any remorse, he didn't show it. 'There was no force last time, just loss of control.' Hers or his, she wondered frantically as her breath caught. 'There *will* be a next time. But don't worry, I'll wait until you invite me.'

'Then you'll wait until hell freezes over.' She spun away from him but his callused hand caught hers. For reasons she couldn't fathom, she halted, looking down at the large, scarred hand that restrained her.

He wasn't taking no for an answer. He kept pushing her and pushing. But she had a trump card. One guaranteed to ward off any male.

'Let me go. I've got my period and I need the bathroom.'

As expected, he released her instantly. She strode to the sanctuary of her bathroom, wondering why her victory felt hollow.

CHAPTER TEN

HUSEYN WATCHED THE DOOR close behind her with a mixture of frustration and pride. Damn, but she was one feisty woman!

And hourly more intriguing.

His wife wasn't the pampered socialite he'd assumed. He recalled her conversation at the treatment works and the respect in which she was obviously held. Not just for her rank, but because she knew what she was talking about.

Then at the perfume factory. Her concern for the disadvantaged in their country was real. But instead of raising money the easy way through charity auctions or galas, she was building something concrete that would allow people the dignity of working towards a better life. She was magnificent, ideal for the role of royal consort.

He paced, fascinated by the barrage of insights into his wife. Not least was the passion in her. When she'd spoken of making perfume she'd lit up from within, as if she'd forgotten she spoke to *him*. That passion—he wanted it for himself. He wanted to obliterate the boundaries she'd put up, and the ones born of his clumsy treatment.

A grim smile curled his lips. She shouldn't be his priority. He still had to cement his rule over the nation. Plus there was a treaty with Halarq to finalise, not to mention one with Zahrat, which was precarious since Sheikh Idris had turned his back on Ghizlan.

A discordant note twanged through him at the thought of Idris. Obviously he and Ghizlan hadn't been lovers, but had there been affection? Did she yearn for him? Or for the mysterious Jean-Paul?

Huseyn swung around, pacing the room.

Ghizlan was *his*. For whatever reason, he couldn't now countenance any alternative. He had no intention of ending this marriage, which had given him everything he needed and more.

Which meant he had to overcome perhaps his greatest challenge—convincing his wife to act like a wife and not a prisoner of war.

Which meant wooing her.

Strangely, the notion appealed.

The prize—having proud, passionate Ghizlan reaching for him of her own volition, satisfying the gut-clenching hunger within—was irresistible.

He'd never had to exert himself to seduce a woman. He'd never had to flatter or even invite since women were only too eager to snare his attention. Relationships were purely sexual, easy and mutually satisfying.

Ghizlan was the only woman to spurn him. Perhaps that's why she intrigued him.

Or maybe because for the first time he was truly *interested.* From the beginning she'd attracted and infuriated him. Now he wanted to understand his contrary, accomplished, fascinating wife. She deserved his attention in her own right, not merely because of their marriage.

He stared at the closed door, remembering the gauntlet she'd flung down. A woman with her period wouldn't want physical seduction. What would she want? He had no idea. His was a man's world through and through. None of his lovers had ever discussed anything so intimate.

His mouth firmed. If she thought to scare him away by referring to such matters she was mistaken. He'd faced starvation, neglect and war. He'd faced down his dog of a father and demanded a chance at life. Everything he had he'd won through sheer determination.

He picked up the phone. His campaign began.

* * *

When Ghizlan emerged from the bathroom, warm from the shower and relaxed from the painkiller she'd taken, she found the bedroom filled with soft light from the lamps rather than the brilliant overhead chandelier. The bed was turned down and her maid had left a hot-water bottle. Had she guessed Ghizlan was suffering from cramps?

The last of Ghizlan's tension eased with the outward rush of her breath. Such peace after the storm. Thank goodness Huseyn had been scared by her mention of—

'You!' Her eyes rounded as the man himself strolled in from her sitting room, resplendent in loose, dark, low-slung trousers and nothing else.

Ghizlan's throat dried as if she'd swallowed part of the Great Sand Desert and her hands went to the sash of her robe, knotting it tight.

His eyebrows rose. 'You speak as if you expected some other man, when we both know you've never had anyone else in your bed.'

He sounded so smug she wanted to slap him. Except that would mean touching him and *that* was a mistake she wouldn't make again. Especially when he was shirtless, the brawny, golden expanse of his torso rugged and appallingly tempting with its dusting of dark hair, its deep bed of muscles and, she realised, seeing him properly for the first time, a collection of impressive scars. Was that an old *bullet* wound along his ribs?

'Why don't you get into bed?' He moved closer and she realised he was carrying a tray. From it came the heavenly aroma of cinnamon-spiced hot chocolate.

'It's too early.' She jutted her chin, falling back on the truth. 'And I don't want you here.'

He shrugged, those massive shoulders riding high in a fluid movement that glued her eyes to his magnificent form. For he really *was* magnificent. Powerfully built like some ancient god and potently male.

'You'll get used to me.' Blithely ignoring her fulminating stare, he put the tray on her bedside table. Not only hot chocolate but her other favourite, rare indulgence, delectable sugar syrup baklava, brimming with nuts and dripping sweetness.

Ghizlan's mouth watered.

Huseyn tugged back the bedcovers further and picked up the hot-water bottle. 'Why don't you indulge yourself? You're worn out. You can tell me off after you've rested. Right now you need warmth and something sweet.'

Ghizlan planted her hands on her hips in a show of defiance, ignoring the impulse to do exactly as he suggested. 'How would you know what I need?'

'I spoke to your maid.'

'You spoke…?'

'To your maid. She said you'd appreciate a hot-water bottle and a warm drink. The baklava was my idea.'

Ghizlan stared at the macho man before her. The warrior who drove all before him, who'd forced the Royal Council to name him Sheikh, who'd forged peace out of the beginnings of war and whose reputation as a hard man was second to none. *This* man had discussed her period with her maid? She'd been sure he'd run for the hills or one of his precious horses rather than think about such things.

'Here.' His touch on her arm was light but compelling. 'Let yourself relax for a bit, then you'll have the energy to fight with me again.'

Was that the shadow of a smile on his sculpted lips? No. He looked merely solicitous as he moved her towards the bed, tugging her off balance so she subsided unexpectedly onto the mattress. Before she had time to argue or get back on her feet, he'd swung her legs onto the bed and pressed the hot-water bottle into her hands, its warmth against her abdomen sheer luxury.

Despite herself Ghizlan subsided on a sigh of relief, clutching the hot-water bottle to her tummy.

'Is it always this bad?' He pulled the covers over her and she stared, undone by the novelty of Huseyn al Rasheed tucking her into bed as if he did it every day.

'No,' she found herself answering. 'Sometimes on the first day.' Ghizlan snapped her mouth shut. She hadn't intended to share even that. But the luxury of sinking into plump pillows, of warmth and softness, undermined caution.

She stared as Huseyn lifted the silver pot on the bedside table and poured the hot chocolate. His movements were economical, easy, as if this enormous bear of a man was quite at home. Of course he was! He ate and drank just like her. Yet the sight of that huge, scarred hand deftly managing the delicate pieces mesmerised her. Just as the scent of him, warm and richly male, and so foreign in her private sanctuary, tantalised.

'Don't you have a shirt to put on?' She sounded waspish. Good. Better than him thinking she accepted his presence.

He shrugged and Ghizlan fought not to stare at a delicious ripple of muscle. She'd never known a man's bare chest could be so distracting. But it wasn't just his chest. Those trousers sat so low she had a perfect view of taut abdominal muscles and the fine line of dark hair bisecting them.

'Be thankful I'm wearing pants. Usually I sleep nude.'

'You're not sleeping here!' She half sat and one large hand pressed her back down, gently but firmly.

'Not yet. I've ordered dinner to be brought here and then I've got several hours of work.'

'Then I suggest you do it elsewhere.' Ghizlan told herself she could do better than this. She should get out of bed, force him out...

But how? Huseyn wasn't going anywhere he didn't want to. She didn't have the physical strength to eject him and her ploy to scare him off by mentioning menstruation had backfired.

'Here. Try this.' He offered the hot chocolate, its rich scent curling through her.

Maybe he was right. Maybe she should recoup her strength before taking him on. Ghizlan slid higher in the bed, plumping the pillows behind her, and took the cup. His fingers brushed hers and runnels of liquid fire spread under her skin.

Obviously she was tired and imagining things.

'Thank you.' It hurt to say the words.

'My pleasure.' He strolled away, around the oversized bed to the other side where, she saw now, a vast wing chair had been placed. Beside it was a small table with a laptop and a pile of papers.

'What are you doing?'

'I told you I had work to do.' He sank into the chair, stretched his long, long legs and reached for the laptop. He caught her wide-eyed stare and his mouth flicked up at one corner. That hard, too-rugged face transformed as the hint of a dimple grooved one cheek. 'Yes, even we provincials can read and write.' Then he turned to the laptop.

Ghizlan shut her sagging mouth. She was about to snap that she hadn't for one minute thought him illiterate. It was more the unwanted *intimacy* of having Huseyn, bare-chested and barefoot, sprawled so casually beside her bed.

Shouldn't he be inspecting his troops or managing some crisis or doing whatever it was that kept his body in such amazing shape?

'That hot chocolate will get cold if you don't drink it.' He didn't even look up. Was she so easy to second-guess? The thought infuriated. Rather than waste effort sparring, she sank back, sipping the delicious drink, and told herself she'd deal with him later.

But later there was no dealing with him. After indulging in an unheard-of rest, Ghizlan was refreshed enough to eat dinner and tackle some of her own paperwork. But as the evening wore on tiredness claimed her and she found herself dozing, the business plan for the perfume factory spread on her lap.

She woke as Huseyn moved the papers away. Amazing to think she'd relaxed enough to forget he was in the room. Not forget precisely, but there'd been something unaccountably reassuring about hearing the quiet shuffle of papers and the soft rhythm of his fingers on his keyboard.

Blearily she looked up into misty blue eyes fringed with thick dark lashes. How had she never noticed how beautiful they were?

Because she'd been too busy watching them narrow in annoyance or disapproval.

'Sleep now, Ghizlan.'

She moved to lift the sheet and sit up but his hand, hot on her shoulder, stopped her. 'Don't fret. I promise to let you sleep undisturbed.'

Dazed, looking up into that open stare, Ghizlan found herself believing him. Slowly she sank back, part of her brain warning that giving in was a mistake. But it was smothered by tiredness. She'd worked non-stop the last few weeks, stressed over the peace talks, wondering about the outcome, and determined to support her people by being seen, calm and supportive, as often as possible. Her schedule had been a nightmare.

Nevertheless, she lay rigid, listening as he put her papers on the table and switched off her lamp. Her breath caught as he moved but it was only to return to the wing chair and his work.

For long minutes Ghizlan watched him, wondering how the line of his broken nose, the firm slash of his mouth and that solid, uncompromising jaw could look so attractive. As for his shoulders and chest, the torso tapering to narrow hips…she shut her eyes rather than let her gaze wander there.

When she opened them again it was broad daylight. She'd slept far later than usual and the sun was high. She lay,

disorientated, until memories of last night flooded back
and she turned her head to the other side of the vast bed.
It was empty, and, when she stretched out a hand, cold.
Yet there was a dent in the pillow where Huseyn's head
had rested and his male scent reached her as she moved.

He'd invaded her space, her privacy, even her bed, and
she'd let him.

Had he really meant what he'd said? That he'd wait till
she invited him to make love to her?

Her lips compressed as she swung her legs out of bed.
She might have a weakness for Huseyn's kisses but even
she wasn't so stupid as to think he'd ever made love to her.
It had been sex. Raw and unvarnished. And if he thought
one evening's solicitousness could make her change her
mind he was in for a nasty shock.

When she returned to her room—their room—that evening, it was a relief to find it empty. Huseyn had flown to
a city on the other side of the country. With her luck he'd
return after she was asleep. The thought of seeing that big,
golden body half naked and sprawled in her space sent a
shiver through her.

Over a cup of mint tea she chatted on the phone to
Arden, the Englishwoman who'd married Sheikh Idris of
Zahrat, abruptly ending Ghizlan's almost-betrothal. Both
women had weathered the storm of scandal that followed
and built a rapport, then a friendship. Of course Ghizlan
had Mina too, but her sister was years younger and busy
with her studies and the delights of France. Besides, Ghizlan and Arden shared similar lives, being sheikhas of
neighbouring countries.

The sound of the sitting room door opening made her
swing round and there was Huseyn, his long legs eating
up the space between them. Ghizlan's heart jolted against
her breastbone.

'I'll have to go now.'

'He's back, is he?' Arden sounded intrigued. 'One day you'll have to bring him to Zahrat so I can meet him. I've heard amazing stories about him—the iron warrior and all that, but I know there must be more to him since you married him.'

Ghizlan bit down a sour laugh. She hadn't told Arden the true nature of her marriage and didn't intend to. Not over the phone at any rate. 'That sounds good,' she murmured, aware of Huseyn behind her. 'I'll call later.'

'Your sister?' She hunched her shoulders as that deep, velvety voice ran across her sensitised nerves.

'Just a friend.' She turned and stopped, aghast, to see him reefing off his clothes.

'What?' He paused, registering her stare. Was that amusement in his eyes?

'I'd prefer not to watch you undress.'

'Then avert your eyes, my lady.' With that he stripped off his trousers and underwear to stand breathtakingly naked.

Ghizlan blinked, telling herself not to look as he crossed to the bathroom. Yet heat blazed in her cheeks as he shut the door. It wasn't just the lithe grace of his movements— a man utterly at ease with his body. It was also the size of him…there. How had they ever fitted together? No wonder it had hurt. Statues she'd seen of naked men had always looked rather limp in that area. Whereas Huseyn looked almost primed for…

She swung away, grabbing her laptop and heading for the sitting room. Work would keep her mind off…him.

Later, at his insistence, they ate dinner in their private dining room. Why he wanted to be with her, Ghizlan couldn't understand. He sure wasn't trying to seduce her. His responses to her few efforts at conversation were short and his mouth tight.

'I'm sorry.' The surprising words jerked her head up. 'I've been like a bear with a sore head.'

Ghizlan raised her eyebrows but refused to ask for details.

'Dealing with some of your officials is an exercise in frustration.'

'*My* officials?'

His mouth lifted at one corner and Ghizlan wished she didn't find the sight so ridiculously attractive. Those occasional hints of humour were too disarming.

'Okay. Representatives of *our* national parliament. I've spent all day trying to get two of them to work together but it's futile.'

'Why bother? Why not order them to obey?' It's what she'd have expected a few weeks ago, before she'd seen the way he'd negotiated a truce with Halarq and convinced even the most bellicose of those in government that discussion rather than confrontation was the way to go.

'I could, but I'd prefer them to negotiate amongst themselves. In the longer run it will save work and time if they're not sending every decision up the line to me.'

He was delegating, reinforcing the role of officials to take responsibility for their decisions. Not demanding every decision be his.

'What is it? You're looking at me strangely.'

Ghizlan shook her head. It wouldn't improve his mood if she told him she was surprised he trusted anyone but himself to make decisions. She was rapidly revising her assumption that his bid for power was all about ego.

'Who's proving so difficult?'

'The Ministers for Education and for Public Works.'

'Ah.' That explained it.

Huseyn sat forward. 'Ah, what?'

'They can't stand each other.'

'Go on.'

'My father used to keep them apart as much as possible but they're both excellent at their jobs, so he didn't want to move them.' She paused, seeing Huseyn waiting for more. 'There was a family rift. One of them had been on the verge of a betrothal when he fell in love with the woman's sister. The marriage contract was changed so he could marry the younger sister. Relations between the women have been strained since and when the older sister married the feud continued.'

'The two bridegrooms are our two ministers?' He shook his head. 'They're well into their fifties. Surely this happened decades ago?'

'Yes, but neither man liked the other anyway. Father said they have very different personalities. One is a methodical planner and the other is instinctive, taking risks others wouldn't.'

She looked up to find those pale eyes fixed on her. 'Your father used to discuss a lot with you.'

Ghizlan shrugged. 'Mainly with Azim, his chief adviser, but, yes, I picked up a lot.'

'He trusted you.' His statement made Ghizlan pause. She'd been frustrated by her father's determination to use her as a political tool and hurt by his inability to *love* her. Yet he'd spoken to her about his work as if she were clever enough to understand and contribute. She'd never thought about it before, but in his own way he'd at least respected her, even if he'd been too emotionally barren to have a normal relationship with her.

'Ghizlan?'

She blinked and looked up into that piercing stare. 'Sorry, my mind was wandering.' And her emotions. Maybe it was hormonal but abruptly she felt her father's loss. He'd been far from a perfect parent but neither had he been a monster. Now he was gone, the only parent she remembered.

'Please excuse me.' She pushed back her chair. 'I'm tired.' It was too early to sleep but she needed privacy.

Maybe Huseyn realised for he didn't follow her into the bedroom. For two hours Ghizlan worked her way through the documents requiring her attention, hoping work would blanket the grief that had overtaken her. It helped, yet still she felt drawn and sad. Finally, packing up her papers, she reached for a paperback. With luck she could lose herself in a good story.

'You're reading a *book*?' Huseyn's inflection made it sound unexpected. Ghizlan looked up, carefully keeping her eyes trained on his face as he undressed. That little skitter of excitement deep inside was surely a bad sign. As was the quickened patter of her pulse.

'I've finished my work and this helps me relax.'

He strode closer. Did he *have* to be bare-chested? Was he trying to remind her how she'd enjoyed touching him? Ghizlan dragged her gaze back to the book.

'You like reading about sex?'

Her head shot up and their gazes meshed. Heat drilled to her core, swirling there in an ache that had nothing to do with her period. She shifted in the bed, stopping abruptly as his eyes narrowed. Could he read her body so easily? Did he know that just the word *sex* on his lips had her remembering the awesome power of their coupling? The urgency for fulfilment that had made a mockery of her denials? Even the disappointing outcome couldn't banish the memory of how wonderful it had been in the beginning.

Ghizlan turned the book to look at its cover. A woman in ringlets and a long gown arched into the embrace of a man in tight breeches and boots. The man was missing his shirt and Ghizlan couldn't help comparing his glossy, hairless chest with that of the man before her. Huseyn looked powerful, huskily male and so desirable her fingers twitched with the need to touch him.

'Not sex. Love.' Her voice sounded strangled and she cleared her throat. 'Well, there's sex in there too but ultimately it's about love.'

'Love?' Huseyn frowned as if she'd spoken a foreign language. 'Is that what you want from life?'

'No.' She'd always known she wouldn't have that luxury. Except for a too-short period when she'd dreamed of escaping with Mina and living a life of her own devising. 'I know love isn't for me.'

'But you believe in it?'

Why was he interested? He stood so close her nostrils quivered at the lush, male scent of him. The calm she'd found reading the historical romance evaporated. How could she relax with him looming over her, half naked?

'I believe it exists. But really, I'm just reading to relax so I sleep.' He opened his mouth and she rushed on, needing to change the subject. 'What do you read?'

'Petitions, proposals, plans.' He shrugged and, to her relief, walked towards the bathroom.

'I mean for pleasure.' Why she was curious she didn't understand. Did she really want to know her husband?

'I've never read for pleasure.'

'Never…?' Ghizlan stared. 'But that's…'

'Reading was a skill I learned because I needed it.' His expression was unreadable. 'It's useful. That's all.'

Before she could question him further he entered the bathroom and shut the door, leaving her pondering a life without the joy of reading. Somehow it fitted her original impression of Huseyn—a warrior, tough and uncompromising, with no time for the finer things in life. But she knew now he was more complex than that. He could even be kind.

Ghizlan had thought she'd sleep well, but her mind circled again and again over intriguing new insights about her father and her husband. Even when Huseyn had finished his own work and turned out the light she lay, trying to turn off the thoughts humming through her brain. She rolled over again.

'What's wrong?' Huseyn's voice was a soft rumble behind her. She'd thought him asleep.

'Nothing. I'm just not sleepy.'

'That's what comes from reading about sex before bed.'

'I didn't…' Ghizlan subsided in a huff. There was no point discussing it. Huseyn would believe what he wanted. 'I've got some things on my mind.' Like her unwilling fascination for her husband and the fact he was far less brutal and far more intriguing than was good for her.

'There's a cure for that.' His voice held a note that ran like fire through her veins.

She'd bet there was. 'I don't want sex.'

'I wasn't offering it.' His tone bordered on smug and her palm itched to slap him. Except that would mean rolling over and touching him and—

Her breath escaped in a squeak of shock as she felt heat behind her and a powerful arm wrapped around her middle, drawing her across the bed.

'What do you think you're—?' Her words stopped as she collided with his body. It curved around her, knees to the backs of her knees, groin to her bottom, solid chest to her back. An arm slid under her head and Ghizlan found herself cushioned by hot, living muscle. Worse was the unmistakably rigid shaft that lay against her buttocks. Huseyn was aroused. So aroused her stomach dipped and quivered in what she told herself was horror. It could not, absolutely could *not* be excitement.

'Making you comfortable so you can sleep.'

'You really think I'll be able to sleep like this?'

'Others have. It's something to do with the comfort of lying against another body.'

Ghizlan swallowed. How many women had taken comfort from Huseyn's body? She screwed up her eyes. She didn't want to know. 'Let me go.' She shoved at his arm but it didn't budge. 'I'd rather sleep alone.'

'But you weren't sleeping, were you? You were keeping me awake. I have a lot to do tomorrow. I need my rest.'

Feeling guilty, Ghizlan lay rigid till eventually his breathing slowed and she felt the rhythm of his breaths in the subtle movement of his body embracing her. It was like being in a hammock, swaying gently, she thought muzzily before finally slipping into oblivion, her hand around the sinewy forearm that held her securely.

Into the night Huseyn lay watching the moon's progress. Lying with Ghizlan was exquisite torture. When she snuffled and burrowed against him his groin caught fire and only his promise not to take her held him still. He'd already broken his earlier promise—not to hurt her. He'd keep his word now. But the combination of tantalising body and sharp mind made his bride daily more rather than less alluring. That had never happened with any other woman.

Huseyn frowned, telling himself that once this became a real marriage, this fascination would lessen and he'd be able to concentrate again.

CHAPTER ELEVEN

TEN DAYS LATER Ghizlan looked across the dining table at the man she'd married and to her shock realised she was *easy* in his company.

It had been a slow process, but inexorable. If she didn't go to sleep with his arm around her she'd wake up in his embrace with no memory of having shifted in the night. Those embraces were a two-edged sword. To her surprise she loved snuggling into his heat, feeling safe as if nothing bad in the world could touch her. Which was bizarre since she was his captive. At the same time her restlessness increased. The stirring deep within spoke of sexual hunger.

But this…acceptance was more than physical. He'd begun asking her opinion about issues that arose during his day and asking about hers. She was growing comfortable as they discussed the one thing that really linked them: their work for Jeirut.

Huseyn looked up. 'What's wrong?'

'Nothing.' She paused, aware of the dragging sensation in her stomach when his misty blue eyes met hers. Despite sharing a bed, he'd kept his word, never demanding sex. Which surely proved he didn't really want her.

Except every night she felt him press against her, making her wonder what it would be like if she invited him—

'Ghizlan?'

She shook her head. 'You never did tell me what happened between you and the Emir of Halarq's nephew when you met on the border. How did you persuade him to champion a peace deal?'

Huseyn watched her so long she thought he might not

answer. Did he guess she was diverting the subject? Finally he shrugged and helped himself to a dish of chicken with pomegranate.

'He's ambitious and eager for prestige, like his uncle. But he's intelligent too. He soon realised the consequences for his country if they attacked. They'd hoped to grab territory while Jeirut was without a leader, but I made it clear I was in control and wouldn't sit idle.' He shrugged. 'Unlike his uncle, his head isn't filled with dreams. The old man deludes himself with visions of honour and great warriors, but real war isn't like that.'

'You speak from experience.' Ghizlan remembered the silvered scars on his torso, her gaze dropping to the marks on his hand as he lifted a forkful of food to his mouth.

His world was so different. Yet he was surprisingly easy to talk with. As if he wasn't her enemy at all.

'I grew up on the border. I experienced raids by the Emir's *gallant* warriors.' Sarcasm laced his tone and an underlying roughness hinted at strong emotions. 'They specialised in attacking at night, terrorising peaceful villagers, looting and raping and...'

'And?' Ghizlan heard the thread of suppressed emotion in his voice. She put down her cutlery and leaned forward.

'One night when I was six they came to our village. My mother lifted me out the window and told me to run to our hiding place in the foothills. It was too late for adults to escape, but skinny little kids could slip through the shadows. Next door Selim's mother did the same, asking me to look after him because he was a child.'

And a six-year-old wasn't a child? Ghizlan's throat tightened. 'Selim? Not—?'

Huseyn nodded. 'Our Captain of the Guard, yes. We grew up together.'

The bond between the two was strong. Ghizlan knew Huseyn trusted the other man implicitly and that Selim was unquestionably loyal. 'What happened?'

Huseyn stabbed a chunk of meat with his fork then put it down. 'We returned at daybreak. We already knew this raid was worse. We'd seen the smoke. The village had been destroyed and it was empty. They took the survivors across the border as forced labour.' His voice was unnaturally blank when he continued. 'We found six bodies, including Selim's parents and my mother. It took us all day to bury them.'

Ghizlan's heart contracted. How could she not have known this sort of thing had happened on their border? Why had her father not told her? Because of the bad blood between him and Huseyn's father that had kept relations with the province of Jumeah so strained? Because he'd sought to protect her?

'I'm so very sorry.' The words were totally inadequate.

'It was a long time ago.' He met her stare, his own clouded. She wanted to reach out and comfort him. As if this self-contained man would welcome that!

'What happened then?'

'You want the story of my life?' His brows crunched together.

'Why not? Unless you prefer that I rely on the stories I hear.'

He waved a dismissive hand. 'People exaggerate.' He paused then went on in a matter-of-fact tone. 'It took us a few days but we made it to the capital. Then, on the day my father held his public audience, I confronted him and asked him to take us in.'

'And he did.' How could he not?

Huseyn laughed, the sound mirthless. 'No, he told me to get lost. My father had sired many bastards and didn't care. He didn't recall seducing my mother when she'd worked as a servant in his home. He'd enjoyed many women and debauching an innocent girl meant nothing to him.'

Their eyes met and Ghizlan's throat tightened. Was that how he thought of their wedding night? Was that why he'd taken such trouble to show another, gentler side of himself, because he felt guilty over taking her virginity?

'His guards were moving us away when I shouted that he was a man without honour. That I'd be better crossing the border and throwing myself on the mercy of his enemy, the Emir of Halarq.' Huseyn's mouth lifted in a bitter smile. 'That shocked the room to silence. I thought he'd order the guards to chop off my head.'

'But it worked.'

Huseyn sat back, rolling his shoulders as if releasing an old stiffness. 'After a fashion. He hated me but didn't turn us away. He set us to work in the stables. We'd bed down with the horses and spend every waking hour working. Eventually his guards accepted us. They liked us enough to teach us some fighting skills when we begged. We practised and practised until finally one of them decided we'd be more use as soldiers than stable hands.'

'And you worked your way through the ranks.'

He nodded. 'I was determined to be the best. I devoted every waking hour to perfecting my skills, learning what I could, including reading and writing late at night. I became a lieutenant, then a commander and finally my father realised I wasn't just one of his best soldiers, but the only man who could take his place when he died and keep the province safe. Believe me, that was a grudging decision.'

'You really did earn everything you got.' Ghizlan's thoughts whirled, trying to imagine what it must have taken to mould himself into the man he was now.

'Except, you would say, the Sheikhdom of Jeirut.' His stare was steady, acknowledging rather than challenging.

Ghizlan waited for the familiar throb of fury that he'd taken her father's place. But it didn't come, not with the force she expected. She chose her words carefully. 'I never disputed your right to be Sheikh.'

He was proving himself a strong, fair ruler, even if he had a lot to learn about the complex layers of responsibility involved in running a nation. None of the other contenders for the position could have done better, she realised.

'Just my right to take you as my bride.' Was it imagination or did that gaze sizzle with silvery heat?

Ghizlan looked down, pushing the half-eaten meal around her plate, her feelings in turmoil. It had been so easy to despise him as a bullying oaf. Now she was faced with a more complicated man. One potentially more dangerous to her peace of mind.

'What you did was unconscionable.'

'Even for the good of the country?'

She felt the tug of reason, of duty and royal responsibility. Hadn't she been trained from birth to act, not for herself, but for the good of the nation?

Ghizlan shot him a look. 'You can't expect *me* to applaud a forced marriage. Anyway, it's a little too late to ask the victim for absolution.'

'Victim?' He swirled his water goblet thoughtfully. 'Is that what you are? I thought you were stronger than that.' Pale eyes coupled with hers. 'I thought you revelled in your role as Sheikha. I couldn't imagine anyone else doing it with such panache or dedication.'

Power arced between them, pinioning her in her seat. It wasn't just the dazzle of those remarkable eyes, it was something else, some force that welded her to the spot.

His approval? Is that what makes you so weak? Because he compliments you on doing your duty?

'It never occurred to you that I wanted to do something else with my life? That I yearned for the day I could make my *own* life? Set my *own* goals?'

It was nonsense, of course. She'd been destined for a dynastic marriage from birth. Only in those few brief days after her father's death had she known the heady excitement of perhaps choosing for herself. Yet she resented the way Huseyn had robbed her of that.

He leaned close, every line of his big frame attentive. 'What would you have chosen to do, Ghizlan?'

The sorry truth was she had no idea. That made her angrier than ever. At herself. Had she been so subsumed by her royal role she couldn't even *dream* for herself?

Suddenly the conversation was too much. She pushed her chair back. 'I have work to do. If you'll excuse me.'

Huseyn delayed joining her in the bedroom, instead visiting the stables. There was something calming about horses. They either accepted you or they didn't. They were honest and loyal, usually more than people.

He took up a curry comb and began to groom his favourite grey stallion, the rhythm of the action soothing.

Had Ghizlan really dreamt of another life? With Idris of Zahrat or the mysterious Jean-Paul? Bitterness filled his gullet at the thought of her with someone else.

He told himself it couldn't matter now. The die was cast. She was his and he wasn't letting her go.

Yet guilt bit. What right had he to deny her dreams? His own dream had been simple. Survival. That's why he'd stood up to his father as a six-year-old in front of a court of mocking adults. Why he'd worked tirelessly in the stables then as a soldier. To survive, and keep his friend Selim alive too. That meant being strong, the strongest of all. If he was the strongest no one could touch him unless they killed him in battle and that was a price he'd always been prepared to pay.

But Ghizlan touched him in ways he'd never imagined, made him feel things he didn't have names for. She even made him wonder if his strength was enough.

More and more he learned from her. He could lead men into battle and even, it seemed, toward peace. But daily he discovered new complexities in his royal role. From advisers but as often from Ghizlan, who had an unerring instinct for politics and good governance.

If she'd been male, Jeirut would have been lucky to have her inherit the throne.

The differences between them struck him again like the kick of an untamed horse. He was rough, tough and baseborn. Ghizlan was refined and well bred. Who could blame her if she pined for Idris as a husband? She'd spoken of having her own goals. Had that been one?

Huseyn's jaw tightened. Marrying him must have been the stuff of nightmares. He tried to imagine what she'd felt—not the spoiled, selfish socialite he'd thought her, but the honourable, hard-working, cultured woman who put duty first.

His skin crawled at what his imagination conjured and he swore, long and low, till the stallion turned and nuzzled him, its dark eye sympathetic.

Huseyn huffed a mirthless laugh.

He mightn't deserve Ghizlan but she was his now. Could he earn her respect? Make her happy? She deserved that.

When he returned to their room she was absorbed in paperwork, not, as usual, in bed, but at the small desk by the window he'd never seen her use. Making a point about keeping her distance? Disappointment stirred. Surely he'd win her over eventually? At least they'd moved from confrontation to a truce.

When he emerged from the shower and found her lying in bed, absorbed in another of those romance books, he smiled. Huseyn liked sharing a bed with Ghizlan, even if it was torment, lying with her and not sating the constant, urgent desire for her.

'What's this?' Beside his chair, on top of the pile of paperwork waiting for him, were some books. He picked up the first, its cover black with gold lettering.

'I thought you might like to read something different.' He turned to see Ghizlan watching him, her expression guarded. 'There's an action bestseller and a non-fiction.'

Huseyn stared, first at her, then at the thick paperback in his hand. He shut his eyes for a second as his skin tingled all over and an unfamiliar sensation churned his belly. He opened them again, staring at but not taking in the words on the cover.

'Huseyn? Are you okay?'

He nodded, not looking up. Not wanting her to see what he now recognised as shock. 'Of course.' He paused, swallowing heavily. 'Thank you. That's...thoughtful of you.' He couldn't quite comprehend it. Did this mean she didn't regard him as the enemy, despite their earlier conversation?

'You're welcome.'

He waited a couple of seconds before looking in her direction. To his relief she'd turned back to her book and he sank into his chair, aware that his knees were loose as if he'd taken a heavy blow. Slowly he breathed out.

His reaction was ridiculous. They were only books.

But they were the first gift he'd ever received.

Growing up on the edge of starvation, he'd never expected presents. In recent years, though he didn't want for material things, everything he had he'd earned. Even the provincial sheikhdom his father had reluctantly bequeathed to him. He'd earned it with his blood and toil and every ounce of his being.

He stroked the cover of the paperback gently.

'It wouldn't hurt you to take a night off and open a book instead.'

He shafted a look across the room but Ghizlan was already turning her attention back to her own reading.

Had she seen his hesitation? His awe?

He was tempted to put the books aside and open them when he was alone but that smacked of cowardice. Slowly he opened the bestseller.

Fifteen minutes later she spoke again. 'If you're not enjoying it, try the other one.'

Huseyn jerked his head up. How had she known?

At his stare she smiled. 'You've been tsking and tutting almost from the first page.'

'I have?' He hadn't been aware of it. 'It's just a little…' he searched for an acceptable word '…far-fetched. If he'd stabbed the man in the spot he describes then he would have died within seconds and the killer would have been sprayed with blood. The victim couldn't have lingered so long, telling his secrets to the person who found him.'

'I really don't want to know how you know that.' Ghizlan shook her head. 'Why not try the other one?'

Huseyn hesitated. He didn't want her to think he didn't value her gift.

'Please? I had no idea what you'd enjoy. Maybe you'll like the other more.'

He did, he discovered. It was a history of Jeirut and the first chapter was about the prehistoric remains he hadn't known were dotted around the region. Fascinated, he lost track of time until he heard Ghizlan's light click off.

Huseyn sat back, thoughts racing. This evening had been remarkable. For the unfamiliar feelings Ghizlan evoked. Then for the way she had knocked him off balance with her precious gift and finally with the discovery he felt relaxed, intrigued and at peace after reading.

He slanted a look at the bed and found her watching him through slitted eyes. He swallowed hard. Always it was difficult resisting the physical temptation of her, but tonight it would be almost impossible. Not only was she beautiful and clever, she had grace and unexpected kindness even in the face of all he'd done.

'Thank you, Ghizlan.' His voice was gravel.

'My pleasure.' Then she rolled over, turning her back.

An hour later Huseyn was still awake. Not surprising since he habitually spent so many hours fighting his animal urges with Ghizlan in his arms. But tonight it was she who was restless even with his outstretched arm as a pillow, which she usually enjoyed. She didn't twitch or shift away, but she lay stiff as a board, her tension palpable.

'Relax,' he murmured, inhaling her sweet scent.

'I'm sorry. I'm keeping you awake. I just can't settle.' She made to roll away but he hooked his arm around her waist, holding her on her back.

'Stay.' Her ribcage rose above his arm as she drew a shuddery breath and he wondered if perhaps Ghizlan too was victim to the strange tug of feelings tonight. Or was she fretting over some distant lover?

Huseyn's jaw tensed. 'I can help you relax.' He lifted his arm, letting his hand graze the soft cotton covering her ribs.

She shook her head, that silky hair splaying over his arm. 'I don't want sex. I think it's better if I—'

'This wouldn't be sex.' He let his hand drift to her breast, plump and perfect, and heard her hiss of indrawn breath. Delicately he circled before cupping her breast, letting it fill his palm. Fire shot straight to his already overheated groin and he gritted his teeth.

He'd waited so long. Wanted her so long.

Okay, it would be sex, but not full sex, so it wasn't a lie. And he was doing this for her, he told himself.

When he gently pinched her nipple she gave a soft, choked cry and almost lifted off the bed. He slid his leg over hers, anchoring her to the bed, though interestingly she showed no sign of fighting him.

'Huseyn!' Her voice was high and throaty, and it did dreadful things to his self-control. 'This is a bad idea. I don't—'

'Let me do this for you,' he said against the cotton covering her breast, then before she could answer, he took her breast in his mouth, suckling hard.

Her moan of delight was everything he could have wished. He wanted to strip away the simple nightgown she wore so he could feast on her skin but he didn't want to scare her. Instead he concentrated on worshiping at one full, delectable breast, then the other, until she was writhing and her breath came in little pants punctuated by throaty moans that made him wonder if he might explode just at the sound of her. His erection, his whole lower body was like forged steel, fiery hot and impossibly hard.

'Huseyn!'

He shifted, looking up to meet her eyes, and desire detonated. Her hips were lifting in time with his caress and he felt her rising excitement. He arrowed his hand down, dragging up her nightdress until his fingers touched the satiny skin of her inner thighs. Instead of stiffening, they fell apart for him, allowing him access to her damp core.

Still their eyes held as he found her centre, stroked her, first softly, then hard and she arched back into the bed, her hips rising, her breathing almost a sob.

'Huseyn, I...'

'It's all right, my lovely. It's all right. Just let go.' And to his delight she did, just as he slid his finger into that slick inner passage. She contracted hard and fast again und again, and nll the time he watched her face, enthralled by the sight of her overcome by the pleasure he gave her.

A great shudder shook him as he slowly withdrew, then pulled his arm from beneath her head. She tested his honour as it had never been tested. Maybe he should go to the stables again, or check the night watch, or—

'Where are you going?' Her voice was velvet, trawling across nerve endings so tense he feared for his control.

'You'll sleep now, Ghizlan.' He pushed back the covers and levered himself up. Except one soft hand closed around his biceps.

He swung round. She was sitting up, her hair a dark cloud around her shoulders, her eyes, even in this dim light, sparkling like stars.

'You need to let me go.' He could break her hold if he

wanted to. But he didn't want to. And he feared what might happen if he touched her again. He'd given his word that he'd wait for her to ask.

'No. I won't.'

CHAPTER TWELVE

'I DON'T WANT you to go.' The words came out in a rush of relief, like air from a punctured balloon. Ghizlan's lungs swelled and filled as the tightness she'd been nursing for weeks eased.

She'd fought this, him, so long…no, fought *herself.* She'd tried to tell herself she didn't want him. That it was a betrayal to want him. But nothing worked. Self-denial had its limits and she'd reached hers.

'I want you,' she whispered, her grip tightening on that biceps that bulged beneath her touch. The admission should have felt like defeat but it tasted like victory. Like a woman acknowledging her desires unashamedly. She desired Huseyn as she had no other man.

She hadn't intended this. Especially tonight when she'd been so confused by the question of what she really wanted from life. But when he'd walked into their suite, rumpled and dusty and smelling of horse, she'd been hard put not to follow him into the bathroom and ask him to kiss her. And when he'd seen the gift she'd put out… The wonder in his eyes, the unguarded emotion that chased across his face, had touched something deep within.

Callused fingers stroked her cheek and she could have sworn sparks ignited from his touch. She cupped her hand to his, pressing it against her face. His hand was big and hard, like Huseyn. But it could be incredibly gentle too. She understood that now.

His gaze searched hers, questioning. She tried to smile but her facial muscles were too tight. Instead she lay down, clasping his hand to her face. 'I want you, Huseyn.'

His features grew taut and his breathing roughened. She

planted her other hand square on that massive chest, shaping the broad band of muscle, skimming the light covering of hair that so fascinated her. Strange how his size no longer threatened her.

To her delight he snatched a sharp breath and beneath her palm his heartbeat pounded.

'You're sure?' His voice was unrecognisable and Ghizlan revelled in the discovery of her power. It made her feel vibrant and beautiful. Not like a woman married for her pedigree but like one he couldn't resist.

Before she had time to think she grabbed the hem of her nightgown and, with a wiggle of hips to free it, reefed it over her head.

Cool air caressed her bare skin as he held still, watching. He sat like that so long her hands crept up to cover her breasts. Instantly his fingers closed on her wrists, gently pulling her arms wide, leaving her completely bare to his gaze. Her breasts rose with each quickened breath and between her legs heat flared anew. She felt self-conscious and at the same time triumphant.

With a guttural groan he lowered himself, his chest against hers so exquisitely arousing that she couldn't keep still. Until his mouth closed on hers and all else faded. His lips were almost reverential as they stroked hers. Their breaths mingled and it was the sweetest, most profoundly moving experience.

His tongue stroked into her mouth and she sighed her delight. Need shuddered through her and she hugged him tight, curving her body into his. The fine cotton of his pants might as well not have been there as she rubbed against that powerful erection, driven by a need she could no longer resist.

With a groan he broke their kiss and slid down her body to capture her breast in his mouth. It was delicious, addictive but not what she wanted.

'Please, Huseyn. I want you.'

In answer he moved again, but lower, hooking her knees up so they splayed either side of his head. Ghizlan blinked, trying to tell herself she wasn't shocked at the sight of his dark head there, or the heat of his breath in that most intimate of places.

Then his head dipped and thought stopped. He'd given her an orgasm before but nothing had prepared her for the carnal power of this caress. She shivered with each touch, each decadent lick, and couldn't take her eyes off him. Abruptly that quake of sensation erupted, starting as tiny ripples and building and building until it consumed her and she flung her head back, crying out his name, clutching at his head with fingers knotted in ecstasy.

Later Ghizlan felt limp, wrecked and elated, her body racked by aftershocks as he moved up the bed, his eyes holding hers. Despite the thrills still coursing through her, the hectic pulse at her core, she'd never wanted anything as much as she wanted this man.

He leaned over her, propped on strong arms so as not to crush her, his breath feathering her. She wanted him closer.

'Better?' She felt the word against her collarbone as he kissed her there. It was the only place they touched, apart from her feet at his ankles, and it wasn't enough.

'It was wonderful,' she gasped. 'But it wasn't what I wanted.' She lifted her hands, curling them around his shoulders and tugging. 'It's you I want. All of you.'

Sated as she was, accepting she couldn't possibly climax again, she wanted that unfamiliar, mind-boggling connection she'd experienced only once.

'Ah, Ghizlan.' There was need in that gravelly whisper and it urged her to take what she wanted. Her hands went to the drawstring of his loose trousers, tugging it undone, sliding the fabric down his hips so he lay hot and rigid against her.

How could that feel like heaven when he'd taken her there twice already? He moved, positioning himself at her core yet still holding back, his face furrowed in concentration, or was that restraint? Did he fear hurting her again?

Boldly she slid her hands round his hips and over his taut, rounded buttocks. They flexed at her touch and her fingers tightened as tentatively she lifted her pelvis.

Ghizlan sighed as he slid forward, that incredible heat filling her slowly, so slowly it was delicious torment. She flexed her fingers and angled her hips higher and saw Huseyn squeeze his eyes shut as he sank deeper.

'Are you all right?'

His mouth twisted up at one corner. 'I should be asking you that.'

Ghizlan stilled, cataloguing the amazing sensation of them together. 'Wonderful, except I want more.'

The words were barely out when he drove in, smoothly but inexorably right to the centre of her and she forgot how to speak.

Gleaming eyes met hers. 'Okay?'

She nodded, breath caught as he moved away, infinitely slowly, till she thought he'd withdraw completely and dug her fingers hard into his flesh. She wrapped one leg up over his, trying to keep him where he was.

He smiled then, but not *at* her. She sensed that for the first time they were totally attuned. That was borne out when he sank into her again and her moan of delight mingled with his deep, guttural groan.

'What should I do?' she whispered when she found her voice.

'Nothing!' She caught the gleam of his teeth as he grimaced. 'Or I won't be able to wait for you to come.'

Huseyn's mouth closed on hers, his tongue delving deep as he withdrew then thrust again, faster this time, a little harder, creating a fizz of excitement she'd thought impossible.

His rhythm was regular yet with a gradually increasing tempo that pushed her closer and closer to that unseen edge. His bulk surrounding her, his salty male scent, his mouth on hers, the bunch and release of muscles beneath her hands, were a potent combination that accelerated pleasure. Ghizlan held tight, kissing him back, giving herself to the rhythm that had taken over her body until on one solid thrust he drove her to a pinnacle unlike any she'd experienced. Bliss was there, waves of tight, bright pleasure, and Huseyn was there too, strong, hard and vital, right at the heart of her.

Ghizlan shattered with a cry and it was as if Huseyn had waited for a signal. The long, rhythmic thrusts became a quick, hungry bucking that drove him hard into her, amazingly prolonging her climax.

Then with a hoarse shout Huseyn arched his neck back, his face fierce yet vulnerable as he lost control and spilled himself inside her.

It must be the clouds of ecstasy, the rush of endorphins filling her, but at that moment Ghizlan felt a profound oneness with him. She lifted her arms, pulling him down until his head sank into the curve of her shoulder, his panting breath against her skin. She never wanted this to end.

Huseyn woke to the sun high in the sky and a sense of well-being so intense he realised he was smiling. He'd never known anything like it.

Because of the woman snuggled in his hold, her hair a silken blanket across his chest. Beautiful, passionate, generous Ghizlan. Despite her exhaustion she'd been eager for him when he'd caressed her awake twice more in the night. She'd given herself unstintingly and each time it had been difficult to ensure her satisfaction before his because his hunger for her grew with each embrace instead of lessening. Only the fact she was still new to sex had held him back from more. He'd held her in his arms for hours, amazed at how much he enjoyed cuddling her, until he'd finally succumbed to sleep at dawn.

It was long past time he was up and about his duties but for the first time in his life Huseyn lay abed. Duty could wait. The sheikhdom wouldn't crumble if he was late today.

He lay there, rough hands on tender flesh, and knew he was the luckiest man alive. It wasn't just the sex. It was Ghizlan. His confounding, obstinate, talented, clever, smart-mouthed, kind wife. Being with her made him feel… better. Not that he'd ever been aware of a lack in his life. All he knew was that now he had her nothing would make him relinquish her. He might have won her through force and blackmail but he'd bind her to him with whatever ties he could.

There wasn't a flicker of doubt, no voice warning about being in thrall to a woman. Because even a man who'd lived his whole life in a rough, brutal man's world, who'd never wanted or expected to want a woman for anything more than sexual release, knew when he held treasure.

He'd set out to tame her, dominate her. But what he really wanted was to win her. To earn her trust and her—

A scratching sound on the sitting room door caught his attention. 'My lady?' It was Ghizlan's maid.

Carefully extricating himself, he slid out of bed, pulled on his discarded pants and strode to the door, opening it a crack.

'Your Highness.' The maid curtseyed, dropping her gaze. 'I'm sorry to intrude. But my lady asked me to bring any package from France to her immediately. She's been waiting for it.'

'That's fine.' He held out his hand. 'I'll give it to her. And you can bring breakfast in half an hour.'

He closed the door, reading the sender's details. Not her sister. His curiosity rose.

'Who was it?' Ghizlan's voice was soft and incredibly seductive with its just awake roughness.

'A package for you, from France.'

'France?' She sat up, excitement in her voice. Huseyn

stood, drinking in the bounty of her beautiful body, until she caught his stare and dragged the sheet up over her breasts. Faint colour tinged her cheeks and throat and he found himself smiling again.

He put the small package in her hands and watched her face light as she ripped it open and worked her way through protective layers. She glowed with excitement and the sight was as enthralling as watching her as she came beneath him, her body slick and welcoming.

'Oh, Jean-Paul!' Her breathy voice cut through Huseyn's thoughts.

'Jean-Paul?'

She didn't answer. Her eyes were closed as she held a small vial to her nose. Her smile was beautiful and infuriating. He didn't want other men making her smile that way.

Huseyn sat down on the bed, hands planted on either side of her hips, forcing her attention back to him.

'Smell this.' She lifted the tiny bottle to his nose and he inhaled, watching the anticipation in her eyes. He smelled sweetness and warmth, something lush and seductive, like the glow in Ghizlan's eyes.

'Roses?'

She nodded. 'And more. It's not overpowering, is it? It's got a delicacy, a freshness that sets it apart.' She bowed her head over the bottle again, her brow pleating in concentration.

'Ghizlan?'

'Hmm?'

'What is it and who's Jean-Paul?' Huseyn was pleased with his even tone. There was no hint of jealousy, though he'd spent too much time wondering about his wife's relationship with both the Frenchman and Idris of Zahrat. He'd never been Ghizlan's choice and the knowledge ate at him, making him wonder if she could ever be truly happy with someone like him. Someone who came from nothing and had fought for everything he had.

'It's a perfume Jean-Paul has developed for me.' She read a note in her hand. There's rose and almond, base notes of vanilla and…ah, that explains the warmth…tonka bean. And—'

'Jean-Paul is a friend?'

What did she read in his expression? Her own changed as she watched him. 'He's a famous "nose". He designs perfumes.'

'And he's been here to Jeirut to design a perfume for your new enterprise?'

She shook her head, ebony hair slipping over her bare shoulders. 'He works from his home in France and I've never met him. We've corresponded.'

'Ah.' Huseyn relaxed and reached for a lock of hair that had slipped towards her cleavage. Her flesh was warm beneath his touch. 'You were so excited I wondered…'

'What? If he was a lover?' Her laughter faded as their eyes met and Huseyn recognised that familiar throb in the air between them. Her eyes widened. 'You *know* I never had a lover before you.'

Soft pink tinged her cheeks and satisfaction slammed into him. Yes, he was primitively possessive where Ghizlan was concerned. Huseyn lifted his shoulders. He refused to apologise.

'The man's in his seventies!'

His hand slid up to cup the fine line of her jaw. 'A man would have to be blind not to want you.'

Her flush turned fiery but the glint of awareness in those dark eyes told him she was thrilled.

'Careful! The perfume! Don't spill it. I need to take it to the factory. We need to name it and discuss production—'

'Ghizlan,' he said against her throat and felt her shiver. 'Call it Ghizlan. It's your scent. Rich and voluptuous but subtle too.'

She pulled back, her eyes round. 'Are you *sweet-talking* me, Huseyn?'

'I've never sweet-talked a woman in my life. I don't do flattery, *my lady*.' He lifted the vial from her hand and placed it carefully on the bedside table. 'I simply call it as it is. Now, why don't you lie there while I wish you good morning properly?'

'You summoned me, my lord?' Ghizlan crossed the echoing throne room where Huseyn had been holding an audience prior to tonight's grand reception.

He turned around, snaring her breath. Even now, after months of intimacy, he did that to her. Even fully clothed. Her gaze skated over his beautifully tailored dinner jacket and down those powerful legs. Something clenched deep inside and she yanked her gaze up. Now wasn't the time. They had a reception in fifteen minutes.

His lazy gaze had turned silver and she knew Huseyn read her expression. She didn't mind one bit.

How times had changed.

'Hardly summoned, *my lady*.' His voice dropped to the low burr that always felt like the slow glide of his hand on bare flesh. It was a lover's voice and she revelled in it. 'I merely asked Azim if he knew where you were.'

He paused, surveying her from head to toe. A smile tilted the corner of his mouth, creating that dimple in one cheek. 'May I say how delectable you look tonight?' He took her hand and turned it over, kissing her palm, then trailing his tongue up to her wrist.

'Huseyn!' It was a gasp of pleasure and shock as she glanced at the closed door. Her nipples budded against her silk evening gown and her skin prickled all over.

'No one will enter without permission.' He drew her closer.

'Because you've warned them not to?' Ghizlan had been surprised and delighted by some of the places they'd made love. Including the stables at midnight after a starlight ride and in their private garden where the setting sun bronzed Huseyn's strong features in the dying light.

'Because no one would interrupt the Sheikh without invitation.' His hands curved round her waist, as always making her feel delicate in his hold.

Ghizlan pressed her hands on his chest, so hard and warm. 'My lipstick,' she murmured as he bent his head. With a sigh he kissed her throat instead, bestowing tiny caresses till she was bowed back in his arms and wished they were anywhere but here, with a crowd waiting for them.

'I want to sweep you off to bed,' he growled, kissing his way past her pearl and tourmaline necklace and heading for her décolletage.

'I want that as well.'

His hands firmed on her waist and he lifted his head, a gleam in his eyes. Ghizlan knew that look.

'No, we can't! We're entertaining the ambassadors of Zahrat and Halarq as part of the peace discussions, remember?'

Huseyn sighed and stepped back. Instantly Ghizlan was bereft. 'It's as well I have you to remind me of my duty.'

She shook her head. That was one thing she'd learned about Huseyn since those early days when she'd thought him brutish and uncivilised. He might be bold and decisive but he took duty seriously. Jeirut couldn't have asked for a better sheikh, albeit one who sometimes struggled to stifle impatience in the face of courtly protocol.

'I have something for you.' He reached behind him and picked up a small, wooden box, beautifully carved.

'It's gorgeous.' She turned the octagonal piece in her hands, marvelling at the delicacy of the work. Each side featured a different flower. As she turned it she recognised each was one being grown locally to supply the perfumery. She traced the curving petals of a perfect rose. Delight filled her at his thoughtfulness. He'd had this made especially. 'Thank you, Huseyn. I'll treasure it. I've never seen work like this before.'

She reached out a hand and his closed around it.

Something beat between them. Something far more than desire. Something solid and comforting and exciting too.

'My province of Jumeah was once known for its craftsmanship, but decades of misrule and threats from across the border all but destroyed our economy. It's only in the last couple of years that there's been a revival.'

Thanks to Huseyn. Not that he'd told her. She'd made it her business to learn about the province that had been a black hole as far as her father was concerned. She'd discovered Huseyn's support was a driving force in turning around the fortunes of his people. She admired him for that.

'I'd like to take you there.' His voice held an unfamiliar gruff note. 'To show you its natural beauty and how the people are starting anew.'

'I'd like that.' She meant it. She wanted to see the place Huseyn had grown up. The place that had moulded him.

'There's more.' His hand squeezed hers then dropped away. 'Open it.'

She lifted the lid and her breath caught. 'It's stunning.' Nestled in a bed of scarlet silk rested the most beautiful piece of glasswork she'd ever seen. 'Also from Jumeah?'

She looked up to read the pride and satisfaction he didn't bother to hide. 'Another ancient art that had all but died. There are only a few old craftsmen left but we've initiated a scheme for them to train the young.'

'If they can create work like this it will be a huge success.' Carefully she lifted the delicate, unusual piece from its bed and held it to the light. It was a small bottle, its body a swirl of colour from pale gold to apricot, peach and amber, with a hint of scarlet threading through, bringing it to life. Its tall, twisted stopper was of intertwined gold and scarlet.

'Your sister designed it.'

'Mina?' Ghizlan's eyes widened. She'd had no idea Huseyn had been in contact with her.

'She did a wonderful job, don't you think?'

'Marvellous.' Ghizlan cradled the precious piece. 'But I don't understand.'

'Since the flagship scent for your perfumery will be called Ghizlan—'

'That's what *you* want.' She still wasn't sure about naming the scent after herself.

He shook his head. 'Your team agrees wholeheartedly. I heard about the vote.' Ghizlan frowned, wondering how he knew. 'Having you as the face of the scent as well as the business will give it a cachet no other perfume has.'

'Flatterer.'

His mouth kicked up at the corner and he trailed the back of one finger down her cheek, the look in his eyes turning her insides to mush.

'I never flatter. It's the truth.' His gaze held hers so long and with such intensity she felt emotions well far too close to the surface. Tender new feelings she strove not to name, but which grew stronger every day.

Huseyn cleared his throat. 'I told Mina the name of the perfume and asked her to design a bottle for it. Something distinctive.' He smiled. 'Your little sister has genuine talent. See how she took inspiration from your name?' His long finger traced the unusual shape of the glass in her hand. 'Knowing you wanted to market this internationally she used the English language letter Z as her model.'

Ghizlan followed his gesture, recognising the letter shape, sinuous and distinctive in Mina's design. 'It's unlike anything I've ever seen. It's utterly beautiful.'

'It works then?' To her surprise he sounded diffident, almost tentative.

She looked up, meeting an unreadable stare. 'How could it not? Any woman would love to own something as precious as this. If it can be replicated?'

He nodded. 'It can. That was part of the brief.'

'Oh, Huseyn.' Suddenly her hands were trembling and he scooped the delicate piece up and into its box, then placed it on a nearby table.

'Ghizlan? What's wrong? I thought you liked it?'

She blinked, telling herself she was overreacting. 'I love it. I never expected anything like this. That you would take the time to plan something so thoughtful...'

'Because I'm a barbarian brute?' He took her hands in his, his hold firm yet gentle.

She shook her head. She'd discovered he was anything but. She'd learned, as they'd discussed politics, made love, and spent time together, that Huseyn was a complex man of integrity and surprising tenderness despite his authoritative streak. He'd even cajoled her back into the saddle, taking her for rides in the countryside. To her surprise she'd found joy in their marriage and a sense of accomplishment as he encouraged her to pursue her interests as her father never had.

'Because no one has ever given me anything so perfect. So thoughtful. I can't tell you...'

'You don't need to. I know. I felt the same way about those books you gave me.'

Ghizlan's eyes rounded. 'That wasn't at all the same. That was easy—'

He drew her closer, the light in his eyes beacon-bright. 'It was the first gift I've ever received,' he said with a stark simplicity that silenced her. 'It meant everything. It made me want to give you something that meant almost as much.' He leaned in, his breath warm on her face. 'And now I've discovered how good it feels to give, I think I'm addicted. If you could only see how beautiful you look right now.'

Ghizlan's eyes grew misty and her throat closed as happiness and awe filled her. The look in those silvery-blue eyes made her feel...

'Huseyn! My lipstick! We've got guests waiting—'

'To hell with your lipstick. And the guests.' And he proceeded to demonstrate how much she enjoyed that authoritative, downright bossy streak in him.

CHAPTER THIRTEEN

GHIZLAN'S STEP WAS light as she approached the stables. After a day apart, each working on their own projects, she and Huseyn were going riding together. She was early, planning to take him to a secluded grove outside the city, a place she hadn't visited for years. When she'd stopped riding she'd never found time to go back to that tiny valley of green in the stark hills. It had always seemed magical with its drifts of wild purple irises and pink cyclamen. Now she wanted to share it with Huseyn.

Once she'd have baulked at sharing such a special place with him. But her feelings had changed. Sometimes it scared her, how much they'd changed and how big a part he played in her life, not through force but because she wanted him there.

That was what made the difference. No force. Every step they took to a deeper, more meaningful relationship was mutual, her decision as much as his. Because she wanted him. Not just sexually.

Happiness filled her, a lightness she'd never known before. Because of Huseyn.

The only dark cloud, and it was minor, was his steadfast refusal to accept Sheikh Idris's invitation, conveyed through his ambassador, for them to visit Zahrat. Huseyn declared it too soon, because peace talks with Halarq hadn't concluded so he couldn't leave the country. Whereas Ghizlan wanted to see her friend Arden, and, she recognised with a smile, to show off her husband.

She reached the stables. Selim was there and greeted her, moving aside so she could see.

She wished she couldn't. For in the centre of the cobbled yard was a scene that took her breath away—Huseyn in riding clothes, looking calm and ridiculously at ease as a dark stallion danced and reared around him.

Huseyn approached with a halter and the horse's lethal hooves flashed. Ghizlan gasped, her hand to her throat as the scene played out—the horse wild and dangerous with its sudden lunges, the man confident and patient.

How long it took, Ghizlan didn't know, but with what looked like consummate ease, Huseyn finally slid the halter on the horse then vaulted onto its back, all the time whispering words she couldn't catch.

'It's like magic,' she breathed as her racing heart began to ease into a normal rhythm. 'I don't know how he does it.'

Selim laughed. 'You're right, he has the gift. But it's not magic. He assesses the horse carefully, a risk assessment, if you like, learning its fears and reactions. Huseyn has always been clever like that, patient enough to take time to see what others don't. And he does care about them, he's always had a soft spot for horses, but, believe me, every step in the process is calculated.'

Ghizlan's gaze narrowed on the powerful man astride the stallion that pranced, not quite docile, beneath him.

Selim spoke again and the words were like tiny shards of ice pricking her suddenly cool flesh. 'Huseyn doesn't give up when he's presented with a challenge. He sets about winning a horse's trust, gentles it until it accepts him, gets used to his presence, even welcomes him. The beauty of it is that when he's finished the animal thinks it's pleasing itself but he's actually taught it to want what he wants, responding to his subtle cues. Make no mistake, he's always the master. But the animal welcomes him.'

Just then the horse reared its head, whinnying and rolling its eyes. It lifted off the ground in a jump designed to unseat its rider and Ghizlan caught the flash of excitement on Huseyn's face as he rode it until it stopped. Its ears flicked back as he leaned forward, whispering soothing words.

So like the whispered praise he murmured in her ear when she accepted him into her body, opened her arms to him, offered herself for his pleasure whenever and wherever he wanted.

A knot of raw emotion, hot and horrible and heavy as the palace's giant foundation stones, pressed down on her chest. It cramped her lungs, pushed her heart to a slow, ominous beat of realisation and betrayal.

Just so had Huseyn made her accustomed to his presence, insisting on sharing a bed, tempting her with that superb body. Had he seen her as a challenge? Of course he had. He'd bragged about all the willing women he'd bedded. Only she had stood up to him. How that must have pricked his pride.

Was that why he'd taken the time to *gentle* her, *tame* her, persuade her that she desired only what he wanted? The single time since he'd seduced her that she'd argued for something *she* wanted—to visit Zahrat—he'd dismissed the idea so quickly she'd wondered at his vehemence.

Because he wants everything his way. What you want doesn't matter unless it fits his plans. He sugarcoats his commands and you eat out of his hand like one of his damned horses.

Ghizlan shrivelled inside, torn between stark horror at the revelation and the wounded part of her that refused to believe it.

But memories flicked through her brain in quick succession, reminding her how patiently he'd searched out her weaknesses and secret desires, then proceeded to give her what she hadn't even known she'd wanted. Tenderness, caring. Acceptance.

He'd given more than she'd ever had from anyone in her life, including her distant father who'd only approved of her when her hard work and dedication had coincided with his own goals. Had it all been a sham?

'My lady? Are you well?'

She blinked and realised she'd slumped against a pillar, her hand splayed on the gritty surface for support.

'I'm...'

Gutted?

Finally seeing my husband for what he is?

And seeing myself, the stupid virgin who believed herself strong but was so easily seduced into compliance.

'I'm fine.' She stiffened her backbone and turned, donning a smile that hurt. 'But I've just remembered something I need to do.'

She turned and marched away, head high, heart bleeding. Only when she was out of sight did she give in to the pain and use the handrail to drag herself up the stairs. It felt as if every bone in her body was bruised.

But the physical pain was nothing to the raw, throbbing ache in her heart.

Slowly she climbed from floor to floor and with each step part of her cried, *It's not true. It's not true.*

And every time another memory surfaced, of Huseyn slowly, carefully worming his way into her world, her affections, giving her praise and tenderness when she hadn't even realised she was needy.

Why had he bothered? It couldn't just be the sex. A man as virile as Huseyn could get that wherever he wanted.

Because she'd thrown down the gauntlet and he'd made it clear he refused to be bested by some 'pampered waste of space'? At the time the words had infuriated rather than hurt. Now she wondered if that was really how he saw her. Did he actually care about the projects she was passionate about, like the perfumery? Or did he encourage her in order to keep her out of his hair while he pursued his own agenda?

Ghizlan frowned. No, that wasn't right. He discussed his

plans with her, got her to help him. Yeah, got her to help him smooth the diplomatic wrinkles. He trotted her out at high powered functions, or when he deemed a woman's charm was useful. She was his ace up the sleeve—born royal, bred to be a hostess, charming and accomplished and useful at negotiating the tangled web of regional politics.

He'd been forced to marry her to win the sheikhdom and he'd decided he might as well get his money's worth.

Ghizlan stopped at the top of the steps to the royal bedrooms and sagged against the wall.

She tried to summon a counterargument. To convince herself she was wrong, but it made too much sense. Everything slotted into place with sickening certainty. Huseyn had deliberately, coldly, seduced her, physically and emotionally. He had her exactly where he wanted her.

Knowing that, she had to break free from him.

A bitter laugh escaped and she shivered at the high, out-of-control sound. She didn't *want* to break free. She enjoyed her gilded cage too much. She tried to tell herself that once she made the break she could follow her own dream for the future, rather than be part of his schemes.

But the dreadful irony was that she didn't *have* a dream for the future. She was living the dream. These last months had been the happiest of her life. The admission scooped her stomach empty.

Despite years trapped in a life driven by duty, she loved what she was doing, now she had the latitude to do it her way and pursue her own interests. There was nothing she wanted more than to see those projects to maturity, to serve her country in ways that best used her skills, and to share her life with Huseyn.

He'd been everything she'd never dared hope for—tender, passionate, challenging, even fun now he'd learned to relax and show the man behind the imposing façade.

Or was that a carefully constructed illusion?

Ghizlan drew an aching breath, facing the ominous truth

that she wanted that man to be real as she'd never wanted anything in her life. Because she'd given not just her body and her trust to him. She'd given her heart too.

With that realisation came pain so deep it was as if her insides were being ripped asunder.

Her breathing ragged, she set her jaw and forced herself to put one foot in front of the other. Soon she'd reach the sanctuary of her apartments.

Their apartments! She no longer even had the privacy of a place to hide and lick her wounds.

Ghizlan's step faltered but she pushed on. One thing at a time. She'd have to find a new haven and a new dream. One that didn't come at the price of her self-respect.

Huseyn's booted feet took the stairs three at a time, impatience riding him. And concern. It had only been after he'd finished working with the new stallion that Selim mentioned Ghizlan had been at the stables early for their ride. And that she'd suddenly looked green around the gills and hurried off.

Ghizlan was never ill. Even when suffering cramps on the first day of her period, she never missed an appointment. But she didn't have her period. This morning she'd straddled him, riding him hard and fast until they'd both collapsed in ecstasy. The memory of her delectable breasts jiggling against his chest, the blaze of delight in her eyes as she climaxed made him tighten anew. It was a position she enjoyed and he was happy to relinquish control of their loving when it gave him the opportunity to watch that shock of rapture overtake her as she milked his body dry.

The thought of her ill sent a niggle of anxiety through his gut.

The other alternative, that she had morning sickness, made him anxious too and triumphant at the same time. Pregnancy wouldn't be surprising, given how insatiable they were for each other. In the beginning he'd wondered if his formidable sex drive would be too much for Ghizlan, especially as it seemed to know no limits when his wife was around. But she was an eager partner. So eager.

The idea of her carrying his child struck at something visceral. An image of Ghizlan blooming with his child made him simultaneously proud, horny and worried as hell.

He pushed open the door to their sitting room and strode to the bedroom, telling himself he was jumping the gun. There was nothing—

An open suitcase lay on the bed.

'Yes, please. That dress and the blue as well. No, not the rest. That's plenty.' Ghizlan's voice came from the walk-in wardrobe.

'Ghizlan?' His voice sounded overloud in the empty bedroom and he found his gaze fixed on the suitcase, already containing a neat stack of clothes.

There was silence for a moment, then she emerged carrying an armful of clothes. She looked pale, too pale. There was a tightness around her lips and a tiny furrow between her brows that spoke of pain. She lay the clothes on the bed as carefully as if they were made of glass, then straightened, her eyes fixed warily on him.

Something shifted in his belly. That stare. He hadn't seen that expression in months. Not since she'd viewed him as the devil incarnate for capturing the palace, and her.

Her maid appeared, bearing dresses on hangers, her gaze darting from her mistress to him.

'Leave us.' He kept his voice steady but still it emerged with a raw, dangerous edge.

Ghizlan's chin lifted. 'We're not finished.'

Oh, they were. They had no trip planned except a visit to his home province of Jumeah next week. And his wife was going nowhere without him.

'Do you really want to have this conversation in front of your maid?'

For an instant longer Ghizlan stood, rigid and unblinking, then she nodded to the maid who placed her burden on the bed and scurried away. Huseyn waited until the outer door shut before closing the space between himself and Ghizlan.

This close he saw a shiver rip through her, and her eyes widen in an expression of distaste.

Huseyn slammed to a stop, a sick feeling in his gullet. 'What the hell is going on?' He hadn't intended the words. Even when he'd seen the suitcase he'd intended to be calm. But seeing his wife look at him like something repellent she'd discovered under a desert rock ate at his good intentions like acid.

She lifted her shoulders in a tight shrug. 'Packing. Even though you can't visit Zahrat, there's nothing stopping me accepting Idris's invitation.'

A red haze misted Huseyn's vision. His fingers curled into tight fists and deliberately straightened them.

'No. You don't leave without me.' It was non-negotiable.

'I *beg* your pardon?' Hauteur turned her features ice cold, a blue-blooded princess outraged by the presence of a rough brute who was more at home in the stables than the royal apartments. 'You don't order me, Huseyn. We agreed I could travel when things had settled.'

She stuck her fists on her hips, destroying the ice princess image and morphing into the passionate, hot-blooded virago who'd driven him to distraction. He was torn between fury and lust. And something else. Something perilously close to fear. After all that they'd shared, she was ready to spurn him?

'So desperate to see him, then?' Bile rose, filling the back of his mouth.

Ghizlan turned and ostentatiously splayed out the dresses that had been dumped on the bed. 'Not so much him, but his wife Arden. She's a friend of mine. And after Zahrat I thought I'd head to Paris to see—'

'The Sheikha is a friend of yours?' Huseyn almost

laughed at how he'd missed the most obvious explanation. 'It's not Idris you've been calling all this time. *She's* your mysterious friend?' He'd tortured himself imagining she had a relationship, even if not a physical one, with Idris. All this time, even when his relationship with Ghizlan had grown so easy, it had been there—a secret shadow marring his contentment, mocking their hard-won closeness.

Ghizlan wheeled, eyes round and mouth open. Then she snapped her teeth shut with an audible click. 'How do you know who I've been calling? Have you been spying on me?' Her stare was as lethal as on the day they'd met.

He stepped closer. 'No. I simply had numbers dialled from the palace monitored in the weeks after I arrived, as a precaution. I didn't know if your staff would respect me as their new Sheikh or try to undermine me while I was away negotiating a peace deal. The report on my return showed calls from your private extension to the palace in Zahrat.'

'And you kept monitoring?' Her gaze kindled.

He nodded, refusing to apologise. Sheer, glorious relief swamped him at the knowledge she wasn't pining for another man. He'd found it hard to believe, especially when they'd grown so close. But the doubt had always been there, taunting him, reminding him he was bastard-born, rough and battle-scarred, the polar opposite of Ghizlan, so refined, elegant and well educated. Would it have been so surprising if his cultured, clever wife had been attracted to a man who'd grown up with the same advantages she had?

'Why?' Curiosity warred with anger in her dark gaze. 'Why not ask me about it? You've never hesitated to confront me before. Why sneak behind my back? Or is that more your style?'

Huseyn frowned. Where had that come from? 'I hoped you'd trust me enough to tell me about it yourself one day.'

Had he? Or had he been scared that if he brought it into the open, made her admit her unrequited feelings for another man, it would be the end of the relationship *he'd* built with Ghizlan?

Huseyn thrust his shoulders back, shaking off the notion. This relationship wasn't ending. He wouldn't allow it.

'Trust you?' Her voice rose to a high, unfamiliar note that worried him. Even at her angriest Ghizlan had never sounded so close to the edge.

He moved nearer and her rapid breathing feathered the V of skin where the neck of his shirt hung open, making his flesh tighten. Never had a woman affected him so easily.

'You thought I was betraying my country by passing sensitive information to another ruler?' Her mouth turned down in an angry pout that notched his belly tight.

'Of course not! You care too much for Jeirut to betray it.'

She stared up at him, her eyes narrowing. 'So you thought it was personal? How many times do I need to tell you there's nothing between me and Idris? It was a dynastic match. The man is head over heels in love with his wife!' She paused, catching her breath. 'And if I had been in love with him, I'd never have told you. Why should I? You and I are nothing but a…a convenient coupling.'

The depth of her scorn seared him, past pride and reason to something far more vital. Emotion pulsed hard, so vehement every muscle contracted as if in readiness for battle.

How could she deny what they had? How dared she?

'Convenient?' His voice was a bass growl, ominous as the thunder preceding the cataclysmic winter storms that occasionally struck the Jeiruti mountains. Storms that tumbled boulders and brought a torrent of white water that could sweep away whole villages in normally dry gullies.

Instinctively Ghizlan backed up a step but huge hands grabbed her upper arms, hauling her so hard against him the air was knocked from her chest.

'You call this *convenient*?' He shook his head, his face

drawn hard and stark as if from pain. 'You're even more innocent than I imagined.'

Then his mouth was on hers, prising her lips apart so he could plunge his tongue deep into her mouth. Her head rocked back with the force of his possession and she clawed at his shoulders, trying to inflict pain and save herself from toppling.

But even as she did, an answering, stormy heat erupted inside her. Ghizlan's tongue met his, lashing and demanding. She sucked him further into her mouth, simultaneously delighting and punishing. Together they felt so good. Even now, when fury and hurt boiled within.

Her body thrummed as electricity struck her breasts, her pelvis, and erogenous zones she hadn't known about.

Then Huseyn's mouth gentled, his hands caressing, as he turned the kiss into something lush and languorous and mind-numbingly tender and Ghizlan found herself powerless to do anything but give him what he wanted. What *she* wanted. A husky sound of masculine pleasure filled her ears and her body relaxed into his embrace. His rock-hard arms gathered her in and his erection pressed, proud and hot against her. She loosened her stance so he could—

No! It was a silent scream against his mouth as she pushed away with all her might.

Hands to his chest, she levered herself away. Knowing she only managed it because he let her made the pain singing in her veins even harder to bear.

'I don't want this.' Even to herself it sounded half-hearted. Because what truly bound her to him wasn't his physical strength but her weakness. The knowledge cut her off at the knees, making her sway in his embrace.

Hot silvery eyes met hers and that silly trembling began along her spine. Surely, if she worked at it long enough, she'd develop an immunity? It was her only hope.

'I thought we'd passed the stage of pretence.' He skimmed one large hand down her side, his thumb brushing in a wide arc below her breast, making her shudder in anticipation of a more intimate touch.

That demonstration of her weakness fuelled both her despair and her determination.

'Let me go, Huseyn.' Her voice was flat.

'Not until you explain.' She said nothing, just stood, shivering in his hold, until he released her, an oath ripping from his mouth. 'Don't look at me like that!'

Ghizlan staggered back to lean against the window alcove, dragging unsteady breaths into lungs that were on fire.

'Are you going to explain?'

'There's nothing to explain. I want to visit Arden in Zahrat and then my sister in—'

'Paris. Yes, I know.' He folded his arms over his massive chest and she was surprised to see how high it rose, as if he found it difficult to breathe too. 'Are you going to tell me what's wrong? Why you're trying to run from me?'

Ghizlan regarded the man who'd become the centre of her world, the reason for her happiness, and considered lying to save face. It hurt that much.

'I discovered what you did.' Emotion throbbed in her voice and she had to pause and swallow. 'I was watching you with that stallion and Selim told me how you worked to tame each one, learning their fears and their foibles, training them to accept you, even *want* your presence. Teaching them to obey your commands, your desires, until they became your creatures…' Her words grew husky and thick and the backs of her eyes prickled but she stared dry-eyed into that silvery-blue stare.

'You enjoy the challenge, don't you? You get your kicks that way, I saw it in your eyes. It's a pity I didn't realise it before.'

'Realise what, exactly?' Not by a flicker did he show a hint of remorse.

Ghizlan stood tall, her chin tilted with all the hauteur

not of a princess but of a woman determined to conquer weakness.

'That you did the same to me. That you saw me as a challenge. You did, didn't you?' There it was, that gleam in his steady stare, betraying him. She'd hit the nail on the head.

'You set about seducing me, calming me, getting me to trust you, to…to *care* for you, like one of your damned horses. You even made me believe—' She snapped her teeth shut before she could reveal how he'd lulled her into thinking he really cared for her.

'Ghizlan…' He reached for her and she put out her arm.

'Don't! Don't touch me.' Her chest was too tight, her throat closing over the words, and raw, tearing pain ripped through her insides. 'You set out to seduce me into caring for you.'

'And if I did?' His jaw tightened. 'If I took the time to try to understand you and give you want you wanted? Is that so bad?' His crossed arms bulged as his muscles bunched and a pulse flicked hard in his jaw. 'What was wrong with respecting your needs and giving you time to make up your mind about me? About trusting you'd come to me eventually?' He shook his head. 'The passion between us was always there, Ghizlan. You can't deny it.'

His expression grew, if anything, harder, his jaw like honed flint. 'Do you think I'd have done that for any other woman?'

Ghizlan stared. 'What are you saying?'

'I told you I don't do flattery. I don't live my life to accommodate any woman.' He lifted one hand, raking his scalp, ruffling his dark hair. 'But that changed with you. *I* changed with you.'

Something danced in his eyes. Something that made her belly tremble and her knees loosen. But she refused to be seduced so easily again.

'You had to change. You realised I had skills and knowledge you could use. How else could you get me to obey when I refused to bow to your every whim?'

Laughter split the air. 'My every whim? That would be the day! You're feisty, stubborn and opinionated, always ready to argue your point of view.'

'All the things you don't want in a woman.' Ghizlan tasted acid on her tongue. She'd thought the hurt couldn't get any worse yet his casual amusement lacerated her.

'I thought you were beginning to know me, Ghizlan.' His voice dropped to a soft note that tugged at her stupid heart. 'Of course I tried to win you over. But you've got it wrong. I didn't do it because I chose to. I did it because I *needed* to.'

Large hands cupped her elbows but that wasn't what welded her to the spot. It was the emotion shimmering in Huseyn's eyes. The ragged note in that deep voice. 'Because I realised long ago that you were more than any woman I'd ever known or expected to know. That you were the only woman I *wanted* in my life.'

Ghizlan's jaw sagged as she met those beautiful, earnest eyes. 'Of course I like it that you can wind ambassadors around your little finger. That you can speak five languages and smooth ruffled diplomatic feathers and act as hostess at a dinner for two hundred. But that's not why I need you.' He paused, dragging in an audible breath as Ghizlan tried not to lean closer.

'I need you because you make me whole. You make me feel like a man I didn't know I could be. A better, kinder man than I've ever been. Is that so bad?'

One long finger stroked her cheek and she swallowed, unable to move, arrested by the words tumbling from those chiselled lips.

'You make me feel things I've never felt before. You make me want what I never expected to want.'

'Like what?' Her voice was as uneven as her pulse. Her skin too tight to contain so much burgeoning emotion.

ANNIE WEST 183

'Belonging. Love.' He cupped her face in his hands and she melted at what she saw in his face. 'You. I've wanted you so long, Ghizlan. Not just as a necessary bride, but as my lover.'

'I fell into your bed so easily.' She was torn between wanting to believe his words and fearing it was another seduction technique.

'Not easily at all.' His crooked smile made her chest tighten. 'But I don't just mean my lover in bed. It's more than sex I need from you, Ghizlan. I'm greedy. I want you all. Body, heart and soul.' He paused and she heard the throb of her pulse heavy in her ears as she tried to take it in. 'Of course I aimed to seduce you. I wanted you to fall in love with me because I've fallen in love with you. I don't want you dreaming of leaving me for some suave aristocrat who's all the things I'll never be.'

His thumbs stroked her cheeks and Ghizlan realised there was wetness there. Tears she hadn't been aware of spilled from her eyes.

'My darling! It's not that bad, surely? I know I wasn't your original choice but I'd hoped you'd come to care for me too.'

That's when she saw it, the fear in Huseyn's proud, harsh features. It was there in his voice and, if she wasn't mistaken, in the sudden sweat beading his forehead.

This was real. Real and true. A perfect mirror to her own devastatingly raw feelings.

Ghizlan slipped her arms over his warm shirt, over that hard-packed muscle she loved to snuggle against, linking her fingers behind his neck.

'Why didn't you tell me?' The wonder of it almost stole her voice.

'I wanted to bind you to me first. I've never set about seducing a wife before. I wanted to know I'd done it right. Completely and thoroughly so you'd never want to leave.' He paused. '*Then* I was going to tell you.'

Emotion fluttered high in Ghizlan's throat, like a trapped bird.

'You would have saved a lot of trouble if you'd told me.' She paused, overcome by the passion she read in his face and his trembling hands. Who'd have thought those big, capable hands could shake with emotion?

'I thought actions spoke louder than words.'

'So they do.' Her lips curving in a taut smile, Ghizlan rose on tiptoe and dragged his head down, kissing him full on the mouth, lingering but light, for she couldn't afford to get distracted.

He grabbed her round the waist, hauling her close. His eyes blazed brighter than any of the fabulous diamonds in the royal collection.

'Tell me!' It was an order, husky and urgent. Ghizlan revelled in the knowledge he was as desperate as she.

'I love you, Huseyn. I didn't want to but I can't seem to help myself.' She leaned in, her lips on his. Her heart thumped a joyous rhythm that mocked her recent despair.

'When did you—? No, tell me later. We've got all the time in the world to discuss the hows and whys. Right now I want a kiss from my wife—the only woman who will ever hold my heart.'

'Is that a command, my lord?' Somehow Ghizlan found she didn't mind his dictatorial ways.

'It is, my lady.' He swept her up off the floor, cradling her with a gentleness that turned her insides liquid. Ghizlan snuggled close, still stunned by the happiness radiating from her heart and the dazzled look in Huseyn's eyes.

There was nowhere she'd rather be than in her husband's arms.

When they kissed again it was a tender promise of joy to come. A gift offered and accepted. A wondrous, heartfelt vow that would last a lifetime.

EPILOGUE

'SO THE STORIES about your husband *were* true.' Arden caught Ghizlan's eye as she sipped iced juice.

'Which stories?' Ghizlan frowned. 'You shouldn't believe rumours.'

Arden chuckled. 'You're so protective, it's cute. Though I've never met anyone who needed protection less.'

Ghizlan leaned back in her seat. 'You're teasing.'

'I am. I like him immensely, especially since he dotes on you. But when we first met I wondered. There was a rumour that he forced you into marriage. And he's such a big man, so powerful, with such an air of determination.' Arden shook her head. '*I* wouldn't like to cross him.'

'Oh, I don't know.' Ghizlan smiled down at her glass. 'It can be quite invigorating.'

Arden giggled. 'I'll bet. Making up with Idris has always been a highlight of our relationship.'

'So it's going well?' Ghizlan barely needed to ask. Arden and Idris clearly adored each other.

'Wonderfully,' Arden breathed, smoothing a hand over her stomach. 'So wonderful we're expecting another baby.'

'Congratulations!' Ghizlan sprang from her seat to embrace her friend. 'I'm so happy for you.'

'Thank you. We're thrilled.' Arden failed to hide her curiosity as her gaze dipped to Ghizlan's flat stomach.

Who knew, perhaps one day soon she and Huseyn would be expecting a baby too. She'd stopped taking the Pill, so nature could take its course.

'There they are now.' Arden frowned. 'Though I'm still not sure Dawud's old enough for a pony.'

Huseyn led a pony across the palace courtyard, talking

gently to both the animal and the small boy on its back. Idris walked behind, ready to support his son if necessary.

They stopped and the boy turned to Huseyn for help getting down. It shouldn't surprise her. Dawud had been fascinated by him ever since she and Huseyn had arrived in Zahrat. And her husband, despite that air of formidable power, was easy and infinitely patient with him.

'I've been ousted in my son's affections,' Idris complained as he kissed his wife.

'I'm just a novelty.' Huseyn's laugh rolled through Ghizlan, low and appealing, turning her bones liquid. He walked closer, the boy tucked easily in his arm, and Ghizlan was struck by how natural he was with Dawud. How easily he'd take to fatherhood when the time came.

Huseyn's gaze lifted as if he read her thoughts. Heat pulsed between them as those misty blue eyes snared hers.

'Here. You'd better let me take him.' Idris reached for his boy. 'Before you forget he's there.'

Huseyn relinquished Dawud with a smile and sank to the grass at Ghizlan's feet. 'Good idea. My wife is far too distracting.' He took her hand and pressed his lips to her palm, sending darts of delight through her.

'In that case, Ghizlan, perhaps you can join us for the trade negotiations. I'm for anything that will give Zahrat an advantage. Your husband's a tough negotiator.'

Huseyn beamed at her in a way *she* found utterly distracting. 'Good idea. Ghizlan is my secret weapon. She'll negotiate us into a better position than I could.' His voice softened meaningfully and his eyes gleamed. 'Which would give us reason to celebrate.'

'Ha! Save us from newlyweds!' Idris laughed.

'Actually...' Huseyn kissed her hand again, then turned to the man Ghizlan knew he already liked and respected. 'If Ghizlan agrees, I've been thinking it would be an excellent idea for her to take the lead in some of the discussions.'

Her eyes rounded but he ignored her shock. 'She was the

architect behind the innovative trade schemes and no one knows more about the joint power proposals.' He turned to her. 'If you'd like to, of course. I know you're going to be busy with the launch of the new perfume.'

Ghizlan stared. It was one thing to support Huseyn behind the scenes. This would break every unwritten law— allowing a woman such an important, public role in the nation's future. Yet his gaze told her he was serious.

'Say yes.' His tone was urgent. 'I want you by my side where you deserve to be. You're more than my wife and lover, you're my partner, my other half. I want everyone to see how important you are, to Jeirut and to me.'

Dimly, Ghizlan was aware of Arden's sigh but she couldn't tear her gaze from Huseyn's. Her heart tumbled as she read warmth, pride and love, above all love, in his eyes. 'The Council will have fits.'

'As if I care. With you beside me we can do anything. It's time our people saw you as you really are: my equal.'

'Oh, Huseyn.' She cupped his face, uncaring of their audience. 'You make me so happy.'

'Excellent.' He leaned in to murmur against her ear, 'That's my long-term goal. To make you so happy you'll always love me the way you do now.' His arm went around her waist as he turned to their host. 'You'd better beware, Idris. My Ghizlan's a force to be reckoned with.'

'I think the pair of you are.'

He was right, Ghizlan knew. Together, she and Huseyn were as perfect a match as love could make. She counted herself the luckiest woman ever, knowing he'd always be there beside her, no matter what the future held.

* * * * *

If you enjoyed
THE DESERT KING'S CAPTIVE BRIDE,
take a look at these other
WEDLOCKED! themed stories!

A DIAMOND FOR DEL RIO'S HOUSEKEEPER
by Susan Stephens
BABY OF HIS REVENGE
by Jennie Lucas
BOUND BY HIS DESERT DIAMOND
by Andie Brock
BRIDE BY ROYAL DECREE
by Caitlin Crews
CLAIMED FOR THE DE CARRILLO TWINS
by Abby Green

Available now!

MILLS & BOON®

EXCLUSIVE EXTRACT

Persuading plain Jane to marry him was easy
enough – but Shiekh Zayed Al Zawba hadn't
bargained on the irresistible curves hidden under
her clothes, or that she is deliciously untouched.
When Jane begins to tempt him beyond his
wildest dreams, leaving their marriage
unconsummated becomes impossible…

Read on for a sneak preview of
THE SHEIKH'S BOUGHT WIFE

It was difficult to be *distant* when your body seemed to
have developed a stubborn will of its own. When she found
herself wanting to push her aching breasts against Zayed's
powerful chest as he caught her in his arms for the traditional first dance between bride and groom. As it was, she
could barely think straight and wasn't it the most infuriating
thing in the world that he immediately seemed to pick up
on that?

'You seem to be having trouble breathing, dear wife,'
he murmured as he moved her to the center of the marble
dance floor.

'The dress is very tight.'

'I'd noticed.' He twirled her around, holding her back
a little. 'It looks very well on you.'

She forced a tight smile but she didn't relax. 'Thank you.'

'Or maybe it is the excitement of having me this close
to you which is making you pant like a little kitten?'

'You're *annoying* me, rather than exciting me. And I do
wish you'd stop trying to get underneath my skin.'

'Don't you like people getting underneath your skin, Jane?'

'No,' she said honestly. 'I don't.'

'Why not?'

She met the blaze of his ebony eyes and suppressed a shiver. 'Does everything have to have a reason?'

'In my experience, yes.' There was a pause. 'Has a man hurt you in the past?'

This was her chance to tell him yes—even though the very idea that someone had got that close to her was laughable.

Zayed had already guessed she might be a virgin, but that didn't even come close to her shameful lack of experience.

Trying to ignore the way his groin was brushing against her as he edged her closer, she glanced up at him, her cheeks burning. 'I refuse to answer that on the grounds that I might incriminate myself. Tell me instead, do you always insist on interrogating women when you're dancing with them?'

'No. I don't,' he said simply. 'But then I've never had a bride before and I've never danced with a woman who was so determined not to give anything of herself away.'

'And that's the only reason you want to know,' she said quietly. 'Because you like a challenge.'

'All men like a challenge, Jane.' His black eyes gleamed. 'Haven't you learned that by now?'

She didn't answer—because how was she qualified to answer any questions about what men did or didn't like?

Don't miss
THE SHEIKH'S BOUGHT WIFE
By Sharon Kendrick

Available May 2017
www.millsandboon.co.uk